TIME SCENE INVESTIGATORS

TSI:
THE GABON
VIRUS

TSI: THE GABON VIRUS

A NOVEL

PAUL McCUSKER &
WALT LARIMORE, M.D.

HOWARD BOOKS
A Division of Simon & Schuster
NEW YORK LONDON TORONTO SYDNEY

Our purpose at Howard Books is to:
- *Increase faith* in the hearts of growing Christians
- *Inspire holiness* in the lives of believers
- *Instill hope* in the hearts of struggling people everywhere

Because He's coming again!

HOWARD
Fiction
A DIVISION OF SIMON & SCHUSTER

Published by Howard Books, a division of Simon & Schuster, Inc.
1230 Avenue of the Americas, New York, NY 10020
www.howardpublishing.com

The Gabon Virus © 2009 Paul McCusker and Walt Larimore, M.D.

Library of Congress Control Number: 2009004825

ISBN: 978-1-4165-6971-8

10 9 8 7 6 5 4 3 2 1

Manufactured in the United States of America

For information regarding special discounts for bulk purchases, please contact: Simon & Schuster Special Sales at 1-866-506-1949 or business@simonandschuster.com.

The Simon & Schuster Speakers Bureau can bring authors to your live event. For more information or to book an event contact the Simon & Schuster Speakers Bureau at 1-866-248-3049 or visit our website at www.simonspeakers.com.

Edited by David Lambert

Interior design by Jaime Putorti

To Elizabeth, Tommy, and Ellie—for their love and patience.

To Barb—for her lifetime of love.

PART ONE

CHAPTER ONE

JULY 15, 1666

REBEKAH SMYTHE LOOKED DOWN at her brother's lifeless body, his eyes staring vacantly toward the heaven he had hoped and prayed to inhabit. With a pale and trembling hand, she reached down and closed his eyelids.

She had done the same for her father and three of her sisters—all lying still now in their shallow graves not far from their home; so silent after their days of suffering and anguish. She could not weep for them. Her tears were spent long ago.

She looked at the makeshift cots on which her mother and youngest sister slept fitfully. They had come down with the symptoms just two days earlier. She dared not hold out hope for their survival. In another day or two, if all went as it had for the rest of her family, they'd be gone and she'd be alone. *Alone.*

By the grace of God, she had resisted the illness. Yet the outcome of her survival would be loneliness. In her darker moments, she wondered how far God's grace could carry her.

Agnes Hull, who lived in the next cottage down, had also survived the Black Plague and claimed that the warm bacon fat she drank was the reason. She left bottles of the wretched liquid at the doors of afflicted families, but unfortunately, it didn't work for Rebekah's family.

John Dicken, who worked in the local mines, was also a survivor. Believing himself immune, he had established himself as Eyam's village grave digger. He would offer his services the instant he heard of another victim. After burying the body away from town, he would return to claim the burial fee—reportedly taking whatever he fancied. Most were too sick to stop him. Besides, what use was their money if they were dead? Few of the men were well enough to take the job from Dicken, and it wasn't as if anyone new would arrive to challenge him. After all, the village was under strict quarantine.

Rebekah sat on a stool, staring at the fire. Pushing a lock of hair away from her face, she was overcome by a feeling of self-pity. *How had it come to this?* Who could have foreseen last September that something as unassuming as a box of cloth from London would start such an epidemic? Mr. George Viccars, a traveling tailor, certainly couldn't have. As he opened the box—wet from a rainstorm—and laid the cloth out to dry, he could not have imagined what he was unleashing upon them all. Within a day, he developed the telltale symptoms of rose-colored spots on his skin and quickly died.

The Earl, the village's patron, sent his personal physician from the castle to examine the tailor's body. The doctor's diagnosis was Black Plague. It had arrived in Eyam.

And so began a year of terror.

The village had rallied together. Catherine Mompesson, the vicar's wife, bravely visited the sick families. Ignoring the risk to herself and her family, she had brought words of comfort and a bouquet of sweet-smelling posies, believing it would ward off the stench of disease.

As she sipped some ale, Rebekah thought about the rhyme sung by local children:

Ring a-ring o' roses,
A pocketful of posies.
a-tishoo! a-tishoo!
We all fall down.

The rhyme went through her mind again and again—

The knock on the door startled her. Few of the villagers would be out and about at this late hour. Perhaps it was the vicar's wife or the grave digger.

She stood and crossed the room to the door. Her hand was poised above the latch when it occurred to her who might be calling.

Him.

Despite the still warm air of the summer night, she felt a chill go down her spine.

The monk.

He came to the families to aid the sick, comfort the dying, and offer peace to the grieving. The women of the village spoke of him as an angel of light. The men called him a demon, unnerved as they were by the mysterious way in which he appeared and disappeared into thin air. Worse was his appearance. Rebekah had not seen it for herself, but the village gossips claimed that beneath his monk's cowl, he had skin the color of deep water. *Blue*, they said. The monk's skin was blue. *A curse*, the men said.

She could not believe that a man of God, one so merciful and compassionate, could be cursed.

She lifted the latch and opened the door.

CHAPTER TWO

AUGUST 10. THE PRESENT.

THE BLACK HAWK HELICOPTER descended toward a small flat outcropping near the top of the icy cliff. It had no markings on its matte black surface, an exterior designed to absorb radar signals.

From inside the helicopter, Army Brigadier General Sam Mosley gazed at the frozen valley below—a vast expanse of ice that stretched between two distant mountain peaks. To the untrained eye, it was a wasteland, but the general knew better. What appeared to be a series of ripples in the valley's floor were actually roofs and camouflage for a large, underground collection of buildings. "The Bunker," they called it; the only inhabited facility for over a hundred miles.

Icy particles sprang up like a cloud of dust as the chopper nestled onto the snowy pad. This was the emergency landing site, a mile from the regular pad located much closer to the facility. The pilot cut the engine.

Mosley swallowed, forcing back the acidic taste in his throat. Was it fear? No, this was the taste of grim determination—the bitter and offensive bile of a tragic duty to perform.

As the ice cloud dispersed, the general looked across the endless white and remembered the champagne celebration they'd had on the day the scheme to build this laboratory was approved. It seemed like genius—or madness—at the time. Imagine building a lab in the middle of Greenland. Yet all the risk assessments told them the site had the highest probability of safety. Only Mark Carlson, the architect of the entire plan, had expressed doubts. "We're arrogant," he said in private, late-night meetings. Often the argument took place over day-old Chinese meals.

"Eventually we'll create something that we can't contain; something that's too potent. Nature always finds a way of escape. It doesn't matter how far into the ice we dig."

Mosley turned to the pilot, who took off his helmet. "Well?"

"Okay to disembark, General."

Mosley nodded. "Thanks, Tom. Excellent job, as always."

"We couldn't have hoped for a better day," the pilot said. "The weather crew at The Hague said the conditions would be perfect."

"Glad they got it right for once."

Nervous chitchat, Mosley thought. He looked out at the snow and ice, frowned and sighed.

"We don't have much time, General," the pilot said.

"No, we don't."

"Would you like me to come with you?" the pilot asked.

Mosley shook his head. "Better that I do this alone." He climbed out of his seat and moved to the rear of the cabin. He dressed quickly and quietly, donning a bright orange suit designed to protect him to fifty degrees below zero.

He glanced at the second suit. The name Mark Carlson was stitched onto the left breast. The thought of Mark gave him pause. *Mark should be here.* But that would have been too much to ask. Four years of Mark's life had gone into making this complex a reality. He'd lost a lot in the process: a wife and a child. Some believed he was now damaged goods as a result of those losses. Mosley hadn't wanted to believe it and continually gave Mark the benefit of the doubt. And yet, he hadn't invited Mark to this occasion. Why risk pushing him over the edge?

The general put his head cover on last, to give added protection to his face and eyes. Certain he was thoroughly protected, Mosley threw open the door and stepped out.

A sledgehammer of frigid air hit him. He braced himself against the side of the helicopter, then reached up to the door, but the pilot was already there, sliding it closed. The two men exchanged glances and Mosley noticed the pilot was wearing a Beretta M9 pistol holstered to his belt. *A precaution. Just a precaution.* He bowed to the elements and pressed ahead, ankle deep in a powdery snow that sparkled like kindergarten craft glitter.

The wind made a mournful sound as he walked toward the

edge of the cliff. Mosley clenched his teeth—not against the cold, but out of a brutal resolve. He stopped and surveyed the scene once more. As a soldier, he hated these moments. As a general, he knew the responsibility was his. For him as a physician, this action went against everything he believed—against the oath he had sworn when he finished medical school. He searched for comfort in the sad thought that the people below were most likely already dead.

He reached into his pocket and retrieved a small black cell phone. Opening the protective cover, he carefully punched in a sequence of numbers. When he came to the last number, he hesitated and glanced back at the helicopter. He saw the pilot through a slim open crack in the Black Hawk's door and knew the pilot had orders to shoot him if he showed any hesitation or attempted to deviate from the plan in any way. The Glock held only six rounds, but one .45-caliber bullet was all that an expert marksman needed to kill him instantly.

Mosley's thumb pressed the final digit and he cursed himself. This was their plan of last resort—the one the experts and the computer models had always said couldn't happen, wouldn't happen. They had insisted the lab was foolproof, that a breach of its safeguards and a failure to contain its virus was unimaginable. Yet the unimaginable had happened, and now Mosley had to do the very thing he'd assured Mark they'd never have to do. From the corner of his eye, he saw the Black Hawk's door open wider. He was taking too long. The pilot was probably taking aim even now.

The general moved his thumb to the SEND button and turned toward the complex. Critical lifesaving work had gone on in that lab. Years of effort. Its potential had been so great, yet so unfulfilled, and now there'd be nothing but terrible loss.

With a defiant gesture, he pressed the button. At first nothing happened. Then, far below, the ground heaved in the center of the complex, rising as if a fist punched the underside of the ice, growing larger and higher until the white earth burst open with an explosive roar.

Mosley stepped back. The ice—and everything that had been the Bunker—blew upward, followed by a massive fireball. The concussive blast hit him, a surprisingly strong wave that nearly knocked him off his feet. He fought it, balancing forward.

In less than half a minute everything was calm again. The secret lab had been incinerated along with its entire staff and an untold amount of data about all things viral.

Mosley stood frozen, his gloved hands clenched. "It had to be done," he said to no one. Turning on his heel, he walked toward the helicopter. He could only hope that the virus had been completely destroyed.

If even one viral particle had survived, it was possible that the world would not.

CHAPTER THREE

AUGUST 11

THE METAL CORRUGATED ROOF caught the blistering African heat and pushed it downward past the wobbling ceiling fans to the meeting room below. The air was heavy with humidity. Even the gathering flies moved sluggishly, lazily, as if weighted by the muggy atmosphere.

David sat on a chair in the center of the small makeshift stage at the head of the room. From here, he could see it all: the flies and the horror of death laid out before him. He scanned the room. No movement. He turned his head to look out an open window, out to the compound.

For all intents and purposes, it looked like an average African village—a dirt road down the middle and pathways lined with wooden huts, metal shacks, and a few makeshift cottages. A gray cement maintenance shed sat in the center of the compound with donated equipment and supplies to provide them with running water and, at least for a few hours a day, electricity.

Beyond that shed were the schoolhouse and the cafeteria. The work house, with the many sewing machines the women used to make the clothing that helped subsidize their community, sat off to the side. A few yards from there, alone and away from the rest of the structures, was David's single-room main office. Through the trees, he could see its flat roof and the small satellite dish mounted on a corner.

David's hands hovered above the laptop resting on his lap. A small icon on the screen told him that he had a strong signal and full access to the Internet thanks to that satellite dish—a dish that he'd fought against installing. It was yet another connection to the corrupt and depraved world that he had struggled so hard to escape.

Why else would he create a commune in Gabon, of all places? Certainly not to replicate his life in America. This had been a chance for him, his family, and his congregation to break free. But his no-contact rule backfired when Hank Hillier came down with malaria earlier in the year. Malaria was a common malady and easily treated, but Hank's had gone to his brain and he developed a near-fatal case of cerebral malaria. Only by the grace of God were they able to contact a local missionary pilot and transport him 150 miles to a specialty hospital in Lambaréné. It was a close call that left David and his congregation nervous about their isolation.

With great reluctance David agreed to install the dish and hardware. Just in time, too. Not long afterward, Sarah McFerran was stricken with appendicitis and, with a single e-mail, she was airlifted to the pediatric hospital in Libreville.

Both Hank and Sarah lay dead in the collection of bodies before him, and now David would use the satellite dish to send out his last words—not as a cry for help, but to ask for forgiveness.

He groaned and rubbed his tired eyes, squeezing them shut. *How did it come to this?* How did he go from being a trendy atheist in college, proud of his intellect, relishing his militant cynicism against all believers in God, to the countercultural pastor of a Christian commune in the middle of a west African jungle?

No doubt, when their bodies were finally discovered, the press would pore over the details of his life in a vain attempt to answer that question.

They would simplify the complexities of his faith and conviction; gloss over the corruptions and decadence of American culture that drove him to take his family and congregation to Gabon; and caricature them all as mindless cult members, rather than the thriving and rigorous group of disciples they truly were.

He ached to think of it, and he closed his eyes as he thought of his missteps, his misguided idealism, and in the end, his business naiveté that put the community on the edge of financial ruin and sent him into the arms of The Corporation for help.

The Corporation. It had seemed like an answer to his prayers. The representatives expressed genuine interest in David's hope and vision, and they were persuasive, offering David a ludicrous amount of money in exchange for some help and cooperation. It had appeared so simple and safe. Only his wife, Rachel, expressed any deep concern. Something in her heart told her it was wrong. "It doesn't feel right," she had warned, but couldn't explain why.

David looked at the bodies closest to the stage. Rachel was there along with his two young, precious daughters and his teenage son. The front edge of a sea of corpses.

The altar sat a few feet from David. It had been hand carved from an ancient oak tree that had fallen outside David's first church—such a long time ago. A wooden chalice beckoned him. A scrap of bread sat on the wooden plate next to the chalice. There was just enough left for him.

David looked down at the laptop computer. He blinked. His eyes burned. He began to type. This was his final confession. A last e-mail to his father—a man who never accepted or affirmed him, much less ever indicated he loved him. What a surprise it would be. He couldn't remember the last time he'd spoken to his father.

David began to type. He was determined not to write with sentimentality or melodrama. He recounted in the simplest terms his hopes and dreams with Rachel and how he believed, as a matter of faith, that their community was created to help save humankind, both spiritually and physically. Lofty goals, but attainable. Even now, David believed they could have succeeded if only he had been wiser and more discerning, if only he'd listened to Rachel, if only he hadn't shaken hands with the Devil.

Now it was all undone. A failure of the greatest kind. A tragedy, just as Rachel had predicted. David concluded his e-mail by asking his father for forgiveness. It was the last thing he needed to do, the most important thing left to do.

A harsh squawk drew David's attention to the back door. A vulture landed in the courtyard. Then another. They knew. They were gathering. Soon, there would be no stopping them. Soon, his compound would contain a congregation of scavengers.

David's eyes filled with tears as he shook off the thought of what would happen to the dead bodies strewn across the meeting-room floor. What were they but empty vessels? God had secured their souls. His gaze fell again upon the men and women, boys and girls who'd put their trust in his leadership.

That morning they had each taken communion, knowing it would be their last. After praying together, they lay down, and went to sleep. David was happy they all went peacefully.

And now, it was his turn.

He finished the note to his father:

> *We were wrong, Dad. Now it's cost me my dream, my family, my community, and my life.*
>
> *It may be a very long time before we are found, since none of the local tribe members come to our compound unless we invite them. I am afraid there will be a cover-up if The Corporation finds us first. That is why I am writing to you. If you can do anything to prevent this evil from spreading, in the name of God, do it.*
>
> *I love you, Dad. I pray that God will touch you—and you'll accept Him—so we'll be reunited in heaven. I'll be waiting there for you.*
>
> *Your son, David*

He reread the e-mail, knowing there was so much more to say. He pressed the SEND button. A box popped up, confirming its passage. He leaned back and sighed.

With little energy, he turned off the computer, stood, and approached the altar. He was surprised at the sweet aroma. He looked at the flowers on the altar. *I don't remember the orchids smelling so wonderful.* He inhaled the fragrance deeply, then dropped to his knees, his hands pressing against the smooth oak.

A prayer from his days as an altar boy welled up in his memory. "Father of mercies and God of all comfort, our help in time of need, we fly unto thee for succor in behalf of this thy servant . . ." He couldn't remember the rest of this ancient prayer. So, he drank the last of the poison in the cup. *God grant that, in this death, there may be true life eternal.*

The poison would work quickly, so he rose and went to his family. Rachel's arm was thrown over her face, as if she had decided not to watch what would unfold. The girls' dead eyes stared at nothing, their expressions serene. Aaron, his son, was on the floor, his face turned away and pressed into the crook of his arm.

David kissed his wife, but couldn't bring himself to do the same to his children. Taking his place next to her, he reached over and pulled her close, his eye catching sight of the telltale red splotches on her arm. Then, as if he needed one last confirmation, he looked at his own arm.

Yes—they were there.

Perhaps he would be vindicated after all. Perhaps they *had* stopped the horror from spreading.

The numbing poison-induced sleep came over him like a soft blanket. He closed his eyes. *Into Thy hands I commit my . . .*

And then he heard a voice.

"Dad."

It came as a whisper.

He opened his eyes. Aaron, stood over him. David attempted a smile, remembering the stories of others who'd come this way before—of the long tunnel with the bright light, of family members returning to walk "over" with their loved one. There to greet him was his boy looking as he had not an hour ago, with his sandy blond, buzz-cut hair and his lean face, which had only just lost its boyish roundness as the passage to manhood had begun. It was a passage that David had stolen from him.

David wanted to speak, but couldn't frame the words. He blinked, trying to clear his eyes.

"I'm sorry, Dad. I'm so sorry," his son said.

David's eyes widened, horrified. His son wasn't an angel. His son was still alive.

"Dad, I'm sorry. I couldn't do it. I couldn't!" Aaron knelt over him, his eyes wide and wet.

David's body lay helpless. His paralyzed vocal chords could make no sound; his arms could not reach up. Not even a tear could form. Why was his son alive? Didn't he know what would happen? He'd been inoculated with the evil along with everyone else. The deadly virus was in his system. His death, inevitable and sure, would be awful.

With a final slow exhalation David knew he had failed once again.

Darkness circled in his open eyes, moving to the center of his vision, obscuring everything to a single pinpoint as he lost consciousness. *Dear God, forgive me.*

CHAPTER FOUR

GENERAL MOSLEY SETTLED INTO the large leather chair behind his cherrywood desk at The Hague. He swiveled away from the mounds of paperwork awaiting his attention and leaned his head back. He rubbed his hands over his face, and let out a long breath. He was still weary from the flight back to Holland the previous afternoon.

Damage control. When did my job become nothing but damage control?

He had debriefed his superiors at the Pentagon and the CIA by teleconference. "Mission accomplished," he'd reported. They commended him on a job well done. He chewed the inside of his lip and thought, *Mission accomplished, yes—if the mission was to bury an unmitigated disaster beneath tons of ice.* But what about the cause of the disaster? Whose mission was it to discover that? And whom would they make the scapegoat?

Not me, he decided. Sure, there'd be appearances before top-secret subcommittees to discern what had happened at the laboratory and how to keep it from happening again. And a disaster like this always had budgetary ramifications, but he wouldn't let them lay the blame on his shoulders.

He groaned and wondered when he'd become such a heartless bureaucrat thinking about debriefings, subcommittees, budgets, and avoiding blame when so many lives had been lost to the failed experiment.

He had known and worked with some of those scientists for over a decade. They had families who, even now, were receiving the terrible news about their loved ones. Not the full truth, of course. Only a handful of people knew that. But all employees had a detailed cover story. Their cause of death would be explained in noble and heroic terms, as if that would soothe the surviving wives, husbands, sons, and daughters. Hopefully, the generous checks they would receive would buy them some comfort.

Mosley tried to console himself with the knowledge that the team hadn't died in vain. They had sacrificed their lives to save untold millions—those who might have died in the future from fatal viruses with names few in the public sector even knew.

He squinted at a large computer screen on the opposite wall. It displayed a map of the world, with multiple colors indicating viral outbreaks anywhere they had been diagnosed in the past year. Some colors remained constant, others blinked to indicate a new report.

He tapped a key on the keyboard to highlight any outbreaks of *Filoviridae,* a family of viruses containing the dreaded Ebola and Marburg viruses. Red dots flickered in parts of the Middle East, Asia, and Africa. Each dot represented individuals who, even as he sat in the comfort of his office, were dealing with these aggressive and relentless viruses. There were far too many.

Filoviridae were a formidable and fearsome foe. He had seen the effects for himself, seen how the virus moved quickly, passing rapidly from person to person. Unknown to most of the world, the mutations of these viruses were becoming far more dangerous. The chances of regional epidemics—even a worldwide pandemic—increased almost daily. It was only a matter of time before the *big one,* the Hiroshima of viral outbreaks, would hit some part of the world and begin its horrific spread. Like a cancer, once it began to metastasize, he doubted it could be stopped—unless his teams could find a treatment.

Mosley looked away from the map and his eye caught a slip of paper by the phone. The message stated that Mark Carlson had called from a medical symposium in Cairo to find out if there was a conclusion to the Greenland crisis. The message detailed where he could be found *only* in an emergency. His cell phone would not be working.

There's a conclusion all right, and you won't like it.

He held the slip of paper in his hand and dreaded how he would explain to Mark that the lab in Greenland had been compromised, and then utterly destroyed. How was he expected to drop that into a conversation?

Standing again, he began to pace. *What had gone wrong? How had the virus broken free in the lab? How had it killed so many so quickly?*

Mosley considered sabotage, a betrayer in their midst. But who? The staff had been rigorously vetted at the highest levels, with extensive psychological testing. No suicide saboteurs in *that* crew. More than likely a careless technician had sent the virus into the air, where the other employees then picked it up, triggering the crisis.

By the time the first rosy death mark had shown up on a technician's chest or arms, the entire facility could have been infected. Excruciating death came quickly—so quickly, in fact, that headquarters had received only one phone call and two urgent e-mails from separate employees. Then silence.

Camera footage, sent over the security system's satellite feed, showed the carnage. The scenes were abhorrent and repulsive. There was no choice but to incinerate the Bunker in the hope that every mutant virus within would be destroyed.

He glanced at his watch. It was nearly time to debrief his executive team on all that had happened. His aide came through the doorway, tapping on the door as he entered.

"Excuse me, General," Major Kevin Maklin said in an apologetic tone.

"What is it, Kevin?"

"I'm sorry, but there's an inspector from Interpol here to see you. Martin Duerr."

"Am I scheduled to see him?"

"No. He said it's urgent."

"Urgent? How?"

"He wouldn't tell me. He said he must speak with you personally."

Mosley looked at his watch again. "All right. I'll give him a few minutes."

His assistant stepped out and a short man with a round face, oval wire-framed glasses, and wild white hair came in. He wore a tan suit that on anyone else would have looked crisp and sharp. On him, it hung like bad curtains.

"General Mosley?" he inquired in a low voice that came as a rumble from somewhere deep inside of him. He had a Swiss accent.

"If it's about those parking fines . . ."

The man chuckled politely. "No, sir. That's the police. Parking fines are not within our jurisdiction." He handed Mosley his credentials: a picture ID and gold badge with the blue insignia of a sword and globe overlaid with the letters OIPC/ICPO—the French and English acronyms for the International Criminal Police Organization, also known as Interpol, the world's largest international police organization. "I'm an inspector for Interpol. I've been sent from our headquarters in Lyon."

"Beautiful city. What can I do for you, Inspector Duerr?"

Duerr looked as if he wanted to sit down, but Mosley didn't offer him a seat. "Have you ever heard of the Return to Earth movement?"

Mosley thought about it. "No. Should I have?"

Duerr shrugged, then produced a notepad from his pocket. Without looking at it, he said, "Return to Earth is an extremist group, a combination of fanatical environmentalists and animal-rights activists who've joined forces."

Mosley gazed at the inspector but didn't react.

Duerr cleared his throat. "They believe that humankind has lost its right to govern the earth because of its abuse of the world and of animals. In essence, they believe that humans should be returned to the earth, as in dead and decomposing, so that the earth can return to its natural state in harmony with the animals."

"I see."

Duerr closed the notepad. "To be blunt, General, they're terrorists—suicide bombers for Mother Earth. They will do anything to take humankind out of the equation. Anything. They'll target individuals, families, industrial plants, factories, polluters, pharmaceutical companies, biochemical research sites, cosmetic companies, and any other entity they deem worthy to put on their hit list for testing on animals or hurting the earth."

"Am I on their hit list?" Mosley asked. "Is that why you're here?"

"Not in the way you think. But your name did come up in one of their meetings."

Mosley scowled. "What meeting?"

"A cell meeting in Switzerland. They have cells worldwide, a loose network that supports and encourages one another. But members maintain enough distance to keep us from effectively tracking them. The individuals often don't know who the other members are. There might be two or more working on the same project and they won't know it. So, when we grab one, the others disappear into the woodwork."

"If you can't track them, then how do you know I was mentioned?"

"One of our agents has infiltrated a cell in Basel. This is a significant breakthrough for us, as you can imagine. We have access to some of their activities as never before. Our agent flagged your name—in connection with some top-secret facility in Greenland."

Mosley felt a cold hand squeeze his heart. He pressed his lips together to keep from speaking.

The Interpol agent nodded. "Yes, I know. I do not have the clearance for you to confirm or deny the existence of any top-secret facilities, but I want you to know that *they* know about it and my agent was led to believe that they were going to take some sort of action against it."

"What sort of action?"

"We don't know," the inspector replied. "Their modus operandi is usually centered around destruction, sabotage, intimidation."

"Hypothetically speaking, if we were to have any sort of facility or facilities, and of course, I'm *not* saying or even insinuating that we do or would, why would they target us?"

"Any facility that experiments on animals is suitable for attack. Or perhaps you were doing something that posed a risk to the environment. Or you may have been working on something that would accelerate their efforts to erase humankind from the earth. Pick one."

Pick one, or all three. Was it possible these fanatics knew what they were testing and believed they could unleash a pandemic by infiltrating and sabotaging the facility? He swallowed an unnerving feeling of fear.

"How strong are they?"

The inspector pursed his lips. "They're, shall we say, resourceful. Not only do they seem to have endless funding, but the ability to find out what a government or company is doing and where they are doing it is astounding. They seem to have followers buried deep within the most guarded enterprises. They insinuate themselves anywhere and everywhere. Some members are experts in various fields, working at the highest levels. Or they plant an employee with, say, an outside contractor for a security firm, the military, or a government on one or more highly secure sites. Or, perhaps a janitorial-service employee works at a secret site. You get the idea."

"What do you need from me?" asked Mosley.

"I want you to be aware, to warn your people in a discreet way, so as not to jeopardize our operation." Duerr thought, then added, "I need access to you in case we need your help. And, of course, I will keep you informed as best as I can."

Mosley thought about Greenland. How differently would things have turned out had he spoken to Duerr earlier? "All right, Inspector. I'll help in any way I can."

Duerr waited as if something else should be said, then bowed slightly. "*Merci*, General."

Once the inspector had left, Mosley called Maklin into the office.

"Sir?"

"Get the team in here. We've got a problem."

"Yes, sir."

Mosley sat down in his chair, his mind working on how he could alert their research facilities about Return to Earth without alerting the terrorists.

A gentle chime sounded behind him and he spun the chair

around to face his computer screen. An e-mail alert. He clicked on the message box.

His body stiffened when he saw the sender's name. The message loaded and the text appeared. As he read, his hands became sweaty and his mouth dry.

It began, *"Dear Dad . . ."*

CHAPTER FIVE

AUGUST 12

MARK CARLSON LAY ON his hotel-room bed and considered the constant noise of the traffic outside his window. He hated being awakened at dawn. *The horns on the cars must be attached to the brakes and gas pedals.* The thought didn't amuse him. He heard the soft whoosh of the air conditioner kick in—a pleasant sound; a soothing sound.

He felt slightly hungover. The dampness from his perspiration meant he would need a shower before taking a cab over to the American University. He was expected to attend a lecture sometime that morning, or was he giving one? He was having difficulty remembering. Something about molecular virology. He rolled over to face the window and winced at the morning light. He'd forgotten to close the curtains.

Through the smeared glass he could see the tops of half-finished buildings, purposefully left that way so the owners wouldn't have to pay taxes on them. *Cairo. What a mess.* High-rises above, hovels below. Smog in the air, rubbish in the streets. It was hard for him to connect this metropolis to the once-great city of the Pharaohs, the place where all the mighty civilizations had come at one time or another. The Greeks, Romans, Ottomans, the French under Napoleon, and British had all come and gone. Here was the city of the Nile, now reduced to squalor and traffic.

He made a feeble effort to sit up and decided against it, allowing his head to fall back onto the pillow. His glance fell to a flashing light on the telephone—a message, maybe several. He had refused to pick up the phone when it rang—rang again—and again. He knew who was trying to reach him.

Donna. His wife. Well, his ex-wife.

Having failed to reach him on his cell phone, she was now trying to reach him on the hotel line. Why did he tell her where he was staying? Why did he tell her anything? They'd been divorced for three years. They were, in theory, leading separate lives. But only in theory.

There was a sharp knock on the door. He rolled over, pulling the pillow over his head.

"Mr. Carlson?" An accented voice. It sounded like the concierge from his floor. "I apologize for bothering you, Mr. Carlson. I know you wish not to be disturbed, but these men have come . . ."

The concierge was interrupted by two other low voices.

Mark groaned.

Someone slipped the plastic key into the electronic lock. It beeped and the door clicked open.

"Dr. Carlson?" A uniformed man entered: American military; a young marine. Another just like him followed.

Mark sat up, swinging his legs over the edge of the bed. "What's wrong?"

"You're to come with us, sir."

"Says who? I'm with the private sector now, remember?"

"Brigadier General Sam Mosley hasn't forgotten and he wants you to move—immediately." The first marine handed Mark an envelope.

This must be about the Greenland facility. He opened the seal. As he did, the second uniformed marine opened the closet, grabbed Mark's suitcase, and began to collect Mark's belongings.

Distracted from the envelope, Mark said: "I can do that," and got to his feet.

"It will be faster if I do it, sir," the second soldier said and handed him a pair of trousers and shirt.

Until that moment, Mark had forgotten that he was standing in his T-shirt and boxers. Mark began to dress. "Where are we going?"

"To the airport."

Mark snorted as he put on his trousers. "No kidding. And from there?"

The young marine looked as if he might not answer, then said, "West Africa. Gabon, to be specific."

"Gabon!" Mark exclaimed. "That's the wrong direction from Greenland."

The marine's brow pinched up. "Greenland?"

"Never mind." Mark turned his attention back to the envelope, assuming that it would explain all.

It didn't.

The message contained a variety of numbers and letters to indicate that it was from Mosley's office at The Hague. It looked like gibberish, but the main message was clear enough to Mark.

The Bunker was compromised. Contract terminated.

Mark found himself slumping back onto the bed. A sharp pain went through his head. His chest felt constricted.

"Sir?" the first marine said from a distant place.

"This has to be a mistake," Mark said, the words falling like dry stones from a desert cave. "All those people . . ."

"Sir?" the first marine inquired again.

Mark pressed his hands against his face as a wave of grief tumbled over him, followed by a swell of fury. "Will the general be in Gabon?"

"I believe so."

Mark was on his feet again. "Then let's go."

CHAPTER SIX

BEAUTIFUL MORNING SUNSHINE GREETED the Reverend Andrew Knight as he stepped from the house that served as his church's rectory. A tall, slender man, he bowed slightly to avoid the stone archway over the front portico—one of the drawbacks to living in a house built in the fourteenth century.

He blew at the steam rising from his fresh cup of tea and began a short stroll through his front garden. He surveyed the variety of colors in the late-summer flowers and shrubs: the lilac blue clematis blooms; the white Japanese anemones; the deep red dahlias; the orange daylilies; the pink, yellow, and white snapdragons; the welcoming circles of yellow and brown rudbeckias; and the vibrant red, pink, and white roses covering the trellis.

He made a mental note to call the church ladies' committee to come and transplant some of the petunias, geraniums, and marigolds to hanging baskets and tubs for decoration in the church.

He smiled as he listened to the birds chirping in the yew trees scattered around the old rectory—his home.

Taking a deep breath, he silently thanked God for the lovely day, the lovely garden, and the lovely life he had as the vicar of St. Lawrence's Church in the tiny village of Eyam. It had been his pleasure to serve there for the past five years.

Ambling across the lawn, Reverend Andrew moved toward the old wooden gate in the high hedgerow that separated the rectory from the church grounds. He knew that once he stepped through that solid old door his duties would begin in earnest.

Eyam may have been a small, ancient village, but it often had modern problems—or so his parishioners told him.

Bob and Anne would be in for their premarital counseling. The Altar Guild expected him to attend their monthly meeting. The Eyam Historical Society also needed his attention since St. Lawrence was a significant stopping point for swarms of tourists and bus tours of schoolchildren. The bishop would be by for a late morning visit to discuss the leadership crisis at St. Mark's in an adjoining parish and all of this *before* lunch.

Andrew shook his head as he reached for the latch to the door, but before his fingers touched the iron, the door was thrown open. Startled, he stepped back, the hot tea splashing on his hand.

"Steady on!" he cried.

A tall man with a plaid cap, stubbled chin, worn overalls, and mud-caked gardener's boots stood framed in the doorway with his heavy brows knitted up in surprise.

"Philip!"

"I'm sorry, Vicar," the man said in a thick northern accent. He pulled off his cap, unleashing a mop of unkempt white hair. "Didn't mean to startle you, but you have to come and see. It's terrible. Terrible."

"What's terrible?" Andrew asked. He immediately thought the old water pipes in the church had finally burst and flooded the floors.

"This way," Philip said, already turning and shuffling up the stone path toward the church. Andrew followed, wondering how bad the damage was and what it would cost to fix, but instead of going straight to the church building, Philip suddenly turned to the right, taking the path to the graveyard.

"The graveyard?" Andrew no longer noticed the hot tea splashing down both sides of his cup.

"Hannah Rogers," Philip called over his shoulder.

Andrew frowned, perturbed that Philip would expect him to remember everybody and every body in the graveyard. "Remind me, please."

"Hannah Rogers died in August 1666—Black Plague."

"Right. What about her?" What could be so urgent about the

remains of a woman who had died more than three hundred years ago?

Philip pressed on, leading Andrew past the ancient headstones, around a large ornate marker, and then stopping abruptly. More tea splashed onto Andrew's hand as he gasped at the astonishing sight.

The grave had been dug up.

He stepped closer, peering into the dark hole with an opened sarcophagus at the bottom, its top leaning open. The inside was completely empty. The body was gone.

CHAPTER SEVEN

MARK HATED THE ANTICONTAMINATION suits. They were bulky and, in this environment, stiflingly hot. There were air-conditioned suits available, but they weren't to arrive until later in the day. He would have to endure the heat, he decided. He hadn't been brought all this way—on such short notice—to wait.

The flight had taken four hours in a military jet from Cairo to Brazzaville, the capital of Republic of the Congo. A military attaché for the general briefed him with only the sketchiest of information about an obscure missionary outpost and a mass suicide with an unknown body count and said that he should expect a World Health Organization (WHO) team to be on the scene. But Mark couldn't discern whether the attaché was being secretive or didn't know what was going on. And there was no forthcoming answer to the obvious question: why was Mark being sent on this assignment? Technically, he was a consultant to the military through Ahaz Pharmaceutical. So why had Mosley plucked him out of Cairo to come to Africa?

In Brazzaville, he had been whisked from the military jet to a Black Hawk for the next leg of the journey. A two-hour flight in the helicopter took him the rest of the way. As he came closer to meeting up with the general again, his thoughts returned to the Bunker in Greenland—and how General Sam Mosley had left him out of any decision making about the crisis there.

But the general had not yet arrived at the compound and the military leadership in the operations tent just outside its boundaries had little to say to Mark. The WHO team, from the regional office in Brazzaville, was in charge for the moment, or so he was told. Thwarted from asking questions or getting answers, he checked in with a rather short and frantic medical officer who had reviewed his clearance and warned him to prepare for the worst inside the compound: "Some sort of mass suicide by a commune of Americans."

Mark suited up and took several deep breaths to confirm that his respirator was functioning properly. It was. But Mark continued to breathe deeply, attempting to fight off the worrisome anticipation of what he was about to see. He stepped from the tent.

Movement overhead caused him to look up in time to see a large flock of Palm-nut vultures circling above. The vultures resembled sea eagles, with an impressive wingspan and equally impressive appetite. No doubt the sudden invasion of living beings had disturbed them from a feast. He could only hope that none of the birds had already begun to feed. If whatever had caused the deaths inside was infectious, then it was possible that the birds, or any other animal, might carry and spread the disease.

Looking at the freakish birds reminded him of when—and how—he'd first encountered them in August 2007. He'd led a medical team to Mweka, deep in the Democratic Republic of the Congo, where the funeral of two village chiefs had triggered an epidemic in four villages. Two hundred and seventeen people fell ill. One hundred and three people died. All from Ebola.

Mark stopped where he was, a deeper concern preying on his mind. Was it possible that the general had other motives for summoning him to this site? What if it wasn't a mass suicide, but a new outbreak of Ebola?

Mark clenched his teeth. Few people in the world knew more about this horrible virus than he did. And the name alone conjured up memories of what it did to its victims: the initial bleeding under the skin, the malaise, the body aches, the high fever. Then, untreated, things would grow worse and the victim would lose blood through uncontrollable vomiting and diarrhea. Dehydration would follow, and then coma. It was a horrible death.

Is that what he was walking into? He looked at the nervous WHO officer. The man gave a humorless smile and the thumbs-up, certifying him to enter the disaster scene. He would be allowed twenty minutes max.

Mark swore to himself and walked through the gate, past the stern-looking armed guards. Somewhere overhead he heard the dull *thump thump thump* of helicopters drawing near. Maybe one was carrying the general.

He looked up, noticing that the vultures had beat a rapid retreat, and squinted at the arriving aircraft. He thought from the design that they might be gunships. As they flew closer and then over the compound, he could see the barrels of the .50-caliber machine guns sticking out each side of the helicopters. His stomach lurched with potent anxiety. Why would they have gunships here? Were they concerned about looters? Were they ready to shoot anyone who tried to break in, or were they afraid someone might try to break *out*?

Inside the gates, Mark walked past the various buildings that surrounded the central courtyard. It was a ghost town. As instructed, he went straight to the structure with a signpost: THE MEETING ROOM. Rivulets of sweat formed and dripped down his face, soaking into his shirt.

He stepped into the large hall and abruptly stopped. His body stiffened. As a trained forensic pathologist, he was expected to be desensitized to death, even gruesome murders and suicides. However, he was not prepared for this.

Corpses were strewn across the pews and on the floor. At least two hundred, he guessed.

A dozen forensic technicians were hard at work, photographing and collecting specimens from the bodies. Another team of technicians had begun to bag the bodies, arranging them in neat rows along a sidewall.

Mark stood where he was, stunned by it all. *This is another Jonestown.* His eyes fell upon a small girl—probably no more than three years old—in a "Sunday best" dress. He looked away. He wasn't ready for *this* kind of job. What was Mosley thinking?

He felt a light touch on his arm and turned to face Dr. Susan Hutchinson, a forensic pathologist with whom he had worked in the past.

The respirator muffled her voice when she said, "Welcome, Dr. Carlson."

He nodded. "Hello, Dr. Hutchinson."

"I'm surprised to see you here," she said. "Does Ahaz have something to do with this?" The question was an accusation.

"I'm a little surprised myself," he said, fixing his eyes on her. "I don't know what this has to do with Ahaz, or me. What's your take on it?"

She turned toward the room. "A charismatic religious leader and his flock all poisoned themselves for some sick reason. We haven't found any notes yet, but we're going to check the computers and the surrounding buildings for any journals or letters. Hopefully, we'll get to the bottom of this. Once we've identified the poison and ruled out any infectious cause—"

"Are you worried about an infectious cause?" he asked.

She raised an eyebrow and then tipped her head for him to follow her. "Look at this."

Mark kept his eyes on her as they navigated through the bodies. He didn't want to look at the victims; he didn't want to see any more dead children. But she led him to the body of a woman, Caucasian, probably in her late thirties. Mark was struck by the feeling that he'd seen her somewhere before. Susan bent and unbuttoned the woman's blouse, revealing the victim's chest and abdomen. They were covered with large pink and reddish spots, a number of them coated with dried blood.

"What do you make of *that*?" she asked.

Mark felt a burning behind his eyes and struggled against the hitch in his throat as he stared at the woman's face. She looked serene. *Where have I seen her before?*

"Mark?" Susan prodded.

Mark turned his focus to the woman's skin and felt a dark dread. He hated it when his worst suspicions became reality. "It looks like this is from a hemorrhagic virus."

"Ebola or Marburg?"

He nodded and stood up. "Possibly."

"Is it possible that it's not a virus, but was caused by a toxin or poison?"

"Let's hope so," he said, but doubted it.

"Mark, what's going on here? Why is The Hague taking an interest in this? How did they find out about it in the first place?"

Mark shrugged. "I honestly don't know."

Susan rose and frowned at him, as if deciding whether to believe him. "All right. Back to work."

As she walked away, Mark's mind reeled from the possibilities. He looked around the room, sweat drenching his face and body. The WHO team was busy at their work. He thought about the personal interest from The Hague. More specifically, he wondered how General Mosley was connected.

Mark squatted to look again at the woman at his feet, at the coloring and texture of the spots on her skin. He shuddered as a horrible thought came to him, and then several pieces suddenly clicked into place. He knew for certain why General Mosley had brought him here. He rose and started in Dr. Hutchinson's direction.

"Susan." He tried to affect calmness in his stride.

The doctor turned.

"You and your team must abandon this site," he said.

"On what grounds?"

"Trust me," he said, wanting to sound friendly and diplomatic. "It would be best for all of you to get out of here. *Now*."

She frowned at him. "We're not taking orders from you."

"I know. But I would suggest you listen to me."

"Spell it out, Mark, or we stay."

"It's possible that though a poison was the cause of death, it was not what led to it."

She moved closer to him, the lines on her brow deepening. "I'm listening."

"It may be that these people had contracted a virus and knew they were going to die. So they poisoned themselves as a less painful way of escape."

Her voice grew louder, "And what makes you suspect that?"

He stared at her for a moment. "I'm not authorized to tell you that."

She threw her arms into the air as if summoning lightning from God. "I knew it! This has something to do with Ahaz and your reckless experimenting. I can't believe you guys."

The WHO team stopped their work and stared at Susan.

"I'm sorry," Mark said softly.

She pushed past him to take the center of the room. "Okay," she shouted, "Everyone out!"

They looked at her, puzzled.

"Leave your equipment and specimens," she ordered. "Everyone out!"

Calmly and professionally the team abandoned their places and filed out.

Dr. Hutchinson turned back to Mark, jabbing a finger at him. "I can only hope for your sake that this is a natural Ebola or Marburg virus—and not one of yours."

CHAPTER EIGHT

AFTER FINISHING HIS VARIOUS calls around the parish, Reverend Andrew Knight returned to the church office and parked his rusting Volvo in his private parking space. He was uncomfortable having a reserved place to park, but the parishioners had insisted.

Still, he made them take down the little sign with his name on it and the cutesy hand drawn symbol of a clerical collar. Climbing out of the car, he took a deep breath. He loved the summer months in Eyam and the smells of the gardens and fresh-cut grass.

A brown Rover sat in one of the guest spaces. Walking past it, he noticed a police radio and clutter of forms and reports on the passenger seat. The police radio could belong to anyone on the force. The clutter, however, had to belong to Ian Glover. Maybe he'd made some progress on the mystery of the missing body.

Andrew picked up his pace along the stone path to the office.

Joan Thompson, the longtime church secretary, stood up when he walked in and thrust a condolence card into his hand. "Sign it before you go in, please," she said. "It's for Myrtle Skinner. Her mum just died and I want to get it off to her before you disappear into your office."

As he signed the card, he motioned toward his office. "Is it Ian?"

"Yes."

"I thought as much."

"He's been waiting for only a few minutes. I took in a cup o' tea."

"Thank you, Joan." Andrew didn't know what he'd do without Joan. She knew about everyone and everything in Eyam, making her an extremely valuable asset for the thirty-five-year-old vicar.

Andrew walked down the short hall to his office. Ian Glover, a detective for the county constabulary, but also a local resident, stood at the window, a mug of tea in his hand.

"Hello, Ian," Andrew said brightly.

Ian turned to him, his bushy eyebrows lifted high in what seemed like a permanent expression of astonishment. He had a round face with ruddy cheeks and wore a brown corduroy jacket over a faded white shirt. His trousers may have been black at one time, but now were an odd gray, well loved and well worn. The entire ensemble reminded Andrew of detectives he'd seen in TV shows from the 1970s.

"Good day, Vicar," he said in a thick Derbyshire accent. "Just admiring the view of your back garden."

They shook hands. Ian took two steps to the guest chair, and Andrew sat down in the squeaky metallic chair behind his desk.

"A peculiar business, this grave robbery," Ian said as he nestled into the chair. "We've been working the case since you rang."

"Have you learned anything new? Is there some kind of nationwide grave robbing going on?"

Ian blew a deep breath from his round cheeks. "Well sir, to be candid, we haven't a clue about it. Whoever dug that hole did a professional job. More than professional, in fact, since it hardly looks like a human being did it. Clean as a whistle. No boot prints or hand marks or tire tracks. Might've been done by someone hanging from a tree like that fellow in the *Mission: Impossible* movie."

He sipped his tea. "And, piling the dirt on a cemetery drop cloth—that was a thoughtful touch. Not your run-o-the-mill body thief, I'd say."

"Have you ever run into one of those?" Andrew asked.

Ian laughed. "Not at all, now that you mention it. It's a mystery, Reverend."

"A mystery indeed."

"You've not had anything like this before, have you?" Ian asked.

"Not in my tenure here."

"Any idea why they'd take that body in particular? Is it likely she'd been buried with something valuable? I need a reason why that grave was chosen. I mean, it can't have been for the body itself. Surely there wouldn't be much left to it. Ashes to ashes and dust to dust and all that."

Andrew rubbed his chin thoughtfully. "I don't believe she was buried with anything valuable."

He glanced down at his notepad. "Hannah Rogers was one of the first to die in the Eyam plague of 1665–1666, if I recall my history."

"You recall it well." Andrew was always aware of being the outsider in these conversations. The locals knew the history of their village in painstaking detail, and took some pride in it.

"Quite a decision your predecessors had to make," Ian said—referring, Andrew knew, to the decision made in 1666 by William Mompesson and Thomas Stanley, two mutually antagonistic clergymen who came together long enough to decide to quarantine the village rather than risk allowing the disease to spread across the countryside.

"It was." The self-sacrifice of a seventeenth century village to lock itself away from all outside contact after the Black Plague appeared was an inspiration to Andrew. Within a year, 257 men, women, and children had died, over half the total population.

"Though it makes for good tourism now, doesn't it?" Ian added.

Andrew nodded. Eyam had become a tourist stop for those who had been captivated by its plague story and for students from schools all over the country who were required to study the event. The church, the rectory, and even the house where the plague started—the Plague Cottage it was called—were landmarks for the hundreds who came through the village every year.

"Is it possible that whoever robbed Hannah's grave was a morbid collector of things related to the plague?" Andrew asked.

"It's possible. There are a lot of freaks out there."

"Has anyone checked any other grave sites to make sure they haven't been burgled?"

"We've checked. Yours was the only one." Ian scratched at his chin. "You know, in the old days bodies were stolen from graves for doctors to use in the medical schools, or for experiments to help science. That sort of thing."

Andrew thought about it for a moment. "I can't imagine anyone wanting to steal a body from here. What if the plague was somehow still alive in those old bones?"

"What if, indeed." Ian sipped his tea loudly again. "That'd be a terrible mess, now, wouldn't it?"

CHAPTER NINE

GENERAL SAM MOSLEY'S helicopter descended onto a field near the compound. The engine was cut and Mark watched the general through the spray of dust. He remained in the cabin and held his head low for a moment, as if in prayer. Then he placed his cap on his head and opened the helicopter door. He walked toward them, but not with his usual energetic stride.

Mark moved front and center with Dr. Susan Hutchinson at his side.

"General," Mark shouted, by way of welcome. He wished he'd had a few minutes to talk to him without Susan. There was no chance of that.

The general shook his hand and said, with an expression full of weariness, "I'm sorry."

Mark nodded. A conversation for another time.

Mosley shook hands briskly with Dr. Hutchinson. "Update?" he asked as he walked with them toward the operations tent. In the past hour it had become the center of activity.

Dr. Hutchinson reported, "Two hundred and seventeen confirmed dead. No survivors have been found."

"Cause of death?"

"I've been waiting for you to tell me," she said. "Obviously there's more going on here than meets the eye."

The general gave her an impatient glance. "Let's begin with what you know, Doctor," he said.

A soldier snapped a salute as they entered the tent. A dozen men in uniform hovered around tables covered with communications equipment, maps, graphs, reports, and assessments. All came to attention when the general entered.

"Privacy, please!" Mosley shouted. All but a single communications officer under a pair of headphones left the tent. The general went to a silver container of coffee and poured three cups, handing them around. "Go on, please."

"My preliminary assessment is that the cause of death was by poison," Susan said. "It appears to be a mass suicide, General."

"What was the poison?" he asked.

"We're running tests. Or, rather, we *were*." She frowned at Mark. "We can't identify the poison yet."

Mosley set the coffee down without drinking any of it. "Do you agree?" he asked Mark.

Mark shook his head. "The formal cause of death might be suicide by poison, but the bodies have the telltale signs of a hemorrhagic *Filoviridae* virus. We would have to evaluate samples to be sure, though all of the samples are in the compound."

Mosley faced his friend. "We can't take the risk of bringing them out."

"Them?" Susan asked. "Do you mean the samples or the bodies?"

"Both."

"We have to know for sure, General," Mark said. "It may not be what we think."

Their eyes met and argued.

"We'll need full autopsies, General," Susan insisted.

"No, Dr. Hutchinson," Mosley said firmly. "No autopsies. No samples. It's too risky."

Susan was undaunted. "What do you mean, too risky?"

Mosley looked at Mark, then back at Dr. Hutchinson. Mark kept his mouth shut to see how the general would answer. Finally he said, "This is not just from poisoning, Dr. Hutchinson, and it's not one of the usual *Filoviridae* viruses. I'm afraid it's something a lot more dangerous."

"Like what?" she asked.

"Like something that can be spread very quickly by secretions and maybe even by airborne particles."

"Just what virus are we talking about, General?" Susan asked. "I don't know of any *Filoviridae* that can be spread by air."

Mark waited. How much would the general tell her?

Mosley diverted his gaze from her to Mark. "This has been a test site for it, Mark. Did you know that?"

"No, I didn't."

Susan stepped between the two men. "This is no time for cryptic comments. Explain to me what you're talking about."

"Am I permitted?" Mark asked Mosley.

"We have no choice," he replied.

Mark faced her. "Dr. Hutchinson, the company I consult with . . ."

"Ahaz," she said, as if she enjoyed saying the name just to express her contempt for it.

"Ahaz and the military have been researching the Ebola and Marburg viruses."

"Researching them? How?"

"We've been working to create a safe version of the viruses."

She looked from Mark to Mosley. "Are you serious? Safe versions?"

"Our theory was that if Ebola could be kept in a viable form, but with the risk of infection removed, then conventional labs could study it."

"How can you keep it in a viable form without the risk of infection? To study it, you'd need the virus to replicate itself in the lab. Take that away and your work is useless."

"Agreed. So, we first made Ebola harmless by taking away the single gene that allows it to replicate."

"What gene did you remove?" Susan asked.

"It's called the VP30 gene," Mark replied.

"The VP30. You took it out and replaced it with what?"

"Researchers from the University of Wisconsin in Madison found that kidney cells from monkeys contained the protein the virus needs to reproduce."

"Monkey kidney cells?" Susan thought about it a moment, then nodded. "I've read about that. Because the cell provides the protein and not the virus itself, the virus could theoretically only replicate within those cells."

Mark was impressed. "That's right. We believed that, even if transferred into a human, the virus would be harmless. Then we could study it further in the hopes of creating a medicine to block the virus and its effects or, even better, to create a vaccine."

"What proof did you have that the modified virus wouldn't slip its leash and spread?"

"We tested it thoroughly in a number of animal models. It didn't cause disease in various live animals, even at extremely high doses."

"And human subjects?" she asked. "Did you test it on humans?"

Mark looked to the general for help. Was he allowed to mention what happened in Greenland? Could he speculate about what may have happened here at the compound?

Susan looked from the general to Mark. "Mark, who were the first human subjects?"

Mark stared at her, unable to answer.

Her eyes widened. "Don't tell me *this* was your first test!" Her face turned red. "You unleashed it on these innocent people?"

"No," Mosley finally said. "This wasn't our first test. I've only just learned that this group was inoculated with what was thought to be the deactivated form of the virus, but the work here wasn't done by us."

"Ahaz did it without your knowledge?" she asked.

"It would seem so," Mosley said.

Susan stormed around the tent, marching in a circle. "Reckless, irresponsible, insane . . ."

"Susan, the animal studies were excellent," Mark said. "There was no reason not to move on to human studies in various parts of the world."

"No reason?" She gestured toward the compound. "There's your reason! You tested your work on over two hundred people here—and it went wrong."

"Will you stop with the accusations and listen? It wasn't one of our sites!" Mark exclaimed, his own impatience rising. "Our partnership didn't sanction these tests. We sanctioned the careful testing of single volunteers in certified BSL4 labs—and never in more than one lab in any one country."

"What difference does all that make if Ahaz has gone rene-gade on you?" Susan went to the tent door. "So where are they? They've got to be around here somewhere."

"I expect to find out as soon as I can," Mosley said.

"I bet you will," she said. "You'll find them so you can work out your cover story. Or have you already got one?"

Mosley glared at her. "There's no cover story."

"Sure there is. It's obvious, isn't it? That preacher was the inside man, ready to take care of the situation for Ahaz if it went wrong. I'll bet he was paid very well to keep the poison ready."

The general held up his hand. "Be careful with what you say."

Susan was clearly beyond being careful, as she turned back to the general. "I can see the well-planted headlines: another mass suicide at the hands of yet another egomaniacal preacher."

"No!" the general snapped. "That is not the plan! You don't know the first thing about it—or him. The young man who led that group was not an egomaniac. He was good and kind. What-ever he did, he did out of love for his people."

Mark was taken aback by Mosley's show of raw emotion.

"Love?" Susan asked, surprised, as she walked back toward Mosley. "First you tell me you don't know anything about this test, and now you seem to know all about the leader of that group. Do you want to explain that to me?"

Mosley looked at her, his eyes hard. "Because the leader of the group was my son."

CHAPTER TEN

DETECTIVE INSPECTOR IAN GLOVER had been gone only a few minutes when Joan Thompson appeared at the vicar's door. She held a tray of tea but he noticed it had two mugs. She placed the tray on the desk and handed Reverend Knight one mug before sitting down in the guest chair with the other.

"We're going to have a talk?" Andrew asked, looking at her quizzically.

"You know, if you want privacy, you really *must* close your door. I could hear everything you and Detective Glover said."

Andrew sipped his tea, waiting for her to continue. She didn't. "Is there something on your mind, Joan?"

"I wouldn't have thought about it if Ian hadn't mentioned doctors and scientists using bodies like they used to."

"And?" Andrew inquired.

"Well, a few years before you arrived, some doctors and scientists from Washington, D.C., came here." She cupped her mug of tea in both hands and rested it on her knees. She looked like a schoolgirl. "It was all to do with a doctor. Stephen Bryant or no, wait, Brian Stephens. He'd done research with HIV, the one that causes AIDS."

"Why would that bring them here?" Andrew was unsure where she was going.

"Because of the plague. They wanted to investigate the similarities between whatever caused the plague and whatever causes AIDS. They thought there was a link. Better still, they thought Eyam might give them a few clues about a cure."

"Why would they think that?"

"They wanted to know how a quarantined village could have any survivors. So a team came to Eyam to find out." She drank some of her tea.

"And how did they do that?"

"Well, first, they had to check out the descendants of the survivors. They assumed that whatever genetic trait had saved the survivors' lives would have been passed down. So Dr. Stephens tested our DNA."

"*Our*?" Andrew asked. "He tested everyone in the village?"

"No, only the descendants." She sat up proudly. "I was his assistant, in a sense."

"Were you?" Andrew smiled. "Well, of course you would be as the church secretary." She would have access to the parish register and the records of everyone who lived and died during the plague period. He thought of the Black Plague survivors name display on a wall in the church.

"Not only as church secretary. I was one of the subjects. My mother's lineage goes back ten generations to the Hancock twins, you know, Frances and Margaret. Margaret survived the plague. So the researchers took DNA samples from me."

"Did they find anything?"

"They did, but I could never explain it to you. All I can say is that it had something to do with our genes. A mutated form, they said. It had a name . . ." She squinted, thinking. "Delta 32, but don't ask me any more than that."

Andrew swung around to his computer and connected to the Internet. A few key words into the search engine and several Web sites appeared. He clicked on one that looked promising: an online encyclopedia with a summary of the Eyam investigation.

"Here it is." Andrew read the article quickly, and then spoke the highlights to Joan. "According to this, Dr. Stephens thought that a genetic mutation—he called it the Delta 32 gene—might explain how the villagers survived since the bacteria that cause the plague and the virus that causes AIDS seem to affect the body in the same way: by getting into their white blood cells and messing with the way they fight off infection and things like that."

"As I just said." Joan reminded him with a wry smile. "Except that bit about the white blood cells."

Andrew continued, "With HIV, the virus travels around the body inside the white blood cells to the lymph nodes. Then the infectious bits break out and attack the person's immune system. In other words, Dr. Stephens's theory was that this Delta 32 gene may have prevented the plague bacteria from entering the white blood cells."

"That's right," Joan said. "Dr. Stephens determined that this Delta 32 thing was found in some of the descendants."

Andrew scanned various links to the article on the Internet and frowned. "I don't see that they've done anything with the information."

"They seemed to disappear," said Joan. "Which is why I asked the next round of researchers who came in and they—"

Andrew interrupted her. "The next round?"

"Oh yes. A few years later some more doctors and scientists came and took more samples, but they weren't from Washington."

"Where were they from?"

"A big pharmaceutical company from somewhere."

"Which one?"

"I don't remember. It had a name from the Bible." She creased her brow, straining to remember. "Ahab. No, that's not right. Ahaz. That's it. Ahaz Pharmaceutical Company."

Andrew had heard of Ahaz Pharmaceuticals from somewhere. However, he couldn't remember much about them. He rubbed his chin. "That's a bad name for a company. Ahaz was one of the worst kings of the ancient kingdom of Judah. He had been willing to surrender his country to Assyria for his own survival. His treasonous actions spelled disaster for the entire nation."

"I wasn't impressed with them. They were very secretive." Joan had lowered her voice and glanced at the study window as if someone might be watching. "They took their samples, paid their bills in cash, and quietly left town in the middle of the night. Which was particularly upsetting to Emily Beecham. You know how she likes to maintain the policies at her hotel."

"Everyone in bed by eleven and not up before six."

"It was very odd behavior for employees of a corporation," she said and leaned in close. "It seemed more like the CIA, if you ask me. They wanted to tear up the graveyard."

"What?" Andrew suddenly sat straight up. "Why?"

"I heard one of them say that they needed tissue from someone known to have died from the plague," she said. "They asked Reverend Jennings for permission to dig up a body but he wouldn't hear of it. He put his foot down and said he didn't want them tearing up the church's grave sites and messing with the dead. It's consecrated ground, he told them, and they better get a court order if they wanted to pursue the matter. We never heard from them again."

"Interesting," Andrew said as he leaned back in his chair. "Even I know that the doctors would have been wasting their time."

Joan nodded. Few, if any, burial services were held in the village during the plague. The victims were placed in graves away from the town. Most of those were unmarked or the graves had been ruined by time.

Andrew drummed his fingers on his desk. "Which brings us to the robbery of Hannah's grave. Do you think that the company came back to get what Reverend Jennings had refused them?"

"Possibly."

"Why now?"

"I don't know."

He drained the last of his tea, then turned back to his computer. He began to type on the keyboard. "Let's see what we can find out about Ahaz Pharmaceuticals."

CHAPTER ELEVEN

"I'M VERY SORRY, GENERAL," Dr. Susan Hutchinson said.

"Here's what I know that you two don't," Mosley said. "My son sent me an e-mail just before he died explaining the hows and whys behind the deal with Ahaz. It was all very straightforward. He thought the financial benefits of this experiment far outweighed the risks. He was convinced by them that the virus had been completely inactivated and thought that this would be an excellent way to keep the community going."

"Sounds crazy to me," Dr. Hutchinson scowled.

"But it wasn't to him. Trust me. The interest earned by the funds from the pharmaceutical company would provide for the needs of the commune for many, many years. But when the sickness started, he recognized it for what it was. When he reported it to the Ahaz reps, they gave him two options: watch his people die a hideous, horrible death or implement their backup plan."

Mark gritted his teeth. "You mean the poison came from Ahaz."

"It was their contingency plan," Mosley explained, his fists clenching. "My son accepted it, believing it would be a gracious and peaceful death for those he loved, as opposed to a grisly and horrible one from this terrible virus."

"You knew nothing about this?" Susan asked.

Mosley glanced away. His voice softened. "My son and I have not been on good terms. I knew he was in Africa, but not that he was working with Ahaz. You can be sure I'll have a few things to say to them once this job is done."

Anxious, Mark leaned close to the general. "What job, General?"

"You know what has to be done, Mark."

"No, General, I do not."

"They're already dead," Mosley said. "Incineration is the only choice. We cannot let even one viral particle escape. Maybe this way, we will save more lives."

"Save at least a couple of the bodies, General," Mark pleaded. "It's the only way we can study what's happening. There are procedures we can follow to ensure that they'll be properly sealed."

"Are they the same procedures we've used elsewhere?" Mosley asked Mark. It was an accusation.

"We'll double—triple—quadruple the precautions."

Mosley chewed his lower lip as a nervous twitch or to keep himself from crying. Mark didn't know which. Then he said, "All right. You have my permission to bring out the bodies of my son and his wife." He produced a photo from his shirt pocket and handed it to Mark. "Here they are."

"Sam . . ."

"Those are the only two I'll allow. No more. And I want them triple bagged. Then I want the exterior of the bags decontaminated and put into a fourth bag. And then I want that bag decontaminated. Fly them to our BSL4 lab in Brazzaville. Full autopsy, full toxicology, full virology, and the initial results on my desk within twenty-four hours. Understood?"

"But, General . . ." Susan protested, "I must evaluate all the bodies. Or, at the very least, take specimens from each of them. We have to do it for the families of the deceased—to be able to account to the surviving family members—not to mention for the myriad legal considerations." She glanced at Mark, appealing for him to help.

The general shook his head. "Sorry, Doctor. Get in there and get the two of them out. That's it. I'll give you no more than two hours, and then the strike package is coming in."

"The strike package?" Susan asked.

Mosley turned away from her and moved toward the tent door. Mark shook his head. She threw her hands up helplessly.

Mark called out, "Do you want to see the bodies, General?"

Mosley did not turn around, but placed his hand against the doorframe. "No. I want to remember them as they were."

The general left the tent.

"We have thirty minutes," Mark said to Susan, taking her arm and pulling her along. "Thirty minutes until what?" she asked.

"Until Armageddon."

CHAPTER TWELVE

FROM HIS TREE FORT a dozen yards inside the thick jungle, Aaron Mosley watched the activity in the distance below him. Soldiers outside of the compound, people dressed in protective suits inside of the compound.

Who were all these people? What were they going to do with the bodies of his family? He couldn't think. His head hurt from fighting the tears that had come and the ones that still wanted to come.

He'd slipped out of the compound after watching his father die. He didn't know what else to do. He'd escaped through the secret gash he and his best friend Jimmy had cut into the chain-link security fence surrounding the compound. Through it they'd been able to come and go unnoticed. None of the leaders of the community ever suspected its existence, but now he was afraid it would betray him. If one of the soldiers happened to find it, it'd be easy enough to follow the footpath to their hideout.

Aaron lay back on the sleeping mat in the center of the tree fort. He watched the camouflaged mosquito netting move in the hot breeze. That was Jimmy's idea. He'd taken it from the storage hut, along with a supply of energy bars and bottled water. It was Aaron who had provided the wind-up shortwave radio. Since his father had banned such devices from the compound, he'd rationalized that he could use it in the tree fort—since, technically, it wasn't part of the compound. He and Jimmy often listened to baseball games from America and sometimes music programs.

But Jimmy was dead now. They were all dead.

The activity in the compound was eerily muted. People moved about, gesturing and signaling. The roar of a truck engine. Helicopters coming and going. The slamming of doors, but no voices. What were these people doing?

Was this the end of all things, the persecution he'd heard so much about? Was that why his father poisoned the wine, to make martyrs of them all? To save them from the end times? To protect them from the persecution? From the tree, Aaron watched and waited.

He struggled against an onslaught of panic. He wanted everything to be the way it was, before all the trouble started. He wanted to be back with his family. He wanted to get rid of the guilt he felt about running away. He wanted to erase the mental images that spun rapidly through his mind: those bodies strewn around the meeting room, his mother and sisters lying down to their final sleep, his father's last wide-eyed expression.

Gone. They were all gone.

Aaron would have shared their fate had it not been for the wine. He never liked the taste of the stuff when his father served it at the communion services. So he did what he always did: he pretended to drink it. And when everyone began to lie down, he knew something was up and decided to do the same. At first he thought it was a practical joke, or some new movement of the Holy Spirit, if only because some wept quietly and others praised God. While lying on the dirt floor, with the fans spinning overhead, the bizarre silence, and, finally, the clicking of his father's typing on the computer keyboard, he tried to work through what had happened.

Jimmy had come down with the red spots first, not long after they had all taken the shots. Then the high fever came. The goons—that's what he called the men from the community who played security guards—came quickly and took Jimmy to an isolation ward in the clinic for observation.

Then things happened quickly. Other folks began to get sick. His dad held secret meetings with a few of the leaders and then a huge meeting for all the adults of the camp. No kids allowed. He had tried to sneak behind the meeting room to listen in, but the goons chased him away. Next thing he knew, his dad called for an immediate service to pray for the sick and to share communion.

The service had all the appearance of normality, but there was an unspoken tension. A few of the women wept as they handed the cup to their children. His own mother hugged him tightly, but she wouldn't look him in the eye.

Soft moans, a few sighs, the shuffle of people taking their places on the floor. Aaron lay perfectly still, frozen from the fear of what was happening. He prayed it was an elaborate prank, and that suddenly the adults would leap up and laugh—a living Sunday school lesson to teach the children about obedience and sacrifice. Or a drill of some sort. A few members in the community talked often enough about the end of all things, how they must respond when Satan's hordes were at the gate to arrest or kill them. This was just a practice, or so he had hoped.

But the feel of Kyle Lawrence's body next to his told him this wasn't practice. Aaron heard his long and final exhalation. And he realized, with mounting panic, that they had all taken their lives.

The wine. There was poison in the wine. This was what the adults had decided in their secret meetings. *Why? What could be so bad?*

When his father was the only one left, Aaron waited. He wanted to sit up and ask him what this was all about, but something in his gut told him not to. Maybe his father had gone insane, the time in the jungle making him crazy. And then his father took a drink from the cup and walked over to his mother and sisters to take his place between them.

The panic in his father's eyes would be branded on his memory forever. And the singular feeling of standing there among the dead, completely alone, would haunt his dreams for as long as he lived.

What else could he do but run?

In the tree fort he had fallen to his knees and prayed for strength, for help.

He thought about running away, but couldn't bring himself to leave his family. So he waited in the tree fort.

He wasn't sure how much time had gone by before the sound of the first helicopter sent him scurrying to the highest point in the tree. It landed and he watched the soldiers leap out, guns ready. They made wild gestures and some had blueprints in their hands and soon they surrounded the entrances to the compound.

Another helicopter arrived, and then another. In what seemed like no time at all, dozens of helicopters had come with more and more military and he knew he would never get inside again.

He thought of the horror stories he'd heard about the end of the age, how the army of darkness would come, looking as if they'd offer comfort and protection, but really bringing pain and persecution. Was this it? Or was he being stupid for not rushing to them?

Torn, he descended into the fort and curled up on the sleeping mat and eventually slept from sheer emotional fatigue.

The pounding of stakes in the ground awakened him the next morning as tents were set up outside the compound. Then people started putting on those protective suits—they looked like weird space suits—and they swarmed all over the place.

From his vantage point, he saw two body bags being carried away. Only two. Were they his parents? His sisters? And what about all the others? What would happen to them?

He finished the last of the snacks and drank the water sparingly. Alert now, he felt agitated, pacing, then lying down, then pacing again, ever watchful of the people in the compound, listening for approaching footsteps. He would make the decision to go to them, but would then change his mind, hoping that God would give him a sign, some sort of clue about what to do. He wept for his family and napped. And upon awakening in the middle of the afternoon, he was aware that something had changed below. There was a different kind of commotion.

Aaron scrambled out to a tree branch and leaned outward, trying to get a clearer view.

Everyone was packing up. The trucks and helicopters were taking the soldiers and equipment away. Within an hour the last helicopter took off, leaving the compound desolate. Were they really going to leave the bodies there to rot?

Not if I can help it. He'd make sure his family was buried properly.

Carefully lowering the rope ladder, Aaron climbed down and crept close to the ground. He was wary about a trap and kept watch for any movement in the trees or brush. He made his way to the gap in the fence. As he began to pull himself through, he heard a roar—familiar because of the trips he'd taken with his grandfather to air shows at Andrews Air Force Base before his grandfather and father had stopped speaking. Fighter jets were overhead.

His gut told him again that something was wrong. He pulled back from the fence and realized why they'd left the bodies behind.

Spinning around, he raced back into the jungle. He thought about returning to the tree fort, but his instincts told him to keep running. Branches and vines lashed at him as he sprinted onward. There was a bright flash and then the sound of thunder crashed in his ears as four F/A-18 Hornet fighter jets zoomed just above his head; they couldn't have been more than a hundred feet above the ground. He stumbled and fell. Rolling onto his back, he watched though a gap in the trees as the jets suddenly pulled up and flew away at a sharp angle. *Just like they do at the air shows.*

He struggled to his feet and continued to run as hard as he could. Somewhere behind him came a *thud, thud, thud, thud.* He didn't dare turn to look. Mere seconds went by. The air around him changed, as if the compound had sucked it in then let it out again. Time seemed to be caught in the vacuum, slowing down.

He stumbled again, falling against a tree. Looking over his shoulder, he saw the fireball—small at first, then expanding upward and outward. One and then another, then a third and a fourth forming a large fiery mushroom cloud. The explosions sent a wave moving at blinding speed through the trees toward him.

He turned to run but the impact blew him off his feet.

This is the end of the world! He felt himself flying though the air. *The great tribulation has begun; the Apocalypse is nigh. Just like Dad and Mom taught me. The end of all things has come.*

Darkness enveloped Aaron.

CHAPTER THIRTEEN

CHIEF WARRANT OFFICER DREW SMITH had flown helicopters his entire military career, but he never loved a helicopter like he loved his Black Hawk. It was a bit clunky at times but, overall, it was a dream to fly.

Drew turned in the pilot's seat to shout back to Tom Mac-Gowan, one of the two young field agents escorting the body bags back to the base. "Estimated arrival is in twenty-two minutes."

"Roger," Tom shouted back.

Rollins, the copilot, engaged the radio to confirm their progress with the base and to establish the protocol for the two bodies once they landed.

The helicopter sped through the air at 180 knots, nearly its maximum speed, turning the brush country below into a blur. It was how the world always looked to Drew when he was at the controls. Flying was second nature, like breathing. On a routine flight, he easily slipped into a daydream filled with the hum and rattle of the helicopter's music, but let there be the slightest change of sound or movement in his machine, or the appearance of an unexpected shape—a building or a road below—and all senses became instantly alert.

His mind wandered to the strangeness of this particular mission: transporting the two bodies from the compound. What a sad business. Tom had said it was another Jonestown. Some kind of religious cult had done themselves in.

But that didn't explain the total annihilation of the area by the fighter jets from the USS *George Washington* anchored just offshore and the extraordinary precautions with the body bags. The community was about as far into the jungle as you could go. Virtually no one would know it had been destroyed. Nevertheless, it seemed like a whole lot of trouble for victims of simple poisoning.

Or was it poison? He glanced back again and wondered if there was more to it than that. If those bodies carried a secret, he'd never know what it was—not buried in all those layers of body bags.

As he turned to face forward, he was surprised by the scent that filled the cockpit. At first he wondered if it might be the disinfectant the field agents used on the body bags, but he had never smelled such a strong, but delicate odor, almost like a perfume.

He felt a sudden itch on his chest. Not in one place, but several, as if an insect had crawled into his flight suit. He patted the area with the palm of his hand. The itching intensified. It reminded him of his boyhood, the hives he'd suffered after eating a mouthful of shrimp for the first time; an unfortunate allergy that had sent him into total body hives and fits of scratching. The difference now, he thought, was that this itch also burned. What had he eaten for lunch?

Drew looked at Rollins, who had a pained expression on his face as he dug his fingers into his chest. "That's weird," Rollins commented. "I'm itching all over."

"You, too?" Drew asked. He reached down, unzipped his flight suit, and clawed at his undershirt. The itching and burning grew worse. *What's going on here?* He ripped at the collar of his undershirt and craned his head down for a look. Bright red splotches covered his torso. "Hey! What's this?"

Rollins lurched forward, clasping a hand over his mouth trying to stop the sudden explosion of bloody vomit.

A wave of nausea hit Drew and he struggled to overcome it. He'd never thrown up while on duty and he wasn't about to start now, but he knew he was in trouble.

"Rollins!"

Rollins threw his head back against the seat, twitching spasmodically. Red splotches dotted his neck and face. He suddenly went limp, his eyes wide open, unblinking.

"Tom!" Drew cried back to the field agent. There was no answer.

He reached for the radio. "I've got a Mayday here." A quick check of the instruments told him he was only five minutes from the base.

Radio static hissed at him and a broken voice inquired about the problem. He could hear Tom in the back talking to someone. He turned to look. Tom was on his cell phone, sweat dripping off his face.

"What are you doing?" Drew shouted at him. "I need help up here!"

Tom dropped his cell phone and began to claw at his collar, gasping for breath.

Drew pressed the button on the radio. "Mayday! I repeat: Mayday! Clear runway 34. Have ambulances ready. We're incoming fast and hard. Code Red status."

"Chief Smith. This is base command," the radio crackled. "Explain your situation."

He was about to answer when Tom, coughing up blood, burst into the cockpit. He threw up bright red blood, spraying the front window and instrument panel. Drew pushed at him shouting, "Get back! In the back!"

Tom fell backward, out of view. Drew caught sight of the other field agent, who was tearing at his skin, trying to fight the invisible forces that had invaded his body.

Drew pushed the throttle to full power. He had to get to the base.

His right arm began to tingle and his mouth filled with the taste of something salty. All the while, the heady scent of flowers became more powerful. *What is this?* He resisted panic. His whole body felt as if it were on fire. He fought to keep conscious. Whatever had infected his copilot and the field agents would *not* master him. He *would* keep control of his wits and his chopper.

The other field agent threw himself around the floor of the helicopter, writhing and shouting a stream of profanities in a pool of his own making.

"Mayday!" Drew cried out again, and it sounded to his ears like a whimper. Then the seizure came and an unwelcoming darkness. He shouted his wife's name before the sound was violently choked off by the constriction of all the muscles in his body.

Drew fell against the instrument panel, thrashing and twitching. The Black Hawk spun out of control and fell from the sky like a rock.

He heard himself scream just seconds before the crash and ensuing fireball.

PART TWO

CHAPTER FOURTEEN

JULY 15, 1666

REBEKAH OPENED THE DOOR. Indeed, it was *him*.

There the monk stood in his long brown robe and a cowl pulled up over his head in spite of the oppressive summer heat. His face was hidden in the dark shadows. His hands were clasped beneath the sleeves, just above a belt made of rope. There was no denying it, Rebekah thought as she stifled the urge to scream: he looked like the Angel of Death.

"Rebekah," he said, his voice deep and warm. "May I enter?"

She opened the door and bowed as he passed. He stopped in the center of the small room and then went to the body of Rebekah's brother. Making the sign of the cross, he said, "I am sorry. I did not know he had passed." He knelt next to her brother's body and whispered a prayer.

After he finished with the dead, he turned his attention to the living, gliding toward Rebekah's sleeping mother and younger sister. He knelt between their cots and reached out to touch each one on the forehead.

"Father of mercies and God of all comfort," he prayed, "our only help in time of need. We fly unto thee for succor in behalf of these thy servants, here lying under thy hand in great weakness of body. Look graciously upon them, O Lord . . ." His voice faded again to a whisper as he continued his prayer.

Minutes went by. Rebekah watched the cowled figure, his arms outstretched like Jesus on the cross. She pressed a hand against her mouth, squeezing her lips to create a pinch of pain. She did not want the tears that now wanted to come.

" . . . grant this, O Lord, for thy mercies' sake, in the name of thy Son our Lord Jesus Christ, who liveth and reigneth with thee and the Holy Ghost, ever one God, world without end. Amen."

Rebekah also whispered, "Amen."

He stood but did not face her. "What may I do for you, sister?"

"It is enough that you have come," she replied, keeping her gaze away from him. "Your prayers are a gift of solace to me."

He moved to the fire; the embers flickered a pale yellow. He reached out and lifted the iron rod, bending to prod the embers into a fuller flame. There was a small burst of light and, for the first time, she saw for a fact what had only been gossip: his hands were blue.

She gasped at the sight.

He looked at her and enough light shone under the hood so she could see his face. It, too, was blue.

"It is true," she whispered.

He straightened and, with a wan smile, adjusted his cowl so that his face returned to shadow. "Rebekah, we must trust in God's mercy. I believe your mother will live. She will not succumb to her illness."

Her jaw fell from astonishment. "Is it possible? How do you know? Are you . . . an angel?"

He shook his head. "I am merely a servant of God."

She took a deep breath. "What of my sister?"

"She will soon join your father, sisters, and brother. Her current sleep is, I fear, her last."

Rebekah closed her eyes. She nodded. "God's will be done." As she said the words, tears flowed down her cheeks in hot streams.

The monk moved closer. Reaching out, he gently wiped the tears from her cheek with his blue finger. "Is there anything I can bring for you, my little sister? Do you need food? Shall I summon the grave digger?"

"No, Brother. I have all I need. Mr. Dicken will surely pass by in the morning, as he always does. I will seek his help then. Tonight, I shall say my farewells, pray, and grieve."

The monk lingered a moment, then moved to the door. "Then I shall depart, and return as the Holy Spirit gives me leave." His hand touched the latch but hesitated. He turned to her again. "Rebekah, I must speak plainly."

She looked at him anxiously. "What is it, Brother?"

"I know of your betrothal to Richard Townsend of Stoney Middleton before the village agreed to isolate itself."

She was puzzled. "Yes?"

"Every soul in this village agreed to the isolation for the good of the other villages, the entire county. Your parents pledged their good name to this cause."

"Why do you feel compelled to remind me?" she asked.

He took a deep breath, but his dark eyes remained fixed upon her. "It is difficult for you not to see your betrothed—this I understand."

"It is very difficult indeed," she conceded.

"And yet . . . you do see him," the monk said, his voice stern but without losing its warmth. "You meet him daily in the Delph."

Startled, she stepped back. *How did he know? How could he know?* She put a hand to her mouth, but did not speak.

The monk continued, "Surely this is a violation of the promise and vow you have made."

She felt her lip trembling and her eyes misting. "We gaze at each other across the moor. It is our way of knowing the other is safe. I love him so."

"Then show your love by honoring your vow as a woman of honor for the sake of your father's good name and the sake of your beloved's life."

She thought for a moment and then nodded her assent.

He raised his hand and she lowered her head. "Then, I bless you in the name of the Father, and of the Son, and of the Holy Ghost."

"Amen," she said.

Before she could look up, he had turned and silently passed through the doorway.

She followed him out and watched as he walked the path to the short hedgerow and the road beyond, turning left in the direction of the church. She wanted to call out to him, to ask him who he was and how he had known to come to their village in this time of need.

Pushed by a sudden curiosity, she moved to the edge of the road and peered in the direction he'd gone. He was now a silhouette at the top of the hill, a mournful figure in the moonlight.

Gathering her skirts up, she followed him. She stepped carefully to avoid the ruts in the road, a dim reminder of the days when the road was used for horses and carts, and not a footpath for the dying. Crickets sang in the nearby woods. She thought she saw the flicker of a candle in the Duffield house. Up ahead, the monk turned into the churchyard, disappearing from view.

She quickened her pace, cutting across a walkway that led to the main door of the church. Rather than risk being seen in the middle of the yard, she went to the church wall and followed it to the corner. Peeking around the edge of the building, she saw the monk walking among the tombstones in the church's graveyard. Again, she felt a chill go down her spine as he moved ghostlike in that place of death.

Where is he going? Beyond the outer wall of the churchyard lay an open field, and then the sharp climb up the hillside to the mines. *Where could he possibly be going?*

A cloud covered the moon and she lost sight of him. She halted, waiting for the light to return or for a telltale sound. A warm breeze rustled the leaves in the trees. The cloud passed and the moonlight returned.

She stifled a cry, for there he was, standing by a mausoleum—facing her. Her body stiffened. Her heart pounded. She couldn't breathe. She felt certain he would call to her, accuse her of following him, and condemn her for her curiosity.

And then, in an instant, he disappeared.

She blinked. Surely the moonlight had played tricks on her, but he had been there one second, and the next he was gone.

It was so remarkable to see someone vanish into thin air that she forgot herself and ran forward to the place in the graveyard where he had been. He was not to be found. There was no evidence of him whatsoever.

Turning in a slow circle, she looked at the empty graveyard and was now convinced that he had done something miraculous. She looked upward as if he might have sprouted angel's wings and flown away.

She shook her head in astonishment and, with nothing else to do, retraced her steps back toward the church. Reaching the main village road, she was struck by the smell of flowers. They seemed so potent tonight, bringing to mind beautiful fields and happier days.

As she navigated the uneven road, her thoughts returned to the Blue Monk and the mystery of his visitation—and departure. Dare she tell her mother about it? And what could she conclude from what she had seen?

She came along a tall hedgerow, within sight of the front door of her house, when a hand grabbed her arm. With a sharp cry, she stumbled backwards, barely keeping balance as she wrenched her arm away. Somewhere a dog barked.

John Dicken stepped through a gap in the bush, his tall and lanky form towering over her. "'Tis an odd time for a walk, Miss Rebekah."

"Mr. Dicken," Rebekah gasped. "You startled me."

"With regrets," he said without regret. "You followed . . . him, did you not?"

Rebekah felt as if she'd been caught doing something wrong. She looked at Dicken without speaking but wanting to discern the grizzled scowl that now scrutinized her.

"There are those who believe he brought the illness to our village," Dicken said. "There are those who desire that he depart and not return."

"Depart? I believe him to be an angel of mercy," Rebekah said.

"Or a demon," he snapped. "What but a demon would exhibit his magical powers? What but a demon would wander graveyards and disappear in them?"

"No . . ." Rebekah whispered.

"You would be wise to keep your distance from him," Dicken said. "And get to your house. This is not a fitting time of night for a young lady to be out and about."

Rebekah nodded and kept her head lowered as she stepped past him.

"You'll be wanting my services tomorrow?" he called after her.

"Yes," she replied without looking back. "I'm afraid so."

Dicken's words were undeniably threatening. Did he have a plan against the monk? Would he dare?

As she approached the doorway to her home she felt a tingle on her arm, a stinging itch as if a thorn had pricked her. At first she thought it was the place where Dicken had grabbed her. Then she realized the sensation was on the other arm. Had she scratched herself in the graveyard? *Foolish girl*, she thought. It's what she deserved for her curiosity. She rubbed her arm. It felt damp. She stepped inside and went directly to the fire. She lifted her arm to the light. There was a rose-colored mark on the skin of her arm.

Her lips trembled. Nausea came over her as she felt an ice-cold panic course through her veins. Her chest and back began to itch. She felt faint and quickly sat down to keep from losing consciousness. As the room spun around her, she heard the appeal of the monk come back to her: stop meeting Richard on the moor, " . . . for the sake of thy beloved's life."

She took a deep breath. Yes, her mother would survive, the monk had said, but he had not given assurance that she would.

Oh God, she began to pray silently then stopped. She looked at the blood that had dried on her fingers and began to sing softly to herself, "Ring a-ring o' roses, a pocketful of posies. A-tishoo! a-tishoo . . ."

CHAPTER FIFTEEN

AARON PUSHED HIMSELF FORWARD through the dense forest, his eyes always on the road that ran parallel to him a few dozen yards to his left. The shock—that numbing sense of survival—left him only vaguely aware of his aching leg muscles and the cuts and bites on his skin. He staggered onward. He'd been walking for over three hours. Another fifteen or twenty minutes wouldn't matter. He had to get to Uncle Win.

Convinced that someone—he didn't know who—was searching for him, he hid when he heard the occasional car drive past. A sudden snap of a branch, a movement deeper in the jungle, made him drop to the ground until he was certain he was safe. At clearings, he crouched low, sometimes crawling, to keep from being seen.

He thought of his family and was unable to get the image of their dead bodies or their incineration from his mind. He yearned for his father, to see and hear him again, to get his advice. *Never again.*

He prayed to God for help as his father had taught him to do, and it was during one of those prayers that he thought of Uncle Win. He wasn't really his uncle, but a pastor named Aloysius Windabe who lived in the small village of Mitzic, a dozen miles from the compound. Uncle Win had been a good friend to the community and an advisor to the leadership. He also took a keen interest in Aaron's prowess at soccer, or football as people called it here. Whenever Uncle Win came to the community, he always allowed an hour or two of kicking the ball around with Aaron, talking of faith and life as they played. Uncle Win would help Aaron. He would know what to do.

From the sounds of town and traffic now reverberating through the woods, Aaron knew he was coming close to Mitzic. Through the trees ahead he could see an open field, with a handful of shacks and huts dotting the landscape. A rusted truck sat off to one side of a house. Laundry hung from lines, the brightly colored clothes flapping in the breeze like flags of warning.

Aaron skirted around the edge of the field and came to a secondary dirt road that encircled the south side of the village. A woman carrying a large bucket of water walked past him, eyeing him as she went. Two men sitting on a makeshift porch chatted without paying him any particular attention. A small group of children were in a game of chase, darting across the road in front of him and disappearing between two houses, their shrieks fading as they ran into the brush. He wondered how life could go on so normally. Didn't anyone hear the explosions? Or had they been heard and ignored, as often happened in this part of the world?

A church steeple came into view just beyond a small grocery. The white wooden cross at the top of the steeple beckoned him. Aaron picked up his pace and followed the dirt driveway that led to the church itself. Uncle Win's house was just beyond that.

In his relief, Aaron very nearly collapsed on the dirt driveway. A sob caught in his throat. He forced himself toward the door. As he reached the edge of a stretch of grass, Uncle Win came out with a broom in his hand and began to sweep the dust from the small porch.

Aaron opened his mouth to cry out, but could only manage an anguished choking sound. Uncle Win looked up and saw him. At first his face registered surprise and then alarm. He dropped the broom and rushed to the boy.

Uncle Win helped Aaron into the house and guided him to the single couch that sat along one of the walls of the main room. Aaron lay down and closed his eyes. He heard Uncle Win slamming cupboard doors and banging cups, and then came the groaning of the water pump. A moment later, Uncle Win was kneeling at his side. "Drink this," he said and held out a cup.

Aaron gulped the water, choked, and gulped some more.

"What's happened, boy?" Uncle Win asked. His face, pockmarked except where white stubble poked out from his chin and cheeks, was pinched with worry. Producing a wet rag, he began to dab at Aaron's face. "Why are you in this condition?"

"They're dead," Aaron said. He whispered at first, but as he spoke he could hear his voice rising, sounding panicked though inside he thought he felt calm. "Armageddon has come, Uncle Win. They're dead. The compound is gone. Planes came. It exploded. A fireball. Everyone drank the cup, but I didn't, and I'm the only one left. Then the others came and . . . and . . ." He began to shiver. Why was he so cold when he knew it was so hot?

"You're delirious," Uncle Win said in a soothing tone. "I'll call the office and speak with your father."

"You can't. I told you, he's dead. They're *all* dead." He heard his voice break in that way it does when puberty is coming and he knew he sounded like an idiot.

Uncle Win patted his arm. "You lie still. Rest. Leave it to me."

Aaron closed his eyes again and heard the tiny beeps of Uncle Win's cell phone as he dialed. A pause, listening. A low signal to indicate that the line was engaged or disconnected. Uncle Win hummed nervously to himself an old hymn. "The Old Rugged Cross." More beeps as he redialed and Uncle Win said into the phone, "Captain Ambrose, please. Yes, I'll hold."

Aaron opened his eyes and sat up. "Captain? Who are you calling?"

"The police, of course," Uncle Win replied. "You must lie down."

Aaron struggled to his feet. "No, Uncle Win. You can't."

"Captain Ambrose is a member of my church," Uncle Win said, coming to him and prodding him back to the couch. "He knows your father. He can help."

Aaron didn't have the strength to resist, but protested as he sat back down. "Don't trust anyone. You didn't see what I saw! The Army of Darkness will come. The world has gone crazy."

Uncle Win gave him a sympathetic smile. "The world has always been crazy," he said, then turned his attention to the phone. "Guy? It's Win. I believe something may have happened out at the compound."

CHAPTER SIXTEEN

THE CHATEAU WAS A fourteen-room hotel in the center of Mitzic. It had seen better days.

And those days were a hundred and fifty years ago, Nathan Dodge thought as he ascended the creaky and lopsided stairs to the set of rooms on the top floor. The wallpaper—if it truly ever *was* wallpaper—was a faded burgundy and gold and sagged on the wall like skin on an elephant. The smell of mold pervaded everything.

Yet Dodge imagined how this house must have looked to the French traders who had first colonized this region. Today, it was still luxurious compared to everything that surrounded it. There was an upright piano in the lobby, and the chandelier in what passed for the dining room must have come from France. So lavish. So wasted.

This was probably a brothel. Too bad it still isn't.

Dodge had secured the four rooms at the top of the hotel and moved in his men and equipment the day before. He went to the first door, knocked twice, and went in. Bernie Toppel, a prematurely balding techno geek, dressed in a Hawaiian shirt, khaki shorts, and University of Florida Crocs, was hunched over a table overburdened with high-tech electronic equipment. Bernie wore a pair of headphones that made the tufts of hair on the side of his head stick out at odd angles. Looking up at Dodge, he gestured for him to come closer and then held up a finger for him to wait.

Dodge circled the room while he waited. Every surface space, even the bed, was covered with unmarked boxes, tangled wires, and components attached to laptop computers, communication devices, and monitoring equipment.

Outside the window, a woman shouted profanity in French, the official language of the country. Dodge parted the thin gauze and peered out. In the alley below, the woman berated a teenage girl, probably her daughter. A domestic spat. Dodge watched them as the woman yelled and the girl hung her head. He wondered, with a wry smile, if the woman would consider their conflict of any real importance if she knew they might all be dead before the day was through. Was this how she would have spent her last hours if she knew what was imminent?

Bernie pulled off the headphones and dropped them onto the table. "This isn't good," he said.

"Of course it's not good," Dodge growled as he turned from the window. "We wouldn't be here if things were good."

"I'm getting chatter off the local scanner. The police. Their dispatch has just radioed a patrolman to drive out to the compound to investigate its condition."

"Oh?" Dodge approached the table. "And why would they do that?"

"Something about a call, a report of trouble. I'm having a hard time understanding their local dialect."

"Who called in?"

"I don't know. They said something about a pastor and a kid. 'Win'?"

Dodge grabbed up a binder and flipped to a detailed map of the village. He found three churches in the area, with sidebars of information about each one. One had a pastor named Windabe. *Win.* A quick turn to another section of the binder and he found a profile on the pastor. The man had regular personal contact with the people at the compound, but how could he possibly know that something had happened? What kid?

"You're certain we have all the communications from the compound, right?"

"Everything from the last twenty-four hours, including all the military and WHO communications; even that final e-mail from David Mosley to his father."

Dodge nodded. They were glad David had taken the initiative

for one last contact with the general. It saved them the trouble of having to get the military involved. Why do all the dirty work when someone else could do it for you?

"No phone calls, no communications in this direction?"

"None at all. That e-mail was the only thing that went out."

So what prompted Windabe to call the police? "How soon before the police arrive at Windabe's?" he asked.

"Apparently the captain was in another village, several miles away, when the call came. He's en route now."

Dodge had to get his people to Windabe before the police. "Pull McAvoy and Keenan from their posts." Dodge pointed to the church on the map. "Send them there."

"To do what?"

"I want to talk to Pastor Windabe."

"And if the police are already there?"

Dodge looked at him impatiently. "They know what to do."

Bernie turned to his console and put on a communications headset.

Dodge paced back to the window. The woman and the girl were gone.

"Then I want you to get me a secure line to the home office," he said.

"Gotcha."

Dodge frowned. Peter Romero, his boss at Ahaz Pharmaceutical, wasn't going to be happy about this latest development.

CHAPTER SEVENTEEN

GENERAL SAM MOSLEY STOOD in the center of the communications tent—part of the newly established Ops Center a mile from the compound. He stared at the collection of communications equipment as if it were complicit in the unfolding tragedy around him.

"General?" a voice asked.

Mosley had heard the *Mayday* from Chief Warrant Officer Smith in the helicopter. He'd heard Smith's screams until they had been cut off and replaced by static.

A team headed by Dr. Susan Hutchinson was now on its way to secure the scene—to check for survivors, unlikely as that might be. He had sent her to implement even more stringent precautions with whatever remained at the crash.

Somehow—and only God knew how—something had gone wrong with their anticontamination procedures. How else had the virus escaped from the bags to kill everyone on that helicopter?

"General," the voice came again.

Mosley turned. "What is it, Mike?"

"Dr. Carlson on the secure line." The young soldier held the phone in his outstretched hand. "He's at the compound."

"There is no compound," the general barked as he took the phone. He had sent Mark back to make certain the destruction was thorough. "Mark."

The line hissed and popped. "General. We'll have to run tests on the air and ash samples we've taken, but I don't believe the site is now any sort of threat."

Mosley noted Mark's careful wording, how he avoided saying anything that might bring images of his family's resting place to

mind. "Good. Tell the sergeant to establish guards around the perimeter anyway—in protective gear—until we get the results of
your tests."

"Will do." Mark paused. "General, did I hear right? The transportation helicopter crashed?"

"Yes."

Another pause. Crackle and hiss. "Was the crew infected?"

"It would seem so. Dr. Hutchinson is on her way to investigate."

"I'll do what I have to do here and hurry back." He hung up.

"You do that," Mosley said to the vacant line and handed the
phone back to the young soldier.

Another communications tech, who looked to be no more
than fifteen years old, stood at the far end of the tent and gestured to the general. "Sir, there's an Inspector Martin Duerr from
Interpol."

Mosley grabbed the mike. *What could this be about?* He pressed
the button on the mike. "Inspector, this is General Mosley."

"Is our line secure, General?"

"Encrypted and secure, as is always the case."

"Good. I've just acquired some information I thought you
would want."

"I'm listening."

"We've identified the members of a special cell within Return
to Earth, a cell that is operating out of The Hague."

"What?" Mosley was surprised, but instantly realized he
shouldn't have been. Some areas of The Hague leaked information like sieves—in both directions. He wondered which areas
were compromised and if any were close to his own.

"I have their identities, General, along with their code names
and communication methods. We've confirmed that some are
under your command."

"My command?" Mosley closed his eyes. He hoped it was a
mistake. If not, he would personally execute the traitors.

"Worse. We intercepted a call within the past hour. It came
from one of your men, on, we believe, a transport of some sort. A
truck, a plane, we couldn't be sure."

"Do you know where he was calling from?"

"Gabon—in Africa. Do you know it? Do you have anyone operating there?"

The general's grip tightened on the phone. "Who is he, Inspector? I need a name."

"Do you have a Tom MacGowan working for you?"

Mosley took a slow, deep breath. "I did—yes."

"Sir?" another communications specialist yelled from across the room. "I have a Captain Ambrose on the line for you. He's with the police in Mitzic. He says it's urgent."

He signaled for the soldier to get more information.

"Are you saying that MacGowan isn't working for you now?" Duerr asked. "Because if not, I need to know who to speak with. He's a dangerous man, General. We believe he's on a suicide mission for Return to Earth."

Mosley stood rigid, feeling as if his bones might snap. *So, that is how the virus escaped from the body bags.* "Inspector, MacGowan may have succeeded with his mission. He's dead, and he took a few others with him."

"We were too late," the inspector said. "I'm sorry."

The tech waved at the general. "You should take this call, sir. Captain Ambrose is on the line about a boy who claims to have come from the compound."

Mosley felt the blood drain from his face. No one could have escaped the holocaust. "Inspector, I'm sorry. I must go."

Duerr began to speak, but Mosley cut the connection and moved toward the other phone as the techie explained, "The captain thought you may want a representative there when he interviews the boy. He's on his way to the address, but is still a few miles out."

Reaching for the phone, Mosley turned to his transportation officer and commanded, "Get me a vehicle to Mitzic."

CHAPTER EIGHTEEN

AARON LAY ON A mat in the back room of Uncle Win's house. He stared at a crack in the ceiling, wishing he could disappear into it. Insects buzzed and birds chirped indifferently through the window over his head.

Uncle Win had paced and fretted for the past half hour, asking Aaron variations of the same questions over and over in an attempt to make sense of what Aaron had told him. The story didn't change and it made no more sense to either of them than it had when Aaron first arrived. Aaron vacillated between feeling annoyed at Uncle Win for doubting him and feeling some vague hope that maybe he was feverishly sick and hallucinated the whole thing. Uncle Win, clearly perplexed, told him to rest and went to the front porch to wait for the police captain. Aaron could hear the swishing of the broom on the wooden slats.

Of course, Aaron couldn't rest. He was now afraid that his uncle might want to drive to the compound to see it all for himself. He was afraid his uncle would force him to go along. He was afraid that the Army of Darkness would capture them.

"Don't trust anyone," Aaron had begged Uncle Win. And now he wondered whether he should have trusted his uncle.

A small laptop sat on a table nearby. Uncle Win had kept it here for him to use when he and his family came to visit.

Aaron got up off the mat and looked at the dark screen, pushing a key to wake it up. The first image was a screen saver of Aaron and his family taken only a few weeks ago. Aaron's heart lurched at the sight of his father, mother, and sisters sitting under a tree just on the other side of the church. A rare occasion when they left the compound and came for a picnic at Uncle Win's church. A happy day.

Navigating the computer, Aaron found a directory of photos which he'd once organized and captioned for Uncle Win. It was going to be a surprise for Aaron's father: a photographic directory of everyone at the compound. Uncle Win seemed to think it would help with fund-raising back in the states. Now, it was a memorial, he thought. He'd have to ask Uncle Win for the photos later, as a keepsake. If they survived.

Standing at the laptop, Aaron felt that something around him had changed. He stepped to the middle of the room, wondering what it was. *The buzzing of the insects*, he realized. *It's stopped. No sounds from the birds.* He looked to the open window, but saw only the jungle beyond.

Worried, he took two steps toward the bedroom door when he heard the rolling crunch of cars driving on dirt approaching the house. *The police?* Aaron positioned himself where he could see through the crack in the bedroom door, into the front room, then through the screen door to the road beyond.

Uncle Win was on the porch and stood watching the arrival of not one, but two vans and an SUV—all black, unmarked, and formal looking. *Definitely not the cars used by the local police,* Aaron thought. The vehicles skidded to a stop, spraying dust. Men in protective clothing leapt from the vans.

The Army of Darkness. Aaron retreated into the room. He turned and bolted for the window as he heard his uncle shout. Heavy footsteps fell on the dirt drive, then the porch. Uncle Win protested as the front door was thrown open.

Aaron hurled himself through the open window and fell to the ground below. He gathered himself up and raced into the sanctuary of the thick brush.

He heard crashes and breaking glass ring out from the house behind him. Indistinct shouts.

Did they see me? Are they chasing me?

Aaron didn't look back.

CHAPTER NINETEEN

NATHAN DODGE PACED THE ROOM at the Chateau, pressing his communications headset to his ear. He couldn't believe what he was hearing. "Has any of this been verified?"

On the other end of the line, his boss, Peter Romero snapped, "How many different ways do we have to verify it? The caller had all the right information down to details only a few people could have known."

"Return to Earth," Dodge repeated slowly, mostly for the benefit of Bernie, who was sitting at his console nearby.

Bernie looked up at Dodge and shrugged.

"I've never heard of it," Dodge said.

"I don't think anyone is *supposed* to have heard of it. That's the point of being a secret terrorist group." Romero's voice was tight as if his very vocal chords were as clenched as his teeth. "But now they've come out. They claim to have sabotaged our work there. They've promised that there's more to come. So we don't know what other projects may be or have been compromised. Probably Greenland. You and your team have to stay on guard."

"Will do." Dodge didn't know how seriously to take this information. It made no sense to him that a group dedicated to destroying humankind and returning the earth to nature would exist, but if his boss was right, then they must be well funded and well connected.

"And if I were you, I'd keep a close watch on the members of your team," Romero added.

"You think these wackos have infiltrated us?"

"They've infiltrated us at some level, or they couldn't know what they know. So, be careful."

Romero hung up and Dodge looked at Bernie, who had his head down and was listening intently to something on his headset. His head suddenly jerked up and he waved at Dodge.

"It's McAvoy!" he said, a harsh whisper.

Dodge punched a button that opened the line. "What's going on, McAvoy?"

McAvoy, one of his agents, spoke from the other end of the line. "The kid isn't here."

"What do you mean he isn't there? Where is he?"

"He may have escaped out of a back window."

"Did anyone go after him?" Dodge asked.

"Have you ever tried to chase someone through the jungle in an anticontamination suit?"

Dodge groaned. "Have the police arrived?"

"Not yet."

"What about the pastor? What's he saying?"

"Not much. He's complaining about our entrance. He says we scared the boy away."

"Did you show your government badges?"

"Yeah, but he doesn't believe they're real."

Smart man. "Was the kid from the compound? Could you confirm that?"

McAvoy was quiet for a moment and his tone changed, softening, as if he wanted to make sure he was out of earshot of anyone nearby. "Yeah, Boss, I'm pretty sure he was."

"How do you know?"

"The pastor's not feeling well."

"Clarify."

"He's showing symptoms."

Dodge looked over at Bernie, who was listening to the conversation on his own headset. Bernie went bug-eyed.

"Get the team out of there!" Dodge shouted.

McAvoy didn't respond.

"Did you hear me?"

"Yes, but . . ." McAvoy began and then stopped.

"But what?"

"Well, since the kid wasn't here all of our men took off their headgear."

"What?" Dodge shouted, and then quickly lowered his voice. "Why would they be so stupid?"

McAvoy was silent again. Then his voice took on a noticeable quiver. "I was one of them, Boss."

Dodge swore under his breath.

McAvoy asked, "Do you think . . . ?"

"Yes, I do."

A whimper came from McAvoy.

"Stay where you are and have everyone put their helmets back on," Dodge commanded. "None of you move. Don't make contact with anyone. And for God's sake don't lead anyone back here."

McAvoy began to speak again but Dodge disconnected the line. He yanked off his headset and threw it across the room at Bernie. "Idiots."

"You can't leave them there," Bernie said.

"This is a disaster," Dodge roared, pacing furiously, running his hands through his hair and over his face. "A complete and total disaster."

"So, what are we going to do?"

"We're going to pack up and get out of here," Dodge said, and moved to the small wardrobe. He retrieved his suitcase and began to throw his clothes into it.

"You're leaving our people?"

"The police will help them," Dodge replied over his shoulder. "Or the military will. You can be sure they're on their way. There's nothing we can do."

"We should try."

Dodge turned on his underling. "You can stay and die if you want. I don't love my job that much."

CHAPTER TWENTY

MARK HUNG ON FOR his life as the military vehicle bounced along the rutted road. The late afternoon sun played hide-and-seek through the jungle lining the highway, creating dark stripes from the shadows of the trees.

Mark had finished his job at the remains of the compound. Everything had been incinerated in all directions, including some twenty yards of foliage. Any potential carriers—human or wildlife—were now ashes. Nothing was left. Not even bones. Everything was reduced to ash.

A soldier with the facial features of an English bulldog turned in the passenger seat to face him. He clutched a radio in his hand. "The general isn't at the Ops Center. He's gone to Mitzic."

"Why?" Mark asked, "What's in Mitzic?"

"Apparently, some boy escaped from the compound."

Mark grabbed the sides of the Land Rover, not because of the road, but to steady himself. *How could anyone or anything have escaped?* "We have a fugitive?"

The bulldog continued, "I guess he's made contact with some local law enforcement."

Mark frowned. "What kind of contact are we talking about? Do we have any reports of symptoms? Do we have another outbreak?"

The soldier shrugged. "No information about that, sir."

After all our efforts, we may not be able to stop this thing from spreading, Mark thought. "Take me to Mitzic!" he shouted to the driver.

CHAPTER TWENTY-ONE

THE GENERAL'S VEHICLE SPED through Mitzic, a small town of a few shops, takeout restaurants, and, surprisingly, a hotel.

Mosley pulled down his cap, adjusted his sunglasses, and made certain the scarf was covering most of his lower face. Not only did he want the protection against the dust, but also he didn't want anyone to identify him.

The driver made a sudden turn to the right, leading them away from the town center and down a narrow road that cut through level countryside of brown grass. Ahead he saw a church—a large hut, really—with a modest steeple topped by a cross. Thick jungle stretched out behind it. The driver veered around the right side of the church to a dirt driveway. If the maps were correct, this led to the pastor's house.

"Watch it," the driver shouted and slammed on the brakes, throwing Mosley forward toward the windshield.

"What the devil?"

"Sorry, sir," the driver said.

Ahead of them, a coal-skinned man in a light brown police uniform was waving frantically as he raced toward them. *"Vous ne pouvez pas avancer!"* He spoke French with the thick accent of a local dialect. He ran to Mosley's side of the Jeep.

"What's wrong?" Mosley believed he already knew the answer.

"Vous ne pouvez pas avancer!"

"In English. *En anglais.*"

The policeman corrected himself. "You must go no farther. There is trouble ahead. Terrible trouble!" His voice was shrill.

Mosley craned his neck to look past the policeman. Black vans, a black SUV, and a couple of four-wheel-drive vehicles were randomly parked around the front of a small house. It looked like a triage center, with a handful of men attending to people lying on the ground; six of the fallen wore anticontamination suits. "Where is Captain Ambrose?"

The policeman pointed. "That's him on the porch."

Mosley squinted and saw a man sitting, his back to the wall of the house.

"They are all ill!" The policeman was on the edge of hysteria. "They told me on the radio. Stay away, they said. I think a couple are dead. I wanted to go to them, to help. But they said I couldn't. I'm afraid."

"You're right to be afraid," Mosley said. He turned to the driver, and barked instructions to have a team from the Ops Center come and seal the area. "Find Dr. Carlson and get him here too. The same with Dr. Hutchinson."

The policeman was shuffling from foot to foot, twisting his shirt in his fists. "What am I to do, sir?" Tears filled his eyes and spilled down onto his ruddy cheeks.

"Keep everyone away. Do you have your radio?"

The policeman pulled it from the back of his belt and held it out.

"Can I talk to your captain?"

"You can try."

Mosley took the walkie-talkie and, pressing the button, asked, "Can anyone hear me? This is Brigadier General Sam Mosley."

The radio crackled and a voice came back. "General, this is Captain Ambrose."

Even at this distance, Mosley could see Ambrose holding a walkie-talkie to his face.

"Captain, can you tell me what you encountered when you arrived?"

Ambrose breathed heavily, his words labored. "My best friend, Pastor Windabe . . . sick, dying. Horrible to see. Men I don't know in some sort of hazard suits. All sick and dying. Six, maybe seven. I approached to make contact. Two of us. I didn't know or I wouldn't have come up to the . . ."

The general clenched his teeth, feeling the responsibility. "I'm sorry, Captain. Had I realized, I would have warned you."

Ambrose's breathing was now labored. "Warned me of what?"

Holding the walkie-talkie away, the general tried to think of what to say. He didn't want to explain on an open frequency— anyone could be listening. "Hold on. Help is coming," was as much as he could muster.

"Help for what, General? What is this?"

Mosley had no explanation. "Be patient, Captain."

"Is there time to be patient?" the captain asked softly.

Mosley looked at the scene again. One of the men who had been standing next to a van, clawing at his body as if trying to tear his clothes off, fell, and was writhing on the ground.

"*Mon Dieu! O mon Dieu!*" the policeman next to Mosley moaned, wringing his hands.

The general spoke into the walkie-talkie again. "Captain?"

A very weak, "Yes?"

"The boy. Was the young boy in the house?"

"Boy?" The captain's voice was fading.

"The one the pastor called you about."

Silence for a moment. Mosley could see the captain beginning to scratch his arms, then: "No. There is no boy here."

He's escaped, and he's taken the virus with him. The general hit his fist against the side of the car door.

CHAPTER TWENTY-TWO

MARK ARRIVED IN MITZIC as the sun continued its descent on the horizon. The shop lights—in some cases, bare bulbs—were on, but the town seemed empty of its people.

"Slow down," Mark told the driver.

The engine whined from the downshift, and Mark looked for signs of life. For a moment, he feared that they'd driven into a contaminated area; then he suspected that the townspeople had been drawn to the excitement created by the general and his team. It was only fifteen minutes ago that Mark got the call about the outbreak at the pastor's house. The news was bound to travel quickly to the locals, so people were either investigating the rumors or staying indoors.

All except for someone loading boxes into a lone SUV in an alley behind a hotel. The Chateau. Mark tapped the driver's shoulder. "Stop."

"General Mosley wants us at the—"

"I know," Mark said. "Give me a minute. I want to check something."

The driver darted to the side of the road and came to a stop alongside a cement structure that claimed to be a restaurant. Mark wondered what they served. He knew that the meat would include anything from the bush: goat, gazelle, or even parrot. A torn poster for Régab beer flapped at him from the wall.

Mark jumped out and backtracked to the hotel, turning at the alley and walking cautiously to the SUV. The back was open and unmarked boxes crowded the luggage area.

"Get away from there," someone commanded from the hotel's rear doorway.

Mark knew the voice and turned his head toward its owner.

Dodge stepped forward, lighting a cigarette as he came close. "Hey, Carlson."

"You shouldn't smoke those things," Mark said. "They'll kill you."

Dodge sneered at him.

"Skipping town so soon?" Mark asked. "The party is just getting started."

Dodge snorted. "Maybe it's your kind of party, but it sure isn't mine. I suggest you get away while you can."

Mark shook his head. "Did you help create this mess or did Ahaz send you in to contain it?"

"I'm just part of the cleanup crew," Dodge said with a slight shrug.

"You haven't done a very good job."

"This is like taking a mop to a tidal wave and I guess you know the contamination—the virus you helped them invent—is out now. You know, the one you said was safe."

Mark took a step toward Dodge, who stepped back. "Do you people know what you've done?"

"You people?" Dodge asked, with a wry smile. "Don't we work for the same company?"

A man Mark didn't recognize appeared at the back door carrying another box. He hesitated when he saw the two men, then continued on, slipping around Mark to throw the box into the SUV's bay. He closed the door. "That's it," he said to Dodge, and he went around to the driver's door and got in. A moment later, the motor roared to a start.

"Gotta run," Dodge said. He waved a hand at the SUV. "We've got room if you care to join us."

Mark glared at him. "Tell everyone at the head office to stop cowering in the shadows. I need information about what they tested at the compound. Was it different from our other test sites? What exactly was it?"

"I'll mention your concerns," Dodge said and walked toward the passenger door, brushing by Mark as he passed. "I'm sure they'll be deeply touched."

Mark grabbed Dodge by the shoulder, slamming him against the SUV. Dodge swung a fist around, but Mark deflected it with his forearm. He quickly grabbed Dodge's lapels with both fists and, with his full weight, slammed him against the SUV again, ramming his knee up between Dodge's legs. Dodge groaned, buckling. Mark hissed in his ear: "Dodge, you've got as much blood on your hands as anyone. So you tell them to get me the information I need—now."

Mark heard the telltale sound of a shotgun being cocked just over his left shoulder.

"We really have to be going," said Dodge's accomplice.

Mark let Dodge go and stepped back, his hands raised. Dodge slumped to the ground, trying to breathe.

"Are you all right, Dodge?" the man asked.

Dodge waved him away and, grabbing the side of the car, pulled himself up. "You need our information?" Dodge said to Mark in a harsh wheeze. He stood up as straight as he could and brushed at his shirt. "Remember? You're a medical messiah. You *know* everything. You save lives! Yeah, right."

Dodge laughed as he and his partner climbed into the car.

"Tell them I quit!" Mark shouted as the door slammed shut. He pounded on the back window. "Do you hear me? I quit!"

Mark watched the SUV pull away and disappear around the corner of the hotel onto the main road. He felt his heart sink. Dodge's sarcasm was on-target. There was nothing he could do. Why did he ever think otherwise? He was helpless.

But leaving was not an option.

CHAPTER TWENTY-THREE

MARK'S FEELINGS OF HELPLESSNESS intensified when he arrived at Pastor Windabe's house. There was nothing to be done for the dying—or the dead. Within minutes after his arrival, a truck with the WHO forensic team pulled up.

The general had stationed his men, all in biohazard suits, at a safe distance around the area, if only to make sure the town's curious and concerned didn't sneak in and risk infection.

Mark informed Mosley about the sampling results at the compound, but left out his encounter with Dodge. Mosley, in turn, informed him that the Gabon Ministry of Health and military had been apprised of the situation and had ordered in their own units to help keep order. They were also providing a special forensics team to assist the WHO's efforts.

A team of local police officers was dispatched to search the jungle, with strict instructions to find, but not to approach, the fugitive. With the death of their captain, the local officers seemed glad to be doing something in this crisis.

"But, sir, if the boy runs, how do we capture him?" a sergeant had asked. Mosley, realizing how difficult it would be for the searchers, reluctantly ordered them to use whatever means were necessary to stop the kid from escaping.

"You want us to shoot him?" another officer had asked.

"Not to kill," the general clarified. "We want him alive, if possible."

Mark imagined that these men had never fired their weapons in the line of duty, let alone fire in such a way as to *wound* the target. Yet, what else could they do?

Mosley addressed Mark. "I want you to suit up and check the status of each person inside the perimeter. I think they're all dead, but I'd like a physician's assessment." He looked at the twilight. "It will be dark soon."

Mark nodded. It took a couple of hours to suit up, examine the bodies, go through the decontamination tent, and then take off the suit.

Mark found the general inside the church, which was now a temporary base of operations. It was a one-room building filled with crudely made wooden benches and, at the far end, an altar alongside a pulpit with a cross on the front. The place unsettled him. He hadn't set foot in a church in a long time. The simple austerity touched him, but his ambivalence caused a keen sense of emptiness. Looking around, he guessed that on a crowded Sunday it might hold fifty people.

He wondered how many would attend church this week now that they'd lost their pastor. If there were an outbreak, would anyone else survive to come?

Susan Hutchinson was with Mosley, sitting at the front of the church.

"That didn't take long," the general said.

"There wasn't much for me to do," Mark said.

"Dr. Hutchinson was debriefing me about the helicopter crash."

Mark nodded to Susan, who looked back at him wearily. He sat on the edge of the small raised stage at the front of the church. "And?"

"First, tell me what you found," Mosley said.

"The bad news is that they're all dead: the two officers, including the police captain. And, of course, there was the pastor. Along with five dead from Ahaz."

Susan groaned.

"How?" Mosley asked. "They looked like they had biohazard suits on."

"They did, but the helmet seals were broken. My guess is that when they got here and there was no boy, they took off their helmets to interrogate the pastor."

"If that's true, why would they put their helmets back on?" Susan inquired.

"I honestly don't know. We'll do a full-scene investigation to-morrow. Hopefully, we'll learn more." Mark looked at Mosley. "How did they know the boy was here?"

The general shrugged. "No doubt they'd somehow picked up the communication about the fugitive. I'm sure they raced to get here before the police—or us."

Mark thought about the boxes that Dodge and his accomplice had loaded into the back of the SUV.

"Idiots!" Susan rubbed her forehead.

"Ahaz is more anxious about this situation than we are," Mosley said. "They're trying to cover their butts." He glanced at Mark. "Have you spoken with them?"

"Why would I?"

Mosley gave him a suspicious look. "Your driver told me that you made a stop on the way here. You met someone at the hotel in town."

"You know someone here?" Susan asked.

Mark felt cornered. "I investigated what I thought might be a team from Ahaz trying to make an escape."

"Was it?" Mosley asked.

"Yes."

"So you have been in touch with Ahaz." Susan was making an accusation.

"'Touch' isn't the word I'd use," Mark said, his voice flat and cold. "Altercation is more like it."

"You should have told me," Mosley said sharply.

"You're right, I should have, but there was nothing to it. No helpful information. No exchange of ideas. No offers to assist. They were covering their butts, like you said."

"And their men were killed for it," Susan said, disgusted. "When are they going to learn?"

"They'll learn when the body count cuts in on their profits," Mark replied. He felt a wave of nausea hit him in the gut.

"That's a harsh thing to say about your employer," Susan said.

"Former employer," Mark corrected. "I quit."

Susan looked at him. "Then who are you working for?"

"Me," Mosley spoke before Mark could.

A door slammed and a soldier entered carrying a small anti-contamination bag. "General?"

"What do you have there?" Mosley rose to face the man.

"It's one of those One-Laptop-Per-Child computers," he replied. "One of the men found it in the house. It may have belonged to the pastor, but we assumed it belonged to a child, maybe the missing boy."

"Send it off to one of our techies at The Hague."

"It'll be faster if my team examines it," Susan offered. "Give it to Dr. LeRoux."

Mosley nodded to the soldier.

The soldier saluted and then retreated with the bag.

"What did you find at the helicopter site?" Mark asked Susan.

"As I told the general, it was nothing but ash." Susan sighed. "We've taken air and ash samples, and they are on their way to our lab in Brazzaville. I doubled our initial precautions. I honestly can't figure out how the virus got out of those body bags. I'll take full responsibility for that."

Mosley shook his head. "That's noble, but it wasn't your fault."

"How do you know that?" Susan asked.

"There is every likelihood that the helicopter flight was sabotaged."

Susan's jaw dropped. "Sabotaged?"

"And not only the helicopter," he added, "but the compound too." He looked squarely at Mark. "Even Greenland."

Mark stood. "What are you talking about?"

Mosley explained about Inspector Duerr and Interpol's infiltration of the Return to Earth movement.

"General," Mark said, after recovering his composure. "Does Interpol realize how hard it would be for these nutcases to incapacitate the lab in Greenland, the compound, and the helicopter?"

"It doesn't matter how hard it was," the general answered. "Apparently they figured out a way to do it."

Susan was incredulous. "But they were suicide missions. The saboteurs had to go in knowing that they wouldn't come out alive."

"It's the new approach to bioterrorism," Mosley said. "For

the life of me, I would never have suspected Tom. He was one of my finest men—a career officer. He had a family."

Mark thought for a moment. "Is it possible that these fanatics blackmailed him? Maybe he did it to save his family."

"I'll mention it to Duerr." Mosley took a deep breath. "Tell me about the bodies, Mark."

"They all exhibit the signs of an overwhelming hemorrhagic disease. There's little doubt that it's the same Ebola that escaped from the compound and I'm afraid it's being spread by airborne transmission."

Susan shook her head. "If this is airborne Ebola, it will be the most virulent form ever seen."

"So we have eight in total here and two hundred and seventeen dead back at the compound." Mosley clasped his hands behind his back and paced the floor.

"That may make it one of the biggest outbreaks in history," said Susan.

The general continued to pace. "And the boy is carrying it."

"What do we do now?" Mark asked. "We don't have a playbook for this type of situation, do we?"

"I suppose we could incinerate all of Gabon," Susan said.

The general paused in his stride and glared at her.

Susan blushed and then spread her arms apologetically.

"The playbook is gone," Mosley said. "We must keep this site secure. We must find that boy before he spreads the virus to others, and we *must* figure out how to beat this virus."

"And how do we do that?" Mark asked.

"The Hague and Washington will give us whatever we need. We have military backup coming in to search for the kid. The WHO team is here from the Congo to collect the bodies and take them back to the lab there for analysis. My team will be working to coordinate everyone."

"Can we do all that without causing widespread panic?" Mark asked.

"Isn't it too late?" Susan said. "Shouldn't we warn the general population about the boy—and the virus? I mean, how can you ask people to search for the boy without telling them about him?"

Mosley gazed at her without answering.

"Oh," she said, realizing the obvious. "You'll let the police believe they're to capture the boy for some other reason."

The general still didn't reply. Mark wanted to signal Susan to let the matter drop, but didn't know how.

Susan—ever tenacious—continued. "What will you do, make him out to be a fugitive cop killer?"

"We're working out a story," Mosley finally said.

Susan squirmed on the pew, stiffening her back and her resolve. "But you can't let them go near him, not without protective clothing. They can't even breathe the air he's exhaling. You don't want another scene like we have outside."

"I know."

"Then what can you possibly do that . . ."

"Leave it to me, Doctor," the general snapped. "You concentrate on your job and let me do mine."

Susan lowered her eyes and shook her head slowly, biting her lip. A little too late, Mark thought.

The general softened his tone. "Susan, I need you to relocate to the WHO facility in Brazzaville. You'll be responsible for coordinating their efforts to fight this thing, and you'll be WHO's bridge to me and to the rest of our military efforts. First priority: pull all of the data together—everything we know up to this point."

Susan looked up at him, disappointment in her eyes. "You're taking me out of the field?"

"I'm putting you where I need you most."

"Technically, you have no authority over me."

"Call your boss. He says I do."

Susan lowered her eyes, her tone restrained. "When do I go?"

"Now," he said. "Go back to the Ops Center and get your things. You'll leave within the hour."

Susan stood up and turned to Mark. "You owe me big time," she said without humor, and marched out of the church, slamming the door behind her.

"That was a bit harsh, wasn't it, Sam?"

"I don't have time to be diplomatic." He sat next to Mark.

"And you'll remember that I didn't want those bodies transported from the compound for the very reasons we've now seen. Good men were lost on that helicopter. The pilot and Tom were both friends of mine."

"Don't forget: Tom was a traitor."

Mosley looked down and said nothing. Mark glanced at him, appreciating how the number of his personal losses was increasing. Nevertheless, he felt he ought to defend Susan. "Susan couldn't have known that there was a saboteur on the team."

"Now we do."

The two men gazed at one another. This sounded like an argument borne out of stress—an unwinnable one.

"What do you want me to do?" Mark asked.

"You're going to connect with a team from the NIH."

Mark was surprised. "You're sending me to Washington?"

"No . . . to London."

Mark frowned, puzzled. "Why would we have an NIH team in London?"

Mosley lifted an eyebrow, an expression telling Mark that he knew more than he was saying. "They're a Special Ops team."

"You're kidding. NIH has a Special Ops team? In London?" It sounded too absurd, and Mark let out a laugh. "Special Ops to do what?"

Mosley sighed. "Hopefully, to end this nightmare."

PART THREE

CHAPTER TWENTY-FOUR

AUGUST 13, 1666

MARGARET SAT ON THE wooden stool by the fireplace, her bony and wrinkled hands clenched together on her lap. A few feet away, John Dicken hammered at the hinge of the door leading into her twin sister's bedroom. Each thud made her blink.

She focused on the ragged edges of his overcoat, faded and stained brown.

"You were saying, Miss Margaret?" Dicken said.

She looked up at him, still blinking even though he had stopped hammering. He stood in the doorframe, gazing at her.

Margaret cleared her throat, a slight cough. "I said, 'For none of us liveth to himself, and no man dieth to himself. For whether we live, we live unto the Lord; and whether we die, we die unto the Lord: whether we live therefore, or die, we are the Lord's.'"

"'Tis beautiful Scripture," Dicken said, and began to wrench the door away from the frame.

Margaret thought of her sister Frances, a competitive woman who determined that she would memorize at least as much of the Bible as Margaret. "For to me to live is Christ, and to die is gain," Frances had quoted just yesterday, then followed with, "Whosoever will come after me, let him deny himself, and take up his cross, and follow me. For whosoever will save his life shall lose it; but whosoever shall lose his life for my sake and the gospel's, the same shall save it. For what shall it profit a man, if he shall gain the whole world, and lose his own soul?"

Margaret hated when Frances quoted long passages of Scripture. "Quoting the Word of God should not be an exercise in vanity," she'd cautioned her.

"'Tis not vanity," Frances had protested, then smugly quoted, "With my whole heart have I sought thee: O let me not wander from thy commandments. Thy word have I hid in mine heart, that I might not sin against thee. Blessed art thou, O LORD: teach me thy statutes. With my lips have I declared all the judgments of thy mouth. I have rejoiced in the way of thy testimonies, as much as in all riches. I will meditate in thy precepts, and have respect unto thy ways. I will delight myself in thy statutes: I will not forget thy word."

Just that morning, Margaret found a verse hidden deep in the book of Jeremiah that she had intended to quote the next time Frances recited a long verse. "Oh, do not do this abominable thing that I hate."

Now, of course, it would not happen.

Dicken had the door free and now carried it clumsily to the front of the small house, banging the wall and the doorframe as he went. He navigated his way out the front doorway to the small garden, where he laid the door on the grass. Margaret sighed.

Dicken returned, slapping his hands against his breeches. He looked sadly at Margaret. "Ah, you poor woman."

It was an uncharacteristic show of sympathy from the man, but Margaret was sure that even Mr. Dicken understood the significance of this latest loss. Margaret was running out of family members for him to bury.

So far, the sickness had claimed three of her younger brothers, strapping men who'd worked in the mines their entire lives, and their three wives. One by one, twenty-two of her precious nieces and nephews succumbed. With each death, the generations of her clan—a family that had helped populate Eyam for as far back as anyone knew—were coming to an end. What a sad surprise. Margaret had assumed that her family and Eyam would be intertwined for many generations to come. Thank God her husband had not lived to see these days—and that her children were grown and safe in York.

"May she be buried in the churchyard, Mr. Dicken? She loved and served that church so diligently, you know."

Dicken shook his shaggy mop of a head. "It is not allowed. By proclamation, we may not suffer burials in the church cemetery. No public or church wakes, or funerals or graveside services for any more than you and the vicar." He spoke as if he had written the proclamation himself.

"Yet, for her to be buried anywhere else must surely be offensive in the eyes of God."

"Possibly so," he said, "but the rules have been set for the common good."

"But she did not die of the Black Death," Margaret protested. "Weak lungs. She always had weak lungs. She wore herself out trying to help those who were truly sick."

The old man looked at her, his brow knitted in tight lines. "Just following the vicar's orders, miss."

Margaret didn't reply. She had spoken to Reverend Mompesson about it and he was immovable. Regardless of the cause of death, he wanted the bodies buried far and wide.

Dicken disappeared into the back bedroom.

Margaret looked at the soot-covered fireplace, empty save for the grate and pile of ashes. Her mind flitted back years ago to a summer afternoon when the entire family had united for the occasion of their father's seventieth birthday. This was before brother Edward had left Eyam to seek his fortune in London.

Father had worried that Edward's ambition would lead him to debauchery. They'd received two letters during the year after he left, and then no more. They had no way of knowing now if he was dead or alive. Perhaps he had fallen to the Black Death there.

Her other brother, Benjamin, had joined them that day, too. *Dearest Benjamin.* He was the quiet and studious one in the family. He had found patronage for his studies in Nottingham and was on course to becoming a cleric. Even now she remembered him sitting next to the fireplace, book in hand, his lovely young wife, Elinor, at his side, so gentle and pure, singing a song to their Lydia, who was only a year old at the time. It had been a perfect occasion—that is, until Benjamin announced to all that he had become a papist.

"Would that you had renounced your faith entirely than to

commit it to that one!" their father had thundered. He shook his finger at Benjamin and cursed him: "In the book of Genesis the word of God records that Rachel named her son Benjamin because it means son of my trouble. Now you have lived up to that name."

Then, to Margaret's and Frances's horror, their father immediately disavowed, disowned, and disinherited Benjamin, banishing him from the village and the family.

Benjamin and his family left that night and were not seen together in Eyam ever again. In the persecutions of the Catholics that came with Cromwell's reign, they fled the country for Ireland.

Joshua Parke, Mr. Dicken's young nephew, now appeared at the door, tipped his hat to Margaret, and then walked past her to join Dicken in the other room. They muttered softly as they went about their work. In a moment they reappeared and shuffled through carrying Frances's body out to the garden. She was wrapped in white linen, her bedsheet. Margaret thought of Lazarus and prayed that God might do a miracle now, as he'd done in the Bible: bring her back so Margaret would not be so totally alone.

They placed Frances on the door and carefully attached her to it with long strips of soiled burlap. Dicken leaned into the doorway again. "If you please, ma'am."

Margaret nodded and stood on unsteady legs. She walked into the fading sunlight, unhappy with its pleasant warmth, as if it had no right to shine on such a forlorn day. Dicken and young Joshua picked up the door with poor Frances jostling on top, and began the slow trek to the field where they would bury her.

Margaret followed, her head held low. As they turned from Church Street onto the Hawkshill footpath, Margaret was aware of the footfalls of another behind her. She glanced back to see William Mompesson, the vicar of the church, following. He wore his black clerical garb with a plain white collar, cuffs, and buckle shoes. He looked at her with large, sad eyes, his face so weathered and lined as to make her doubt that he was only twenty years of age. To be so young and to have endured so much seemed an unreasonable demand from a merciful God. The vicar tipped his head toward her in respect, then lowered his gaze, his lips moving in silent prayer as they walked behind Frances's body.

They reached a setting of fir trees on the north side of Eyam. Mr. Dicken and Joshua Parke stopped at the edge of the grove and placed the door onto the grass next to a grave dug earlier in the day. The vicar moved around to Frances's head and opened a small *Book of Common Prayer*. He began the service for the burial of the dead: "'I am the resurrection and the life,' saith the Lord, 'he that believeth in me, yea though he were dead, yet shall he live . . . '"

Mr. Dicken and his assistant stepped back. Margaret moved to Frances's side and knelt next to her, one last time.

The sun was all but gone when Margaret struggled to her feet. She was alone. The vicar, John Dicken, and Joshua Parke left after the body was placed in the grave and covered over, but Margaret was not ready to leave her sister. Not yet.

She stood there and remembered the life now gone, and she prayed for God's mercy on both the departed and the detained.

With aching knees she turned to make her way home. A sharp snap of a branch somewhere in the grove of fir trees made her jump.

"Who is there?" she asked in a coarse whisper.

"Fear not," a deep baritone voice intoned from the shadows. It was a familiar voice, yet she couldn't place it exactly.

"Fear not?" she asked, her tone defiant. "Then come out to where I can see you."

The figure stepped into the dull gray light of early evening, emerging from the shadows, but still looking like a shadow. He wore a long monk's robe and his face was lost in the circle of darkness beneath his cowl.

Margaret willed her legs to stay firm. If this was the Angel of Death come to collect Frances, then perhaps she might bargain with him. Perhaps he would take her as well. "Well?" she demanded.

"I have come not to harm thee, but to bid thee peace."

Margaret squinted at him. "Then bid me peace in an appropriate manner. Show me your respect and your face."

He paused, as if considering the suggestion. "You were always tough as leather," he said, his thin smile radiating from under the cowl.

The intimacy of the statement caused her to start. Then slowly he lifted his hands to the cowl. The sleeves dropped ever so slightly and even in the dim light, Margaret could see the legendary blue tint to his skin. She stifled a gasp.

The man pushed the cowl back slightly, just enough for her to be able to see his face.

She thought she would swoon at the sight of his blue features. Indeed, her knees buckled and he reached out for her with strong hands, steadying her. Her head tilted back, and she looked up at his face, now so close to hers.

"Father in Heaven," she cried out.

Then all went dark.

CHAPTER TWENTY-FIVE

AUGUST 13

THE BLACK TAXI PULLED to the curb in front of a modest brick townhouse. There was nothing about it to betray that it was the English home of the National Institutes of Health's Special Department of Historical Research and Data Development—affectionately known to insiders as TSI, or Time Scene Investigators.

With access to state-of-the-art medical and scientific technologies, the team was tasked with investigating historically relevant medical mysteries to establish applications for modern public-health conundrums or emergencies. It was a new enterprise, but the team had already assisted the FBI and CIA in several cases. It was the cold-case unit of all cold-case units.

Nora Richards, PhD, tucked a wayward lock of her blond hair behind her ear and quickly double-checked a text message on her cell phone to be sure they'd arrived at the right place.

"Number Three, Rectory Road," the driver announced in a thick East London accent, his eyes flashing at her in the rearview mirror. His eyes had done that a lot during their drive from Heathrow. It was a wonder they hadn't crashed into something along the way.

"Thank you," Nora said from the back of the cab. He cut the taxi's motor and got out.

Rectory Road was a quiet street in Chiswick, London. The only noticeable sound was the low rumble of the trains passing through the Turnham Green station. Still concentrating on her cell phone, she punched in a series of numbers and hit the SEND button. This was to let the guards inside the townhouse know it was she and not an unexpected guest.

The driver opened the passenger door, pausing long enough to gaze at her legs before he leaned in and grabbed the suitcase from the floor in front of her. He was disturbingly close now, his leering smile only a fraction away from getting damaged by her fist.

"Shall I carry the suitcase inside for you, ma'am?" he asked. There was a lascivious hope in the question.

"No, thank you," she replied. "Just put it on the porch, please."

He gave her the once-over yet again before retreating from the cab with her suitcase. She sighed, picked up her briefcase, and followed.

A three-foot-high wall lined the front with a small gateway, adorned on each side with cement orbs, leading to a stone pavement. The grass in the small front garden was neatly trimmed, and the flower beds under the ground-level windows were full of purple, yellow, and red snapdragons. She walked up the pavement to the porch—a portico, really—at the front door.

The driver stood there next to the bag. She was now willing to bet that he would mention her eyes, and then he would suggest, in what he thought were subtle terms, that he didn't have another fare and perhaps they might go to the pub around the corner for a drink. Or, in lieu of that, they could go directly inside.

"There you go, miss," he said. "It's no trouble taking the suitcase inside. It's a bit heavy."

"Honestly, I've got it." She placed her briefcase on the porch, reached into her purse, and handed him the appropriate number of British pound notes. "It's yours. I appreciate the service."

He tucked the money into his shirt pocket. "American, is that right?"

"I am, yes."

"I'd have thought you were Scandinavian with your blond hair and those eyes. You have amazing blue eyes."

She prepared herself for the possibility that the guard just inside the door might have to physically remove this horrid man.

"That's a long ride, coming all the way from America. You must be parched. There's a pub the next street over that—"

"No, really. I can't."

"You'd rather go inside, then?" he chuckled in what he obviously thought was a flirtatious voice. "I'm happy to oblige. Just hand over the key . . ."

At that moment the door opened and Nora took a step back in case of violence.

Startled, the driver swung around.

"Darling!" cried Theodore Burns, better known as Digger, a six-foot redhead with the body of the Michelin Man under an oversized Hawaiian shirt. With outstretched arms, he pushed past the driver, and came to her.

She stifled her amusement as he said, "Hello, sweetheart. I'm so glad you're home."

Digger came to her for a quick embrace and then surprised her by kissing her lightly on the lips. "I was getting worried. So were the children. 'Where's Mummy?' they kept asking over and over." And then he turned back to the driver. "Thank you, my good man. You are dismissed."

The driver, embarrassed and disappointed, gave them a quick salute and returned to the car.

Nora could hear the engine start and the cab pull away as she smiled at Digger. "Thanks," she said.

"No problemo," he responded. "It was either me, or Bruno the Human Pit Bull. He was going to come out and tear off several appendages."

"You were watching? Then why didn't one of you come out and rescue me earlier?"

"We were having too much fun viewing the situation. Better than what's on British TV."

They walked to the door, laughing as Theodore passed by her suitcase without offering to carry it in.

"Digger?" she called out.

He turned in the doorway. "Yeah?"

"A little help, please?"

"Sorry." He turned, reached out, and took her small briefcase.

"Thanks," she said. "Oh, and if you ever kiss me again, I'll dissect your private parts while you're asleep."

He grinned at her and disappeared into the house. She lugged the suitcase inside. It was heavy.

The front hallway of the townhouse led to an open lobby with an antique desk, wingback chairs, and, on a table behind the desk, a series of security monitors showing points from around the townhouse, including the front porch. A stout American soldier in uniform stood behind the desk, his hand resting on the gun in his holster.

"You must be Bruno the Human Pit Bull," she said.

"Welcome, Dr. Richards. I'm Sergeant Brian Johnson. My friends call me Bruno." He glanced at Digger. "And, so does Dr. Burns." He had a warm and welcoming smile. "Please step into the box, look straight into the retina scanner, and place your hands on the fingerprint reader."

"Of course," she said and moved to the wall where a machine that looked like a phone booth waited. She entered it, the detectors of the electronic sniffer engaging. Looking directly at the eye scanner she also placed her hands on two hand-shaped pads. Meanwhile, puffs of air hit her from all sides to make sure she wasn't hiding any explosives. A light turned green just above her and she stepped back out.

"You're clear," Bruno said. "I'll get your suitcase to your room."

She smiled. "Nice to know there's at least one gentleman at TSI."

A door opened to her right and a short perky girl with blond dreadlocks and a white lab jacked entered. "Hi, Nora," she said brightly.

"Hi, Georgina."

"Did you just get here?"

"Just."

"Then you haven't seen the place. You'll love it."

"From the outside it looks awfully small."

"Don't let that fool you. It's really huge. We've knocked out the walls to the townhouses on both sides of us."

"I'll bet the neighbors loved that."

"Our neighbors are the CIA, MI5, and, I think, MI6. We're not really supposed to know, but one of the agents with MI5 asked me out."

"Oh really? And what did Digger think of that?"

"Digger?" she giggled and blushed. "Why would he think anything?"

Nora gave her a knowing smile. "Where's Mac? I should check in."

"Actually, he's supposed to meet us in the lab in a minute. You should come in. It's really cool."

"Which way is the lab?"

"Back this way." Georgina led Nora through the door and they walked only a few steps down a narrow hall to what appeared to be a wall, but as they approached, Georgina swiped her ID over a scanner and the wall magically opened. Georgina stood back and allowed Nora to go first.

Nora gasped. "Good heavens."

"Didn't I say?"

Nora stepped into a large lab that extended well beyond the walls of the single townhouse.

"Take a look around. I'll go find Mac." And she was gone.

The center of the room was filled with desks, each with two or three large flat-screen translucent monitors. Nora immediately was able to identify Digger's and Georgina's desks. Not only were they pushed close to each other, but they were also strewn with journals, papers, coffee cups, and, in Digger's case, several plates of food items of a variety of ages.

At the end of the room, on the other side of large plate-glass windows, was a beautiful conference room. Around the sides of the room were a variety of forensic labs, also set behind large observation glass. Nora was very impressed; no expense had been spared for this effort.

Digger was in one of the well-equipped lab rooms, now wearing a white lab coat and standing over a gurney that held what appeared to be a corpse. Nearby was Henry Colchester, PhD, a very dapper-looking white-haired gentleman dressed in a tweed suit. He also scrutinized the form on the gurney, looking over his half-rim spectacles perched perilously close to the end of his nose. Nora walked to the glass door and knocked.

Digger turned and signaled for her to come in. As she entered she could see the corpse was extremely decayed and wore a torn and ragged soldier's uniform from, she guessed, World War I.

"A doughboy?"

Henry looked up at her and smiled broadly. "Nora, my love!" he exclaimed in a posh English accent. Henry was the only non-American scientist on the team and a vital diplomatic link to the British government. "I'm so glad you've arrived. Having a true historian and medical anthropologist in our presence has dramatically elevated the academic quality of the room. Have you published any more academic papers since I saw you last? Just six weeks ago, I believe."

Nora laughed. "Yes. My latest is in the journal, *Medical Anthropology*."

Henry raised his eyebrows. "Truly?"

"It's called 'Love Injuries: Verbal Violence Among Immature TSI Forensic Pathologists.'"

Digger, still working on the body, smiled. "Look, just because you two trained together at Boston University doesn't mean that you can go around disrupting team morale."

She went around the gurney, where Henry gave her a very polite embrace. In the European tradition, he kissed her on each cheek.

"Hey! Why don't you mind when *he* kisses you?" Digger complained.

"He doesn't smell like last night's curry," Nora answered, then gestured to the corpse. "What do we have here? An addition to your collection?"

Digger nodded. "I retrieved him last night from a graveyard in Camden Town."

Nora waited for a further explanation. When one didn't come, she asked, "And why did you steal this poor thing?"

"It's a hobby," Digger said as he leaned in to examine the corpse. He held a pair of tweezers and appeared to be picking at the skin.

"Our friend here," Henry said, waving a hand over the corpse, "was one of the estimated forty to fifty million who died of a pandemic form of influenza toward the end of World War One. We believe a similar strain has broken out in Siberia and we're now looking for parallels between it and the 1918 version."

"I remember studying about it. It was called the Spanish Flu."

"Or *La Grippe*," Henry added.

"A global disaster. The most devastating epidemic recorded in world history," said Nora.

"Our job," Henry commented, "is to investigate how to prevent another."

"Has there been an outbreak?" Nora asked.

Henry shook his head. "There's been a problem in Siberia. Nothing to panic about. Yet."

"But waiting to look for a cure *after* a pandemic starts might be a little late," Digger said and straightened. He gazed at the corpse with great affection. "He's a beauty, isn't he? If we can't get what we need from him, then we won't get it anywhere."

Suddenly a deep and booming voice sounded from the doorway. "Where is he?"

Retired Colonel James MacLayton, the leader of TSI, stormed into the room and shot their way like an arrow. Nora always thought he was the spitting image of Sean Connery, especially when he was angry about something Digger had done.

"Digger!" he raged.

"Yeah, Mac?" Digger feigned indifference.

"Perhaps we should step back," Henry suggested softly to Nora.

"What were you thinking?" Mac shouted, though he was now only a few feet away.

"About what?" Digger asked.

"Hi, Mac," Nora offered.

"Not now," Mac snapped at her, keeping his attention on Digger. "Are you trying to create an international incident? Do you want to blow our just-established and, I might add, impeccable cover, and get us all deported?"

Digger looked up at the ceiling, as if thinking. "No, Boss, not today." Then, he looked at Mac. "Why?"

"Then what in the blue blazes were you thinking when you went grave robbing last night? It's all over the newspapers. Scotland Yard is involved."

"Why?" Digger asked, as he leaned forward again to continue his work on the corpse.

"Why?" Mac shouted. "I'll tell you why. This body happens to be a relative of the Duke of Buckingham."

"Good God." Henry's eyes widened.

Digger shrugged. "He must have been a poor relative if he was buried in Camden Town."

"Good point," Henry conceded.

"I don't care," Mac growled. "We can't draw attention to ourselves by stealing the bodies of members of the Royal Family."

Henry held up a finger. "Well, technically, he wouldn't be a member of—"

"Stop it, Henry!" Mac ordered.

"Right." Henry bowed slightly, like a butler accepting an order for drinks.

"Well?" Mac snarled at Digger.

Digger looked up at Mac. "Would you like me to put him back?"

The veins in Mac's forehead looked as if they might burst, and they might have had Georgina Scott not appeared at the door. "Mac?"

"What?"

"Mrs. Benson told me to tell you that you have an urgent call in your office, on the red phone."

"Coming," he said. "Digger, I don't know what I'm going to do with you—or, with him." He pointed to the corpse. "I may order you both buried." He then spun on his heel and headed for the door. Over his shoulder, he shouted, "Hi, Nora. Good to see you!"

After Mac left, Digger said to Nora and Henry, "You see? That's what happens when you put an uptight, nonscientific, nonmedical, former-soldier-type guy—an SES, no less—in charge of a group like ours. He doesn't appreciate what lengths we'll go to in the name of solving cold cases and unsolved mysteries."

"I don't trust him," Georgina scowled.

Digger grunted. "He's a bureaucrat."

"Give him a break," Nora said. "Mac had a distinguished career in the army, before he retired. Some pretty important higher-ups convinced him to transition to the Senior Executive Service."

"I wish he did it somewhere else."

"We're not the easiest group of people to manage," Nora reminded him.

"Too true," Henry chimed in. "If we could get real jobs, we certainly wouldn't be here."

"Speak for yourself," Digger said. "Johns Hopkins was desperate to get their hands on me."

"Dead, or alive?" Nora asked, laughing.

Mac had a small office on the second floor of the townhouse. He suspected that, in another age, it had been a servant's room and any charm it might have had was now replaced by metal furniture and filing cabinets. *No aesthetics here.* Nice furniture was for people who didn't have to move out at a moment's notice.

He looked at the red phone on the credenza behind his desk. The first line flashing, waiting, just as Mrs. Benson had promised. He knew who it was without being told.

Snatching the phone, he snapped, "Colonel MacLayton."

"Colonel," said a low, resonant voice. "We have a situation."

"What kind of situation?"

The voice on the other end of the line explained about unfolding events in Gabon, Africa: the testing that had taken place there; the outbreak at the compound; the mass suicides; the compound's destruction; the boy who now seemed to be a carrier; and the efforts by American military to control and contain the outbreak.

Mac listened quietly, his anger rising to alarming levels. "Why am I only hearing about this now? Why wasn't I informed that you were testing in Africa?"

"We inform on a need-to-know basis. Now it is imperative that you know."

"Why? It's your mess. What's it have to do with me?"

"Because Brigadier General Mosley is going to call and ask for help from your team."

"I know Mosley."

"Good. We want to stay a step ahead of this situation. We want the cure, if one can be found."

"Do you have other people working on it?"

"That's not for me to say. We'll expect regular reports from you."

Mac hung up the phone and drummed his fingers on the desk.

Then the intercom buzzed at him. Mrs. Benson's thin voice announced, "There's a General Mosley on line two. He says it's highest priority."

"Thanks, Margery," Mac said.

One step ahead, he thought, *but barely.*

CHAPTER TWENTY-SIX

NORA SAT IN THE conference room and stared at her laptop computer screen. She wasn't looking at anything in particular—just some notes she made at a conference she attended in Chicago—anything to fix her mind on something other than the mindless banter between Digger and Georgina. She liked them well enough, but their mating ritual was sometimes distracting. Now they were passionately arguing over which Martin Scorsese film best represented a nihilistic worldview.

She looked over at Henry, who sat on the opposite side of the table absorbed in a leather-covered book. How was he able to block out all the noise to read?

"*Taxi Driver*," Digger said, as if those two words were a complete argument unto themselves.

"*The Departed*," Georgina countered.

She was a patient woman but now found herself searching for excuses to walk out. One came to her. She could go to her room and unpack. A bath in one of those quintessentially deep and long British tubs would be heavenly. Let them summon her when they were ready to discuss her reason for being here.

As she closed the lid on the laptop and moved to gather her things, Mac came through the door—just in time to see Georgina throw a wad of crumpled paper across the table at Digger.

Mac scowled at her. She smiled back at him angelically.

"We've got a problem," he announced.

"What'd I do now?" Digger asked, with a jaded affectation.

"For once, it's not you. Let me show you our next assignment."

Mac walked around the large table to a bank of translucent panels on the far wall and retrieved a button-covered glove from a holder. He pulled it onto his right hand, punching the buttons on the wrist. The screens lit up and maps appeared with world clocks and menus. "I just got a call about an outbreak of a new strain of Ebola in the remote jungle of east central Gabon."

Digger sighed loudly. "Oh no. Don't we have better things to do than get involved with another sick flock of gorillas?"

"A group of gorillas is called a troop, not a flock," Henry corrected.

Using the glove like a wireless computer mouse, Mac moved his hand and the images on the three panels obeyed, sweeping maps off to one side and bringing a map of Africa to the center. With a few movements of his fingers he zeroed in on Gabon. He turned to his team. "Here's an animated mortality map. Of people, not gorillas." He frowned at Digger before turning back to the screen and beginning an animation that appeared like small starbursts on the map.

The team gasped, almost in unison. Nora sat up straight, her eyes wide as she tried to take in what she was seeing.

"It started with a commune of more than two hundred Americans who, upon realizing that they were infected, chose suicide to stop the spread of infection. Only one person survived: a young boy who somehow escaped."

Mac waved his hand and pointed to the menu. Numbers appeared next to each starburst. "These are the approximate times of each incident. It's pretty clear that as the boy moved away from the commune he took the disease with him."

"He's our vector," Digger said.

Mac nodded. "A very potent one. In just over twenty-four hours he's infected nearly fifty people."

"Holy cow!" Georgina gasped.

"Fifty!" Nora said. She could hardly believe so many could get sick with Ebola in such a short amount of time. Usually the incubation of Ebola is four to six days. "Are they sure it's Ebola?"

"Yes. And it appears to be the first Ebola transmitted via airborne spread."

"Where are they being treated?"

"Treated?" Mac said. "That's fifty dead—on top of the suicides."
A stunned silence.

Nora struggled to comprehend it. "What about the sick, those who haven't died?" she asked.

"The mortality rate appears to be one hundred percent," Mac said.

Digger threw himself back in his chair, groaning. Henry leaned forward and began to scribble notes on a pad.

Georgina pointed to a laptop screen now open in front of her. "Why isn't it on the news? You'd think the web would be filled with reports. I don't see anything."

"They're trying to keep a lid on it," Mac answered.

"Which 'they'?" Digger asked. "Us 'they' or someone else 'they'?"

"A combined 'they.'" Mac said no more.

Nora walked around the table and studied the map. "The timing of the incidents shows the movement of the boy. He went from the compound to—is that Mitzic?—and then down to Lalara. Where is the boy headed?"

"Best guess?" Mac placed a hand on a city near the coast. "Libreville. We don't know why. Possibly because there's an American consulate there. But the city is large and crowded."

"So if he gets there, you can kiss most of the population good-bye," Digger said.

Mac turned to the team. "This isn't just about Gabon. The WHO thinks this has the potential of becoming at least a regional epidemic, and perhaps even a worldwide pandemic. If news of this gets out, the panic would only add to the disaster."

"Wow," Digger said, and then pulled out a palm device. "Just the impact on the financial markets alone will be huge. I better call my stockbroker."

"You're not calling anybody," Mac said.

"I'm still confused," Nora said, working it through. "How exactly did this thing start?"

Mac pulled off the glove and walked to his chair at the head of the conference table. "The problem was first uncovered in Greenland."

"Did you say Greenland?" Georgina asked.

• • •

After Mac finished explaining the circumstances behind the destroyed lab in Greenland and the vaccine-experiment-gone-bad in Gabon, the team sat back to consider it all. Nora's mind was reeling as she tried to think through what they might do to battle the spread.

Georgina turned to her and asked, "Nora, do you think Ahaz's tests caused the inactivated Ebola virus in the vaccine to mutate? Is that what's going on?"

"I wouldn't think so," Nora answered. "Somehow the virus must have been activated and then regained its ability to reproduce. Maybe people have an unrecognized protein in one of their organs that activates it. If I remember correctly, researchers in Wisconsin saw this happen when they tested an Ebola vaccine on monkeys."

"I dated someone on that research team," Digger said.

"One of the monkeys, no doubt," Georgina said.

Digger opened his mouth to respond, but Mac cut him off. "Stay focused, people. Millions may die if we can't figure out how to stop it."

"What do you mean 'we,' Kemo Sabe?" asked Digger.

Mac nodded. "That's our job."

"Surely not alone?" Nora exclaimed.

"Samples of the virus have been sent to the BSL4 labs at the National Institute of Allergy and Infectious Diseases and to the U.S. Army Medical Research Institute of Infectious Diseases. Those labs have revoked all time off and all vacations to keep their people on it. They're calling in experts from around the world to begin a top-secret project to find a vaccine, a cure, or a treatment. Everyone will be working 24/7, including us."

"What do they expect us to do?" Henry asked.

"Yeah, we're here in London, pretty far away from the U.S. labs," Georgina complained.

"As usual, they expect us to come at it from a different angle. We have to look for similar epidemics in history to find clues to help the other research teams. That's where we start."

No one moved. Mac gazed at them a moment.

"I mean now!" he barked.

Nora watched as the others leapt to their feet and moved for the door. She stayed where she was, gazing at the computer panels, her mind racing through epidemics from history. *Moses and the Egyptians. Rats and the plagues of the Orient and Europe. The Spanish flu epidemic . . . so many to consider.* Then one epidemic came to mind.

"Nora?" Mac asked.

She looked up and realized that the entire team was looking at her.

"What's wrong?" she asked.

"You've thought of something," Digger said.

"How do you know that?"

Georgina smiled, as if the question was too obvious to ask. "Your lips are pursed and you've got that little V shape between your eyebrows."

Nora felt self-conscious and tried to relax her face.

"What are you thinking?" Mac asked.

"Maybe . . ." Nora began as she went over to the bank of screens. She put on another glove and began to move the maps and stats of Africa off the monitors. "The symptoms of this outbreak in Gabon might be similar to . . ."

A few gestures with the glove and she found a web page with pictures of a quaint English village. One showed a modest stone church. Another had a row of Tudor-style cottages. Another with a small green park had an old stockade in the middle. "Here it is—in the countryside."

"It's Eyam, in Derbyshire," Henry said. "The Plague Village."

"Plague Village?" Georgina asked. "What is it, the Disneyland of disease?"

"Explain, Nora. We don't have much time," Mac said.

"Henry's right," Nora said. "Eyam became famous during the Black Death of 1665 to 1666. When the plague arrived, the villagers heroically decided to contain the disease by quarantining themselves—to keep it from spreading to their friends and family in nearby villages."

The team members looked at each other, still not getting it.

"Most of the villagers died, but a significant portion survived," Nora added. "Unit recently, no one's been able to explain why. Don't you guys ever watch documentaries or read journals?"

"You're going to have to spell it out for us," Mac said.

Nora continued, "For years the assumption was that the plague in Eyam was caused by *Yersinia pestis*, a bacteria carried by fleas; but researchers now think it might have been something else."

A lifted eyebrow from Mac. "Ebola?"

"It may have been an Ebola-like virus," Nora replied. "Or an anthrax-like bacteria."

"Keep going," Mac said.

"Based on the symptoms and data we saw from the WHO, it's possible we may be dealing with an illness in Africa like they had in Eyam. That's our parallel, but what makes this particularly helpful is that Eyam quarantined itself."

"Meaning that, since everyone should have died but some didn't, we can investigate the survivors," Georgina said, the light appearing to dawn on her.

"Exactly. How do a large percentage of people survive in a quarantine situation?" Nora said. "That's the question a friend of mine from the NIH had. So he checked out the descendants and determined that a portion of Eyam's population was genetically unique and naturally immune to whatever the disease was."

Mac moved toward the screen. "And you're suggesting we go to Eyam?"

"It's a strong lead," Nora replied. "There, we'll have an environment to explore the nature of the disease, in a situation where we have access to the bodies of those who survived the epidemic and to their descendants."

"Brilliant!" Henry exclaimed.

Nora added, "And we should be able to recover viral fragments or bacterial particles, as well as samples for DNA testing. The combination may help us crack the code."

Mac thought for a moment as he gazed at the screens. "Well, unless someone can come up with a better idea."

No one spoke. Nora realized the flaws of going after her first idea. "I think we all need to research other possibilities to see if there are any better candidates."

Mac shook his head. "No time. Your instincts have served us well in the past, so I'm willing to gamble on them now. Digger, you and Henry work out the equipment and technology the team will need—including the most advanced communication gear you can carry."

"Right," Digger said with a salute, then turned to Henry. "Are you ready, Q?"

"Yes, Mr. Bond."

Mac pointed to Georgina. "Get with our pals at MI5 and make arrangements for a cover story, documents, travel, vans, lodging, and the like."

"Aye, aye," she said.

"Nora, who else do you need on your forensic team?"

"I have an idea," Nora said, and turned back to the monitors. A few sweeping hand movements and she began to pull up head-shots on an academic website. She was aware that the team was now lingering at the door, waiting to see whom she would suggest.

The phone in the center of the conference table rang, and Mac picked it up. "What is it, Margery?" he asked, then put a hand over his free ear and turned away from the team. "Again? Put him through."

While Mac took his call, Nora scrolled through the various photographs on screen. Finally, she landed on one that was familiar to everyone there. "That's who I want."

"Oh, no!" Digger protested. "Not him, Nora. Not Malachi."

Nora corrected him, "He's Mark."

"Maybe he's Mark if you're cozy with him," Digger said, "but in grad school, he was called Malachi. Sometimes we called him other things, when he wasn't around to hear."

"I don't care about your personal history," Nora said.

"It's not my history I'm referring to—it's his. He's damaged goods."

Georgina stepped next to Digger. "What are you talking about?"

"He's not reliable."

"Why do you say that?" Henry asked.

Digger snorted as if the question was too obvious to answer.

"He's legendary for being assigned to projects and not showing up. Or he'll show up and then bail out as soon as things get stressful. He even had to take a job with Ahaz because neither the government nor academia wanted him anymore. I heard the higher-ups would only work with him as a contractor so that someone else could take on the headache of managing him."

Georgina moved to the photo. "But that doesn't line up at all." She pointed to his photo on the screen and the caption next to it. "It says he's medically brilliant. Some people call him the Sherlock Holmes of forensic pathology."

"He's one of the best," Nora finally said, having bitten her tongue throughout the entire conversation.

"He *was* one of the best," Digger corrected her. "But he hasn't been right after what happened to his kid and after his wife walked out on him. Who you bring in to this team affects all of us, Nora. Everyone knows Mark's a shadow of his former self. His best years are behind him. He could hold us up or threaten our mission altogether. We can't risk it."

Nora didn't answer, but looked at Mark's photo on the screen. She recognized the pain in the eyes looking back at her. He could be a risk; there was no denying it.

"Look," Digger said, as if making one last appeal. "Even without all of that, he's a consultant with Ahaz. Greenland was his project, wasn't it? How do we know he wasn't the one who screwed up and started this crisis in the first place?"

"He's better than that," Nora said.

Digger snorted. "You're only saying that because you have the hots for him."

Nora spun around, rage filling every empty space in her being. "I'm being professional about this and I resent the implication that—"

"Must every conversation on this team wind up as adolescent nose pulling?" Henry asked wearily.

Georgina shrugged. "I don't know what you're arguing about. It's up to Mac, isn't it?"

Mac hung up the phone, his face sculpted into another scowl. "No, it isn't up to me. Brigadier General Sam Mosley has made the decision for us."

"He's sending someone?" Nora asked.

"The general has already sent someone. He flew from Gabon overnight. He's on his way from Heathrow Airport right now."

The team reacted with indignation.

Henry said, "It's remarkable to me that this general has the authority to assign people willy-nilly to our team."

Nora was curious and asked Mac, "Why didn't Mosley tell you earlier?"

"He said he forgot to mention it before. More than likely, he thought we'd have an argument about it, the way you just did."

"Why would he expect an argument?" Georgina asked. "Who is it?"

Digger appeared relieved. "Frankly, I don't care. Anybody he sends has got to be better than Malachi."

"Well? Who is it?" Henry asked Mac.

Mac shot a wary look at Nora. "You really have to be careful what you wish for." He hooked a thumb toward the photo on the screen and walked out.

Digger slumped into a chair. "Oh no."

Nora put a hand over her mouth to hide the smile.

CHAPTER TWENTY-SEVEN

STUCK IN TRAFFIC ON the Chiswick high road, the military attaché hit the horn of the Peugeot and inched the car forward, as if closing in on the bumper in front of him would make the multitude of cars ahead move faster.

In the rear seat of the car, Mark put his head back against the headrest. The military flight from Gabon had been turbulent and sleepless.

His cell phone rang in his carry-on bag. Assuming it to be Mosley, he hit the TALK button before looking at the number. He realized his mistake immediately.

"Mark!" his ex-wife shouted.

"Hello, Donna."

"Where have you been? I've been trying to reach you for days."

"Sorry. I've been busy trying to save the world from a pandemic."

"I don't care. You should answer your phone when I'm trying to call."

"I'm still at your service, is that it? It seems to me that the terms of our divorce—"

"I don't want to hear about that."

"Oh? Then what would you like to hear? Sweet nothings? Musings of my undying love?"

"Don't be stupid. I need money."

"I've sent you this month's alimony check. Come to think of it, I've also sent you next month's, and the month's after that. In fact, by my estimation, I'm paid up through the end of the year."

"It doesn't matter to me what you've sent. I need more."

"What is it this time? A boyfriend with bad gambling debts? The Mob is going to break his legs tomorrow if you don't pay up?"

"Now you're being mean. I'm not seeing Richard anymore."

"Terrific. Then why are you bothering me?"

"I had an investment opportunity and now I'm broke."

Mark laughed, without an ounce of pleasure. "What is it this time? Another restaurant? Or are you trying your hand at another little crafts store? What was the last one? I remember now, it specialized in those authentic homemade Native American jewels and pottery. What happened to that? Oh that's right, they weren't authentic or homemade because you bought them from some cheesy company in China. That was a clever idea."

The line was silent for a moment. "Are you enjoying yourself?" Donna asked, icicles hanging on each word.

"Not at all."

"Mock me all you want, but this is a sure thing."

"What is?"

"A spa."

"What do you know about spas besides going to one as often as possible?"

"That makes me more qualified than a lot of people," she said. "Besides, André has found a location—"

"André? Who is André?"

"A friend," she said. He knew what that meant. Then she added, "He's a massage therapist."

"I see."

"Why are you being so difficult?"

Because hundreds or thousands could die in this epidemic and you're talking to me about massages, Mark thought. "I'm really busy, Donna."

"Fine," she said, "but I need that money."

"Go find it somewhere else."

"You know as well as I do that I could have gotten a lot more alimony out of you. This is what I get for being kind."

Mark squeezed his cell phone, and feared it would break in his hand. "In the fallout of our relationship, Donna, 'kind' is not a word anyone would use about your behavior."

"You want to talk about behavior? Then let's talk about your behavior leading up to . . ." She stopped herself, but only for dramatic effect. "Don't make me say it."

"Go on," he said, his head now aching. "You've never stopped before. Play the guilt-and-manipulation card."

"If you feel guilty, Mark, then maybe you should stop to remember why."

He took the phone away from his ear and looked at the driver—rather, at the back of the driver's head. The traffic was now moving slowly in feet rather than in inches. Mark sighed. He brought the phone back to his ear. "I'll give you another month, but that's it. No more. I'll have my bank handle it the usual way."

"I won't bother to say thanks. It's the least you can do, considering—"

He snapped the phone closed and threw it back into his bag.

"I'm sorry about the delay, sir," the driver said from the front.

"Take your time," he said. "There's nowhere I'd rather be than right here with you."

The driver looked at him in the rearview mirror and chuckled.

Mark was taken to the townhouse on Rectory Road. He stood at the end of the pavement while the attaché carried his belongings inside. He didn't want to go in. In all probability, he knew some of the people working there, and he knew they knew him.

Nora Richards appeared in the doorway and he felt both relief at seeing a friendly face and a profound dread. Nora, more than anyone else he'd ever worked with, had an uncanny understanding of him and, he suspected, a misguided hope for him. He had openly teased her that it was due to her staunch devotion to Roman Catholicism.

"Catholics can always smell the guilt in people like sharks to blood," he had once told her.

"And the Episcopal Church suffers no guilt and it should," she had replied.

"It's nothing to me," he'd concluded. "I don't believe in anything anymore."

"We'll work on that," she'd said.

That seemed like a lifetime ago.

She walked toward him and he would have been less than human not to notice her beauty, her lithe form, and her catlike walk.

"Hi, Nora," he said.

"I've come to save you," she replied and, without breaking her stride, caught his arm and guided him away from the townhouse.

"Where are we going?" he asked, allowing himself to be saved.

"I want to debrief you—away from the rest."

They walked along the silent street. Mark wondered if all of the houses belonged to the government or if there were normal humans living normal lives behind some of the doors and windows. Along the length of the street, the only activity was across the road where a man in overalls moved around the back of a small green van. DEADMAN'S PLUMBING was painted on the side.

"That's an unfortunate name for a company," Mark said to Nora.

She looked over and smiled. "Not if you make hearses."

As they passed, the man in overalls—a large, scraggly-headed beast—gave them a nod and then bent into the back of the van, where pipes banged against one another.

Mark and Nora walked to the end of Rectory Road, turned left, and came to a pub called The Strongman's Arms. The sign hanging over the door was shaped in the form of a bulging and tattooed bicep.

Inside there were only a few customers at the bar. Nora led the way to a booth in the quietest corner—a scarred table positioned against a paneled wall. A faded-gold plastic lamp hung precariously from the wall. Mark sat down opposite her. The bartender came over to inquire about their needs. Nora ordered a diet soda, Mark asked for water with a slice of lime. The bartender went away with an air of annoyance.

"I think he would like us to drink more substantially," Mark said.

"I'm sorry to disappoint him, but we have to keep our wits about us."

"And why is that?"

Nora leaned forward, her arms crossed on the table. "You were in Gabon. Tell me about it."

Mark gazed into her blue eyes and knew that Gabon was the last thing he wanted to talk about, but he knew he should, so he told her everything that had happened there.

The drinks came and Nora leaned back, shuddering as if from a sudden chill down her neck. "It must have been horrible."

He sipped his drink and expected her to begin grilling him about the medical and scientific details of the virus.

Instead, she asked, "How are you doing?"

"Me?"

"All those bodies. There were children, I assume."

"Many. Yes."

"So?"

His head dropped and he had to decide whether to allow her to scrape the scab off the wound that was already smarting from Donna's call. He sighed. "I'm all right. You know me: heart of stone, resolve of iron." He frowned. "Or is that *head* of stone and resolve of iron?"

"Uh-huh, and your emotional stability?"

He looked at her, wounded. "Is this an interrogation?"

"Maybe." She leaned forward again. "I want to know how you're *really* doing, Mark."

"Is this personal or professional?"

"Both."

"I'm doing well enough to tackle this assignment," he said, his voice wooden. "After what I saw in Gabon, I think I can handle just about anything. Thanks for asking."

She looked pained. "Look, this isn't about me. I trust you, but you're not Mr. Popularity with some in our group."

"Like who?"

"Digger Burns, for one."

"Digger's a moron."

"He's a genius at what he does and he thinks you're damaged goods."

"Genius or not, he's still a moron, and I don't care what he thinks."

"But I do," Nora said and lifted her drink. "That's why you have to prove him wrong."

"How do I prove him wrong?"

Nora frowned at him. "Tell me you're up for this. Tell me that you'll stay focused, that you won't flake out."

He nodded. "I can do that."

She watched him silently for a moment and he could tell that she was reading him with the same expertise that she could read a crime scene—and he *knew* he could not fool her.

"How's Donna?"

"The same as always."

"She won't leave you alone."

"I'm her cash cow."

"Mark," she said. "Can you keep her and your past at bay during this project?"

"I already said yes."

"Good."

"But I don't even understand what this secret little team is supposed to do. What's it about?"

"History," Nora replied.

"That narrows it down," he chided her. "Can you be more specific?"

"Let me tell you about Eyam."

The skies were overcast and a few drops of rain fell as Mark and Nora walked back to the TSI townhouse.

Mark thought the whole idea about Eyam was ridiculous. But, he had no choice but to go along for the ride. At one time he thought that Ahaz was his last employment opportunity. Now it appeared to be TSI.

The Deadman's Plumbing van was gone and the street seemed extraordinarily still and lonely. Even the traffic and train noises from the main roads of Chiswick seemed to have stopped.

He thought, *This is what it will be like if we're the only two left alive after humankind is destroyed by a pandemic.*

CHAPTER TWENTY-EIGHT

MARK SAT ON THE edge of his bed in the small room provided by the TSI team at the headquarters building. It was as functional as any hotel room, but without a television. His fists were clenched and his eyes were squeezed shut.

He had lost the knack for dealing with the raw edges of his emotions. He no longer knew how to react to pure and unadulterated feelings. But he had to. He had to keep his promise to Nora.

He looked at the clock. 4:00 p.m. Teatime in some parts of the country. He was due for a meeting downstairs and didn't want to go. Seeing Digger and some of the others for the first time since arriving would not be pleasant, and he had Eyam to deal with. Why did they have to go to Eyam?

Standing up, he tucked his white oxford shirt into his jeans. He ran his fingers through his hair in an attempt to bring it to order. He looked back at the bed and thought how pleasant it would be to lie down again for just a few minutes more. Let the team wait. They could start without him.

No. Growling, he grabbed his briefcase and walked to the door. *You promised Nora.*

That was the clincher. He would rather face a dozen critical Diggers than a single disappointed Nora. He would not let her down.

He forced himself out of the room, slamming the door behind him.

· · ·

"Cool politeness" was the phrase Mark thought of to describe the welcome he received from the assembled TSI team members. Colchester and Mac quickly shook his hand. Georgina nodded at him, sizing him up as she did. Digger was slumped in a chair and wiggled his fingers in an indifferent hello. Nora hovered anxiously until Mark was seated and they could get on with their business.

Mac took charge. "Now that we're all here, let me tell you what I've learned from General Mosley in Gabon." He held up a sheet of paper and squinted at it. "The mystery boy is still on the run. Thirty-seven more people are dead in the jungle: two hikers, five itinerants, and thirty small-village workers. The boy must have approached them, or they approached him; we have no way of knowing for sure. The WHO teams are gathering and beginning their preliminary work on identifying this sickness. Dr. Susan Hutchinson is the liaison between the WHO and the military."

"Did he mention the fanatics?" Mark asked.

Mac looked puzzled for a moment, then asked, "Which ones? The religious nuts in the compound or the environmental crazies?"

"Either would be interesting," Digger said.

"The general said you would explain the animal-rights folks more fully," Mac said to Mark.

All eyes turned to Mark. He cleared his throat and told them what he knew about the Return to Earth Society, including Interpol's suspicions that the society had infiltrated the labs in Greenland and Gabon, and the military helicopter transporting the two bodies from the compound.

"Well, that's an interesting twist," Digger said.

"It's more than just interesting," Mark said. "These people are dead serious."

"No pun intended," said Georgina.

Mark continued, "They're terrorists who will resort to suicide to accomplish their mission; with their resources and inside knowledge, it wouldn't surprise me if they know about this team and are watching us now."

"Isn't that a bit paranoid?" Henry asked.

"Maybe," Mark said, "but I believe they had a truck out front."

Nora turned to him. "The plumbing van? What made you think it was them?"

"For one thing, I checked and couldn't find a Deadman's Plumbing listed in the telephone directory, Yellow Pages, or on the Internet for London or anywhere else in Britain. For another, when the man we saw bent over to reach into the back of the van, I saw a gun holstered on the inside of his overalls. I assume the plumbers in Britain don't usually carry firearms."

"Well, you're just a regular Sherlock Holmes, aren't you?" Digger said.

Georgina looked worried. "He could have been with British Intelligence. Or the CIA," she offered hopefully.

Mark shrugged. "Possibly, but they have no reason to spy on us, do they?"

"I'd bet my money that it was Ahaz," Digger said.

"All right," Mac said, holding up his hand. "The point is we have to keep our eyes open while we work. Now, back to the mission at hand. Nora?"

Nora was looking at Mark as if she still didn't know what to make of his revelation about the plumbing truck. Then she suddenly snapped to. "Yes. As I've already suggested, the symptoms of the outbreak in Gabon are similar to the symptoms reported in the Eyam villagers, though Gabon is more potent and accelerated. But since we have to start somewhere, Eyam is as solid a candidate as we have. I believe our first line of investigation is to find out why some of the Eyam villagers survived in a highly contagious quarantine environment. I've compiled booklets for each of you with theories about the survivors' descendants and the results of their DNA samples from the NIH research there. I've included a few of the scientific debates about whether the infection was from an Ebola-like virus or anthrax or *Yersina* and the like. Admittedly, some of the theories are complex, contradictory, and controversial, but at least we won't have to retrace those steps."

"What steps are you recommending we take?" Henry asked.

Digger cracked his knuckles. "We will have to find and examine actual bodies of plague victims," he announced.

"How surprising that you'd recommend that," Georgina said.

"Why?" Mac asked. "What are you looking for?"

Nora replied, "We'll be looking for any remaining infectious particles and taking genetic samples."

"Why?" Mac asked again.

"To see if there are any similarities between the dead: both the victims of the sickness and the survivors who lived to later ages. I'll compile a list of the plague survivors and have sources to direct us to where they're buried," Nora said.

Digger let out a hooray.

"But it won't be grave robbing," Nora quickly added. "We won't be digging up corpses but using our equipment to retrieve the samples from the graves."

Digger let out a small whine.

"I also have a list of the descendants of the survivors," she said.

"In the meantime," Mark interjected, "I think I can get access to the work of the team who checked into all this a few years ago—to reevaluate the samples of distant survivors so we can look for any other genetic similarities."

"Well, aren't you the well-connected little doctor," Digger teased.

Mark gazed at Digger. "In the human realm, it's called networking. I don't know how you do it with your dead bodies."

"Ah!" Digger cried out. "A retort. And a half-decent one at that."

Mac hit his hand against the table. "You're like children in a nursery," he complained. "Henry, please guide everyone through their cover stories for Eyam."

"Happily," Henry said and stood up, though there was no reason for him to do so. "You are an American film crew who has come to do a documentary on Eyam. This would explain your boxes of technical equipment. It also explains why you'll be wandering the village and asking questions.

"The team will essentially take over all the rooms of the Rose and Crown bed-and-breakfast on the outskirts of the village center, not far from the church itself. It has a large meeting room on the bottom floor and a converted attic that is well suited for our lab equipment. I'll be handing out your personal packets at the end of the meeting—with your false drivers' licenses, passports, petty cash, and other rudimentary items." Henry sat down again.

Mac leaned on the table. "Listen, people. You have to stay anonymous. Don't interfere or do anything to draw attention to yourselves there. It's a small village and the locals will talk."

"As if a horde of Americans with a lot of technical equipment won't draw attention," Digger mocked.

"Pack your things," Mac snapped. "You're leaving at 1800 hours."

"*Tonight?*" Georgina asked. "Why do we have to go tonight?"

Mac looked at her as if she were an imbecile. "Well, besides the part where we talked about this being a race against time to save the world from a potential pandemic, I'd rather you arrived by cover of night so you can get unpacked and installed without the watchful eyes of the villagers."

Georgina sighed and feigned a disappointed pout. "But I have a date."

Mac roared and marched out of the room.

"I was only joking," Georgina said.

CHAPTER TWENTY-NINE

NORA TOOK ONE LAST look at the equipment in the back of the two vans before signaling that she was satisfied. The drivers—soldiers in plainclothes—climbed in. The rest of the TSI team, chatting amiably, also chose their respective vans and disappeared inside.

Mark stood alone on the curb, waiting. Nora eyed him for a moment.

"I feel like the last boy picked for the school baseball team," Mark said with a boyish pout.

"I'm taking a rental car," Nora said, gesturing to the silver Peugeot. "You can ride with me."

"Can I? Thanks!" He went to the right-side door—what would have been the passenger side in an American car—realized his mistake, and went around. "I keep forgetting that the British do it the wrong way around."

"Not the wrong way," she corrected him. "Just opposite."

Once inside the car, Mark said, "I guess this makes you the new Mother Teresa." He buckled his seat belt. "Getting stuck with a leper."

She giggled and programmed the GPS system for Eyam. She turned to him, suddenly glad to have this extended time alone together. "Ready? Do you need to use the bathroom before we go?"

Mark smirked at her. "I'll use my coffee cup, if necessary."

The vans pulled away from the curb ahead of them, and Nora guided the car in to take up the rear.

Getting out of London was no easy task as the traffic seemed congested in every direction. Nora clenched the wheel, straining to keep her patience. More than once she thought that even the GPS voice prompter sounded irritated. But once they reached the M1, the motorway north toward Luton and Sheffield, things eased and the navigating was less arduous.

They sped past the rolling green countryside, their passage marked by off-ramps to obscure towns and villages. The occasional smokestacks thrusting up in the distance added character to the scenery. Nora and Mark chatted easily about their work, conferences they'd attended, and articles they'd read about advancements in viral research. She was impressed by the degree to which he'd kept up with his reading and was reassured by the extent of his knowledge, even in the details of the work being done. Whatever his problems, his mind had not gone slack.

During a lapse in their conversation, Mark noticed a small pouch in the cup holder and reached for it. "Ah, what do we have here?" he asked playfully, as if there was something questionable about the pouch. He picked it up and opened the small drawstring.

"It's nothing that would interest you." She glanced his way.

"A necklace?"

"Wrong."

He held it up. "A rosary?" He moaned. "Aw, I had hoped for something scandalous."

"The rosary is scandalous for some people."

"Beads and string," he said, putting the rosary back into the pouch.

"Oh? And the cross is just an intersection of two pieces of wood?"

Looking straight ahead, he hesitated, his face momentarily catching the golden light of the setting sun. "Sorry. I don't want to have this conversation."

Never one to flinch from a hard topic, Nora pressed forward, her intellectual curiosity aroused as much as anything. "I know you've been through a very painful experience, Mark—the worst imaginable. But have you really dispensed with God entirely?"

"More or less."

Nora thought for a moment, aware of where she was treading, but also yearning to understand. "So . . . what kind of deal did you think you had with God in all those years you did believe in him?"

"Deal?"

She nodded, putting her theory forward. "Isn't that why people lose faith? They think they've made a particular deal with God, and then something happens that makes them decide that he double-crossed them, so they ditch him altogether. They conclude he hates them, he's unreasonably cruel, or he doesn't exist."

"I said I don't want to talk about this."

They rode in silence for a few minutes. She was sorry to have ventured into such a painful topic, having hoped that he might be able to talk about it. She was about to apologize when he spoke.

"I don't know about a deal," he said, "but yes, it seemed unreasonable that we would have to suffer the way we did."

"Isn't suffering part of the package?" she asked. "Considering the state of the world, shouldn't we be suffering all the time? What measure of grace stops that from happening?"

He took a deep breath. "Look, I can accept my suffering, but not the suffering of—" He stopped himself abruptly. Then he said more quietly, "I would have taken all that suffering on myself if I could have."

She nodded. "Then. But not now."

"Now?"

"You can't take the suffering now."

"What are you talking about?"

"I mean, rather than believe that God wants to participate with you in your suffering now—and that he wants you to participate in it with him—you've pushed him away. Is that an accurate way to put it?"

"An accurate way to put it? Are we having an academic conversation?"

"I'm sorry," she said, realizing she'd gone too far. "I thought that if we talked on that level it might be easier for you to . . . never mind. Bad idea."

He turned, and she could feel his stare burning into her. "If you were anyone else, I'd slug you."

She flinched and instantly felt contrite. In a small voice, she said, "I'm only trying to understand."

"You couldn't possibly understand."

She felt a sharp pain deep inside, thinking instantly of all the ways she did understand and the hard experiences that had given her that understanding. "Can't I?"

"How could you?"

She frowned, resisting her own desire to fight back, to prove him wrong. She offered a quick prayer for help and then said with great restraint, "I won't play one-upmanship in the suffering contest, Mark. But I'm trying to understand how it is that some people suffer and are drawn more closely to God while others suffer and move away."

"I can't account for others," he said, "but I can give you four words to explain my path: death of a child."

Nora knew the conversation was over and that she'd completely mishandled it. Along with her regret, she felt sudden relief when the van in front of them signaled to take an off-ramp to a roadside restaurant.

CHAPTER THIRTY

THE ROSE AND CROWN bed-and-breakfast was a large Victorian-style house tucked in the woods at the end of a meandering driveway off the main road, only a quarter of a mile from Eyam's town center.

In the glare of their headlights and a single lamppost over the small parking area, Nora could make out the large cream-colored stonework of the large windows, and the expansive front door. A light in the foyer illuminated a stained-glass window in the center of the door depicting a rose and crown.

The porch light came on and a tall middle-aged man with styled gray hair came out. He wore a polo shirt and casual trousers that looked newly pressed. "Sophistication" was the word that came to Nora's mind. He was a match for Henry.

And it was Henry that the man went to, speaking loudly in a clipped Oxford accent, "Welcome, one and all. I am Matthew Cunningham, the owner of this modest establishment. I'm so delighted that you chose us as your base of operations."

"Right," Henry said to Mr. Cunningham as they shook hands. "Thank you for taking us on such short notice."

"My pleasure. I won't try to get all your names, but rest assured that the house is, in essence, yours. You will have complete privacy and security. I stay in a cottage in the back and can be reached whenever you need me. Allow me to show you our facilities."

He turned on his heel as if in a military parade and strode toward the house.

Henry, Digger, and Georgina followed as the two soldiers began to unpack the equipment.

Nora and Mark looked at each other, shrugged, and also began to follow. Nora's cell phone rang, and she quickly retrieved it from her jacket pocket. The screen showed a three-number code to indicate the headquarters in Chiswick. She waved for Mark to go on as she took the call. He nodded, but rather than go into the house, he began to help unload the equipment.

"This is Nora."

"Mac here. Have you arrived?"

"Just now." She drifted toward the front of the house as she talked, noticing the lush flower beds under the ground-floor windows. Yellows, purples, and violets. *No one gardens as well as the English.*

"I saw that Dr. Carlson rode with you. A shrewd move on your part."

"Shrewd?"

"To evaluate him."

Nora was amused by the idea. "That wasn't my intention."

"Well, I still need your professional assessment. Is he up for the job?"

Nora glanced around to be sure Mark wasn't nearby. "I believe he'll do his best."

She heard a tapping sound and imagined it was Mac flicking a pencil against his desktop. "Nora, your success depends a lot on his ability to behave professionally under extremely stressful circumstances."

Nora turned her back to the house, cupping her hand over the phone. "What do you want me to tell you, Mac? He has a lot of unresolved anger and pain, but he promised me that he'll do the work and I believe him."

A pause. "I want regular reports."

"I'll keep an eye on him," she said. "If there are any problems, I'll remove him from the mission."

"Good. We'll talk tomorrow."

She hung up the phone and glared at it for a moment.

"A contingency plan already?" Mark asked from directly behind her. His eyes were daggers.

So he'd heard. "Mac is worried. It's understandable."

"I'm sure he thinks so."

"Look, Mark, the pressure is on me to make sure you be-have—or release you."

Mark lifted an eyebrow. "So you're Mother Teresa and Donald Trump all wrapped up in one. How fun. Am I fired or forgiven?"

She frowned at him and walked into the house.

Irritated, Mark walked in the other direction, back down the tree-shrouded driveway toward the main road. He wondered if the local pub was still open. Maybe he'd pop in for a drink. Or maybe not. To disappear to a pub and return with alcohol on his breath would only affirm what the team already thought of him.

He grimaced and kicked at a stone. How had his professional reputation become so tainted? He'd always done good work. He defied anyone to point to a slipup or error that could be attributed to him or to his circumstances.

Or was that entirely true? Might the facility in Greenland have been saved if he had had a clearer mind? Would he have spotted the infiltrator from Return to Earth if he weren't so consumed by his own problems? He'd never know.

He thought of the conversation he'd had with Nora in the car. He knew her well enough not to distrust her intentions. She had an insatiable mind and an open heart. Her questions were fair ones, but they were painful too; until he could figure out how to manage his pain, he was going to react in less than academic or diplomatic ways.

It would be so much easier if people would leave him alone. Just give him a lab to work in—alone, with a challenging assignment—and he'd be fine.

He reached the end of the drive and stood next to a tree that skirted the road. For a moment, he again considered going to the pub. What was it called? The Miners' Arms. That was it. It existed in the time of the plague: the drinking hole for all those who had worked in the bowels of the earth.

To the left a tiny flash—a flicker of something—caught Mark's eye. He stepped back into the shadows, narrowing his eyes to look.

Approximately twenty yards down the road, a vehicle sat to the side. The flicker, Mark surmised, was from a cigarette lighter or maybe the sudden glow of a cell phone screen.

Mark recognized the shape of the vehicle. He had no doubt that if he walked past it, he'd see the telltale markings of Deadman's Plumbing on the side.

PART FOUR

CHAPTER THIRTY-ONE

AUGUST 13, 1666

THE COWL-COVERED MAN MUST have carried Margaret back to her cottage, for when she awoke, she was lying in a makeshift bed by the fire in her front room. He dabbed a cool damp cloth on her forehead.

She looked into the strange blue face, then reached up to touch it. There was no doubt about it, now that she was recovering from her shock. He was older, deep lines had spread across his forehead and from his eyes. She knew those eyes. "Benjamin, how can this be?"

"Margaret, I'm truly sorry for startling you. Truly, had I realized the extent of Frances's illness, I would have come to you sooner." His eyes were moist.

"Are you the one?" In the flicker of the candlelight she peered closely at him. "You must be. How many cowled figures with blue skin could there be?"

"Do I have to convince even you? Shall I remind you of how, as children, we made boats of stick and raced them down at the creek? I remember well how you took a stick to James Simpson when he was mistreating me."

Margaret smiled and then burst into tears. "Oh dear, dear brother! We didn't know what had become of you. We feared you were dead."

"Did you not wish it? Did mother and father not declare me so when I became a papist? Did father not curse and disown me?"

"So they did and to their regret." She placed a hand on his arm. "But, where have you been all these years? Where are your dear wife and child?"

"Gone to Christ," he said.

"No!" Margaret sat up. "How, dear brother? Spare me none of your account."

He looked at her as if weighing how much he might say, then nodded. He explained how tragedy had struck the boat that he, his wife, and child had taken from England for Ireland. They capsized during a storm on the waters between Holyhead and Dublin. Both Elinor and Lydia were lost. Benjamin survived—barely—only a shell of his former self. A grief-stricken man. In time, he accepted the call to become a monk.

"You have been living in a monastery?"

"Many monasteries in many countries," he replied. "Only after the restoration of King Charles to the throne in England was I able to return."

"That was five years ago," Margaret complained. "Why did you not write to me? Why did you not come to visit?"

"It was forbidden by the head of our order. We were not allowed to communicate with our families. At first, I believe it was to avoid discovery and possible persecution for our Catholic faith. Later, I came to understand that our identities were to become one with Christ in our order and no longer bound to our family names."

"I may have a few words for the head of your order, if ever I were to meet him," she said.

He shook his head. "That is unlikely in this lifetime."

"Was it also by his order that your skin would turn blue?"

He chuckled and held up his hands, as if seeing them for the first time. "A condition of my habitat."

"What habitat is that?"

"A place of the earth." He said no more.

She leaned toward him and spoke in a near whisper. "You must know that there are those who believe the worst of you. You are a source of fear and consternation, in spite of your charity and compassion. I hear all of the talk."

"And contribute to it, no doubt." He smiled.

Margaret felt her cheeks blush. "Some believe you are a demon or a sorcerer. Others call you the Angel of Death himself. Where do you live? What shire?"

"I am not far from here."

Margaret's eyes widened. "Near Eyam? Where?"

"In a secret place, within the mines."

"You live in the mines?" Margaret asked. "Why?"

"It is part of the vow I made to my order."

"'Tis a strange order to require its brothers to live in mines. What are you, moles?"

He laughed, a full laugh until it was cut off by a deep-chested cough.

"It must be terrible."

"On the contrary, dear sister, it's beautiful. There are caverns as spectacular and as tall as any cathedral. There are underground rivers with fresh water. The placement of the cave openings gives us fresh air and ventilation. We are able to burn fires there without any inhalation of smoke ourselves. We live there. We worship there, in a magnificent cavern that has become our cathedral of prayer. We have adorned it as such."

He spoke in such joyful tones that Margaret found herself smiling, pleased for him. "But how is it that you live there secretly? Why have the miners not found you?"

"There are tunnels and caverns as yet undiscovered by the miners. Our order has served there for over thirty years and we are still discovering new shafts."

"Thirty years!" She pondered this for a moment and then asked, "But whom do you serve, besides God?"

"We have served the miners."

"How?"

"By praying for their prosperity and safety. We have also provided food and necessities for their families. We minister to them all in their time of distress. And, for those who will accept it, we give communion."

Margaret suddenly remembered the talk about mysterious baskets of provisions that had been left on the doorsteps of cottages. They had been unaccounted for, and many believed it was the work of a secret Good Samaritan. The villagers eventually decided not to speculate about who had been doing the good deeds, for fear they might stop. "'Twas you."

"My order."

"How many are you?"

"We were nearly sixty."

"Were?"

"Alas, yes. Now, we are . . . one."

"One? You alone?"

He nodded.

"Why did the others leave?"

"They have all died, Sister. The skin of each one turned blue, like mine. We believed it was God's mark—a sign of holiness, of our calling, and so it was."

"It was your calling to die?"

"No. Ours is to live in the earth and serve the miners, as we have, but there was a price to pay for our sacrifice, as there always is in service to our Lord."

"What price, dear brother?"

He paused and took a deep breath. "Slowly, each of the brothers became sick. Their minds would fail them, and then pain would rack their bodies. They each saw their suffering as a share in Christ's suffering. Then God, in his wisdom, took them, leaving only me." He lowered his head and she could see the blue tint of his scalp at the center of his tonsure.

"Speak no more, Brother, if it distresses you."

He slowly shook his head. "They are with God. If I am distressed, it is because I am here alone to carry on the work—and I am inadequate."

"You are not!" she protested. "You have helped so many."

"Perhaps, but did not the Lord say that the harvest was bountiful, yet the laborers few?"

"Why will your order not send more to your aid?"

"None have volunteered, preferring the monasteries to the mines near a plague village."

Margaret nodded, understanding. "I'm sorry, Brother," she said, as she reached out to take his hand.

He took hers and patted it gently. "In time, I have a great surprise for this village. When this season of death passes, I will show everyone where I live and the wealth with which God has blessed my order. I will share it with all and, by the grace of God, prosperity will return."

Margaret was perplexed. "Wealth? Do you mean spiritual or physical?"

"You will see, at the right time. But not sooner. What I have to share might corrupt those of wicked hearts."

She pondered his words and their meaning. They made little sense to her.

He continued to pat her hand and spoke softly. "I came to you now because, too late, I learned of Frances." He gazed at her. "I am so sorry."

As Margaret was about to respond, she heard the groan of her gate being opened. The wind? No, something else. Suddenly she was afraid. "Dear brother, I fear for you."

"Do you? Fear not, my sister. Remember the words, 'To live is Christ, to die is gain.'"

Suddenly the door was kicked open. Margaret cried out. Benjamin quickly threw his hood over his head and was on his feet, standing between his sister and the door.

A crowd of men pressed at the doorway, their faces haggard distortions of grief, weariness, fear, and drink.

John Dicken, the grave digger, emerged from the crowd and slowly walked toward Benjamin, an iron bar in his hands. "Ah! So it is you," he said to Benjamin. "With so much death today, we are not astounded to see you."

The men behind murmured their agreement.

"And no graveyard through which to escape us this time, aye, mate?"

Margaret struggled to her feet and faced the man, though Benjamin's arm came up in front of her to keep her at a distance. "Explain yourself to me, John Dicken!" she demanded. "What are you and these—these ruffians—doing here?"

The man was wild-eyed and smelled of a pungent drink. "Did we not bury your sister today?" he asked, keeping his eyes on Benjamin.

She replied, "We did, but I do not see how—"

"And did I not bury me own mother this morning?"

Margaret was taken aback. She had been so absorbed in the grief of losing Frances that she had not heard of other deaths. "If so, Mr. Dicken, then I am sorry for you and all your kin."

"Sorry for me?" his face contorted and his mouth became a snarl. "You would share company with this demon of death and express sorrow for me?"

"This is no demon!" she shouted at him.

"If he is no demon, then he is a companion of demons. It's all the same to us."

A few of the men at the door had now slipped into the room. One or two brandished crude weapons. Margaret saw a rope and felt sick with fear.

"It is he who brought the sickness," Dicken said, his speech slurred.

"You are drunken fools!" Margaret shouted at them with all the defiance she could manage.

Dicken ignored her, his eyes still on Benjamin. "Will you not speak to us, Monk?"

Benjamin did not answer.

"Say something, Benjamin," she pleaded with him and then turned to the mob that seemed to be growing in her house. "He is my brother. Do you hear me? My brother!"

"You are bewitched," another man shouted.

"Aye," said Dicken. "'Tis well-known by all that your brothers are far away from here."

"Ne'er to come while the village is isolated!" Joshua Parke added.

"Yet, *he* comes and goes as he pleases," Dicken sneered.

"No," she cried out and took a step forward as if some inner sense told her that violence would now erupt.

It did. From no impetus that Margaret could discern, the men rushed forward, their weapons and fists raised. She screamed.

CHAPTER THIRTY-TWO

AUGUST 14

THERE WERE FEW HOTELS in the world Susan Hutchinson hated more than the Charles De Gaulle Hotel in Brazzaville. The beds had horribly uncomfortable mattresses and pillows that had an unpleasant smell; the air conditioning was erratic and unreliable; and the elevator, when it worked, was like a NASA gravity test for astronauts. To make matters worse, this was probably the best accommodation in the city and the most expensive, but then everything in Brazzaville was expensive, she reminded herself.

The only reasonable fee she had to pay was the two-dollar cab ride she had to take to and from the hotel to the WHO compound, which was located in the more reputable Cité du Djoué section of the city. The ride took her by the Basilica of St. Anne, the largest church and the only cathedral in the city, where she occasionally slipped in for a worship service or prayer.

Brazzaville had been a relatively well-developed and thriving city before the civil war began in 1997. Now it seemed that most of the services and buildings were either falling apart or into disrepair—except for the WHO facility. The staff and labs there were still world-class, which was a comfort to her considering the crisis they were in.

For the first two hours after arriving at her hastily organized office, Susan and her team monitored the reports coming from their various teams in the field. They had completed a survey of the villages and cities in the infected areas of Gabon. She checked and rechecked the reports, talked to the leaders of at least three field teams, then gathered up her papers and headed down the hall to report to General Mosley.

"Good morning, Kevin," Susan said to Mosley's aide as she approached his desk.

"And to you, Dr. Hutchinson," Kevin responded, looking up at her from his computer. He paused, keeping his gaze on her.

Susan always had the feeling that he wanted to ask her out—which wouldn't have been an unwelcome invitation—but then, for some mysterious reason, did not. She waited, then took the initiative: "You can call me Susan, you know."

Kevin smiled and then tilted his head in the direction of the open door. "Go on in . . . Susan. He's waiting for you." Then he leaned forward. She thought it might be the moment. Instead, he whispered, "Be careful. He's in a bad mood."

Susan nodded and whispered back, "Thanks."

As she took a step to enter the office a voice bellowed from inside, "I'm not in a bad mood. I'm in a *horrible* mood!"

Susan cringed and walked in. The general was at his desk reviewing a small mound of paperwork.

"It doesn't stop," he complained without looking up. "Wherever I go, the military chases me with paper." He quickly signed a letter, thrust it into his out-box, sat back in his huge office chair, and sighed. "I hope you have some good news for me."

She shook her head. "I'm afraid not, General." She walked to his conference table and unrolled a map that her staff had just printed for them.

As Mosley walked around his desk to the table, Susan commented, "The reports through the night have been terrible."

"Explain." He leaned over the map.

Susan pointed. "Here's the road from Mitzic to Lalara. As you can see, the death count is growing. The pattern we're seeing is that some die very quickly when exposed to the virus—"

"Some? Like who?"

"The Africans, it would seem, but there are others who don't show symptoms until a period of time after exposure."

"Non-Africans?"

She nodded. "However, their symptoms arrive within a few hours—even a full day—after exposure."

Mosley studied the map. "So, according to the times you've indicated here, we're seeing a second wave of death."

"That's right. We now have another seventy-eight victims since yesterday. And so far, one hundred percent of the cases are the new variant of Ebola, which we're calling the Gabon Ebola. It's now, officially, the largest and most virulent epidemic ever reported."

"The worst epidemic ever reported." Mosley sighed, "And, it could get worse?"

Susan nodded as she stared at the map, aware that the colors, codes, and numbers betrayed the humanity behind each victim. She realized the numbers were in danger of becoming just numbers to her. There was a point, she knew, when the mind simply couldn't comprehend the reality of the figures.

The general rubbed his chin. "Has this hit the news? Are we public yet?"

"The government of Gabon thinks that they may be able to keep a lid on it today—maybe tomorrow—but, the news will eventually get out. So the leadership at the WHO in Geneva is discussing whether to have a news conference this afternoon as opposed to waiting for a report to escape. The staff here believes they'll do the former."

Mosley pointed to an area on the map. "But it doesn't look like the deaths are spreading beyond the immediate region. Is the epidemic limited to this area?"

"It would seem so, and, fortunately, there have been no new cases this morning—likely due to the fact that as soon as someone in the area is symptomatic, they and their immediate contacts are quarantined."

"Voluntarily?"

"Mostly, but a few have required forceful quarantines. The Gabonese military presence has been helpful. So far there has been no backlash, and if one arises, they're ready for it."

Mosley nodded and, in the silence, seemed to sense something. He turned to Susan. "Is there something else?"

She took a deep breath, working through how to say what needed to be said. "The fact that the deaths seem to have stopped in Lalara raises a terrible possibility—or hope—depending on your point of view."

"Go on."

"There is the possibility that something has happened to the boy—maybe he's died—and the problem has resolved itself."

The general seemed to think about this as he walked back to his desk. He picked up his cup of coffee without drinking from it. "Or?"

"Or he may have moved deeper into the jungle and hasn't encountered anyone. Meaning that he could still surface somewhere else."

The general nodded. "Or?"

"Or he's still moving to a larger town, without encountering anyone along the way, and will suddenly appear in a populous area."

"Which would make containment nearly impossible."

Susan looked helplessly at Mosley. "I don't want to even think about it."

Mosley took a sip of coffee. "Well, we can't sit around and wait. We need to meet with an expert on Gabon who can review maps and transport possibilities with us. And I want to have a conference call with the chiefs of staff of the president of Gabon and the director general of the WHO."

Susan looked at him, her expression obviously reflecting the question she wanted to ask.

"We have to work out a plausible cover story," he explained. "And, I want to put a bounty on the boy."

"A bounty?"

"That's right. If the Gabon police and military can't find him alone, then a bounty will get more people searching."

"But General, that would mean more people will risk exposure to capture him."

The general turned his face away from her. "I don't just want him captured. I want him stopped."

Susan felt a burning behind her eyes and she realized what he intended to do. "He's just a teenager," she said.

"Listen, Susan, this isn't the time to be squeamish. This has to be brought to an end—by any means possible."

"Any means possible?"

Mosley nodded, "Dead or alive; he must be stopped."

CHAPTER THIRTY-THREE

THE TSI TEAM GATHERED the next morning in the dining room of the Rose and Crown, where Matthew Cunningham, looking fresh and groomed, bid them good morning and announced, "The fare includes a full English fry-up, with fried or poached eggs, fried and toasted bread, ham, bacon, tomatoes, mushrooms, baked beans, and black pudding. We also have fresh-squeezed orange juice, tea, and coffee. You're welcome to any variation."

"I'll have all of the above," Digger said.

Georgina scowled. "It's a heart attack on a plate."

The others chose variations from the menu. Mark opted for toast and coffee and avoided eye contact with the rest of the team by reading the *London Times*. He wasn't concentrating on the news. The print was a blur. His mind was sifting through the information he spent studying most of the night: research papers, articles, data, and lab results that might give him a clue or an insight about how to fight the virus in Africa.

He glanced at Nora. She looked tired too. No doubt she'd also spent the night as he had. He shook his head as he returned to the newspaper. Had they not had their little spat, and had he not been worried about the rest of the team's gossip, he would have suggested that they spend the night researching and brainstorming together.

Mark's toast and coffee arrived. The coffee was strong. Just what he needed—a wake-up jolt for his dulled senses.

After Mr. Cunningham served the last of breakfast, he withdrew. Digger, with uncharacteristic subtlety, stood up with a small square electronic device and casually walked around the dining room, holding it up in the air, pointing it at corners and plants and under the tables and chairs. It beeped rhythmically without interruption. After a moment, he sat down again.

"No bugs," he declared.

"Thanks." Nora stood up and leaned forward on the dining table. She spoke on the edge of a whisper. "Henry, you, Digger, and Georgina will set up and test the equipment in the designated rooms with the appropriate security. Mark and I will begin scouting around Eyam for samples."

"Hopefully not each other's," Digger said.

Mark kept his eyes down, but could feel Nora glare at Digger.

Georgina groaned. "Do you have to be so crass?"

Digger shrugged. "It's an art."

"You'll be taking cameras, of course," Henry said to Nora. "You're filming a documentary, you'll recall."

"I have them ready to go."

Mark cleared his throat, but didn't look up. "I suggest you be extra diligent about security around here."

"No worries," Digger said. "I've brought a quick and easy security system that I'll set up in all our rooms. I also set a system up on the outside of the B&B, and laser beam detectors on the edge of the property."

"And we have our body guards," Georgina added, nodding her head toward the soldiers who'd brought them up.

"Why?" Nora asked, looking at Mark—obviously aware that it was an unusual statement for Mark to make.

For the first time that morning, Mark looked at her fully. "Our pals from Deadman's Plumbing were parked out on the road last night."

All eyes fell to Mark.

"Let's roust them out," Digger exclaimed, making as if to get up.

Mark held up a hand to stop him. "That's a bad idea. Chase them away and they'll only find another place where they can watch us. I'd rather leave them where we know they are."

"Tell me again who they are?" Georgina asked. "Back to Earth?"

"Return to Earth," Mark corrected her, "but it might be someone else."

"Ahaz," Digger smirked. "They want to keep an eye on you."

Mark ignored the remark and turned his attention back to the
newspaper. He struggled to hide the shaking of his hand when he
lifted the mug.

In front of the Rose and Crown, Mark stood on the gravel drive
and gazed at the endless sky, the deep blue color of pacific
waters. He took a deep breath and enjoyed the fresh air. The
scents of the sycamore and ash trees came to him, rich and
sweet.

Nora came up behind him. "It's a restorative place, isn't it?"

"It would be, if we were here for other reasons."

She held out a digital camera to him. He took it, gave a quick
once-over of the functions, and then dropped it into his sports-
coat pocket.

"The village is close by. Shall we walk?"

He nodded, noticing for the first time that she was dressed to
the hilt in a hiking outfit: dark green long-sleeved T-shirt, khaki
shorts, knee-high socks, and hiking boots, complete with a large
backpack that looked, from the outside, as if it was packed to the
seams. He contrasted her outfit to his own sports jacket, white
shirt, jeans, walking shoes, and carrying case. "Where are you
going that I'm not going?" he asked.

"Grave hunting."

They headed down the driveway toward the main road. He
wondered if now was the time to tell Nora about his previous
visit to Eyam, but decided to wait until it was absolutely necessary. Why bother her with such things now?

After a moment of silence, she said, "I'm sorry about what
happened last night. I was insensitive and thoughtless."

"Let's forget about that," he said. "What's our plan?"

"I've worked out a map that identifies plots of land where
various groups of plague victims and survivors were buried. I'll
check those out to see if we have any candidates for samples to

study. I'd like you to explore the church and graveyard. You also have a list—"

"Of descendants of the survivors." He reached into the inside pocket of his sports coat and pulled out a sheet of paper, which he held out to her. "Why don't you do that part and I'll search for the graves?"

She looked at him, suspicious. "Why?"

"No reason. I'd enjoy the walk."

"You look more like a television producer," she said. "And you're not dressed for a walkabout."

She had him on that one.

"Let's stick with the plan. You talk to the descendants. I suggest you start at the church."

Mark grunted his obedience.

"We'll want samples from them, too. Unless you were able to get the lab results from the NIH's investigation a few years ago."

"I downloaded their data last night. It's not as helpful as I'd hoped." Nor was the material from Ahaz, he wanted to add, but decided against it.

"Then we'll want new samples to examine for ourselves."

He raised an eyebrow. "It'll be hard to convince people to give samples to a documentary crew."

Nora gave him a knowing smile. "Let me show you something."

She squatted by his carrying case and opened it up. "Of course, you have the camera and tripod so that you can look as though you're videotaping interviews." She rustled deeper into the bag and pulled out a folder of papers and a small black bag. She opened the folder. "These are the consent forms people have to sign for you to tape them. Every television crew must do this—and these folks have been filmed enough to understand this."

"Got it," Mark said, wondering what else was in her bag of tricks.

She unzipped the small bag. "This is the best of all. Take a look." She unsnapped the container and Mark looked closely.

"It looks like an ink pad."

She smiled. "It's supposed to." She closed the case and picked up a consent form. "If you look here, you'll see how there's a space for a fingerprint. The substance that looks like fingerprint ink is actually a specially formulated adhesive. When you swipe their finger across the adhesive and then push it on the consent paper, it will painlessly pull off tens of thousands of epithelial cells."

Now, it was Mark's turn to smile. "DNA samples on paper, eh?"

"Indeed, and each consent is legally worded to include the signer's permission for us to test their DNA."

"Brilliant."

Nora grinned at him. "I know."

CHAPTER THIRTY-FOUR

EACH HOUR SEEMED TO be longer than the one before. Aaron hid, he slept, he watched, and he ran. The previous two nights he had crawled into the crook of giant trees—far enough off the ground to be protected from the lower-flying insects, as well as the two- and four-legged hunters that often stalked one another in the darkness.

His parents had always insisted that his sisters and he sleep protected by a chemically treated mosquito net. The nasty little bugs were notorious for the diseases they carried: malaria, dengue, yellow fever, and the West Nile virus. Some of his friends at the compound had caught these diseases in spite of all their family's precautions, and here he was out in the jungle with no change of clothes, no supplies, and certainly no protection.

He felt he was growing weaker. And, he felt a wave of dread. "What if I've caught malaria?" he asked aloud, aware that lately he'd taken to talking to himself.

Aaron felt exposed and vulnerable and very, very alone.

Yesterday, he had circled the small town of Lalara, searching for food in the garbage cans and praying for some semblance of hope: a clue, a hint, about what he should do next. He paced, prayed, and pondered, but was often distracted by his hunger and by the suspicious looks from passersby. He'd never been so hungry before, yet he still felt guilty for his petty thievery: nabbing a bowl of fruit that had been left on a porch table.

He promised himself that one day he would return and pay the owner.

He felt even guiltier about taking a Bible from a chair outside a small hut, for he knew how valued a family Bible was. But he needed its consolation, and he was desperate to remember all he'd been taught about the coming Apocalypse. Surely the Bible would give him clues on how he might recognize the friends or enemies of God. It was so hard to tell. Some people reached out to him as if they wanted to help, but he avoided them for fear that they might want to trap him or turn him over to the authorities.

He had spent the better part of a day reading and rereading the books of Isaiah, Daniel, and Revelation. Nothing in these ancient books gave him advice about what to do, so he turned to prayer, believing that God might talk to him. A still small voice. Something. Anything.

But all that ever came to him were the noises of the jungle and distant village, and the grumbles and moans of his stomach.

Jesus had fasted for forty days in the wilderness. Could he last that long, if necessary?

He scratched at the bite marks on his arms. "I hate those bugs," he complained to himself as he tore at the raised rosy spots.

Bugs, disease, hunger . . . *I've got to get help.* But he had run out of people he could trust.

Out of frustration, he began to weep. He didn't want to die in the jungle. He didn't want to die alone.

Looking through the branches above his temporary home, he whispered, "Lord, if you're not going to come rescue me, then tell me what to do!"

He was quiet for a few moments, but no reply came except for the mocking cry of a bird.

Aaron remembered the story in the Bible of the birds arriving to feed the prophet Elijah when he was hiding from King Ahab. Elijah was the prophet that had felt so alone that he'd complained to God and God told him that he wasn't alone; there were lots of others like him. Aaron closed his eyes and whispered, "God, I need your help. Show me others like me: my brothers and sisters in Christ." He thought of a prayer from the Bible: a man calling to Jesus as he walked on a road somewhere. "Have mercy on me, Lord Jesus."

Then, to his surprise, he thought he heard a voice.

He opened his eyes and looked around expecting to see someone. No one was there.

What had he heard? The words "Sisters" and "Mercy." His own words. Was it an echo of his prayer?

No. The voice he heard wasn't his own. It was no echo. It was like a whisper in his ear. "Sisters" and "Mercy."

Sisters? Was he thinking of his dead sisters?

He leaned back and groaned, "I must be delirious. Sisters and Mercy?"

Then it came to him: Sisters *of* Mercy. That's what he had heard. "Sisters of Mercy."

They were nuns who lived on the outskirts of Libreville, the capital city of Gabon. His family had gone there to visit when they'd first arrived in the country. The Sisters of Mercy. His father had always spoken respectfully of them. His father trusted them.

Suddenly, Aaron knew he had to go *there*. They'd give him a place to hide. He knew it. He just *knew* it.

But Libreville was over two hundred miles away.

How will I get there? God, how am I to get there?

In his mind, he heard his mother's voice: "A journey of one mile or one thousand miles both start the same way: with the first step."

He climbed down the tree and began his journey.

CHAPTER THIRTY-FIVE

MARK AND NORA WALKED up the main road toward Eyam's town square. They passed patches of woods intermingled with old homes, bed-and-breakfasts, modern homes, and various types of businesses. The Miners Arms was off to the right.

"Apparently it was built in 1630," Nora observed for no apparent reason, though Mark suspected that she knew what he was thinking.

"We'll have to pay it a visit."

"After we've finished our work."

"A late lunch, then. Two o'clock? We'll compare notes."

"See you then."

At the square, which was really a junction of several roads, Nora said good-bye and veered off to the north, heading for the noted burial sites. Mark went straight onto Church Street and felt his first wave of apprehension about being recognized.

He strolled past driveways for a primary school and for various historic cottages and houses adorned with holly and lilac trees. The architecture of the village was of mixed character and styles. Light sandstone and limestone seemed to be the building material of choice, and the structures appeared to represent a style from each century over the past seven hundred years.

He crossed the drive leading to the rectory and came upon St. Lawrence's Church set back from the road beyond a collection of crypts and graves looking like jagged teeth thrusting up from a trim bed of green. The church was Normanesque with a square bell tower and traditional arched windows. Some sections had been added later, he could tell, probably during the Victorian era, but the overall look was consistent: a classic English church nestled in a quaint English village.

As he continued on, he noticed the added embellishments of a clock above the main entrance and a sundial above a side door. An ancient-looking cross sat nearby. He moved closer and tried to remember what he'd read about it. The Saxons had built it, he believed, and the artwork was Celtic with interlacing patterns and runic knots. At the top was a carving of Madonna and child and angels holding long horns.

He followed the avenue that cut between the church and the rectory, lined with lime trees that stood like sentries. The Church Centre, a modern building that housed the church offices and classrooms, sat at the end—an architectural contrast to the church itself. He braced himself as he approached the double doors that served as the entrance. Opening one, he stepped in.

Her name came to him immediately—not only because she was on the descendants list, but also because he remembered her. Joan Thompson. She sat at her desk in a receptionist's enclave complete with sliding glass window. He stepped up to the glass and she reached up to open it.

"May I help you?" she asked, and her eyes drifted up to his face. Her expression changed for only a second as she seemed to struggle to place his face.

"Hi, I'm with an American television-production company," he lied. "We're here to film portions of a documentary about the plague."

"Yes, I've heard about that," Joan said.

"I'd like permission to wander the grounds and snap some photos of the plague victims' graves, if I may."

"Of course you may. Tourists do it all the time."

"I may also want to interview you and Reverend Knight. We're looking for descendants of the villagers who endured the plague."

"That would include me," she said with a touch of pride. Then her face shadowed again. "Have we met before?"

Mark affected a light chuckle. "Why would you think that?"

"You look familiar to me."

"I occasionally appear in our documentaries. Maybe you've seen me on television."

"Maybe so," she said, clearly unconvinced. "Shall I show you around?"

"I don't want to inconvenience you," he said, hoping she recognized that he was politely saying he didn't want her to.

"It's not an inconvenience at all," she said and stood up. "I didn't catch your name."

"I'm Mark."

Mark learned more than he ever thought he'd want to about the Church of St. Lawrence. People had worshipped there for more than nine hundred years, though it was known as St. Helen's Church until parish politics changed the name in the nineteenth century.

The nave was a traditional design of arches and stained glass, with dark wooden pews and an ornate altar at the east end. Though some of the structure was dated to the fourteenth century, it was thought that much of the work was accomplished in the sixteenth and nineteenth centuries.

More than anything, Mark was struck by a variety of paintings on the nave walls: partial and faded representations of the tribes of Israel, calligraphies of the Apostles' Creed, and banners of Christ with children. Mark stopped at the banner and felt again the emptiness he'd felt in the church in Gabon. Now, though, it was more like an ache.

The church gave quite a bit of space to the plague history, with racks of brochures and booklets and a cupboard that purported to be made from the box that had originally brought the "infected cloth" from London in 1665.

A display on the north aisle contained a facsimile edition of the parish register opened to September 1665 when the plague deaths began. A beautiful illustrated manuscript of the names of plague victims was encased in a glass display on the south aisle.

Mark tapped the glass and asked, "How many of these plague victims are buried in the churchyard?"

"Not many," Joan replied. Again, she looked at him as if the question had tickled her memory and she was renewing her efforts to remember him.

Outside the church Joan pointed out the highlights: the Celtic cross, the sundial above the priest's door, Catherine Mompesson's tomb, and several other graves of note including a "Cricketer's Grave" dedicated to the memory of someone named Bagshaw.

Mark's eye was drawn to a newly dug grave, but it had a worn tombstone. He asked Joan about it.

"That's Hannah Rogers's grave," she explained. "She died in the plague."

"But the ground has been dug up."

Joan looked displeased and then lowered her voice to a conspiratorial whisper. "We had a robbery here."

"A grave robbery? Does that happen often around here?"

She shook her head. "Not at all. Never, in fact—at least until now."

"I assume it's significant that they robbed the grave of a plague victim."

"Probably," she said. "The police are investigating. It only just happened."

"Was anything stolen?"

"The body." She wrapped her arms around herself and, even in the heat, shivered. "It's sick, really."

Mark didn't want to press his luck by asking for more information, but he was fairly certain he knew who had dug up the grave. With a nagging sense of paranoia, Mark looked around the churchyard. At the far end of the property, near a stone wall adjoining the neighboring field, a tall, thin man watched them.

"Do you know who that is?" Mark asked.

Joan followed his gaze. "Oh, that's Philip, our groundskeeper."

"Has he worked here for long?"

"Over thirty years as groundskeeper, but he's lived in Eyam his whole life."

"I'll want to talk to him later, I'm sure." Mark continued a slow scan of the area.

"Are you looking for something?" she asked.

He improvised his answer. "Just thinking about various places and angles for the camera. We'll want shots that'll show off the area."

"Shots," Joan said in a tone that caused Mark to glance at her. Her face was suddenly troubled.

Mark knew that Joan now remembered him. Shots—needles—blood samples.

She opened her mouth to speak, but a banging door drew their attention to the rectory. A man, dressed in clerical collar, stepped through.

"That's the reverend," Joan said.

Another man wearing a well-cut suit followed the reverend. Mark clenched his fists as he recognized Nathan Dodge.

CHAPTER THIRTY-SIX

THE REVEREND WAVED AT Joan, who waved back. Nathan Dodge was distracted closing the gate behind him. Then he turned and saw Mark. He hesitated for only a second, enough for Mark to know that Dodge's mind was now reeling like his own.

"Come meet Reverend Andrew," Joan said and began walking toward the two men.

Mark followed her anticipating his encounter with Dodge.

"This is good timing," Joan announced as they drew closer. "Reverend Andrew Knight, this is Mark Carlson from the American film company you heard about."

"A pleasure," the reverend said, thrusting out his hand.

Mark shook his hand, fully aware that Joan had given Mark's last name though Mark had not given it earlier. Her memory had fully placed him, which would make this meeting even more interesting.

Reverend Andrew smiled and said, "Ah! We have two Americans in our midst. Mr. Carlson, this is Nathan Dodge. He works with an American pharmaceutical company."

Mark shook Nathan's hand and both men squeezed extra hard as they did, their eyes locked with the same fierceness as their hands.

"Which company?" Mark asked.

"You've probably never heard of it. Ahaz Pharmaceuticals."

"I've heard of it," Mark said. "And what brings an American pharmaceutical company like Ahaz to Eyam?"

"Reverend Andrew had some questions about our firm," Dodge replied.

"And you came to answer him personally?" Mark said, feigning astonishment. "I had no idea that pharmaceutical companies were so diligent with their customer service."

"I happened to be in the area."

Mark noticed that Joan was watching them both with a stern expression, her hands clasped in front of her like an annoyed schoolteacher. He wondered if she would blow their cover.

"And what's the interest of an American film company in Eyam?" Dodge asked.

"We're doing a documentary about the plague," Mark said.

"Interesting," Dodge said.

The two men gazed at each other.

Dodge broke the moment, turning to the reverend. "Well, Reverend. I must be going." He shook Knight's hand. "Thank you for your time."

"Thank you for coming," Andrew said.

"I believe your van is around the corner," Mark said to Dodge.

"My van?"

"From Deadman's."

"You're mistaken," Dodge said. "I have a car."

A final nod to the reverend and a quick thanks to Joan and Dodge walked away from them, down the drive to the main road.

"You must have had some difficult questions for a pharmaceutical company to set up a personal visit," Mark observed.

"I did," Andrew said. "Shall we go into my office to chat?"

Joan offered to make tea as Mark sat down in the clergyman's office. Reverend Andrew lingered in the hall with her for a moment then entered, and crossed to the chair behind his desk. He brushed a hand over his salt-and-pepper hair before placing his elbows on his desk and smiled at Mark.

"Well," he said, then pressed his lips together.

"Well," Mark repeated, noting the reverend's change of attitude. "You have a beautiful church."

"Thank you."

Joan entered and quickly handed a small card to Andrew. With a look of disapproval at Mark, she left again.

He looked at the card, chuckled, then handed it to Mark. "Joan keeps everything," he said.

Mark took the card. It was an Ahaz business card. Mark's name was on it.

"It's uncanny," the reverend said. "Imagine the coincidence of you having the same name as a doctor who worked for Ahaz and who came here a few years ago to study the plague."

"Imagine," Mark said and tossed the card onto the desk.

The reverend seemed pleased with himself. "From your facial expressions I assume you and Mr. Dodge truly didn't know you were both here."

"No, we didn't."

"And it's not likely that he just happened to be in the area and stopped by to visit me."

"No. Not likely."

"And you're not here to film a documentary."

"No."

"Then why are you here?"

Joan entered with a tray of tea, dropped it onto the desk with a rattle, hastily poured two cups, and then spun on her heels to leave again. At the door she stopped. "My memory is slower than it used to be, but eventually I remember. Did you honestly think I wouldn't? I don't give my blood or health history to every stranger who comes along, you know."

"I'm sure you don't."

"Was it necessary to lie?" she asked him, and he wondered why she seemed so wounded.

"In this case, yes," he said calmly. He then addressed them both. "I'm here on business for the U.S. government."

"Not Ahaz this time," the reverend said.

"No. Not Ahaz."

"Then perhaps you should explain."

"Before I answer, I have to ask where Mr. Dodge sat when he spoke with you."

"In your chair," the reverend replied.

Mark reached down, running his hands along the bottom edge of the desktop, then under the metallic edges of the chair.

"What are you doing?" Joan asked.

His fingers found a small bump, which he pried from the frame. He held up a small listening device. Joan gasped. Andrew tilted his head, impressed.

"We'll talk soon," Mark said to the device, then dropped it onto the floor and crushed it under his heel. He relished the thought of Dodge or his cronies going deaf from the noise in their headphones.

"This is getting interesting," Reverend Andrew said.

"It's important that I remind you of your government's Official Secrets Act. What I'm about to tell you falls well within that. If you leak a word of this to anyone, you could go to jail."

He and Joan nodded to one another. He said, "Consider us both reminded."

Joan frowned. "You were a lot nicer when you were here as a doctor."

"I'm here as a doctor now, though when I came before, it was strictly for developmental research. I'm here now because of a crisis—one that could have international ramifications if we don't get some answers."

"Oh dear," Joan said.

Mark gestured to her. "You may as well sit down and have a cup of tea with us," he said. "This will take a few minutes to explain."

Andrew leaned back and scrutinized Mark. "This had better be the truth, Dr. Carlson. I'll know if it isn't. I can always tell when I'm being lied to."

"How did you do with Mr. Dodge?"

"Him? Oh, I knew he was giving me a load of old cobblers the minute he opened his mouth."

"You're wise."

"And he'll get nowhere in this village without my cooperation. Come clean with me and I'll do all I can to help."

"Count on it," Mark said, and he began. By the time he had finished, the tea was cold and Joan was pale. Andrew had his hands pressed together in front of him, his fingers interlaced, and his expression grim.

"You haven't said much about Ahaz," Andrew observed. "Obviously they play a role in this somehow or they wouldn't be here."

Mark had purposefully stayed away from any speculation, accusations, or theories about Ahaz. Even now, he didn't want to speak of them. "What should I say?"

The vicar smiled. "You confess to us about a pandemic, but you're going to hold back about a pharmaceutical company?"

"I don't want to confuse the situation by discussing outside parties," Mark said as a matter of fact.

"And your loyalties aren't with them or you wouldn't be here now."

"My loyalties aren't with them because I'm a former employee. My loyalties are with finding a cure for this virus."

"Isn't that what Ahaz wants to do?"

"Is that what Dodge told you?"

Andrew smiled sardonically. "Actually, my guess is they want to find the cure first, so they can save the world, all with a nice profit. Is that it?"

Joan frowned at her boss. "That's a terribly cynical thing to say."

"Am I wrong?" he asked, but his question was directed to Mark.

"Money is a great motivator for the private sector," Mark said. "Maybe that's why they got here ahead of the government."

"How do you know they got here ahead of you?"

"I saw the grave."

Mark noticed Andrew and Joan exchange another glance.

"Well, if they were after a plague victim, the body in that grave won't do them much good," Joan said.

"Why not?"

Another exchange of glances. Mark suspected that she was fearful of saying too much. Andrew smiled at her and she turned back to Mark. "It is a secret, known only to the church's vicars and a few other people."

Andrew explained, "Not long after Hannah Rogers's death, her body was removed from that grave and buried in Eakring nearer to her family plot."

"Then what body did they dig up?"

"It belonged to a servant girl who died of a broken neck from an accidental fall over one hundred years after the plague. The vicar at the time, who had great affection for the poor girl, decided to bury her properly in Hannah's grave rather than use a pauper's grave outside of town."

Mark felt a great flush of pleasure. "So any tests they conduct on the girl will be useless."

"Correct."

"Is there any way to ensure that my team gets to the right graves?" Mark asked.

Andrew looked to Joan. "Well?"

"Do you trust him?" she asked.

He considered Mark for a moment. "This isn't only about trust. I'll have to talk to my bishop."

"Can you do that now?" Mark asked. "You understand the urgency of the situation."

"I do indeed."

CHAPTER THIRTY-SEVEN

NORA SCRUTINIZED THE MAP of Eyam and looked down beyond the steep field of green patches and stone walls toward Eyam below. She held up the map again, studying the various Xs she had placed there to mark the plague victims' burial sites. Her sources were historical—some likely valid, others probably apocryphal—and most had yielded only marginal results after hours of searching.

According to the map, she was in an area known as Barkers Piece. A handful of graves might be found in this area but, by her own notations, it seemed unlikely.

She stopped for a moment to appreciate the beautiful view of the valley stretching out to the horizon. Hope Valley it was called, which seemed ironic, all things considered. The sun disappeared behind thick black clouds.

A footpath cut eastward through Barkers Piece, touching the southern edge of some woods, and the top end of Water Lane. That lane led back to the Miners' Arms, where she was to meet Mark in half an hour. Adjusting her backpack, she trudged along, wanting nothing more than to sit down for a meal.

After reaching Water Lane, she looked longingly in the direction of town. One last glance at the map before folding it up. There were rumors of graves behind the Miners' Arms. Then her eye caught a notation in the midst of a thick collection of trees just to the northeast called Furniss or Furness Wood. The note indicated a possible burial site, but she couldn't remember anything in her research about burial sites in the woods.

She was tempted to forget about it. There was no point in

getting lost in the woods for a grave she wouldn't find anyway, and it was about to rain. She could smell it.

But . . . The thought nagged at her that a grave tucked away in the woods might be the best one of all. How would she know unless she investigated?

Groaning, she pushed aside her fears and turned left onto a footpath headed north. When she thought she was parallel with the burial site, she turned right into the woods. Since she didn't know what she was looking for, she simply craned her neck back and forth, searching between the trees and tangled undergrowth for clues or signs pointing to a burial place. She knew instantly that she was making a huge mistake. There was no footpath, and her walk consisted of mostly half stumbling.

Ready to give up, she stopped. "You have one last chance to make yourself known," she said to the grave.

She turned full circle, and was startled to see something she hadn't noticed before: a figure through the trees. It seemed to be dressed in a robe with the hood pulled over its head and it stood perfectly still. She thought it must be a statue of some sort, perhaps a memorial, and wondered why it was out in the middle of nowhere.

She took a few steps, intending to investigate, but then the figure lifted an arm and pointed to her.

Nora froze where she was, her heart lurching. The eeriness of it made her knees weak. She found herself offering a silent prayer.

The specter's arm slowly moved and pointed to her right.

She didn't want to take her eyes off the figure, but forced herself to look in the direction indicated. She saw nothing but trees and thick undergrowth.

Snaps and clicks sounded around her as the rain began to fall. She glanced up at the thick green ceiling above her, then back to the figure. It was gone. She muttered a prayer for protection though she didn't know why she felt she needed protecting.

She shivered. The rain fell harder. Frowning, she pulled her jacket over her head and chastised herself for not following her first inclination. She looked again to her right—where the figure had pointed—and realized that it was south, the direction she needed to walk, and it was as good a pathway as she might find retracing her steps. She was grateful that she'd be walking downhill—a small mercy.

The figure stayed in her mind. Someone dressed like a monk in the middle of the woods made little sense. She knew of no churches or monasteries in this area, at least none that appeared on any maps, and it had disappeared so quickly. Was it possible that she had imagined it?

She looked back in the direction where it had stood, hoping to see a tree from a different angle, wanting to believe that it was her eyes playing tricks on her.

She was so focused on the spot where the specter had been that she didn't see the small log in front of her. With a cry, she stumbled and fell over it. She tumbled forward, her arms outstretched to keep from landing face-first. A sharp pain pierced her ankle as she hit the ground.

Still rolling, she twisted to her side, sliding down the slope of the hill for several feet until she skidded to a stop. The pack kept her from rolling onto her back: she lay on her side for a moment. She flexed her ankle and it rebelled with another sharp stab of pain. Hopefully it was just a sprain and not a fracture. Annoyed, she struggled to sit up.

"Terrific," she said with a groan.

She was facing a thick overgrowth of bushes and vines that looked like a tent, the sort of natural enclosure an animal might use for shelter—though it would have been a large animal, considering the size of the green canopy. It was a little over four feet high from the ground to the top. Leaning in a little, she tried to get a better look. Just a few feet in she saw something in the shadows. With deference to her painful ankle, she took off her backpack, unzipped the side, and removed a small flashlight. She turned it on and trained the thin beam into the darkness.

The object was a stone cross.

A grave, she thought.

She grabbed a knife from another zippered pocket and hacked at the brush and vines. Crawling on her hands and knees, she reached the cross, which was crudely cut from stone. It was about two feet high and ensnared in more vines, which she cut and pushed out of the way. Expecting to find a name and date, she was surprised to find instead a symbol where the crossbeams met. The cross was smudged with dirt and leaves, which she wiped off. The symbol looked as if it had been hand cut into the stone, probably with a dull tool.

The image consisted of an outer circle split into two halves. The upper half appeared to be an intertwining of olive branches. The lower half looked like a representation of a vine and flowers—the flowers were in the shape of lilies. Inside this floral circle was a carving of a lamb sitting in repose—with lines radiating from above it like sunbeams. Also, above the lamb hovered a bird with a rough resemblance to a dove.

Nora stretched her memory back to her Catholic education in an attempt to recall what the symbols meant. If they were Christian, and not a pagan configuration, then the symbol of the dove probably meant peace or the Holy Spirit. *Or did it?* She thought again. No, earlier representations used two doves for peace, whereas, a single dove meant . . .

"What does a single dove represent?" she asked aloud, as if dear old Sister Bernadette might appear to give her the answer. The sister didn't, but Nora suddenly remembered that a single dove symbolized hope. Maybe humility.

The lamb often meant love, or gentleness, or represented Jesus. The radiating lines might represent holiness or the light of the world. Lilies more often than not symbolized chastity or purity. The olive branches represented peace or harmony.

Curious to see if there was an inscription on the opposite side of the cross, Nora wrestled with the branches, pushing and snapping them aside. The back of the cross was blank, but the new angle allowed the light of the flashlight to shine farther into the dim hollow. Inside were many more crosses, perhaps a dozen, just like this first one.

She crawled the several feet to the next cross, her better instincts telling her not to be foolish, since she knew little about the indigenous snakes or animals in these woods. The next cross bore the same symbol as the first.

Who is buried here? she wondered. *No names or dates, just the symbol. Was it a family? A religious order? Might this be from the time of the plague?*

Unsnapping the cell phone from its holder on her belt, she used its built-in camera to take a picture of the cross and the symbol.

She backed out of the enclosure and only then realized the rain had stopped. Standing, she brushed herself off and turned to continue on her way back to the town. Each step sent a bolt of pain up her leg.

Only a few feet ahead of her, the cowled figure stood, its face covered in shadow.

Nora gasped. "Who are you?" she asked in a tight voice.

The specter didn't speak, but lifted its hand and pointed toward the burial site. The exposed hand was a deep blue.

Nora took a step backward, stumbling again and falling on her back, the backpack knocking the wind out of her. In spite of her breathless pain, she spun on the ground and got to her knees, bracing herself for anything that might happen.

But the figure was gone.

CHAPTER THIRTY-EIGHT

THE MINERS' ARMS WAS built in the Tudor style with black timbers accenting its white walls.

Mark walked inside, blinking against the change from daylight to the pub's ambient dimness. Game machines flashed at him from a corner. A man with long whiskers nodded at him from behind the bar. He was surprised to see that Nora was already there sitting at a table in the far corner against a brick wall and unlit fireplace. She was hunched over a drink and staring vacantly at the hearth. As he came closer, he saw that her brow was knitted into a worried expression, and that she was pale.

He made his way through the pub, aware of the other diners, wondering if any were from Ahaz or Return to Earth. No one looked suspicious or seemed to pay him any attention.

"Hi," he said to Nora.

"Hi," she said, without looking at him.

"What's wrong? You look like you've seen a ghost," he said.

The comment seemed to startle her. "Don't say that."

He'd never seen her look so troubled. "What's wrong? Bad news?"

"No," she said quickly and took a drink. "Nothing. I'm thinking. Sit down."

He took the chair across from her. "More than thinking."

"I'm tired too."

He could see the weariness in her eyes, but sensed that something more was at work. "How was your search?"

"I found a few candidates. We'll meet with the team at five

o'clock and talk about them." Another sip of her drink and her eyes slid back over to the fireplace and rested there.

Mark flagged the barman and signaled for a drink. He perused the menu, choosing a "Plowman's Lunch" of cheese, chutney, pickles, and bread. "Did you order?"

No reply.

"Nora?"

She looked at him as if he'd just arrived. "Hi."

"Have you ordered?"

"Yes, but I'm not hungry."

Mark gave his order to the barman and then turned fully to Nora. "What's wrong with you?"

She looked at him steadily for a moment. "Something curious . . ."

Mark waited, but she didn't speak again. "You'll have to give me a clue."

"I don't want to talk about it now." She straightened and shook her head as if shaking off the cobwebs of her thoughts. "What happened with you?"

"Well, it's a mix of good and bad news," he said.

Nora lifted an eyebrow.

"The good news is that I had a nice chat with the church secretary and the vicar."

"And the bad news?"

"That chat took place after I bumped into an old crony from Ahaz."

She frowned. "So they're here."

The barman arrived with Mark's drink and set it down on the mat in front of him.

Nora waited until he departed, then asked: "And the Deadman's Plumbing van belongs to Ahaz?"

"I don't think so. My former coworker seemed genuinely surprised when I mentioned it."

"Which means somebody else is with us. Return to Earth?"

He shrugged. "Unless there's another group we don't know about."

"It wouldn't surprise me." She sighed. "We should hold a convention."

He smiled. "It's funny, really."

"Is it?"

"If we could figure a way to get out from between Ahaz and Return to Earth, they'd obliterate each other."

"I wish they'd hurry up and get it over with. We have a lot of work to do."

Mark tapped his carrying case. "I have a fingerprint with epithelials from the church secretary. She was on the list of the descendants."

"Great."

"Except she was a bit reluctant to participate."

"Why?"

Mark downed half of his drink. "Ah, well . . . that might fall into the category of 'bad news' that I mentioned earlier."

"Meaning what?"

"She knew I wasn't a film producer."

Nora cocked her head. "How did she know that?"

"Because she recognized me from when I was here before."

Nora stared at him for a moment, as if unable to register what she'd just heard. Then she banged her drink down onto the table, jarring the cutlery and small vase of flowers. Aware of the stares around her, she leaned toward Mark and spoke in a harsh whisper. "When were you here before?"

"A few years ago. On assignment for Ahaz. As part of our preliminary research in . . ."

Nora lowered her head and groaned.

"It's not a problem."

She gaped at him and clenched her fists as if she might take a swing at him.

"I'm sorry," he said. "I should have told you before, but I didn't want it to complicate things any more than they already are." His explanation sounded feeble even to his own ears.

Nora breathed in and out for a moment, an exercise to restrain herself. She spoke softly. "All right. So the secretary recognized you. What did you say to her?"

Mark could think of no easy or diplomatic way to break the news, so he simply stated: "I explained to her and the vicar what we're really doing here—and why we're doing it."

Nora threw herself back against her chair, banging against a painting of foxhunters and dogs directly behind her. The painting tipped a little. Her cheeks were a deep red and her eyes blazed. She spoke on the hard edge of the whisper. "You divulged top secret information—without clearance, without approval—to a couple of *civilians?*"

He spread his arms in open appeal. "I think we'll make more progress with them than without them. The vicar has given me a list of grave sites and the bishop's approval for us to test several of the bodies in the graveyard tonight."

"Is that so?" she fumed. "Well, I'm so glad you got that for us. I'm sure Mac and the team will be reassured to know that you blew our cover to get us permission to access the very place we were going to access anyway. I know it makes me feel comforted down to my toenails. Thank you so much, Dr. Carlson."

The barman arrived with their lunches. Mark stared at his, unsure of what to say next.

Nora took a bite of her club sandwich before suddenly pushing it away. "Why do you make things so much harder than they have to be?" she asked standing, grabbing her knapsack, and marching out of the pub, limping slightly as she went.

Mark watched her go, as did everyone else in the dining area.

The barman looked at Mark from behind the counter and said, "I guess you'll be paying for lunch, then."

Everyone laughed except Mark, who turned back to his lunch. "Ah, that dry British wit," Mark grumbled as he picked up a piece of cheese from his plate. "It's why I love this country so much."

Mark walked back to the inn following a footpath that wound behind the businesses and houses along the main road. Skirting along the sloping fields and small groves that marked the north end of the town, Mark had a chance to think through his lunch with Nora. He wanted to believe that she'd overreacted. Maybe it was a follow-up to whatever was troubling her when he'd arrived at the pub. *Why had she overreacted?*

He had to admit that the question of permission or authority had never entered his mind when it came to telling Reverend Andrew and Joan their real mission in Eyam. He was used to a certain amount of trust and autonomy when it came to major decisions, but here he seemed to be little more than a worker bee and a damaged one at that. He had no doubt that the team would verbally make mincemeat out of him.

"You make things harder than they have to be," Nora had said. Was it true? Exactly what kind of tangled mess had he become? He knew the answer and it hurt to think about it. How long could he allow his personal tragedy to impair his life? When had it changed from a valid reason and become merely an excuse?

Beyond a line of trees, he could see the roof and chimneys of the Rose and Crown. He cut along a different path that looked as if it was the most direct route—then stopped quickly and drew back behind a tree. The path was an access road of some sort, and sitting at the far end nearest the road was the Deadman's Plumbing van.

Maybe it's time to end the mystery. He set his carrying case down behind a fallen log and, moving from tree to tree, crept to the back of the van. Someone was in the driver's seat. Straightening himself, Mark casually walked from behind the tree and to the open window.

"Good day for a stroll," he announced.

The man in the driver's seat was unsurprised and merely looked at him impassively through the eye sockets of a ski mask.

The surprise fell to Mark at this unexpected sight, and he quickly took a step backward.

It occurred to him that he should never have turned his back to the woods: too many places for a person to hide.

A sharp pain exploded white light in the back of his head, and he fell to his knees.

"There's a good lad," a voice said.

And then he felt a pinprick in his arm.

As he slumped to the ground, he thought again of Nora's question: "Why do you make things so much harder than they have to be?"

CHAPTER THIRTY-NINE

DR. SUSAN HUTCHINSON STOOD at her office window looking out at the campus surrounding the WHO's regional headquarters in Brazzaville. There was a certain serenity about the people going about their business as if life was and would always be normal.

She watched a small gray bird the size of a finch perch on the ledge of the building. Its head jerked this way and that, and then it took off again, gliding to one of the many trees dotting the campus. She remembered a wish she'd often had as a small child: to escape her troubles at home or with friends at school and simply fly like a bird, soaring over great cities and vast landscapes, seeing it all without being touched by any of it.

"We're sending out for Chinese food. Want some?"

Jerked back to reality, she turned to a young WHO staffer, Jimbo Kimbabee, a Nigerian with both a master of public health degree and a PhD. His dark skin was as smooth as marble and unblemished, unlike many of his WHO colleagues; he had an ever-ready ivory smile that always brightened Susan's day, no matter how bad it was—and today was bad.

She offered a faint smile. "Thanks, Jim, but I really don't have much appetite."

He nodded. "All the same, I'll have them bring an extra plate of bean curd with black mushrooms. I know you love it."

Before she could protest, he was gone, and with the absence of his smile, her own dour expression returned. She picked up a report and photographs from her desk, checking and double-checking the information, hoping for a mistake. She couldn't find one. Just as she hadn't found one five minutes ago—or five minutes before that—or the five minutes before that when the material had first come to her. She'd immediately put in a call to General Mosley, but was informed that, though she said it was urgent, he was in a video meeting with The Hague and the White House and couldn't be interrupted.

She took a sip of her now cold tea and decided that he had to be interrupted anyway. Gathering up the papers, she took a deep breath, and headed down the hall.

When she arrived at Mosley's office, she was surprised to see Kevin's desk sitting empty. She walked to the door, which was open slightly, and saw the general typing on his computer keyboard. He had a heavy touch, which sounded as if he was furiously attacking the keys. Maybe he was. Susan craned her neck to see if anyone else was in the room or if the videoconference was still going, but he seemed to be the only one there. She knocked.

"Come in, Susan," the general commanded, without looking.

"How did you know it was me?"

"Everyone has their own style and sound to their knock—as unique as their walk or handwriting." He spun around to face her and gestured to a large overstuffed chair. "Have a seat. Kevin said you wanted to see me, but I had to get an e-mail off to the Pentagon first."

"General . . . our staff has finished the analysis of the laptop computer found at Pastor Windabe's house."

He waved his hand to the papers on his desk. "Yes, I received that report. From your Dr. LeRoux."

She bit her lower lip anxiously. "Have you looked at it?" He couldn't have, she knew. He wouldn't be chatting with her so amiably if he had.

"No. I went directly into a videoconference." Mosley leaned forward. "Why? Did your team figure out who the computer belonged to? Was it connected to the compound?"

"We're pretty sure it belonged to the pastor, but we believe he let some of the kids from the compound use it when they came to visit. It had a lot of video games, Bible-type exercises, and stories."

"I assume Pastor Windabe was close to the people at the compound. That would explain why the boy went to him."

"Windabe seemed to be a spiritual advisor and mentor to the leader . . ." She stopped and corrected herself. "Your son, I mean. The captions referred to him as Uncle Win."

"Uncle?" Mosley repeated vacantly, and he lowered his eyes, curling his hands into fists and pressing them against his desk blotter. His shoulders hunched forward and Susan braced herself, sure that his pent-up emotions were about to break free. A moment went by and then Mosley looked up at her again, his eyes red. He cleared his throat. "What captions?"

The question surprised her and she stammered, "There were photos on the computer."

"Of what?"

"The various families and individuals at the compound. Windabe may have been compiling some sort of flier or directory for fund-raising or support, or something. It's hard for us to tell. But many of the photos were captioned with names."

"I'd like to see those photos."

"We'll get them to you," Susan promised. "Though Dr. LeRoux put a photo of your son and his family in the report."

"That was kind of him. I haven't seen a recent photo."

"It wasn't out of kindness, General."

Mosley looked uncertain. "Get to the punch line, Susan."

"The police in Mitzic found various witnesses who claimed to have seen the boy when he was walking to Pastor Windabe's. We e-mailed the photos to the police, who showed them to the witnesses. Without exception, they identified him."

"But that's good news. Why are you being so morose about it?"

"This is in your file, but . . ." Susan pulled out a photo with the face of the identified boy circled in black. She handed it across the desk.

Mosley reached out and looked at the photo. His expression, which had been passive, sharpened. His eyes narrowed and his jaw slackened. He looked up at Susan, dazed. "This can't be right. Aaron Mosley?"

"I'm afraid so, sir."

"Aaron." Mosley swallowed hard and, when he found his voice again, muttered, "The missing boy is my grandson."

Susan wanted to do something, to say a word of encouragement, to comfort him, but there was nothing she could offer.

The photo fell to the desk as his eyes widened with a new and horrific realization. "I've issued a death warrant for my own grandson."

CHAPTER FORTY

"STOP, PLEASE! PULL OVER! I'm going to be sick!" Aaron cried out
to the couple in the front of the ancient Renault station wagon.

The driver, a man, looked panicked. He spoke in French to his
wife and Aaron picked up enough of the language to understand
that he didn't want the boy throwing up in his car.

The man swung the station wagon to the side of the road.
Aaron opened his door and, with a feigned stumble, lurched into
the jungle.

The wife got out of the car, but lingered by the passenger
door, watching him. She'd been watching him for the past hour,
in fact, glancing over her shoulder with an anxious expression,
speaking in hushed tones to her husband. They were wary of this
white boy and his story of getting to Libreville to surprise his
family. That Aaron was carrying a Bible seemed to reassure them
initially, but they began to look at him with suspicion. He knew
he must have looked awful: dirty and sickly.

Aaron had become suspicious too, believing that they might
hand him over to the authorities at the next town. Then the traffic
jammed up and slowed down and he heard the driver say something
about a checkpoint on the road ahead. He wondered if the checkpoint was for him, though checkpoints weren't unusual in Gabon.
Better to play it safe. He contrived sickness as a way to get out.

Once he was just inside the tree line, he hunched over with
his back to the road and pretended to vomit, with the worst
retching noises he could make. He glanced around, checking his
options. Then, once he established the quickest path deeper into
the jungle, he bolted.

The woman called after him and the man hit the horn on the car—for the woman, or for the police up ahead, Aaron didn't know.

His plan was to follow the jungle around to the north, then rejoin the main road to Libreville on the other side of the checkpoint. His hope was to hitch a ride with a friendly local.

But that was later. For now, he had to get around that checkpoint.

He followed the path of least resistance, moving deeper into the jungle while trying to stay parallel to the highway. From various vantage points, he saw police and military cars on the road or sitting to the side. He had gotten out of the way just in time.

Reaching a small hill, he struggled to crest it and had to stop alongside a large tree to catch his breath. He was growing weaker, he knew, but there was nothing to be done about it until he got to the Sisters of Mercy. They would know what to do. They would protect him.

Amidst the birdcalls, occasional screeches, and buzzing noises of the jungle, Aaron heard a man's voice. He got to his feet quickly, anticipating the sight of a policeman or soldier. No one was coming from the road. So he slipped around the tree and looked toward the jungle.

He saw that the backside of the hill he'd just crested descended to a small dirt road that cut through the jungle; more like a walking path with double lines of tire tracks. It looked rarely used and was littered with fallen branches, stones, and deep ruts. Aaron guessed it was once a means of transport before the main highway had been built.

On the road sat a dented pickup truck that might have been red at one time, but was now spotted with dark gray primer and green splotches as if the owner had hand painted a camouflage look to it. A banged-up camper shell covered the rear bed, the small windows spray painted black.

A dark-skinned man in a sweat-stained T-shirt and baggy shorts paced around the truck, swearing at it in several different languages. He was old, thin, and slightly stooped, but he kicked at the side of the truck energetically and Aaron realized the problem: the rear-left tire was stuck in a rut.

The old man went to the bed of the truck and lifted the camper shell door, then dropped it. Still swearing, he reached in and began to push what looked like dark cloth one way and then the other, searching for something.

Aaron peered more closely and realized that the dark cloths were actually animal skins. Gorilla and monkey skins, he suspected. It was an illegal and profitable trade. Several times, the men of the compound had to deal with poachers in the nearby jungle. If this man was transporting illegal fur, it would explain why he was on a back road and not the highway.

Aaron stepped to get a better look and a branch snapped under his foot. The man quickly closed the bed door and swung around, his right hand moving to his pocket. He had a pockmarked face with a patchy gray beard and worried eyes. In a husky voice, he shouted in a language Aaron didn't recognize—a demand of some sort.

Aaron held his arms out and said, "*Bonjour, monsieur*. Do you speak English?"

The man eyed him up and down. "Why do you say *bonjour* and then ask me if I speak English? What are you doing here?" His eyes darted around the jungle to make sure Aaron was alone.

"I'm going to Libreville."

The man hooked a thumb in the direction of the highway over the hill. "It's that way."

"I was looking for a ride."

The man again hooked his thumb in the direction of the highway. "You'll find one that way."

Aaron ventured closer. "You're stuck. Do you need help?"

The man snorted. "You have the strength to push me out of this ditch?" He swore again and kicked at the truck.

"Maybe two of us could do it."

The man appeared to consider the idea, leaning against the side of the truck and looking the boy over. He picked something off his lip and flicked it away. "You want to avoid the checkpoint, is that it?"

Aaron was about to make up a story, but suspected from the man's expression that he wouldn't believe it. He opted to tell the truth. "Yes. I want to avoid the checkpoint."

"Are you running away from home? Going to Libreville to seek fame and fortune?"

Aaron said, "I'm running away from home, but I'm not looking for fame or fortune."

The man gazed at Aaron, making a decision. "You help me get out of this ditch, and I'll take you as far as I'm going."

"Are you going to Libreville?"

"Close enough."

The man showed Aaron how to shift the gears so he could rock the truck back and forth in the ditch. The man would push from the back and leverage the forward momentum to get the truck out.

It was a trial and error effort as Aaron, who had no experience driving a vehicle, sometimes stalled the engine, backed up too fast, or went forward too fast, spraying the man with dirt.

In time they got the rhythm just right, and the truck leapt out of the rut. Aaron was pleased with himself. The man seemed pleased too, as he came up to the driver's side. "Move over, partner," he said.

Aaron crawled to the passenger side, and the man got behind the wheel. With a smile that showed more gums than teeth, he stepped on the gas, and they began a very bumpy ride.

Aaron leaned back, both relief and weariness flowing over him. He untucked the Bible and held it close to his chest.

"I am Pierre," the man said, glancing at Aaron and then the Bible.

"I'm Aaron."

The man nodded to him and turned his gaze back to the road ahead.

"You carry only a *Bible*?" Pierre asked. "No clothes or food, but a *Bible*?"

"That's all," Aaron said.

"You are a missionary child?"

"I was," Aaron said, and squeezed the Bible harder at his use of the past tense. "But now I am a missionary."

"Missionaries are good," Pierre said. "I like missionaries."

Aaron closed his eyes, putting his head back, holding the Bible close, and appreciating the breeze blowing on him from the open window.

There was a click, then the sound of static. Aaron lifted his head again to look. Pierre had turned on a CB radio just under the dash and was switching channels. The static gave way to a barrage of chatter, excited voices in French.

"That's interesting," Pierre said. "On the radio they say there is a search for a teenage boy."

Aaron turned his head away, considering how he might jump from the truck without breaking his neck.

"A driver claims to have seen him recently."

Aaron didn't say anything.

"Funny. It was in the area where we just were. The police are rushing there now."

Aaron slowly turned to Pierre, who had a mischievous smile on his face.

"It is a good thing you are with me," Pierre said. "Otherwise, someone might mistake you for that boy."

Aaron adjusted his aching body in the seat. "It's a very good thing."

"You are safe with me," Pierre said. "Partners, *oui?*"

"Partners. *Oui,*" Aaron said and wearily closed his eyes again.

CHAPTER FORTY-ONE

NORA CLOSED HER CELL phone, but held on to it in the hope that Mark would call her back. The team was assembled in a small meeting room at the Rose and Crown, waiting impatiently.

"What a flake," Digger grumbled.

"Perhaps he's embarrassed by his faux pas," Henry suggested.

"He knows the level of sarcasm you can dish out, Digger," said Georgina.

"Rightly so," Digger said, proudly.

Nora shook her head. "Mark's too professional for that."

Digger scowled. "I wouldn't use the word 'professional' in the same sentence with 'Mark.'"

Nora opted not to argue. She was worried about Mark, but knew this wasn't the group to look to for sympathy. "Let's get started," she said then gestured to Georgina.

Georgina tapped the keys on her laptop and announced, "The meteorologists in London have predicted sunset at eight thirty p.m. Being nineteen days after the full moon means the moon phase is between the new and quarter moon, and the weather crew is predicting moonset at nine forty-two p.m., meaning that we won't be protected by the cover of darkness until about ten."

"I love it when you talk like that," Digger said, leering at her.

"Let's plan to make our move at ten," Nora said. "We'll go to the graveyard at St. Lawrence first."

"How are we going to do that without Mark's list of grave sites?" Georgina asked.

"I have a list of victims' names that I've compiled from other sources," Nora said.

"But not their location?" Digger groaned. "We're going to walk from grave to grave looking for the right names or dates?"

"I'm sorry, but until we get Mark's list, there's little else I can do."

"You could go back to the vicar and ask for another," Digger challenged.

"Good idea," she responded. "I'll just explain that Mark has gone missing and the list with him and would he mind giving us another. That will impress him."

Digger shrugged. "It's your call."

"It won't be an issue since Mark will show up," she said.

The team simply stared at her, and she was sure they didn't believe her.

"Is the equipment working properly, Henry?" she asked, to change the subject.

"The equipment *always* works properly," Henry said with a condescending sniff.

"I know it does," Nora said. "I mean, work properly in the sense that it will do what we need it to do. We have to assess the accuracy of the ultrasonic bone detector."

"Of course," he said.

Nora continued. "Also, the scopes will have to work at a length of six feet down or more—in front of or directly under the grave markers."

"Are you sure it'll be six feet? Some of these British graves are less than that," Digger said.

"I understand that the six-foot rule was created during the plague to ensure that any contagion was thoroughly buried."

Digger turned to Henry, "We'd better make sure to bring the longer extensions in case the graves are deeper than that. I don't trust those medieval measurements."

"Technically, it wouldn't be medieval since the Middle Ages ended early in the fifteenth century," Henry corrected him.

Nora tried to get them back on track. "Since we'll have to disassemble the equipment to carry it in our backpacks, I suggest we practice taking it apart and putting it together."

Georgina pouted. "Why?"

"Because the graveyard is behind the church in the dark. Do you know how to assemble the ultrasound equipment in pitch black?"

Georgina lowered her head and looked chastised.

"A great idea," Digger said, suddenly clapping his hands together. "I get to be the drill instructor!"

"Why you?" Henry asked.

"Because I have the most experience with using this equipment in dark graveyards."

"We have to get this right," Nora said. "The clock is still against us, and this may be our only chance to get the samples we need."

I wish it would stop! Mark's brain screamed. The excruciating pain permeated his whole body. Even the movement of his closed eyes hurt, as if his corneas were scraping against sandpaper on the inside of his eyelids.

He struggled to maintain consciousness, but knew he was slipping into other realities. He felt feverish with the blur of sense that comes with it.

There was a moment—just a brief moment—when he'd opened his eyes enough to see that he was in a stone building of some sort. Old and cold, in a dank cellarlike way. And it stank of rotten meat. He could hear flies buzzing. He thought he heard crying. An adult. A man. His heart began to race as he thought he was back at the compound with all those dead bodies—those dead children.

He closed his eyes again, willing the pain and the place to be a dream. He thought he felt a hot breeze against his face.

He opened his eyes again—or had he?—and he was in his car, screeching into a hospital parking lot, narrowly missing a light post as he brought the car to a hard stop. The building looked like Holy Cross Hospital in Silver Spring, Maryland. There was only one reason for him to be here, and his heart pounded like a jackhammer now as he dashed toward the Emergency Department doors.

The revolving front door barely slowed him as he sprinted through the lobby and to a staircase. He took the stairs two to three at a time, the rivulets of sweat streaming down his face. His lungs began to burn.

At the fifth floor, he burst out of the stairwell and into a hall and slowed to a rapid walk as he approached the nurses' station.

Doris, a tall, redheaded nurse, recognized him and stood up. "Oh, Dr. Carlson . . ." Her eyes filled with tears as she pointed. "Room thirty-six."

He hurried down the hall, the adrenaline of his panic pumping through every vein. He stopped at the door to gather his wits and offer a small prayer for mercy.

"Mercy," he heard himself say aloud as he half opened his eyes.

"Of course," said a man in a black ski mask.

Still, somewhere, a man was crying and Mark wondered if it was his own voice he heard. Was he crying yet again for this memory, the one he'd lived through over and over?

He closed his eyes and saw himself stepping through the door into the hospital room, which looked as if it had been made of old stone. His wife sat by a bed, leaning forward, her head turned away from him and pressed against the crisp sheets. Was she asleep or crying?

On the bed, stretched in repose, was his sweet Jenny. She was pale, but she was always a pale child, her silky skin milk white and beautiful.

The scene was familiar, as if she'd fallen asleep while her mom had read her a bedtime story.

He quietly approached the bed. For a moment, he believed the outcome might change, the horror would be altered, but then his terror built as he realized his Jenny wasn't breathing. The monitors were darkened, still and silent.

Oh God. No. No! The grief poured over him anew.

The pain in his head was throbbing mercilessly as he grabbed Jenny's limp wrist, hoping against hope that there would be a pulse. This time, please. Mercy.

Her skin was cold, hard, and lifeless, and he felt as if he were holding on to a plastic armrest.

He opened his eyes—had they been closed?—and realized his hands were clenched around the arms of a steel gray chair. His arms were fastened to the chair with duct tape.

His wife came into his field of vision. "It's *your* fault, Mark. *Your* fault," she whispered to him. Then she began to shake him by the shoulders and screamed, "*You* killed her! You killed her!"

He closed his eyes tight again. "I know," he said, beginning to weep.

The hands continued to shake his shoulders violently. He opened his eyes, wondering where his wife had gained such strength. A black ski mask faced him.

What is this?

The eyes within the mask were black cauldrons.

Then Mark winced at a burning sensation in his nostrils. He jerked his head away, one direction, then another, but the smell continued. "All right, all right, enough with the smelling salts already."

"Are you with us, Dr. Carlson?" The man in the ski mask had a slight Eastern European accent.

"Yeah, I'm here." Mark tugged at his legs, realizing now that they were also bound. He took a deep breath, and the stench returned, as did the piercing pain in his head. The stone room was real enough now, with a dirt floor and iron rings and hooks hanging from the walls and the ceiling. A row of stalls stretched along a side wall.

"An abattoir?" Mark said. He wondered how many animals had been slaughtered here.

"In continuous use from the late seventeenth century until just before the Second World War," the man said as he pulled a chair in front of Mark and sat down. "A hellish place."

Mark sniffled and realized his cheeks were wet.

The man sat with his hands folded in his lap. "Yes, you were crying. It's a side effect of the drug we use. Memories become real. People weep like babies over lost hamsters, a hug from a grandparent . . . a dead child."

Mark ignored the reference. "What drug?"

"Nothing you would have heard of. We have our own supply."

"Did you test them on animals?" Mark asked glibly.

The man chuckled. "Only the worst: man."

"So, you're with Return to Earth?" Mark asked. "I win the office pool if you say yes."

The man leaned forward. "Why don't you leave the questions to me?"

Mark wondered if the drug had not only knocked him out, but also had served as a truth serum. What questions had they already asked him? What answers did he give them?

A sob echoed from somewhere and Mark turned to look. Through a doorway, in another room, he saw a man strapped to a chair in the same fashion as he was. Another man in a ski mask hovered over him.

Mark tensed as he realized that the man in the chair was Nathan Dodge. Dodge's head bobbed up and down and he moaned loudly, the sound coming from a deep and painful place.

"Is he drugged or have you been torturing him?" Mark strained against the tape again.

"There are things we need to know," Mark's captor said. "As workers with Ahaz, we figured you two could tell us."

"Dinner and a few drinks might have been more of a persuader."

The man grunted. "Don't make this harder than it has to be. I'd like to know exactly what Ahaz and the U.S. military are doing here."

"You already know. Didn't I blab everything while you had me drugged?"

"No. Unfortunately, you kept muttering about your daughter. Jenny, was it? And your wife blames you for her death? How boring. That's the problem with the drug—it's hard to keep people focused."

"I'm so sorry for you."

"So, back to the subject at hand. What are you doing here?"

"We're trying to put a stop to what you started in Gabon."

"What *we* started?" The man feigned his disapproval. "Oh no, *you* started it. We simply want to see it completed."

"Let's not quibble."

The man's eyes narrowed. "All right. Simply tell us your plan and you're free to go."

"Plan?"

"What are you looking for in Eyam? What's your strategy?"

"That's easy," Mark said. "We're looking for samples from the bodies of the plague victims. We think there's a connection between what happened here and in Gabon."

"I want details."

"Are you a doctor? A scientist?"

The man didn't answer, but reached into his pocket and produced a small digital recorder. "Tell us your theories, all your guesses, even the most absurd, and give me the name of every person and organization that is working on this project."

Mark shook his head. "That's going to be difficult."

"Why?"

"Because I don't want to."

The man looked surprised. "Oh?"

"Helping you destroy the human race isn't part of my creed."

The man sighed and then waved a hand to his accomplice in the other room.

From where he sat, Mark couldn't see clearly what was happening but suddenly Nathan Dodge began to scream. It was a hideous sound.

"Wait! Stop!" Mark cried out. "What are you doing?"

"It's an abattoir," the man said. "We're cutting up bits of meat."

"But he doesn't know anything," Mark protested.

"We've already established that," the man said. "That's why we thought we'd torture him—to get the answers out of you."

CHAPTER FORTY-TWO

GENERAL SAM MOSLEY TRIED to concentrate on the task at hand. It was difficult. His eyes kept moving to the photo of his son's family on his desk. They sat under a tree somewhere looking happy and content. It was a perfect photo except for the black circle like a target around his grandson's face. The missing boy, the carrier, who was now unknowingly responsible for the deaths of dozens, maybe hundreds—maybe thousands or millions before this whole business is concluded.

And the conclusion might come by the general's own order: to kill his own flesh and blood.

He had been hopeful only a couple of hours ago when reports came of a sighting to the west of Alembe. A pair of tourists had given a ride to a teenager who fit Aaron's description, but he had jumped out of the car and disappeared into the jungle just as they came up to a checkpoint. The tourists, a husband and wife, were showing symptoms of the virus, as was the squad at the checkpoint who'd intercepted them.

It was now guesswork as to how many others who passed through the checkpoint had been infected by the newly contagious police officers. The virus could be traveling unrestrained through the entire region. All because a couple of tourists gave a helpless boy a ride.

Mosley looked at the map. There was no question now that Aaron was headed for Libreville. But why? Who did he know there? The general's team had examined everything they could from the compound's computer files and found nothing to explain what Aaron hoped to find in the country's capital city. The

U.S. Embassy? The airport? A church? A supporter of the compound that they didn't know about? Any guess seemed equally valid. Whatever the reason or the place, he braced himself for a new trail of victims. And once Aaron reached Libreville, their worst nightmares would likely come true.

Kevin appeared in the doorway. "General . . ."

"What now?" he asked. *What could be worse?*

"Inspector Duerr from Interpol is on line one. He says it's urgent."

"And why shouldn't it be?" Mosley reached for the phone. "The world has run out of its quota of nonurgent business."

Kevin walked out, a puzzled expression on his face.

"Mosley here," the general said into the phone.

"I'm glad to have reached you so quickly, General."

"What's going on, Inspector?"

"We have news from our agent," Duerr said. "Bad news, I'm afraid."

"Let's hear it."

"A Return to Earth cell in England has nabbed one of your people."

Mosley sat up. "Nabbed? You mean, kidnapped?"

"Essentially, yes."

Mosley's mind raced through the possibilities. For a minute, he struggled to remember all of the people he had in England. "Do you know who it is?"

"One of the members of the team you've placed in Eyam."

"A name?" he asked impatiently. "Do you have a name?"

"Dr. Malachi Carlson."

"They've got Mark?" Mosley let loose a string of obscenities. Kevin returned to the doorway, watching expectantly. "Why? What do they want with him?"

"Information, I'm sure. The more they know about what you're doing, the harder they can work to stop you."

"Do you know where they have him?"

"We have a fairly good idea."

"Good." Mosley signaled Kevin to get ready to take notes. "Then we'll send in a Special Ops team and—"

"With respect, General, I'll ask you not to do that."

"I'm not leaving my man hostage."

"Nor am I suggesting you do, but a Special Ops team will tell the cell members that they have a spy in their midst. I can't allow my agent to be exposed."

"Then what are you suggesting?"

"Something a little more accidental."

A call from Scotland Yard was the last thing Detective Inspector Ian Glover expected. Even more surprising was the nature of the call and his subsequent assignment, which had originally generated from MI5 itself.

Eyam was suddenly becoming a rather exciting place to work these days. A grave robbery, an unspecified international crisis, a television production company . . .

"Sir?" Police Constable Harry Pullen sat on the chair next to Glover's desk. "Everyone's ready in the briefing room."

"Thanks, Harry."

"We're a little confused, though."

No surprise.

"We're surrounding the old Wallace abattoir to search for a missing child who isn't actually missing?"

"Right."

"But, in reality, we're looking for a television producer who may be held hostage by a radical animal-rights group?"

"More or less." Glover stood up and gathered his notes for the briefing.

Pullen rubbed his chin thoughtfully for a moment. "Why would an animal-rights group take a television producer hostage?"

Glover shrugged. "He wore a fur necktie to the BAFTA Awards—how am I expected to know?"

Mark's head was slumped onto his chest. He was physically exhausted from straining against the tape that bound him and emotionally numb from Nathan Dodge's horrific screams. Then

Dodge's screams had stopped and Mark relaxed, but not for long.

"I've told you everything I know," Mark said in a hoarse whisper.

"I wish I could believe you."

"Believe it," Mark said, lifting his head and looking into the cold eyes of his captor. "You know all there is to know. Not that it'll help you much. Now why don't you slither back to your little hole with the rest of your cowardly snakes."

The man came nearer to Mark, his gloved hands clenched. "Cowards, is it?"

"You think hiding behind a ski mask is brave?" Mark asked. "You think it takes courage to torture two bound men?"

The man grabbed Mark's throat and squeezed. "You think hiding behind military superiority is brave? You think it takes courage to kill helpless animals or to destroy the planet so you can drive faster or live in obscenely large homes?"

His air cut off, Mark squirmed against the gloved hand, gasping, fighting back the black spots that began to appear before his eyes. Suddenly his captor let go as yet another masked man appeared in the doorway leading outside.

"What?" Mark's captor asked sharply.

"The police are coming."

"The police! Why?"

"We picked up on the scanner that they're looking for a missing boy from Middlevale. They believe he was last seen in this area. They're coming here to mount a massive search in the area."

"Now?"

"Now."

"That's . . . inconvenient." The man turned to Mark. "They're really coming for him."

The man at the door asked, "How would they know he's here?"

"How indeed?" Mark's captor said. "Any ideas, Dr. Carlson?"

"It's your club. Why would I know anything about your members?"

"We have to go," the one at the door said.

The accomplice from the other room appeared. "What do we do with them?"

"Leave them."

The two men rushed out. Mark's captor pulled a small case from his pocket, opened it, and took out a scalpel. "I'll know where to find you if I need any more questions answered," he said with a vindictive smile. With a deft slash, he used the scalpel to cut the tape holding Mark's right arm. "See you around, Doctor. Your patient is waiting."

He strode out of the abattoir.

Mark pulled his right arm free, the tape tearing at his skin and hair. He then began working at the tape on his left arm. "Dodge? Dodge! Hang on. I'll be there as soon as I can. I don't know what they've done to you, but . . ." His left arm was free, and he attacked the tape that bound his ankles to the legs of the chair. It was a slow and frustrating effort.

Outside, he heard a car pull up. Then another. Doors slammed.

"In here!" he shouted.

Free, Mark leapt from his chair and then fell to the ground. His legs were numb, the circulation cut off. He began to crawl in the dirt toward Dodge. The man was slumped over. Mark couldn't be sure, but believed he saw ribbons of blood dripping down the frame of the chair. "Hold on, Dodge."

The first police officer, in uniform, stepped through the door. "Hello?"

"Here!" Mark cried out.

"What's all this?" the officer asked, then stepped back outside and called, "Detective Glover!"

"This man needs urgent medical help!" Mark shouted to whoever was listening.

"Call an ambulance!" a plainclothes policeman commanded as he entered. He ran to Mark. "Help him," Mark said, and struggled to sit up to rub some circulation back into his legs.

The plainclothes policeman said, "I'm Detective Ian Glover," and rushed to Dodge.

Other uniformed police entered and fanned out. Two rushed

to Mark. "I'm a doctor," Mark explained. "I can help him if you'll carry me over."

An officer held each arm and Mark got to his feet, the warm pins and needles stabbing into every muscle of his legs. They moved towards Dodge, but Glover returned and stood in their path. He looked sick. "Don't bother."

"But, I have to try," Mark pleaded.

"No!" Glover shouted, then instructed the two officers, "Take him out to the car."

The two officers, one under each shoulder, carried Mark from the building.

Mark slumped into the backseat of the car and put his arm over his face. He thought of death—and hated it.

It was nearly 9:30 p.m. when Detective Inspector Glover dropped Mark off at the front door of the Rose and Crown.

Nora rushed to the car as Mark climbed out. He was stiff and still ached from the interrogation. The three hours he'd spent talking on the phone with General Mosley, three MI5 agents, and two busybodies from the local constabulary didn't improve his overall well-being.

Seeing Nora, her brow puckered with worry, was a tonic.

"Some people will do anything to get a little sympathy." She looked at him at arm's length, hugged him, and then looked at him at arm's length again. He thought she might cry.

Mark closed the door and tapped the side. Glover waved and pulled away.

"Are you all right?" Nora asked.

He put his arm through hers. "Walk with me."

Surprised, she asked, "Are you sure? Don't you want to rest?"

"I've been sitting for hours." He guided her down the driveway.

Mark was aware of a shadow behind him and he immediately jumped, his body tense with anticipation. It was one of their military bodyguards. "Don't sneak up on me like that!"

"Sorry, sir," the soldier said. He must have been six foot two or more and held his body fully erect, which betrayed his military training regardless of the casual clothes he wore. He had a lean face and close-cropped hair.

"Jankowski is now officially our godfather," Nora explained. "And, three more soldiers are coming up from London to watch over us."

"A little late." He continued walking down the driveway to the road. Jankowski followed at a discreet distance behind them. "It reminds me of a Jane Austen story," he said, nodding back to Jankowski. "The chaperone following the two lovers."

She didn't respond. Then he noticed that she still walked with a slight limp.

"What's with the limp?"

"I tripped during my hike today. A slight sprain on my ankle." She grabbed on to his arm tighter. "Where are we going?"

"Back to the place where they grabbed me. I shoved my carrying case behind a log." He half-turned to the soldier. "Jankowski, are you carrying a penlight?"

"Yes, sir."

"Good."

They walked on. Nora said, "Mac briefed the team about what happened to you. He called us after you spoke with the general."

"Did he say anything informative?"

"Only that Ahaz is going to retreat from the area and let us do our work without interference."

Mark thought of Nathan Dodge. "Détente, is that the idea?"

"I suppose so."

"I don't believe it for a minute." Mark knew Ahaz too well. They were too mercenary to allow the murder of one employee to affect their opportunity here. "Did Mac say anything else?"

"Not much. Except that he made you out to be some kind of hero."

"Oh." He pulled away from her, and then asked brightly, "Does that mean Digger will lay off me for a while?"

"Five minutes grace. That's all you'll get from him."

"And you? Have you forgiven me?"

Nora looked away. "I may have come down on you a little too hard."

"Are you going to tell me what was wrong with you at the pub?"

She sighed. "Later."

They reached the end of the drive. Mark glanced left and right just as a precaution, though he didn't expect to have any direct trouble from Return to Earth for a while. "This way," he said, and they went right toward the town. "There is a small dirt road or path. That's where I found them."

"I was very sorry to hear about your coworker from Ahaz." Nora said softly. "Nathan Dodge, right?"

Mark nodded. "I didn't like him very much, but I never would have wished for him to die—especially the way he did."

"Mac didn't say. How did he die?"

Mark took a deep breath to steady his voice, but it shook anyway. "They cut him to pieces." He felt his body grow tense again. "What kinds of people do that?"

"The kind of people who would purposefully cause a pandemic," she said.

"I hope MI5 finds them—and does to them what they did to Nathan. Surely there's some medieval law still in place that allows them to do that."

Nora didn't respond, but squeezed his arm and walked quietly at his side.

"Here," Mark said, and they moved down a dark path, which Mark guessed was an area for trucks to back up to either collect or deposit livestock. "Penlight?"

Jankowski stepped forward and handed him a military-issue penlight. Mark turned it on and imagined he could guide airplanes in with its brightness. He walked to the end of the dirt road then turned to the left, hoping he had his bearings straight. A yard into the trees he found the fallen log. He was relieved to find his carrying case behind it.

He held it up to Nora. "This has everything: names of all the descendants and the graves worthy of our attention. Both victims and survivors. If Return to Earth had gotten their hands on this, they would have sabotaged the graves and destroyed the bodies. We'd never find a useful sample."

"But . . . didn't you tell them everything?"

"No. I told them only what was obvious or easily discovered."

"Even while they tortured Nathan?" She sounded genuinely troubled. "Even when they threatened to torture you?"

"I assumed they were going to kill us both," Mark said. "They certainly weren't going to let us buy our way out with information. So why give it to them?"

She wrapped her arms around herself and shivered. "I couldn't have done that. I would have told them anything they wanted to know, hoping that . . ."

Mark held up his hand. "You see? That's the difference between us. I've given up hope when it comes to my life."

"Give me that," she said and took the penlight from his hand. She turned it on again and shone it upward, just enough to take his face out of the shadows. She considered him for a moment. "I don't believe you. You still have hope, in spite of yourself. It may only be a flicker, but it's still there."

He looked at her and felt affection welling up inside. "I'm glad you think so."

Nora turned off the penlight and was silent again as they walked back toward the road. Then she asked, "So why didn't they kill you?"

"That's a good question," Mark replied. "I've wondered the same thing myself, and I have a theory."

"Oh?"

"I think my interrogator was a physician—or used to be."

"How do you know?"

"Some of the things he said, the questions he asked, and the way he held a scalpel to threaten me and to cut my bonds. He held and wielded it just like a surgeon."

"How could a doctor allow his cronies to do what they did to Dodge?" asked Nora.

"I didn't say he was a *good* doctor."

"But how does his being a doctor explain why he left you alive?"

"Believe it or not, somehow I think it was professional courtesy." He paused, then added, "Or he intends to capture me later to torture me for more information."

Jankowski cleared his throat. "Sir, ma'am, you may want to pick up your pace. It's almost ten o'clock."

"Is that important?" Mark asked Nora.

"It's the witching hour," she replied.

CHAPTER FORTY-THREE

THOUGH NORA TRIED TO persuade Mark to remain at the Rose and Crown, he wouldn't hear of it.

"I want my five minutes of grace with Digger," he said. "I worked hard for it."

She laughed. "You've certainly earned it."

As the team gathered in the meeting room of the inn and divided up the equipment into four backpacks, Henry and Georgina welcomed Mark back and seemed genuinely glad that he was safe and sound.

Digger gave a small grunt and growled, "Yeah. Glad to get that list for the graveyard."

Mark looked at Nora, who rolled her eyes.

Mark smiled at Digger. "Digger, I want you to know that you were on my mind constantly during my ordeal."

Digger frowned suspiciously. "Really?"

"Something about the smell of that old abattoir reminded me of you."

The team laughed, and in spite of himself Digger grinned. "One to you," he said.

Nora took charge of the meeting and reviewed their plan: "Henry and Georgina will walk together on the south side of the road. Digger, Mark, and I will follow a minute later on the north side. We'll look like tourists heading to the pub for a drink."

"Will Jankowski and his buddies be around?" Digger asked, referring to the additional contingency of soldiers who'd arrived to protect them.

"They'll be around," Nora said. "Even if you can't see them."

Henry chuckled. "All these people whom we can't see, will they be bumping into each other behind the trees?"

Nora continued, "We'll meet up in the graveyard on the north side where we won't be seen from the street. I assume you've all memorized the locations of the graves you're going to search?"

"In the three minutes we've had them? Yes! Completely," Digger complained.

"Any questions?"

Mark raised his hand. "For the sake of authenticity, maybe we should stop at the pub for a drink."

Nora ignored him. "Let's move."

Mark felt a sense of déjà vu as they took the same route he'd taken earlier in the day. Though the sun was gone, it was still hot and muggy. By the time they entered the church grounds, sweat was dripping down his back. They passed the gate leading to the rectory, and he remembered Nathan Dodge stepping through it with the vicar.

Was it after that meeting that the thugs from Return to Earth grabbed him? Had Mark's reference to Deadman's Plumbing drawn Nathan's attention to the van? Maybe he also went up to investigate and they caught him, just as they'd caught Mark.

"It's all your fault," Mark could hear his ex-wife saying, as in the dream. Jenny's death. The lab workers in Greenland. The people at the compound. Nathan Dodge. Somehow it all came back to him and something he did—or didn't do—in time.

"What're you thinking?" Nora asked softly.

Mark looked at her shadowed face. "I'm thinking that it's been a very long day."

An evening wind rustled through the leaves and branches in the trees above them. They caught the lights from the street-lamps on the road. Haunting shadows danced across the tomb-stones.

The team gathered in the darkness behind the church. The graveyard stretched out away from them. Mark rubbed his arms, trying to calm the gooseflesh that rose up there. He didn't like graveyards at night. For that matter, he didn't like graveyards at any time.

As they walked out of a shadow and under a streetlamp, Digger stepped next to him. "Creepy, isn't it?"

"Very," Mark said.

Digger smiled. "I like creepy."

"Let's keep the talking to a minimum," Nora said then signaled the team to fan out to their assigned positions. "Remember, we meet back at the inn at eleven thirty."

The team moved off. Mark took a step, but Nora put a hand on his arm. "You stay with me," she said.

"Still don't trust me?" he asked.

"Call me a mother hen," she said. "I don't want my little chick to get lost again."

They drifted into the graveyard. The flashlights Henry had issued them cast a red light, which was less likely to draw attention than a conventional white light. Nora pointed to a gravestone and took off her backpack.

Mark followed her lead, and they silently unpacked and assembled the equipment. He helped as he could, but knew that she had practiced the job. Nora had told him how Digger had made them disassemble and reassemble their equipment over and over again, first in a lit room and then in a dark room, until each team member could handle his or her equipment quickly and with a minimum of fuss.

"'The art of good grave robbing,' he told us," Nora whispered, "'is in speed, efficiency, and silence.'"

Nora fit together the sections of the ultrasound. Mark thought it looked remarkably similar to a metal detector except this had a screen that could only be seen in the pair of night goggles that were placed on the head, like ski goggles.

"Hold this," Nora said to Mark, handing him the ultrasound while she put the night goggles on.

Mark held the ultrasound machine in front of him. "Give me a yellow shirt and a pair of plaid shorts and I could be one of those guys looking for quarters on the beach," he said.

"Shush," Nora said.

Mark chuckled to himself as he watched Nora switch the machine on and begin to pass the instrument back and forth across the ground in front of the tombstone. Mark noticed in the red hue of his flashlight that the grave belonged to a William Watson who had died on 3 October 1665—shortly after the plague broke out. He leaned toward her and whispered, "I hope Mr. Watson doesn't mind you peeping in on him like this."

"Shh," Nora responded. "And, turn off your flashlight." He did as she began moving the head of the ultrasound slowly over the top of the grave. She pressed a trigger and Mark heard the soft whish of a fluorescent spray paint hitting the grass. She moved carefully, with great concentration, up and down the grave, spraying up and down and from side to side. Then, when she finished, she knelt down on the ground and took off the goggles, gesturing for Mark to join her.

As Mark knelt down, Nora turned on her flashlight. A fluorescent-green image of the skeleton six feet below the earth appeared, painted on the top of the grave.

"Meet Mr. Watson," Nora whispered. "The paint was designed to disappear in a few minutes. We need to work quickly."

Mark nodded his approval and almost laughed out loud when he saw the marking Nora had used for his skull: a happy face.

Now it was his turn to go to work. He pulled out and unwound the eight-foot specimen-gathering scope, which contained an ultra-quiet high-speed drill that could easily bore through stone or concrete, along with an encased light source and high-powered suction pump. Even as Mark finished the assembly and attached the contraption to the night goggles so he could see its screen, he worried about the volume of sound they might make, but Henry had assured them that no one beyond ten feet would hear a thing.

They were about to find out if Henry was right.

Mark put on a pair of latex gloves and positioned the goggles. He placed the end of the scope, perpendicular to the ground, over the green paint indicating the location of the upper leg bone. The femur would provide the best sample.

Nora leaned toward him and whispered, "Depth is forty-eight to fifty-two inches."

Mark nodded and wiped the sweat from his forehead with

his arm. He turned on the drill, its shrill whine reminding Mark of his last visit to the dentist—although much more muted. He pressed the tip into the ground. Through the goggles Mark could see the scope advancing through the soil. It moved with such unlimited ease that Mark wanted to thank someone—he didn't know whom—for allowing him to be a doctor in this day and age. The marvels of such technology never ceased to amaze him.

Nora watched the marking on the outside of the scope's tube, tapping Mark when he'd reached the twelve-inch mark indicator. Mark pressed a button and the flexible tube suddenly stiffened so that the first foot of the scope became rigid.

They repeated the process foot by foot until they reached the forty-eight-inch mark. It had taken less than a minute. *Amazing!*

He had not seen any evidence of a stone or wood coffin, but Digger had warned they hadn't always used them. "Finances and social status determined everything about what or how a person was buried," Digger had advised.

Mark slowly advanced the scope, millimeter by millimeter. Then a new image emerged amidst the dirt.

"Bone," he whispered to Nora. He pushed the drill against the bone, and as he did he activated the suction that would pull the bone fragments up the scope and deposit them into a special container on the ground next to him. The system was entirely self-contained so there was no chance of any particles escaping into the air or of any outside air contaminating the particles.

As the end of the scope moved into the bone, Mark switched off the rigidity of the distal segment of the scope, turning it ninety degrees so he could continue up the bone, sucking out the desiccated remains of the marrow.

His heart raced as he felt the exhilaration of his work. These moments made him forget the angst and cynicism of the medical world and took him back to the thrill of his first medical school experiences and discoveries.

After grinding and removing four to six inches of bone, Mark turned off the drill, light, and suction tube, and indicated to Nora that he was withdrawing the scope. He could hear her opening the canister of disinfectant, which she sprayed onto the tube and scope as he pulled it out of the grave. The aroma of the chemical made him wince.

Without a word they collected the equipment and moved to the next grave. Within thirty minutes they had extracted samples from four graves. Mark suggested to Nora that they press on and take more time to get samples. Nora drew a finger across her throat, indicating that they needed to stop.

Mark finished packing up his equipment and stood to stretch his aching body while Nora packed the last of the ultrasound. He was aware that Digger, Georgina, and Henry would be at the far end of the graveyard, so the unexpected movement he caught out of the corner of his eye startled him.

He froze and slowly turned as casually as he could. Not thirty feet away he saw someone standing next to a tomb. The lights from the street, lashed by the tree branches, flickered on the figure, which stood perfectly still and seemed to be dressed in some sort of robe with a hood over its head. Perhaps it was an adornment to one of the tombs, like an angel or Christ figure.

His hand ready with a flashlight, Mark slowly walked toward the figure. It didn't move. But a sudden breeze shook the trees, the streetlight flickered on the figure, and Mark was sure that it had lifted an arm. Alarmed, he quickly brought up the flashlight and turned it on. To his shock, no one there.

Mark could hear Nora padding across the grass toward him. He turned the flashlight on the rectangular tomb, examining it closely. There was no angel or Christ figure on top, not even a cross—nothing to explain the appearance of the figure. He shone the light down on the tomb itself, but the name of the deceased had long worn off the stone.

"What are you doing?" Nora whispered.

Mark didn't answer. Instead he moved around the tomb, checking the sides. In the center of each side was an unusual symbol, a floral circle with what looked like a lamb and a bird of some sort.

Nora was next to him now and saw the symbol. She gasped.

Mark turned to her, just as Digger, Henry, and Georgina rushed up.

"Did Mark decide to blow our cover again?" Digger whispered.

Mark kept his gaze on Nora, her eyes wide. "Do you know what that symbol is?"

Suddenly they were engulfed in a blazingly bright light. Mark raised his hands to protect his eyes and made out someone in silhouette. Whoever it was had a shotgun trained on them.

"Put your hands up!" a voice commanded.

The team raised their hands.

"We don't have weapons," Nora called out.

"I do," the voice growled and cocked the shotgun to prove it. "Now don't make any sudden moves."

"Listen," Mark said as he took a step in front of Nora, "we're not grave robbers, if that's what you think."

"As if I'd believe you," the man said.

"You're Philip the groundskeeper, right?" Mark asked.

"It's none of your business who I am. Just stay where you are until the police get here."

"Your vicar knows who we are and why we're here," Mark said. "And I suggest you lower that gun before somebody gets hurt. Especially you."

"Me?" the man laughed. "I don't think you're in a position to . . ."

With a loud *oof*, Philip was knocked down and instantly restrained by two soldiers who had been strategically hiding around the churchyard.

"Don't hurt him!" Mark called out as he raced to the men.

Philip swore loudly, just before something covered his mouth.

"Not another word," Jankowski ordered as he approached.

Mark reached up on top of a headstone and turned off the industrial-sized flashlight Philip had shone on them. The absence of light was blinding—and each member of the team had the same idea to turn on his or her own flashlights.

What they saw was a tangle of soldiers in fatigues and face paint, pinning down the tall and wiry groundskeeper, who still struggled against them.

"What's all the ruckus?" a voice shouted from several yards

away. The flashlights trained onto Reverend Andrew, who came through the rectory gate dressed in a robe and slippers. He marched up to the scene. "I thought you lot promised to be quiet!"

"We did our best," Mark said.

The soldiers got to their feet with Philip still held between them.

Andrew was puzzled. "Philip?" He looked accusingly at the soldiers. "Do take that tape off his mouth, if you please."

Jankowski ripped the tape off.

Philip swore and rubbed his sore lips. "These hooligans jumped me while they were robbing our graves!"

They stood in silence for a moment, then the vicar said, "Right. Who wants a cup of tea?"

CHAPTER FORTY-FOUR

MARK AND NORA WERE the only two to join Andrew at the rectory for tea. The rest of the team opted to take the samples back to the Rose and Crown and begin the lab work on them.

The soldiers half-heartedly apologized to Philip, who suggested that their apology would be more meaningful if it was attached to a pint at the Miners' Arms. With Nora's permission, Jankowski agreed to take the old man there for that purpose. The remaining soldiers escorted the team back to the B&B.

The rectory was roomy, but cozy. After introductions, Andrew gave Mark and Nora a very brief tour, ending with the study where Reverends Mompesson and Stanley met to discuss the quarantine of the village in 1666. Mark was astonished. Having imagined a large room with a big desk and walls filled with books, he was surprised to see a fairly small and narrow room that felt as if the three of them were a crowd.

With the pot of tea and mugs on a tray, Andrew led them into an adjoining dining room where they sat down. He poured the tea and said, "It's my fault, really. I didn't think to tell Philip about what you were doing. It never occurred to me that he might stake the place out. Poor man."

"I'm sure the Miners' Arms is soothing to his bruised body," Mark said.

The vicar laughed. "Without question." He eyed them both for a moment. "Did you get what you were after?"

"We hope so," Nora replied. "Thanks to the list and locations you provided, we were able to get samples from both the plague victims and the survivors."

"And that will do the trick?" he asked.

Nora shrugged. "We don't know."

He sipped some of his tea, then asked, "Is there anything else I can do?"

"Not at the moment," Nora replied.

"I have a question," Mark quickly said.

Andrew and Nora both turned to him as if they'd forgotten he was there.

"There's a tomb in the graveyard with some strange markings on it—a symbol with branches and a lamb and . . ."

" . . . a dove," Nora finished.

Mark remembered Nora's reaction when she saw the symbol on the tomb. "You've seen it before?"

She shrugged, and then asked Andrew, "What is it?"

"I was curious about it when I first arrived here," he said. "I looked through the church archives and some of the private papers left for the rectors, but the information was vague, downright legendary."

"Try it on us," Mark said.

The vicar held up a hand and left the room. He returned a few minutes later with a large leather-bound book. He set it on the table and pointed to the open pages. A drawing of the symbol was there, with the words *Lumen Christi* beneath it.

"That explains the symbol of the lamb with the beams of light radiating from it." Nora looked at Mark and then the vicar. "The Light of Christ?"

"Yes. It was the name of an order of Catholic monks for about three centuries. It's believed that this was their symbol."

For the first time, Mark got a close look, and noticed that the circle was actually two halves of a circle. He pointed to the top part. "What are those branches?"

"Olive branches," the reverend said. "And this line on the bottom is a vine with lilies."

"Symbolizing what?" Nora asked.

"The olive branches symbolize peace, while the lilies symbolize purity."

Mark pointed to the inner circle. "And the rest of it?"

"The single dove represents humility. The lamb in repose

represents the love of Christ, while the radiating sunbeams represent light or holiness." Andrew turned the page to one covered in detailed calligraphy. "All of these virtues were part of the order's vocation—to exhibit them wherever they went. It's spelled out here, but I won't try to read it to you. My Latin isn't that good, and my eyes are even worse when it comes to this scribbly, scrolly-type writing."

Nora leaned closer and appeared to be reading the script. Or trying to.

"Was this order part of your church?" Mark asked.

"Not that I'm aware of," he answered. "And if it was Catholic, it would have been a secret effort."

"Then why is there a tomb with those markings in your graveyard? Was one of the monks buried there?"

"No one has ever opened it to look." Andrew sat down again and picked up his mug of tea. There was a curious twinkle in his eye. "Why are you so interested?"

Mark sat down and reached for his own mug of tea. He hoped to look casually disinterested. "No special reason. The symbol caught my eye, that's all."

Nora looked over at Mark. "Caught your eye? From where we were working? In the dark? Even in daylight you couldn't have seen it from there."

"What are you talking about?" Mark asked, bothered by her tone.

"You saw something else," Nora said. "You turned on your flashlight, risking our entire effort tonight, because you saw something."

"All right," Mark challenged her. "Since we're confessing in front of a priest . . ."

"I'm an Anglican minister." Andrew corrected him with a smile in his eyes. "Anglo-Catholics consider themselves priests. I'm a staunch son of the Reformation."

"Then in front of a *man of God*," Mark amended, "tell me where you've seen that symbol before. You gasped when you saw it on that tomb."

"There are some graves on the hillside with that symbol on them."

Andrew sat up straight, nearly spilling his tea. "You've seen the graves?"

"This afternoon," she replied, puzzled by his reaction. "Why?"

"There was a journal entry by one of our vicars—I can't remember which—alleging that some of the monks had been buried on a hillside around here. I think some of the remaining members of the order came looking for them back in the nineteenth century, but no one ever found the graves."

Nora seemed please. "I'm pretty sure I can lead you to them."

"Yes, please. I'd like to see them."

Mark was still irritated by Nora's interrogation. "Why didn't you tell the team about them?"

"Because there was nothing to indicate that they were from the period of the plague." She turned to the reverend, "Were they?"

"No. Those monks probably died before the plague came."

"There," Nora said to Mark. "That's my big confession. Now, how about yours?"

Mark squirmed in his chair for a moment. "There's nothing to confess." It was one thing to see something in a dark graveyard, and another thing to admit to it in a cozy dining room with two adults staring at him.

"Well?" Nora folded her arms, a very motherly posture.

"I thought I saw something," Mark explained. "A statue. A shadow. I don't know. My eyes were playing tricks on me after looking through those blasted goggles for an hour."

"But what was it?" Nora asked, her tone taking on an appeal. "What do you think you saw?"

Mark shook his head. It seemed silly to mention it now. "Nothing. I shone the flashlight in the direction of it—and there was nothing there. So, let's drop it."

"You're holding back," Nora said.

"Why are you being so persistent?"

"Why won't you tell us what you saw?"

Suddenly, Andrew laughed and banged a fist against the table. The tray of tea rattled.

Mark and Nora turned to him, bewildered.

"I'll tell you why he won't confess," Andrew said. "It's because he thinks it will sound ridiculous and strange, and maybe even a little crazy."

"What will?" asked Nora. "What did he see?"

"A ghost," Andrew stated.

Mark was indignant. "I didn't say that! I didn't say anything about a ghost. I don't believe in them."

The vicar waved his hands at Mark. "Oh, calm down. You're not alone. He's legendary around here."

"Who is?" Mark asked.

"The Blue Monk," said the reverend.

CHAPTER FORTY-FIVE

"THE BLUE MONK?" MARK exclaimed.

"I'll give you bits and pieces of the legend as I've been able to assemble them over the few years I've been here," Andrew said.

Mark and Nora leaned forward to give him their full attention like two kids anticipating a good story.

"Before the time of the plague, the Lumen Christi Order helped out in this area, mostly ministering to the miners and their families, but, according to some sources, the monks became ill from some unknown cause and slowly died off. They were buried, but no one was sure where." He tipped his head appreciatively to Nora. "Until now."

She smiled back at him.

"When the plague hit, a mysterious man in a monk's cowl, who, it is assumed, was a member of the order, began to help the sick and dying, usually at night."

"Why at night?" Nora asked.

"Because of his appearance. His skin was said to be blue."

"The monk really was *blue*?" Mark asked.

Andrew nodded. "Legend has it that he was the last of the order, at least in this shire, and that he was the one who had to bury his brothers as they died."

Mark's mind began to work out the reasons for such a phenomenon and landed on the most obvious answer, but he kept quiet and allowed Andrew to continue.

"Some villagers considered the monk a blessing, others thought he was a curse. He brought comfort and solace and even blessed the bodies and graves of the departed. But a few people thought he might be in league with the devil, while others blamed him for bringing the plague to the village."

"He helped them, but they still blamed him?" Nora asked with disbelief.

"You'll remember that the Pharisees accused Jesus of using Satan's power to cast out demons," Andrew said.

"And you'll remember Jesus' answer to that," Nora said. "A house fighting against itself will fall."

Mark wasn't interested in a Bible story. "What became of the monk? Did he die of the plague?"

"Not that we know of."

Nora's face lit up. "He came in contact with plague victims again and again, yet survived?"

"It would seem so."

"I'd love to find *his* grave," Mark exclaimed, realizing the opportunity. "If he didn't die of the plague, a sample from his body might yield solid help. His immune system must have been remarkable."

"Maybe he's buried with the other monks," Nora suggested.

"Maybe," Andrew said, but with a skeptical tone. "Except . . ."

"Except what?"

"We don't know that he died in this area. He disappeared under mysterious circumstances."

"What kind of mysterious circumstances?" asked Mark.

"A scandal or a curse of some sort."

"Scandal? Like, he had an affair with the vicar's wife or took off with the church funds?"

"We don't know," Andrew replied. "I'm using the word 'scandal' because that's the word used in several places in the records. No specifics, only a reference to the scandal that led to the monk's disappearance, and then a reference to a curse in other places."

"Maybe they considered his blue skin a curse," Mark suggested. He hoped they hadn't already reached a dead-end.

"I'll take you to the graves of the other monks tomorrow," Nora mused, "but the graves don't appear to be near any sort of monastery or house. Where did the monks live?"

Andrew shrugged. "That's part of the mystery."

Then, in an instant, an idea struck Mark. "I know where they lived."

Andrew and Nora looked at him.

"In the mines."

Nora looked surprised. "What makes you say that?"

"Argyria."

Nora nodded and said, "That makes sense. Lead mines, blue skin."

"Argyria?" the reverend asked.

"Silver poisoning," Nora explained.

"Silver will turn you blue?"

"Every square inch of your skin," Mark said. "I saw a case in medical school and will never forget it. The guy looked like a Smurf."

"But," Andrew asked, "what does silver poisoning have to do with lead mines?"

Mark explained, "Well, lead mines are often laced with veins of silver."

"Have you heard of colloidal silver?" Nora asked the vicar.

"I think I've seen it in some of the health-food stores."

Nora explained, "Some people believe that, taken orally, colloidal silver will prevent or heal all sorts of illnesses: from the flu and colds to infections and chronic fatigue to emphysema and stomach ulcers—even tuberculosis."

"You're joking."

Mark added, "It's no joke. Some say it can be used for allergies, arthritis, blood parasites, bubonic plague, and even AIDS."

"Are you telling me that it really does treat all those things?" Andrew asked.

"I doubt it," Nora said.

Mark shook his head. "Most of the experts I've read believe prolonged exposure to silver is unsafe. Not only does it accumulate in the skin, but it can also build up in the body and damage the nervous system, the kidneys, and other organs."

Nora said, "If the monks lived in the mines and the mines had any silver in them, the monks could have been exposed, which would have had terrible effects on their health, even killing them."

"That last monk was likely exposed to it as well, which is why he was blue," Mark said. "But if he survived for a long time, then he must have had a powerful resiliency. Another reason to find him."

"But how?" Andrew asked.

"Maybe he died somewhere in the mines," Mark said. "In which case, we might be able to find his remains and get a sample."

"You'll have a task there," Andrew warned them. "There are miles and miles of tunnels interweaving beneath Eyam."

Mark pondered their dilemma. "Regardless, there must be a sensible place to start. He didn't live in *all* of the mines, but must have found a central spot to call home, something with easy access to the village. Surely the town has documents and surveys identifying the mines over the years. It was one of the primary sources of business, after all."

"We have plenty of those kinds of things," the reverend said, "but this order was very secretive and private. They wouldn't have set up shop in an area that anyone could simply wander into."

The three considered the puzzle in silence for a moment.

Suddenly, Andrew's eyes lit up. "Wait! I've just remembered . . ." He stood, opened the large leather book on the table, and flipped through the pages. "In 1712, the vicar of the time, named Brooks, drew his own map. He was an avid bird-watcher and wanted to note the locations of certain bird species. Along the way, he identified the entrances to some of the mines as markers. I suppose he assumed that everyone around here knew where the mine entrances were."

"But over time the abandoned mines would be forgotten," Nora said.

"Right," Andrew confirmed. "For example, not long after I arrived, I came upon Brooks's map and, out of curiosity, used it for a few of my hikes in the hills. I was intrigued that some of the entrances he noted didn't line up with the official maps, and some didn't seem to exist."

"Are you sure?" Mark asked.

"Mind you, I didn't do a detailed search, and we're talking about a time period of almost three hundred years ago so it's possible the entrances are there, but have completely collapsed or been covered with foliage." Andrew suddenly stopped flipping pages and pointed to a crudely drawn map of the area. "I mention it only because it might be helpful."

Mark and Nora gathered around the book.

"Good heavens," the reverend exclaimed. "I don't remember *this* from before."

His finger fell on a section of the map. It was the symbol with the lamb and dove, the Order of Lumen Christi and the word "Cathedral."

"Why would Brooks put that symbol there?" Mark asked and then turned to Nora. "Is that where the monks are buried? Maybe he stumbled onto their burial site as you did."

Nora studied the map. "I don't think so." She ran her finger from the symbol to an area several inches away on the map. "The monks are around here somewhere. Quite a distance."

"Then what does the symbol signify?" Mark asked Andrew. "And what does 'Cathedral' mean? Was it the site of a cathedral at some point? Is there a ruin there?"

Andrew shook his head. "I've hiked up there myself and didn't see anything significant. Just trees and rocks. Definitely no cathedral or ruins of any sort."

Mark rubbed his chin. "Would you mind if we look tomorrow?"

"I don't mind," Andrew said. "I'll go along. All this talk has me curious again."

Nora looked unhappy. "Hold on, Mark. This is all very interesting, but we have to keep focused on our task at hand."

"I am," Mark said. "If we can find the remains of the Blue Monk, then we might have a perfect specimen to help us with our work."

She looked at him skeptically. "You go, then. I'd rather not be a part of it."

Mark considered her, a nagging suspicion flagged. "Because it's a waste of time—or for some other reason?"

Nora didn't answer, but looked away.

Andrew caught on to Mark's thinking and brightened. He turned to Nora. "So, you saw him also!"

Nora looked at them both sheepishly.

Mark playfully gasped. "You little hypocrite! When did you see him? Tonight at the graveyard?"

"No," she said, contrite. "This afternoon in the woods. When I found the monks' graves. In a way, he led me to them. That's why I fell and hurt my ankle."

"And that's why you were acting so strangely at the pub," Mark said. "Why didn't you tell me?"

"For the same reason you didn't want to admit it. It sounds crazy. Whatever it was scared the living daylights out of me."

"You should have said something," Mark gently teased her.

Nora wouldn't respond, but asked, "Do you believe in ghosts, Reverend?"

"Every vicar who has lived in this house since the mid-eighteenth century has reported seeing the ghost of a woman on the stairwell. She sometimes weeps at night."

"Every vicar? You've seen her?" Mark asked.

Andrew nodded. "I have. More than once."

"And how do you explain it?" asked Nora.

"I don't," he replied. "Some things simply are what they are. You either believe or you don't. No explanation will persuade you one way or the other." Then he was quiet and seemed deep in thought.

"Is something wrong?" Nora asked.

"I was just thinking about Paul's admonition to the church in Corinth. He told them, 'So we fix our eyes not on what is seen, but on what is unseen. For what is seen is temporary, but what is unseen is eternal.' Maybe what is seen at times and not seen at other times is in between the temporary and the eternal."

"Or, maybe it's eternal," Nora added.

"How so?" Andrew asked.

"Isn't it the book of Hebrews that says something about our being surrounded by a great cloud of witnesses?"

He nodded. "And?"

Nora smiled. "Maybe some allow themselves to be seen."

CHAPTER FORTY-SIX

AARON COULD HEAR VOICES. They were rousing him from a deep, deep sleep. *What were they saying?* he wondered.

"I don't care," he mumbled to himself as he rolled over and burrowed into the straw mattress, which, considering the past few days, felt as comfortable as a thick feather bed.

But the voices continued, and Aaron roused himself enough to remember where he was: a shack somewhere in the middle of the jungle. Aaron was sure it was Pierre's hideout for his illegal fur business.

After bouncing along the dirt road for a few miles, Pierre guided the truck back to the main highway after he was certain there would be no other police or checkpoints to deal with.

They drove for many miles until, just before dusk, Pierre turned off the main highway and followed a dirt road back into the jungle. A couple of miles later they arrived at the shack.

"Is this your home?" Aaron had asked.

"A stopping point on our journey," Pierre said with a dismissive laugh.

He then had insisted that Aaron go straight into the shack, where he would find a bed in the back room. "You're exhausted. You need your sleep."

Aaron had thanked him, guessing that Pierre was really less interested in Aaron's sleep and more interested in making sure Aaron didn't see him unload the skins from the back of the truck and put them in the locked hut next to the shack.

He now felt sluggish from his lack of sleep, but the words "The Army of Darkness" suddenly came to his mind and he realized he must wake himself up. When he opened his eyes, he saw through a window that it was nighttime. What if the police had found them? Did Pierre call them, as Uncle Win had? What if, even now, they were in the other room discussing his capture?

He sat up as the door to the room was thrown open and a blinding light turned on. He tried to roll in the opposite direction away from the large, unshaven figure that lunged across the room.

An enormous hand fell on his arm and yanked him to his feet. Then he was dragged to the other room. The stench of tobacco and alcohol was overpowering. Aaron kicked at the man and shouted for Pierre's help.

"Stop kicking me!" the man commanded in a Gabonese-accented English. He punched a fist into Aaron's side, knocking the wind out of him. He then swung Aaron heavily onto a wooden chair and clamped down on his shoulders to keep him from getting away.

As Aaron struggled to breath, another man, equally large and scruffy, walked into the room followed by Pierre. Wheezing, Aaron clutched at the chair. *I was tricked. Betrayed.*

The man who walked in with Pierre held out his hand. "Show me!" he commanded.

"Yes, Boss." Pierre produced a piece of paper from his pocket, unfolded it, and held it up for the boss to see. The boss bent over and squinted, then snatched the paper from Pierre and held it next to Aaron, looking back and forth from the paper to Aaron's face. He stepped back as a broad grin crossed his face.

"Yep. That's him all right. You were right to contact me." The boss leaned toward Aaron. "Did you know the military wants you? And the police, too? And the Americans? They've put out a reward for you—dead or alive."

Dead or alive? Aaron knew it was just as the Bible said it would be for Christians in the time of the Antichrist.

The one Pierre called boss pulled a giant knife from the sheath on his belt. "I say we kill him here and now. Easier to take them a dead body than a wiggling one that will try to escape."

Pierre stepped forward and grabbed the boss's arm. *"Tu ne tueras point ici!"*

Aaron knew enough French to get that Pierre didn't want the boss to murder him in this place.

The veins in the leader's neck popped out. He clenched his fist as if he might strike Pierre, but then released it and took a deep breath. "Don't worry. I won't kill him here." He sheathed the knife again.

Pierre stepped toward the boss and said. *"Je veux mon argent!"*

Pierre wanted his money, Aaron translated.

The boss turned to face Pierre, then shoved a hand in his pocket and produced a large wad of bills. He handed it over. Pierre took it and, licking his fingers, counted it quickly.

"That's part of it. You'll get the rest when we get ours." The boss turned to the second man and nodded. He yanked Aaron to his feet.

Pierre pocketed the money and scratched at his arm. "Sorry, boy. Business is business."

The boss and his accomplice led Aaron to the door. Pierre continued to scratch at his arm then muttered, "What is this?"

The sound of fear in his voice caused the boss to turn and look. Pierre held out his arms. They were covered with bloody splotches.

"Did you sleep in a nest of something?" the boss asked, laughing.

Pierre exclaimed something in French and began to wildly scratch at his chest, pulling and tearing at his T-shirt.

The sight of the old man squirming in panic riveted the attention of the boss and henchman. Aaron, seeing a chance of escape, eased toward the open door.

A hand fell on his shoulder. "Not so fast," said the accomplice with a stern look. He pushed his shirttail aside and drew a small pistol from his belt.

Aaron froze where he was.

In French, Pierre cried out for help as he stepped toward the boss. The splotches on his arms were also on his chest. He clawed at them.

"I don't like this," the boss said, worried, backing toward the door.

If this is your help, God, then give me a clear chance to run, Aaron prayed.

Then Pierre vomited blood with explosive violence.

Both the boss and his accomplice threw their hands up to protect themselves, stepping in opposite directions and away from Aaron.

This was Aaron's chance. He threw himself out of the door and scrambled for the darkness of the jungle.

"Stop!"

As he reached the edge of the jungle, he heard a loud pop. The bark of a tree to his right splintered, and he felt the stinging spray of the wood. He dodged quickly to the left. There was another pop and the tip of his left ear suddenly felt as if someone had placed a burning match against it. He threw himself to the ground, crawling on his stomach for several yards in the direction of the rear of the shack. He could hear the boot heels on the gravel, but they were farther away now, back where he had first entered the jungle.

"Did you hit him?" the boss yelled.

"I think so," the henchman replied. "He should be around here."

Aaron continued to quickly inch away. Then, when he was confident of his place in the darkness, he positioned himself into a crouching position and sprang up, grabbing the low branch of a tree. He pulled himself upward, moving monkeylike from branch to branch, going higher and higher.

They'll look for me on the ground, he thought. *They'll expect me to run.*

From where he sat, he could see the two men, mere shadows, searching for him, moving in the wrong direction. He touched his ear, wincing from the pain. Then he watched and waited. He was getting good at that.

CHAPTER FORTY-SEVEN

AUGUST 15

AT BREAKFAST, THE TEAM debriefed their mission from the night before. Digger, Henry, and Georgina had immediately begun to catalog and analyze the samples they'd taken from the church graveyard, and they'd sent a portion of each sample to a lab in Cambridge via military courier.

The three looked exhausted, which was understandable, but Nora noticed that there was an unusual amount of sniping among them at the table. Even Digger and Georgina seemed at odds.

"What's wrong with everyone?" Nora asked. "I know last night was hard and late, but there's something you're not telling me."

"Oh, are you interested?" Digger's sarcasm was obvious. "I assumed your late-night *tea* with the vicar was the only thing you had on your mind this morning."

Nora glared at Digger. "If there's a problem, then spell it out, Digger."

Silence around the table. Henry finally spoke up. "Our preliminary look at the samples didn't yield anything new."

"From the victims?" Mark asked.

"The victims *or* the survivors," Henry replied.

"It's everything we've already seen, discussed, and dismissed," Digger said. "We're circling the same old drain."

"But we knew that coming in," Nora said. "We're going to have to dig deep for an answer to this problem. It's not going to jump up and surrender to us."

"Unless we're chasing a rabbit," Digger said. "This whole expedition could be a diversion."

Nora struggled not to feel defensive about the comment. "A diversion from where? If we shouldn't be looking here, then where?"

More silence as the team avoided eye contact with one another. An uncomfortable shrug from Georgina.

Mark spoke up. "We're going to have to come at this in an unorthodox way. If the samples we found last night don't help us, then let's go out and find more."

Digger scowled at Mark. "Look, I know you suffered for the team yesterday, but please don't bore us with a pep-rally speech. All right?"

"It's not my job to encourage you to do your job," Mark said.

"Good thing," said Digger.

"Pout if you want," Mark said, "but our late-night tea with the vicar gave us a possible lead."

Nora caught Mark's eye, wondering how much he was going to tell them.

He picked up a piece of toast and buttered it as he spoke. "Let me tell you about the Blue Monk."

"The *what*?" three voices asked in unison.

Over the next ten minutes, Mark explained to the team everything they knew about the Blue Monk. Nora was relieved that he left out the part where they thought they saw the apparition the previous day.

"And you're telling us this *why*?" Digger asked.

"Weren't you listening?" Georgina said to him. "This monk must have had some sort of incredible immunity."

"Could he be the super specimen we need?" Henry asked.

Digger still seemed unimpressed. "Great. Any idea where he's buried?"

"No, but we have a few clues," Mark said. "The vicar and I are going to investigate areas today."

"So you get to go hiking while the rest of us work," Digger complained. "Frankly, I think it's a waste of time. You're looking for a blue needle in a black haystack."

"Maybe."

"Or," Georgina said, "maybe he'll find the monk with all kinds of artifacts and jewels buried with him like the Egyptian pharaohs and he'll be called *Monk Tut* and we'll all be famous and fabulously rich."

The team looked at her, collectively mystified.

"Georgina," Henry commented, "you're a wonder."

Nora stood and said to Mark, "As curious as I am about this, we can't afford for you to spend much time on it. There's too much else to do. If we are chasing rabbits, as Digger has already diplomatically suggested, then we have to find out and then find the right track."

"That was my mood talking," Digger said, "but I'm feeling much better now that Mark is going to chase a more useless rabbit than we are."

"I'm here to make you feel good about yourself, Digger," Mark said. "Never doubt it."

"Around you, pal, anyone would feel good."

"Point to you, Digger," Mark said.

"All I'm suggesting," Nora said, "is to look around with Reverend Andrew this morning, but get back to us fast."

"Aye, Captain."

Nora looked at the group, suddenly feeling the weight of their work. "I assume we all realize how unlikely it is that, even if we find this monk, the body will be of any use to us."

Muttered assent except from Mark, who commented, "A famous athlete once said, 'You miss one hundred percent of the shots you don't take.'" Nora's cell phone rang. She looked at the screen. "It's Mac," she said. "Which is *another* reason we have to work fast. He gave us two days or he'll scrap the mission." Nora flipped open her phone and said, "Hello," and walked from the dining room into the hall.

"How are things, Nora?" Mac asked.

A young soldier, whose name Nora had forgotten, sat on a chair by the door. He stood as she entered. She nodded to him and he sat back down by the door.

"We're busy with the samples we collected last night," she said and drifted to the foyer of the B&B. It was an open area that served as the intersection of halls going in separate directions, with a broad staircase leading up to the bedrooms. Nora spied an alcove to the side of the stairs, a cozy nook with a small wingback chair, end table, and Tiffany-style lamp. She sat in the chair. "Any news from Africa?"

"Yes. The missing boy is on the move and people are dying in his wake. Worse yet, some people he apparently infected passed through a police checkpoint, infecting some of the police, who, in turn, infected others they stopped. Now, mini breakouts are being reported in a dozen or more places. It's a growing disaster."

Nora closed her eyes and wondered if their work was in vain—was it already too late to stop this nightmare? "What are the reports from the other lab sites?"

"We'll all find out at noon our time. Get Henry or Digger to set up for a videoconference, linked with me. I'll connect the others."

Just then, Digger came around the corner to head up the stairs. Nora waved to get his attention. He peered over the banister. She mouthed, "Noon. Videoconference."

Digger nodded, then continued up the stairs.

"Did you get that?" Mac asked.

"Noon," Nora affirmed. She glanced at her watch and only then realized it wasn't on her wrist. She frowned, unsure of where she'd left it. "I'll make sure we're set up."

"Be prepared, Nora," Mac said. "The pressure is on."

"Understood."

Georgina also came down the hall, cell phone in hand. She was either texting or dialing a number and didn't see Nora. She glanced around furtively and then slipped out the front door. Nora wondered whom she'd be calling at this time of the morning.

"Are you somewhere private?" Mac asked.

"Private?" She looked around. Apart from the soldier still stationed near the dining room, no one was around. "More or less. Why?"

"I'm forwarding some information we've received from Interpol. A connection related to Return to Earth. You need to look at it as a matter of priority."

"Why? What's it—"

"Be sure you're alone. It may not be what it seems, but we have to take every precaution."

Mac's cryptic statements disturbed Nora. "All right. I will."

"Call me back." He hung up.

Nora looked at her phone, mystified and concerned.

"You're frowning," Mark said from the stairs.

She shook it off. "Mac. Pressure. You know."

"I take it from your comments at breakfast that you're not coming with me to search for the monk?"

"No. The situation in Gabon is worsening by the minute. We have a videoconference at noon. I want to be prepared."

"And you don't want to be seen chasing rabbits," Mark said with a smile. "Or ghosts."

"Thank you for not mentioning it," she said.

"I'll need your map."

"Map?"

"You have to show me roughly where that burial site is. We won't find it on our own."

"I drew one up after we got back last night." She reached into her briefcase, found it, and handed it to him. "I wrote down the landmarks I could remember."

"Thanks."

"Mark," she said, "please don't get kidnapped again."

"I'll do my best not to," Mark said. He darted up the stairs and around the landing to their rooms.

Nora followed, slinging her case over her shoulder and trying to imagine what Mac had sent to her that required so much privacy, but if it had something to do with Return to Earth, she assumed it couldn't be anything good.

Back in her room, she opened her laptop on the small courtesy desk and logged on. Henry and Digger had set up an encrypted wireless system, bypassing the one provided by the B&B, which assured her that no one could eavesdrop on their work.

She clicked into her secure e-mail account and found the message Mac had sent half an hour before. He had forwarded it from an Inspector Duerr with Interpol, who had sent the original message to General Mosley.

The e-mail looked formal with case numbers and other bits of bureaucratic information in it. The main portion, which someone had highlighted, stated that the attached photograph had come from a cooperative archive shared with Britain's MI5: a photo file of suspected members of subversive groups that they'd been monitoring in the United Kingdom and throughout Europe.

Duerr's question to General Mosley was whether he could confirm the person in the photograph as a member of one of his units. If so, this person might be an infiltrator for Return to Earth. In other words—a spy.

The photograph was tagged as coming from surveillance of a Return to Earth march in London in July—five years earlier.

Nora clicked on the attached photo and it uploaded quickly, but in increments. She could see a crowd with placards—angry expressions as a small group seemed to clash with the police. At first, Nora wasn't sure whom she was supposed to be looking at, but then an inset close-up appeared in the lower corner of the main photo. To the left of the central action, a woman stood, placard in hand.

The face was unmistakable.

It was Georgina.

CHAPTER FORTY-EIGHT

MARK DRESSED FOR THE day in the most casual clothes he had: a basic light blue polo shirt, dark blue hiking trousers, and sneakers. He stuffed his backpack with bits of information about the area, resource material the team had collected, and a poncho for the rain that the weather report had promised for the afternoon. He also packed a .38-caliber pistol, a safety measure provided by Mac after Mark's encounter with Return to Earth.

Mark found Jankowski in front of the Rose and Crown. He wore a crisp white shirt, crisp khaki trousers, polished boots, and dark sunglasses.

"You look like you've been ironed and starched from head to toe," Mark said.

"Sir?"

"Can't you rumple yourself up a little? You look so . . . *military*."

"I *am* military, sir."

"You'll draw too much attention. Go back inside and change into something more casual."

Jankowski looked himself over. "This is all I have."

"Then roll around in the dirt or something. If we walk anywhere together, people will assume I'm some sort of official and you're with the Secret Service."

Jankowski looked offended. "I understand, sir, but—"

"I don't want to be late. See what you can do and meet me at the church."

"My assignment is to protect you, sir."

"I understand that. Don't worry, I'll keep to very public places and promise not to get kidnapped until after you show up."

"If you'll wait for a minute—"

Mark walked off, glancing back to wave. Jankowski watched him, an indignant expression on his face.

Mark reached the rectory right at 8:00 a.m., the time he'd agreed to meet the vicar. He strolled across the wide, neatly trimmed lawn to the large two-story house, and appreciated it more fully in the morning sunlight.

He knew from the vicar that one wing dated back to the sixteenth century, easily marked by the tall, uneven windows. The rest had been added to in subsequent years, but maintained the look of the original. He tapped on the front door using the large knocker. The sound seemed to echo throughout the village. He waited. No one answered. He knocked again. No answer.

He drifted around the house, thinking that the vicar might be tooling about in the garden. Nestled as it was among the trees, the house seemed isolated though it was only a stone's throw from the church to the west side, a neighbor's house to the east, and the main road to the south. From the garden Mark could see the sun pressing a white gold on the rising hills and forest they planned to explore—if he could find the vicar.

He knelt, opened his backpack, and took out the gun. He wasn't going to be caught without one a second time. "My job was never this complicated in the lab," he said to himself.

There was a wrenching sound that caused Mark to jump. A window opened on the second floor of the rectory and Andrew leaned out. "I'm terribly sorry, Mark. I had an emergency call first thing this morning. Pastor business."

"Is everything all right?"

"Yes, but it's made me late. Give me a few minutes, if you don't mind."

"I'll meet you in the churchyard," Mark called back.

Andrew retreated and Mark circled around the house to the gate leading to the church. Once through the gate, he walked down the lane to the tomb where he had seen the Blue Monk. It was a chipped and moss-covered rectangle, nondescript except for the symbols embedded on each side.

"Still curious," Philip said with diffidence.

"Still curious," Mark affirmed, wondering how the grizzled

old groundskeeper had snuck up on him so easily. So much for being on guard. He was struck by the man's face close up—a pinched mouth, long nose, and dark eyes that sat in his pale skin like black buttons in snow. He also had a long neck and an Adam's apple that looked like a stork trying to swallow a turtle.

"Not sure why you're wasting your time," Philip said.

"We have to consider every possibility. Do you know who's buried in here?"

He shrugged. "Some fellow from the 1500s. Wealthy. The poor folks couldn't afford a fancy box like this," he grunted. "The man didn't get his money's worth if you ask me."

"Why not?"

"There was an inscription on the lid," he said, putting his hand on the top. "Long since worn away. Poor craftsmanship."

"What about the symbols? They're still here."

Philip stepped back to look at one. "Those were added later."

"How much later?"

He shrugged again and shoved his hands into the pockets of his overalls. "I couldn't say, but a man gets to know these stones after years of working around them. The style and craftsmanship isn't as crude as it was in the 1500s."

"Do you know what the symbols mean?"

"No idea and no interest," he snorted. "Something cultish, no doubt."

"Cultish?"

"Demon stuff. All tied into that Blue Monk, if you ask me."

"What do you know about him?"

"Only what everyone gossips about. He supposedly shows up as a ghost from time to time."

Mark kept his eyes on the tomb. "Have you ever seen him?"

"Me? Never. It's a load of codswallop."

"Why?"

"No such thing as ghosts."

"Are you sure?"

"How sure do I have to be? Besides, how can a monk be a ghost, eh? If he were a true man of God, he'd be in heaven now, wouldn't he? Holy men aren't doomed to wander the earth as ghosts."

"Is that formal Anglican theology or your own?" Mark teased.

"I'm only saying that if he's a ghost—and I'm not saying there are such things—then it follows that he was a cursed man. That's all I'm saying."

"A good point."

"And if he's cursed, then it follows that he'll bring nothing but curses to the people who mess with him."

Mark turned to the groundskeeper to ask him to clarify that statement, but he'd already shuffled off to a wheelbarrow and shovel that Mark hadn't noticed before. Philip laid the shovel across the bed of the wheelbarrow and pushed it along the path until he disappeared around the corner of the church.

A cursed man? Mark wondered. He thought for a moment, allowing himself to think back to those distant days when he had gone to seminary. What had he learned about ghosts? They were generally considered demonic, the spirits of the damned, but the Bible hinted at other things. In the Old Testament, there was the story of the spirit of the prophet Samuel returning to chastise King Saul. In the New Testament, the disciples of Jesus were at times fearful of Jesus' miraculous appearances, thinking he was a ghost. Surely they wouldn't have considered him a demonic ghost knowing what a holy man he was. Yet, Jesus had to declare "Be not afraid" or "Peace" to them as reassurance.

Andrew slammed the gate to the rectory. Mark looked up and the vicar waved at him. He walked in long, quick strides. He wasn't dressed in clerical garb but, like Mark, wore hiking clothes. It was odd to see him without his collar. "Where is Nora?" he asked.

"She can't join us today," Mark replied. "Meetings."

"Ah. Too bad. I enjoyed the idea of spending some time with her."

That makes two of us.

"Is she married?"

"No."

"Ever?"

"No."

"You?"

"Once. It didn't turn out very well."

"A shame."

"How about you?"

"Once, but that didn't turn out very well either."

"Divorce?"

"No—death." Andrew sighed. "Cancer. A nasty business."

"I'm sorry."

"Let's go up to the church office. I made copies of the map from the book I showed you last night."

"Nora gave me a rough map of the burial site too."

"Excellent. Let's make a move, then."

As they walked to the church office, Mark said, "I don't think Philip approves of our being here, or of our interest in the Blue Monk."

"Philip's an interesting man," the vicar observed. "Very down-to-earth. Unseen realities don't interest him, which, I suppose, makes him a good gardener."

Mark nodded. "He gave me an earful about the Blue Monk being a cursed man."

"Well, that's more than I could ever get him to say on the subject." Andrew laughed. "I asked him early this morning about the reference to the Cathedral on the map."

"And?"

"Impatience. Disdain."

Mark urged the reverend on. "But you could tell he knew something about it."

"A lot, as it turns out," Andrew replied. "He claims that the idea of a cathedral is an old mining legend: that beneath Eyam there is an underground cavern that is cathedral-like and even has an altar, but better than that, it contains a lost treasure trove of religious art work and artifacts."

"Artifacts?"

"Gold and silver chalices, crosses, relics, icons, gold-leafed statues; things hidden during the various persecutions, from the time of Henry the Eighth to the Restoration." Andrew chuckled again. "According to Philip, it's no different than stories of buried treasure by pirates or pots of gold at the end of rainbows."

Mark mused on the idea a moment. "Legends sometimes have a basis in fact, a starting point somewhere."

"Agreed," said the vicar. "There are miles and miles of tunnels, shafts, and caves beneath us. One was only recently discovered under the town square."

"So it *might* be true that there is a huge cavern somewhere below us or in those hills."

"It's possible."

"And since we suspect that the monks from the Lumen Christi Order lived in the caves, it also makes sense that they would have set up a place to worship."

Andrew considered the notion, and then said, "It makes perfect sense."

"So, it isn't a wild goose chase for us to explore the markings on that map. It may get us closer to the Blue Monk than any other effort."

"Indeed it might," Andrew said, and then looked at Mark quizzically. "Has somebody suggested that it is a wild goose chase?"

"Only everyone I work with."

They reached the church office just as Joan Thompson drove up in her car. She waved at them as they went inside. Mark followed Andrew down the hall to his office. It looked unchanged from the day before. He circled his desk and looked perplexed. "That's odd."

"What's wrong?"

He came back around the desk, and Mark followed him into the hall and two doors down to a small closet-sized room with a photocopier in it. He checked under the lid and in the trash can and on the supply shelves nearby. "It's gone."

"Gone?"

"I made a copy from the book and . . ." he shrugged. "Oh well, I'll make another." He slid past Mark and they went back to his office. The leather book was on his desk, but when he opened it to the correct page, he exclaimed, "What is going on here?"

"Is there a problem?" Joan asked from the door, her handbag and car keys still in hand.

Andrew spun the book around from the desk. "The page is gone. It's been torn out!"

Mark observed that in England no problem is so great that a cup of tea can't help. Joan went off to make a pot while Mark and Andrew discussed the situation.

Andrew, completely perplexed, talked through every step he'd taken that morning. He had walked to the office from the rectory with the book in his hand and made copies of the map. He left the book on his desk and returned to the rectory, where he ate a quick breakfast, showered, and was then interrupted by the call from Jan Carol, a woman whose mother was very ill. He hung up, saw Mark in the garden, and the rest Mark knew.

Mark frowned. "Was the office locked?"

Andrew shook his head. "I wouldn't think to lock it during the day. We never worry about people coming in."

"*You* never worry," Joan said, entering with the tray of tea. "But I do." She distributed the tea and sat down.

Agitated, Mark paced the small office. "Someone knew of the map's importance."

"Are we being watched?" Andrew asked.

"Yes."

"By whom? Ahaz?"

"Possibly. Or a group called Return to Earth."

"Return to Earth?" Joan asked.

Mark explained the movement to them.

She made tsking sounds and lowered her head.

The reverend looked aghast. "I consider myself an environmentalist, but that's insane."

Mark didn't respond, knowing his silence was response enough. He dug into his backpack. "We still have Nora's map. It's worth checking the monks' graves." He handed the map to Andrew. "If the Blue Monk is buried there, then we may have a fighting chance of finding him."

"The Blue Monk!" Joan nearly spilled her tea. "What does he have to do with this?"

"You know about him?" Mark asked.

"You can't live here your entire life and not know about him."

"Have you ever seen him?" Andrew asked her.

She looked at him through narrowed eyes, paused, and then said, "You can't live here your entire life and not see him."

Andrew sat up. "Joan!"

Joan shrugged and sipped her tea.

"Philip claims he's never seen the Blue Monk," Mark said.

Joan looked as if she might disagree, but thought better of it. Instead, she asked, "What's the Blue Monk have to do with your business here?"

Mark spelled out his hope to her—however ridiculous—that the body of the Blue Monk might give them vital information to fight the sickness in Africa.

Joan looked doubtful. "You believe the Blue Monk might help stop the pandemic?"

"We have to explore all our leads," Mark said.

Joan looked thoughtful for a moment. "That's why you're so upset about the page being torn from the map."

"Exactly," Andrew said.

He and Mark exchanged glances. There was something about Joan's knitted brow and the way she looked at her hands that struck them both. She was making a very serious decision.

"Joan?" Andrew asked, prompting her attention.

"I'll see what I can do to help you," she said, and suddenly stood, gathered the teacups, and left.

"I have no idea what that was about," Andrew said.

"Do you remember enough of our lost map to get us in the general direction of the Cathedral?" Mark asked.

"It's worth trying," the reverend said.

CHAPTER FORTY-NINE

JANKOWSKI WAS WAITING FOR Mark in the churchyard. He now wore a T-shirt with torn sleeves, jeans, and sneakers. He gave Mark a "happy now?" expression.

"Much better," Mark said to him.

"I work out in this shirt," Jankowski said as if the thought of wearing it any other time was reprehensible to him.

"Thank you for making a personal sacrifice."

Mark reintroduced Andrew and Jankowski. "I remember him from last night," Andrew said. "You tackled my man Philip."

"He had a gun," Jankowski said.

"I wasn't being critical," Andrew said. "Shall we be off?" They headed on the path along the church graveyard toward the hill beyond.

"We'll follow this up and around to Barkers Piece," Andrew explained as he held up Nora's map. "Then we'll go around to the forest where Nora found the graves."

At the rear edge of the graveyard, in the shade of a large oak tree, Mark saw a fairly new headstone. As they passed by it, he noticed that it belonged to an Ariel Keenan, with the date of her birth and death only four years apart.

"That's a sad situation," Andrew said, noticing where Mark's attention had gone. "It was a case of a fungal sinus infection gone wrong. She was more ill than the parents knew, and by the time they realized, the infection had gone to her brain. She died shortly thereafter. They have not been able to forgive themselves. Pity."

With startling speed and clarity, Mark's memory shot back to the death of his own daughter, as vivid to him as yesterday due to the drug given to him by the Return to Earth thugs. He swallowed back the emotion that came with the memory, surprised by how raw it made him feel.

"You know something about that," Andrew said.

Mark turned to him; an unspoken question furrowed Mark's brow.

"It's in your biography on one of those online search sites," Andrew explained. "I looked you up after we met. I wanted to find out more about you."

"And?"

"Losing a loved one never stops hurting," Andrew said. "Especially a child. I think the longing always persists."

Mark didn't reply.

The reverend continued as they walked. "But buried grief can be like toxic waste in a bad container. You bury it, but it seeps out and affects everything in some very unhealthy ways."

Mark kept quiet as they cleared the graveyard and began an ascent up the hill.

"You once studied to be an Episcopal minister," Andrew said.

Mark grumbled, "I really should seek legal action against those Web sites."

"Oh," Andrew said, disappointed, "it's not true?"

"It's true, but it's not relevant."

"What isn't? That you studied to be a minister, or something else?"

"All of it," Mark said. "Studying to become a minister and the reasons for it are no longer important."

Andrew was silent for a moment, and then asked, "Because of your daughter?"

Mark hitched up his backpack and glanced at Jankowski, who walked a few feet behind them and didn't seem to be listening. "I'm sorry, Reverend, but I'm not going to talk about this."

He nodded. "Of course. I didn't mean to pry."

They hiked on. Mark wondered why his daughter's death had suddenly become so prevalent. Was it because of the children he saw dead in the compound? The latest argument with his ex-wife? The discussion with Nora? The drug from Return to Earth? He didn't know, but he found it unnerving.

They reached the area of the map called "Barkers Piece" and swung eastward. Mark had a strong feeling of walking in Nora's footsteps, seeing the beauty of the views around him and wondering what she thought of them as she saw them. He wished he could ask her.

They reached a point on the south edge of some woods. Andrew pointed toward the road heading to the town and said, "Water Lane. This goes back to the town square." He gestured to the north. "According to her map, Nora followed the path north. She's made a few notations that I hope will make sense when we see them."

On they went, and Mark's legs began to ache as if they were on the verge of cramping. The reverend, thin and wiry as he was, seemed exhilarated by the walk. Jankowski wore the look of a man who was fondly remembering forty-mile hikes and bivouacs of days gone by.

"'Lightning tree trunk,'" Andrew said.

"What?"

"It's what she wrote. I assume it's a tree that she thought was struck by lightning."

"Or," Jankowski suggested, "it's a tree that looks like the shape of lightning." He pointed up ahead on the right, and sure enough there was a tree with a crooked trunk that could easily remind a passerby of lightning.

"A remarkable woman," Andrew muttered. "I guess we go into the woods here."

They did, departing from the sunlit path and into woods shadowed under thick branches and leaves.

"Due east, I think," Andrew said.

There was no set path, so the three of them had to do their best, stepping over logs, fallen branches, and collected forest debris. Mark already felt that this would prove to be a huge waste of time even though Nora mentioned seeing the Blue Monk in these woods; he had to wonder if this mysterious being would reappear.

"Jankowski?"

"Sir?"

"Do you believe in ghosts?"

"No, sir."

"Not even as a kid?"

"No, sir. They made for interesting stories, but I took them only as that: stories."

"So, how do you explain that people claim to have seen them?"

"I don't explain other people's experiences, sir. Since they aren't mine, there's nothing to explain."

"How wonderfully simple," Andrew said from up ahead.

"How about you, Reverend?" Mark continued. "You say you believe in them, but how do you explain them theologically?"

"I don't know that I can," he said over his shoulder. "Theories abound about what happens after death, but most are loosely extrapolated from Bible verses that could easily be interpreted a number of different ways. I base my theory on a key word used in the Bible to convey the idea of death: sleep. The sense of being asleep certainly isn't a final condition. It can be interrupted. So, when King Saul and the Witch of Endor awakened the prophet Samuel, he seemed grumpy and annoyed with them, as one would when rudely awakened. Jesus raised a girl from the dead after announcing that she was only asleep. The point is that this sleep can be interrupted, but our theology falls short of explaining the hows and whys of it. In the biblical examples, it was God himself who allowed the sleep to be interrupted for specific purposes."

"Not a bad theory," Mark said, not really believing it.

The reverend stopped for a moment to get a drink from his water bottle. "It's possible that the Blue Monk's sleep has been interrupted to help us. He led Nora to those graves. He led you to the symbols on the tomb."

Jankowski gazed at Mark. "You think you've seen a ghost?"

"I don't know what I saw," Mark said. His credibility was already stretched with the team. He didn't want this to get back to them. "You're not to mention it to anyone. We're not here because of a ghost. We need a body."

Jankowski looked away, seemed to flinch, and quickly pulled out a revolver. "Down," he said, crouching.

Mark and Andrew obeyed. Mark swung his backpack off and dug out the .38 from the side pocket.

Andrew eyed the weaponry with an expression of alarm. "Did you learn to use that in seminary or medical school?"

"Part of my training to work as a military contractor," Mark said, then whispered to Jankowski, "What did you see?"

"Light reflecting off something."

"Why is that a problem?" the reverend asked.

"It could be light reflecting off the scope of a rifle. Wait here." Jankowski quickly and quietly moved down the hill, taking cover from tree to tree.

"A rifle?" Andrew asked. "Does he think someone is going to shoot us?"

"Why not?" Mark felt tightness in his stomach as he waited to hear shots firing. He searched for Jankowski, but couldn't see him through the trees.

"What do we do if any shooting starts?" Andrew asked.

"Hiding would be my first idea," Mark said.

Suddenly, they heard Jankowski shout, "Hey!"

Mark peered in the direction of the voice and finally saw Jankowski in a thicket, waving his arm at them. Mark stood, with Andrew close by.

"It's clear," Jankowski said. "And I think I found what you were looking for."

Mark and Andrew made their way down the hill to Jankowski. Mark arrived first and Jankowski looked at him rather smugly. "This was sitting on that," he said, and held up a woman's watch. He nodded to the densest part of the thicket and Mark saw a crudely carved cross with a symbol in the center of it.

Andrew was breathless when he arrived. "A watch?" he asked and looked at Jankowski with admiration. "Are you telling me you saw light reflect off the face of that watch?"

"I must have," he said. "It's the only thing here that could have reflected any light."

"And it was *on* the cross?" Mark asked.

"Draped over the right arm," Jankowski said.

Mark and Andrew looked into the deep cavelike area where the cross sat. "That's impossible," they said in unison.

Jankowski shrugged and handed the watch to Mark. "It's inscribed to Dr. Richards."

Mark took the watch and looked at the silver back. *To Nora, with great affection, Father Francisco.* "I'll see that she gets it," he said and put it into his pocket.

"We never would have found this with Nora's map," Andrew said, clearly astonished. "If he hadn't seen the watch—"

"We don't have time to think about it," Mark said. "This must be the burial site." He took out a hunting knife and began to hack away at the thicket to give them better access. Jankowski joined in. Andrew pulled away the cut branches.

With more light, they now saw not only the first cross more clearly, but also other crosses beyond, and something was wrong. The crosses were tilted to one side; some were fully knocked over. The ground around the crosses had been dug up. This wasn't how Nora described what she found yesterday.

Mark groaned loudly as the realization struck him. "Someone got here before us," he said. "The graves have been ransacked."

"Well, I'd say Ahaz came and grabbed the bodies for their own research," Mark said, "or Return to Earth did this to thwart us. Take your pick. Either way, someone's out to wreck us."

The three men were several feet away from the burial site, Mark on a log, Andrew against a tree, and Jankowski on his feet eyeing the area.

"How could they do it so fast?" the reverend asked.

"If they followed Nora, then they've had since she was here yesterday afternoon to do it," Mark said. "That's plenty of time."

"What should we do now?" Andrew asked. "If they've destroyed this site there's no telling what they've done to the other one."

"You mean the one marked on the map that we don't have because it was stolen from your office?" Mark asked bitterly.

"That's the one," Andrew replied. He struggled to his feet. "I think we should have a look anyway. What's the harm, even if only to confirm our worst fears?"

"Do you think you can find it?" Mark asked.

Andrew shrugged his backpack on. "I'll try."

Mark got to his feet. "Which direction?"

Andrew pointed to the northeast and, just as he did, there was a loud ground-shaking explosion from that direction. Mark could feel the force of it crawl up his legs and into his back. Dirt and smoke rose skyward a short distance away.

"What was *that*?" Andrew asked, wide-eyed; he looked at his finger as if he'd somehow caused it.

"Come on," Mark said, moving toward the dust and smoke. He was certain of what they'd find.

Someone was still a step ahead of them.

CHAPTER FIFTY

AARON AWAKENED AT FIRST light after sleeping fitfully under a lean-to he crafted out of thick branches and soft ferns. The bed was comfortable enough, but he seemed to jolt awake at every unusual sound.

He lightly touched the wounds on his head and ear. He tried to remember how he'd gotten them. A spray of splinters after a bullet had hit a tree nearby and a second bullet that must have grazed his ear. *That was a close call*, he thought. The wounds still hurt, but hadn't bled much.

He wasn't sure how far he had run. He eventually reached a river and, for no reason he could imagine, felt strangely safe. He thought it was the Ogooué River, one that he and his father had kayaked.

He knew that if he heard the distant baying of hunting dogs, he could slip across the river. Yes, there was the very real possibility of a crocodile getting him but he had decided those odds would be better than facing dogs and the Army of Darkness. The river would protect him from them—but, not the mosquitoes. They became more bothersome every minute.

His arms itched and he looked down as he scratched the red marks. *Are these bites,* he wondered, *or some tropical disease?* He thought of what happened to Pierre and wondered if he had caught the same thing. He remembered the violence of the illness and prayed that God wouldn't let him suffer the same. Maybe the nuns at the Sisters of Mercy Convent would be able to figure it out—if he could get to them. He guessed he had one hundred and fifty miles left to go.

It was a daunting thought. How would he get there? If what those men had said was true—that he was wanted dead or alive—then he knew the main road would be too dangerous. But it was the only reasonable way to Libreville. He knew that trying to make it through the jungle would take too long and drain the last of his strength.

He bowed his head. *Father, thank you for letting me escape last night. Thanks for protecting me. Please show me the way to go.*

Aaron tilted his head as a delicious aroma came to him, something mouthwatering and smoky. Like bacon. Was it his imagination? What could it be, here in the middle of the jungle? He lifted his head and breathed in deeply. It was bacon. It had to be!

He followed the smell along the river and soon could hear sizzling sounds. He stopped, crouching behind a small bush, and carefully separated the branches. On the shore of the river, a young African man was hunched over a campfire frying eggs and bacon in a skillet. Aaron couldn't believe his eyes.

Although every shred of his common sense told him to back away, his hunger was too strong. He was willing to risk his safety for just a little of that food. He slowly stood and stepped out from behind the bush.

"Hello!" he shouted.

The man looked up and smiled as if he was expecting a guest to arrive. "Hello, back." Then a wave forward. "Come on down."

Aaron looked cautiously up and down the riverbank and could see no signs of life. A small tent was erected a few yards behind the man, and scores of fish were nailed to trees around the camp, apparently drying. A skiff with a tiny outboard motor sat on the shore of the sandbar. Aaron figured the man was a local fisherman.

"You look hungry," the man commented with a heavy accent. "May I offer you some breakfast?"

"Why don't you speak French?" Aaron asked as he walked over.

The young man laughed lightly. "*Mon frère, je parle français,* but since you called out to me in English, and since you don't look local to me, I thought English was worth a try." He held out his hand, "My name is François."

Aaron shook his hand. "Hi. I'm Aaron."

"Are you running away from something, my brother? Or running toward something?"

Aaron blushed. "Both, I guess."

"Well, have a seat. My home is your home." François went to a supply box, opened it up, and pulled out an extra plate and fork. He walked back to the fire, sat down, and served one half of the eggs and bacon on a plate, and handed it to Aaron.

As Aaron began to shovel the food into his mouth, François reached over and patted his forearm. "Eat slowly, my brother. There is no hurry. The Lord has provided us plenty of food." He gestured to the trees. "If we run out of eggs and bacon, we'll cook some fish." His smile was warm and welcoming and Aaron found his anxiety melting.

"François," Aaron asked, "why do you call me brother?"

"Because, I am a follower of Jesus. And you?"

Aaron hesitated. Should he trust this man or not?

"Are you not sure? Because if you aren't, then I would be happy to tell you how you can know God's love."

Surely an enemy of God wouldn't talk like this. Aaron nodded. "I'm a Christian."

"Excellent! We are two, and where two or more are gathered . . . well, any number of wonderful things could happen."

"I don't think anything wonderful will happen now," Aaron said.

François eyed him. "No? And why are you so gloomy?"

"Because it's the end of the world."

"The end of the world?" François asked. He leaned toward Aaron. "Do you mean Armageddon, my little brother?"

"Yeah. The Apocalypse."

François put down his plate. "What makes you think so?"

Aaron looked around, wanting to make sure no one was around, and then he told François everything that had happened to him over the past couple of days.

François listened carefully and, when Aaron was done, shook his head and looked downriver as if a response might drift toward him like a branch.

"Well?" Aaron asked.

François looked at him with misty eyes. "Aaron, my brother, you have traveled a difficult road—a road many older men would not walk, but you have done it as a young man."

"Do you believe me?"

"There are three things I can tell you for certain. First of all, I was at my pastor's home last night and we watched the BBC World News. There was no mention of an Apocalypse, or of Armageddon—at least, not yet."

Aaron began to protest, "But . . ."

François held up a hand and smiled. "The second thing I know is that if you love our Lord, Aaron, and if you are called according to his purposes, then all things will work together for good. *All* things, my little brother. God's word could not be more clear."

Aaron lowered his head. "I know."

"And there's a third thing I know, Aaron." He paused for a moment.

"What's that?"

"I know how you can get to the Sisters of Mercy Convent without walking on the road or in the jungle or even by the river."

Aaron's eyes widened. "How?"

"Just across the river, maybe a mile into the jungle, are the tracks of the Trans-Gabon Railway. It goes to Libreville. If you wait by the tracks, it will stop to pick you up. I have done it myself many times."

"The train. Why didn't I think of that?"

François laughed.

Aaron was quickly sobered by a hard realization. "But I don't have any money."

"Money?" The black man pointed back at the fish drying on the trees. "Aaron, my brother of little faith. The Lord says that he will give us everything we need and more so that we may freely give to others. If you will allow me, I will purchase your ticket. It will be my honor."

• • •

The two arrived at the railroad tracks by midmorning. François looked up at the sun and then down the tracks. "If the train is on time, which is not always certain, it should be here in about two hours. While we wait, I want to show you something extraordinary."

Aaron followed the black man across the tracks and into another part of the jungle. The trail climbed gently up a mountain slope until they arrived at the edge of a large clearing. François crouched and signaled for Aaron to do the same.

"They are here," François whispered.

"Who?"

"Just be quiet a moment. Listen, and no matter what happens, don't move a muscle. Do you understand?"

Aaron nodded, sat down, and listened.

After a few moments, he could hear rustling in the deep grass. Someone, or something, was moving toward them. He looked at François, but François kept his eyes on the clearing. The sounds grew nearer, and Aaron could see the tops of the grass moving. He felt beads of sweat break out on his forehead as his heart began to race. *What could it be?*

As the sounds grew closer and closer, Aaron held his breath. It was all he could do to keep from fleeing into the protection of the jungle, but his natural curiosity and his trust in François kept him steady.

At that moment, a tiny pair of wrinkled, stubby black hands reached out of the tall grass and separated the tall fronds. Aaron gasped as a tiny furry black head peered out and stared at him. Then a baby gorilla stepped out of the grass, only a few feet from Aaron. Smiling, Aaron looked at François, who was also smiling.

"His name is Mubagu. At least, that's what I call him," François whispered. "He's only a couple months old, but don't move. His mother is likely to be very close. Whatever you do, don't move a muscle."

At that moment, a very large gorilla sprang out of the tall grass and ran full speed toward them. Aaron froze with fear as the massive gorilla came at them like a freight train.

"Lord," Aaron whispered.

Then, at the last possible second, the beast slid to a halt and sat down directly in front of François. The hair on its back was thick and dark gray, while its head hair was a dark red. Its chest looked like shiny leather.

"Hello, Mama," François said, his head remaining bowed, a sign to her of his submission.

The gorilla placed a hand on his head and shook it.

François laughed.

The gorilla turned to Aaron. He looked up at the massive creature, which tilted her head down to look back at him. She reached out her hand and gently rubbed his arm. He thought it might be a gorilla ritual of some sort until he realized that she was caressing the bites on his arm. With a pang of sadness, he thought of his own mother.

The gorilla suddenly jerked her head up, as if listening to the air. She then stood and turned, inhaling deeply.

"She smells something," François whispered.

The gorilla grunted, took the hand of her baby, and the two of them ran into the deep grass.

"Come quickly," François whispered. He stood and ran into the jungle. Aaron followed as quietly as he could. When they were safely in the jungle, François stopped and looked behind them.

"What is it, François?"

"The mother sensed a danger. Someone—or something—must be coming up the other side of the clearing."

Aaron thought of the poachers he'd met the night before and wondered if that was how they caught their prey.

François turned and silently led Aaron down the mountain toward the tracks. He then reached into his pocket and pulled out a money clip. Carefully counting out the bills, he handed several to Aaron.

"Here, my little brother. This should take care of the cost of the ticket and a meal on the train, if they are serving. But don't eat any meat you can't identify," François said, chuckling. "Be sure to let the conductor know where you are going. They will stop the train to let you off at the convent. It is on the outskirts of the city."

"Thank you, François."

"I must leave you and get back to my boat before someone borrows it. Before I leave you, I'd like to pray for you."

"Okay."

François laid his hands on Aaron's head and began, "Our dearest heavenly Father . . ."

François reluctantly left the boy by the railroad tracks, certain that the train would come soon.

As he made his way back to the river, he felt a great satisfaction for the gift of this morning and its guest—almost deliriously so. A strange smell of flowers seemed to envelop him.

Back at the river, he prepared his boat for the next part of his journey. Packing his fish, he thought of Jesus and the Disciples, simple fishermen like himself, living off nature, God's own provision. Where else could he meet such interesting people? God often brought them to him, and he relished the chance to minister to them in some way.

He stopped at the bow of the boat for a moment, a momentary dizziness coming upon him. He shook it off.

He thought he heard a train whistle in the distance. *Ah, thanks be to God. The sisters will care for that dear orphan. What a tragedy for him to have endured in Mitzic. If all of what the boy said was true, then it is little wonder he believed the Apocalypse had come.*

François began to push his boat back into the water, and then suddenly stopped. *The fragrance of the jungle is strong this morning,* he thought. It was so potent that he lifted his head to take a deep breath, wondering why it would be so strong so suddenly. *Amazing bouquet.*

He quickly slapped his forearm, a well-practiced habit of killing the mosquitoes when they first landed on his skin, before they could bite him and spread their diseases.

He looked at his arm and was surprised to see not a squashed mosquito but a number of blood-filled blisters. He held his arm up and looked at it curiously. *What is this? What could this be?* His other arm was covered with the same grotesque sores. *Where did these come from?*

There was only a moment for him to think of the gorillas in the tall grass, the boy by the railway tracks, and the Apocalypse, which promised a time of pestilence and death, before a convulsion wracked his body.

François stumbled against the boat before falling into the water, thrashing and writhing until his last breath.

CHAPTER FIFTY-ONE

NORA DIDN'T WANT TO believe that Georgina was a member of Return to Earth, but she also didn't want to take any risks. She couldn't have her attend the noon briefing, but knew excluding her would draw attention, so she also excused Henry on the pretense that she wanted them both to check and double-check the samples, looking for any mutations, aberrations, or unusual traits in the DNA and virus.

Nora could see in Henry's eyes that he recognized it as mere "busy work" but was too loyal and discreet to say so.

She now sat at the conference table in a large room at the back of the Rose and Crown. She sipped a cup of coffee, harsh and bitter stuff, which had probably been sitting in the canister since breakfast.

Digger buzzed around her, setting up the equipment for the videoconference.

Somewhere outside, a loud *ka-boom* echoed through the valley. Nora and Digger looked at each other.

"That can't be good," Digger said.

Nora dismissed the sound and studied her notes for several minutes. Then she stood up and paced the room, looking at it fully for the first time. The walls were covered with dark paneling and framed oil paintings of the English countryside, horses, sheep, and pastoral villages. Three leaded windows adorned the far wall, with outside covering provided by thick tree branches in need of pruning. A large bulky wooden dining table with matching chairs dominated the center of the room.

Digger sat down at one end of the table, banging the keys of a poor, abused laptop. A projector threw dull light onto a screen behind him. He alternately swore at the laptop and then glanced at the screen. Then, four white boxes appeared. A few more keystrokes and the box in the upper left-hand side of the screen presented Mac, sitting at a desk.

Nora leaned onto the table. Digger turned his laptop around so its internal camera would capture her for the four teams gathered elsewhere.

"Smile for the camera," Digger said before coming around the table and sitting across from her.

"Good morning, TSI," Mac said.

"It isn't all of us," Nora said. "Just me and Digger."

"Understood," Mac said. "I've got General Mosley and Dr. Susan Hutchinson on the line from Brazzaville. Dr. Jim Dillard and some of his colleagues at USAMRIID"—which he called U S Am Rid—"and we've got Dr. Vicki Prentice and some of her team from the Laboratory of Molecular Biology in Cambridge too. I think you've worked with that lab, Nora."

"I have. It's one of the best medical research labs in Great Britain, if not Europe." She also knew Dr. Dillard, who was the director of the U.S. Army Medical Research Institute of Infectious Diseases—USAMRIID—as they had worked together on a number of projects.

"Unless there's something you need to tell me confidentially, I'll bring them on," Mac said, and then paused. "Anything I need to know?"

Apart from possibly having a spy in our midst and Mark chasing ghosts . . . no, not a thing. Nora thought it, but said, "We're ready."

"Okay, let's get on with this." Mac leaned out of the camera's view for a moment, a few clicks of the mouse, and then the three remaining screens filled up with all the people he had mentioned. It struck Nora how haggard the general looked. And Susan Hutchinson, whom she knew from other projects, appeared sallow cheeked and dark eyed. Little wonder.

"I'll forgo introductions so we can get to the heart of the matter. General, may we start with you?"

Mosley positioned himself in front of the camera. "Yes." He

cleared his throat, "We are keeping the government in Gabon and of the surrounding countries fully informed. The officials in Gabon have given us their complete cooperation. In the meantime, the president and the Joint Chiefs of Staff in the U.S. have been notified and are receiving daily updates from me. In fact, I'll be talking to the president as soon as I'm off this call. He understands the implications should this virus break free of the region. He has made all available research and military resources accessible to us at a moment's notice." He glanced away from the camera and then said, "That's it from me. Susan?"

Susan leaned into the camera. "Good morning everyone. We have some good news and bad news. The bad news first. The boy we believe is carrying the disease has not been found yet. We have only his trail—which, sadly, is a growing registry of victims." She glanced toward the general and then continued. "Fortunately, we've had no outbreaks in areas outside the region, but that could change at any time. We have cause to believe he is headed for the capital city of Libreville, which has over seven hundred thousand people. If he gets there, well . . . Anyway, we're doing all we can to find the boy, but in a way to avoid mass hysteria."

Nora appreciated the effort, but couldn't help but wonder if they were misjudging the "masses" and might save more lives if they spelled out to the public what was going on.

Susan paused to look at her notes and then looked back at the camera. "We've also positively identified the virus. It is indeed Ebola and it appears to be an extremely potent strain, perhaps the most potent we've ever seen or heard about. Infection to death takes only hours, sometimes less, and it spreads very easily and quickly, even via air."

"Dr. Hutchinson," Digger called out to the small microphone. "Have you typed it?"

Susan nodded. "We have and it appears to be a new strain. We're tentatively calling it the Gabon Ebola virus. We'll get the genetic information of the virus to each of you via e-mail this afternoon." She paused and then said, "Jim? You have something else about the boy, I believe."

Mac, playing moderator, drew attention to Dr. Jim Dillard. "Dr. Dillard? Thanks for getting up so early on our behalf."

After a slight pause for the words to transmit several thousand miles, Jim said, "Happy to help, Colonel MacLayton. We have some information about our vector." He paused, then added awkwardly, "I mean, Aaron."

Nora watched the screen projecting General Mosley's image. He tilted his head only slightly, but his eyes reflected his intense interest.

Jim continued, "With the help of General Mosley, we were able to obtain the family's medical records. There we learned that Aaron's parents banked his umbilical-cord blood at birth and were paying a facility to have the sample maintained."

"Isn't that a little weird?" Digger asked. "It seems awfully trendy for a missionary type."

Mosley leaned into the camera. "Maybe so, but the boy's parents, David and Rachel, had altruistic reasons. Apparently, a member of their congregation suffered from leukemia and, based on advice from their doctor, David believed that the stem cells of Aaron's cord blood could be used to help fight the disease. Their church put up the money to have it stored. And, as sometimes happens, it was forgotten—a bill that somebody paid without asking about it. I only just learned of it yesterday."

Nora quickly scribbled a note to Digger and pushed it over as Mosley spoke: *Aaron is the general's grandson.*

Digger looked at the note, then Nora, and made as if to slap his forehead with the palm of his hand.

"How does this information help us?" Nora asked Jim.

Jim replied, "Because of that find, we were able to obtain and test some of Aaron's cord blood. We discovered that he inherited the Delta 32 gene from *both* of his parents."

"Is that a good thing?" Mac asked.

"Our research indicates that people who inherit a double whammy—one gene from the mother and one from the father—are far more protected from viruses like HIV and Ebola."

"Is 'double whammy' a scientific term?" Digger asked.

Jim chuckled, but pressed on. "I believe Dr. Prentice has new information that will affect our tests. But, to put it simply, we think this may be why Aaron has survived the virus in his system."

"Will he survive indefinitely?" Nora asked.

"Indefinitely?" Jim asked.

"Will the gene keep him from dying?" Nora clarified. She hated to ask the question in Mosley's presence.

Jim hesitated. General Mosley leaned into the camera again and said, "Probably not."

Jim nodded. "Unfortunately, with an infectious agent this virulent, it will likely overcome his genetic protection. Unless we find him and provide a treatment . . ." He didn't finish his sentence.

The general sat back, but remained on camera. "Look, folks, I don't want anyone walking on eggshells around me because of this. We have to keep our information objective and our jobs on task."

"With that in mind," Mac said, "let's get Dr. Prentice into this conversation."

An exotic-looking woman of Indian descent with long, wavy black hair, olive skin, and large, penetrating eyes appeared in the camera. "Good afternoon."

Digger groaned and said under his breath, "That's simply wrong. An expert in molecular and genetic biology shouldn't be allowed to look like that."

"Good afternoon." Dr. Prentice spoke in an impeccable British accent. "We received the samples and information that each team provided, the most recent coming from Eyam early this morning. Initially, it looked as though the samples yielded nothing new. In fact, it appeared to us that the Delta 32 gene mutation hypothesis was a dead end."

Nora asked, "Can you elaborate on that, Dr. Prentice?"

"As was true for our NIH colleagues, we could only identify the mutation in about fourteen percent of the descendants of the Eyam epidemic and that included the samples taken by the NIH a few years ago. The more recent samples you provided seemed to follow that same pattern."

"What about the Gabon samples?" Digger asked.

"The mutation did not occur in any of the victims in Africa. They had no natural protection at all against such a powerful virus."

Digger said, "Meaning that if the Delta 32 mutation really had prevented the Eyam infection in the survivors, it should have been found in more of the survivors and their descendants."

"Correct," Dr. Prentice said. "However, we may have found something else." Dr. Prentice gestured to someone off camera. "This is Dr. Sharon Donaldson. I'd like to ask her to explain."

A short and rather plump scientist stepped to the center of the screen. She wore large glasses and looked scholarly in a bland and stringy-haired way.

"That's what a lady scientist should look like," Digger said.

Nora scowled and threw a pencil at him.

Dr. Donaldson said, "The Delta 32 mutation occurs in a particular gene called CCR5. The effect of the mutation is to block viral infections like HIV and Ebola, and bacterial infections like *Yersinia*. We looked at this gene in all of the samples and made a surprising discovery." She paused a second—either to collect her thoughts or to add drama to the meeting, Nora wasn't sure—then continued, "There's another mutation associated with the CCR5 gene. It's called the m303 mutation. We found it in nearly all the specimens of the Eyam survivors."

"Ancient and recent?" Nora asked.

"Yes. We found this mutation in all of the Eyam survivors and in almost all of their descendants. We didn't find it in a single person who died in Africa. It looks as though this may be a clue for finding a treatment, if not a cure, for our modern Gabon plague."

"And," Dr. Prentice added, stepping back into view, "we found no *Yersinia pestis* particles in any of the ancient Eyam specimens from plague victims."

Surprised, Nora and Digger looked at each other. Before they could speak, Mac jumped in. "You'll have to spell it out for the layman here. What does it mean that you found no *Yersinia pestis* particles in the Eyam villagers?"

Dr. Prentice looked puzzled for a moment, as if the question was too obvious to not understand. "Well, it means that the Eyam deaths in the seventeenth century were not from the Black Plague."

"Then what was it?" Mac asked.

"See for yourself," she said and produced electron-micrograph pictures from the Eyam specimens. Next to those were pictures of the Ebola specimens from Gabon.

They're the same. Nora was astonished. She could hear a gasp from her colleagues in other parts of the world.

"Yes," Dr. Prentice said. "As you can see, they are a near match."

"Well, well, well," Mac said, then addressed Nora and Digger, "looks like the pressure just increased for your team."

"Pressure? What pressure?" Digger asked.

"What do you need from us?" Nora asked.

Dr. Prentice responded, "We need tissue from someone exposed to the Eyam Ebola virus . . ."

"Haven't we given you enough already?" Digger said.

"We need samples from a survivor and samples that are better preserved," Dr. Prentice explained. "Ideally, if we could get the blood-storing organs, say the spleen or blood marrow, from someone who survived at least a year after being exposed to the Eyam Ebola outbreak, then we could perform rapid tissue culture growth of their cells and test them against the Gabon Ebola virus and some of the medications we're developing. It's the only way we can think of to beat this thing. Any possibility of finding that for us?"

Mac looked skeptical. "You're asking for a nearly perfect corpse, preserved for over three hundred years?"

"Essentially, yes. I know it's virtually impossible."

"Is it, Nora?" Mac asked.

Nora looked at Digger, then the camera. "It'll be like looking for a blue needle in a black haystack, but we'll do our best."

Jim smiled. "I have no idea what that means, but if you found such a superspecimen we could quickly test for possible treatments among several experimental medications we already have here at USAMRIID. Then, if the experiment worked, we could get emergency approval to use these medications on the missing boy—*if* he's ever found. Then we'll use it on future victims. Again, this is contingent on finding a perfectly preserved corpse."

"We have some leads," Nora explained. "In fact, that's where Mark—I mean, Dr. Carlson—is at this very moment."

CHAPTER FIFTY-TWO

MARK REACHED THE SCENE first. The explosion was in the area that had been marked on the old map, hidden in a thick part of the woods about a quarter of a mile from the road that followed the top of the ridge. A few hikers and tourists were gathered around the mouth of a cave now completely obstructed by fallen rock and debris. At a glance, Mark could see that trees and vines nicely covered the cave itself. Few would have found it unless they knew exactly where to look.

"Did anyone see what happened?" Andrew called out to the crowd.

"I was walking past, just up the road," said a young American in hiking clothes. He held a cloth to his forehead, and then pulled it away to reveal a small gash. "Then there was this humongous explosion, which threw rocks and stones all over the place. One nicked me, and I think there was a van pulling away—it got hit in the rear window."

"A van?" Mark asked. "Can you describe it?"

"A commercial van, I think," he said, "but I don't know what make or what company it belonged to. It was green."

Return to Earth, Mark thought.

Andrew was on his cell phone, calling the police and the fire brigade.

"These old mining caves occasionally blow up," said an older woman in a thick northern accent. "For no apparent reason."

Mark carefully moved closer, suspicious that Return to Earth may have set a second device, if only to indiscriminately hurt passersby and onlookers.

"I wouldn't go any closer, sir," Jankowski said.

Mark stopped where he was. "Yep, the view is fine from here," he said. He looked at the rocks and stones on the ground. A large chunk in the shape of an archway was blown several yards from the mouth of the cave. Mark knelt to examine it. The Lumen Christi symbol was evident.

Andrew joined him. "You won't get into that cave, if that's what you're thinking. It'll take weeks to dig it out."

"I don't have weeks," Mark said.

He sat down on the fallen archway. *What are we expected to do now?*

"I wonder if it destroyed the Cathedral," Andrew asked absently.

"I suppose that depends on how far in it was." Mark stood up and kicked at a stone. "It's hopeless."

"I wonder," Andrew said.

Mark looked up at him.

"I suggest we return to the rectory. Two pairs of eyes on those old documents are better than one. Maybe there are other clues, other ways in."

Sirens wailed in the distance.

"I think our search for the Blue Monk is over," Mark announced to Nora on his cell phone. He was trudging back down the various paths toward the vicar's rectory.

"What?" Nora asked, surprisingly alarmed. "Why?"

He explained to her about the dug-up burial site and the explosion at the cave.

"I heard that explosion," she said. "No one was hurt, right? Are you okay?"

"We're all fine, but we're going to have to come up with another scheme."

"But there isn't another scheme," Nora said. "I've just come off the conference call with the various teams. They need the superspecimen—they're holding out for us to deliver the Blue Monk somehow."

"Wait a minute. How did we go from denying we saw him to full-blown acceptance?"

"I have confidence in you."

"Well, you better pray to whatever saint your church has in charge of lost monks because we're going to need all the help we can get."

"I'll mention it to all of them," she said. "What are you going to do?"

"Andrew and I are going back to the rectory to see if there are any other clues in his archives though I can't imagine the point."

"Is there anything we can do?"

"Yeah, find out who our mole is. Somebody knew about that burial site and the reverend's map. I'll buy into the idea that you were followed, but the map puts things a little closer to home. Either Ahaz or Return to Earth is paying somebody on our team."

There was a pause, then, "I'll check into it."

After hanging up from Mark, Nora immediately dialed Mac.

He snapped up his cell phone with a terse, "What?"

"Destroyed burial sites and blown-up caves, that's what," Nora replied. "I want permission to interrogate Georgina."

Mac paused. "Let me send in a professional."

"Do that if you want, but I'm going to talk to her now." She realized her hand was tightly wrapped around the cell phone. Snapping it in two would have been easy.

"If you insist, but make sure one of your bodyguards is around."

"I will," she said, "and I suggest you go back to Ahaz to make sure they're not still jerking us around."

"They promised they wouldn't."

"This is Ahaz we're talking about, right?"

Mac sighed. "You're right. I'll call them."

"Tell me you're not involved," Mac barked to Peter Romero at Ahaz Pharmaceuticals. They were on their computers using the secured video-communications link.

Peter Romero was a strikingly handsome man with dark skin, thick moustache, and perfectly coiffed hair. His gaze exuded warmth and trust, which his actions often betrayed. "I can assure you, Colonel, that whatever is happening in Eyam has nothing to do with us. Losing Nathan Dodge was a terrible and tragic blow. We left, just as I told you."

Mac paused. "If it proves otherwise . . ."

Romero smiled. "You're not resorting to threats, are you?"

Mac was, but realized he had little ammunition to back them up.

"Besides," Romero said, "we've withdrawn our operations to allow your team to do what they do best. And, of course, I'm counting on you to keep us thoroughly informed on every detail."

"Right."

"*Every* detail, Colonel," Romero said.

The screen went blank.

"Sure," Mac said to no one. "I'm reassured now."

CHAPTER FIFTY-THREE

NORA, WITH CORPORAL BRAINERD following, walked to the top floor of the Rose and Crown where the lab equipment had been set up. Georgina was hunched over a microscope. Digger and Henry were at a small desk looking intensely at imaging on the computer monitor. They clicked back and forth between images that for the most part looked identical— looking for minute differences. Nora's arrival caused all three to look up, like grazing deer that have heard a shotgun blast.

"Georgina?"

"Uh-huh?"

"I need to talk to you," Nora said.

"Oh, you're in trouble now," Digger teased, his eyes back to the computer screen.

Georgina followed Nora back into the outer hall, looking first at the bodyguard, then Nora, then down at the briefcase in Nora's hand. "Is something wrong?"

"Let's talk in your room."

They descended the stairs one floor to their individual rooms. Georgina unlocked her door and they stepped in. The room was similar to Nora's: a double bed, large wardrobe, small TV, and writing desk. A laptop sat open on the desk.

"Am I in trouble?" Georgina asked, now looking worried. She sat down on the edge of the bed, her hands tucked between her knees like a little girl. The bodyguard followed Nora into the room, closed the door, and leaned back against it, his arms crossed over his chest.

Nora suddenly had her doubts. Georgina was a bit wild, a bit flakey—the kind of woman who would name her children things like Bran and Tofu—but a spy for an environmental terrorist group? It didn't line up. But Nora knew what she knew and had to follow up.

"Tell me about Return to Earth," Nora said.

"The radical group?" Georgina asked, her brow bunched between her eyes. "You know more than I do."

"But you have heard of them before?"

"Sure, via RSS news feeds."

"Not at a rally?"

"Rally?"

"You know, a rally—as in a protest—as in a protest in London. Surely you haven't been to that many."

Georgina eyed her warily. "Nora, what are you asking me?"

Nora pulled a photo from the briefcase. "Look familiar?"

Georgina took the photo. Her eyes went wide, and the color drained from her face. "Where did you get this?"

"Never mind that," Nora said. "What are you doing in that photo?"

"I don't know."

"You're holding a placard and you don't know it?"

"I was on Oxford Street in London. Shopping with . . . a friend. A protest was parading down the street, blocking traffic. We thought it was fascinating, all those people marching down the street like that. We went to the curb to look, and someone shoved a placard in my hand. I waved it up and down, just to be silly, and handed it back. That was all."

"It was that innocent?"

"Yes!"

"Who was the friend?"

"I don't remember."

"Couldn't have been much of a friend."

"We had only met the day before. He was in London for a layover and . . . well . . ."

"You became his layover."

"There's no point in being nasty."

"I have to be nasty, Georgina. Right now you're a suspect."

"A suspect for what?"

"For being a mole for Return to Earth. This photo links you to them. That's you holding a Return to Earth placard at a major protest in London. It turned violent. Shop windows were smashed. Thirteen people were hospitalized. Sixty-two people were arrested."

"Come on. Be serious."

Nora leaned toward her. "Mark was kidnapped and they nearly killed him yesterday. A man from Ahaz was tortured and murdered by them. I couldn't be more serious."

"I'm not one of them, not then, not now. I'm telling you, I was shopping." She shook her head, her eyes getting misty. "Do you really think I'd betray our team?"

"I don't know, Georgina. I don't know what to think. These people are apparently ruthless. For all I know, you are too. This could be a great act."

"Then it's a lifelong act," Georgina said, her voice taking on a girlish whine. "This is *me*, Nora. You know me."

"It would help to get your layover's name."

She thought for a moment. "It was Steven. No—Stefan. He was from Russia or something like that."

"Were you working for the government then?"

"Yes. The NIH."

"Did you tell him that?"

"I don't know. I really don't remember."

"Did he tell you what he did for a living?"

"I got the impression he was a doctor, but I don't know why I thought that."

"Maybe the way you played doctor . . ."

"Don't be so self-righteous."

"I can afford to be. My job isn't on the line because of poor choices in one-night stands."

"Oh, and you make *good* choices?" Georgina retaliated.

Nora wouldn't be diverted. "Where did you meet him?"

"At a pub. He came up to me and started talking. He was nice. Personable, but intense—very serious in that Russian way."

"Be more specific."

"I don't know . . ." She groaned, then thought about it.

"He didn't like my being silly very much, especially at the protest."

"What do you mean?"

"He was annoyed that I took the placard and got into the crowd. He yanked me back, probably right after the photo was taken."

"Is he in the photo?"

She looked, and then pointed to a blurred profile right behind her. "I think that's him."

Nora looked closely, but couldn't make out the features of the man's face. Nora then wondered if Inspector Duerr had photos of any Return to Earth suspects. "If you saw a photo of him, would you remember him?"

"You mean, like, mug shots? Is he wanted for something?"

"I don't know," Nora said. "I'm considering all the angles—as though I believe you."

"You have to believe me, Nora. I'm no spy." Then she hesitated as if a thought had occurred to her. "Wait a sec. I might have a picture of him." She stood and walked toward the desk.

"Here?"

Georgina opened her laptop computer, then her fingers whirred across the keyboard.

"I keep files of personal photos on this thing, and I think . . ." She navigated to one file, then another. "Here it is."

She hit a button and a collection of thumbnails appeared on the screen. Many of them were the usual tourist shots: Big Ben, Parliament, Tower of London, mixed in with Georgina in close-up with various traveling companions. It looked to Nora like an endless party.

"Got it!" She opened one of the photos.

Nora stepped closer and studied the image. Georgina was very close to the camera, mugging with a contorted expression.

"That's me," she said, as if she needed to. "I took this in my hotel room with the internal camera on the laptop, and that's him." She pointed to a figure sitting on the bed in the background. From the coloring on his face, he seemed to be looking intently at a television off to the right. The light gave a clear view of his facial features: strong profile, hard chin, handsome face. He appeared to be naked.

"He didn't know you took this," Nora said.

"No." Another flash of memory seemed to come to her. "Now that I think of it, he didn't want me to take any photos of him. I assumed he was married or something."

Nora held back her disgust at Georgina's cavalier attitude about such sacred things. "What was he watching on television?" Nora asked.

"Probably the news. It seemed like he had it on constantly. Not an aphrodisiac for me, if you know what I mean."

"Was this photo taken before or after the rally?"

"Before, I think. He left me right after we visited Oxford Street."

"Whose idea was it to go to Oxford Street?"

"His. I never would've thought of it. This was my first time to London and I didn't know Oxford Street was such a big shopping deal."

"So he would have known the rally was going on."

"Maybe." Georgina looked at Nora carefully. "You're a very suspicious woman."

"I'm considering how your whole encounter may have been a setup. Didn't they train you about that?"

"I was doing routine lab work for the NIH—nothing top secret. Why would anyone bother with me?"

"If I know the drill, groups like this get as many early recruits as possible. Then, as they rise through the ranks, they can provide more information. Did you give him your personal information?"

"My home e-mail address."

"Did he ever contact you again?"

"Once or twice, just to say hello."

"Would you still have his e-mail address?"

"Yes," she said, then corrected herself, "No. The last time I wrote to him, his address kicked back as undeliverable."

"How long ago was that?"

"A couple of years ago. I don't remember."

"Why would he contact you, then give you a bad e-mail address?"

"I wondered the same thing at the time. He said he was going to be in D.C. and wanted to have dinner."

"But that didn't happen."

"No. It's strange. When I wrote back to him, I copied it to my work address, just to remind myself not to work late that night."

"Your e-mail address at the NIH?"

"Yeah. He wrote back once more to say that his plans had changed. When I wrote to him, the address kicked back."

He got spooked by the government e-mail address. They're monitored; addresses that can be traced. "A very cautious fellow," Nora said, and then gestured to the screen. "E-mail me that photo."

"I'll do it now." Again, Georgina went over the keys with lightning speed. "Do you really think he was tied to Return to Earth?"

"I don't know. Maybe the whole encounter was nothing, but I have to follow all the leads, to determine your guilt or innocence."

"That would be innocence."

"Meanwhile, you're under house arrest."

"What? No way!"

"Consider yourself lucky. I could throw you to MI5 or Interpol for a real interrogation."

"But my work . . ."

"I can't let you near any of our data or equipment, and your wireless connection will be cut off too." Nora held out her hand. "Cell phone, iPod, and computer, please."

"That's not fair!" She protested but relinquished the equipment.

Nora handed the electronics to Corporal Brainerd, with the exception of the cell phone, which she opened. She scrolled through the called numbers. "You made a call this morning right after our meeting. To whom?"

Georgina lowered her head and bit her lip.

A low and threatening tone. "Georgina."

"It's funny, but this is why I thought I was in trouble."

"Why?" Nora tapped the screen. "You called a local number. Who was it?"

She pursed her lips, then said, "It's the gardener—Philip."

"Why did you call him?"

Georgina hung her head.

"Oh, no. Not another one-night stand?"

Georgina looked up. "No!"

"Then what?"

"I went to the Miners' Arms with him—and Jankowski—last night. I felt so bad about what happened to the poor man that . . . I promised I'd let him know of any other happenings around the church, so he wouldn't be taken by surprise again."

Nora glowered at her. "You didn't."

"I'm sorry. I felt so sorry for him."

"You're a walking sieve of security, do you know that?" Nora said as she went to the door.

"You're locking me in?"

"Corporal Brainerd will be on guard outside."

"Brainerd?" Georgina frowned at the soldier and then looked up at Nora. "Why the short one with the broken nose? I want Jankowski."

Nora and the soldier turned to leave the room. As she pulled the door shut behind her, Nora whispered, "Watch her like a hawk."

Back in her room, Nora sat at her computer and took a deep breath. Her hands were shaking. Playing the tough interrogator didn't come easily for her, but she had to smile: her entire performance was based on the example of Sister Mary Alice, one of the nuns at the convent school Nora had attended. Sister Mary Alice was a master when it came to finding out which girl had done what naughty thing.

Nora went to her e-mails and retrieved the photo from Georgina. She then sent it with a cover note to Mac, using the address from Mac's original e-mail to copy that Inspector at Interpol. Hopefully, they could work their magic with the photo and figure out who this guy was.

Nora realized that the entire incident could have been coincidental, but as a practice Nora didn't believe in coincidences. With her belief in a God who was involved in every detail of every life at every second, coincidences simply didn't fit into the scheme of possibilities.

But she hoped for Georgina's sake that the girl was telling the truth.

CHAPTER FIFTY-FOUR

"I KNOW IT'S HERE somewhere," Reverend Andrew said and rifled through one stack of books and file of papers, then another.

Mark flipped through a yellow-leafed book, once bound in leather, but now crumbling. Flakes of the spine spilled onto the table. The book was part of a collection of archives held in private storage by the various rectors of the church. Mark realized that by "archives," they meant a hodgepodge of junk in boxes.

"Have you ever thought of cataloging this stuff?" Mark asked.

"Who has time?"

Mark looked over at the eight file boxes stuffed with papers, not to mention the assortment covering the dining room table. "We don't," he said.

Andrew looked up at him. "Right. Sorry. A fair point. I'm looking for a small sheaf of papers from one of my predecessors. Reverend Wright, I'm sure it was. He did his own little investigation of the Blue Monk legend back in the 1950s and scribbled out a list of the facts as he could discern them. You'll know the papers by his scrawl at the top: his name in large letters.

Mark began sorting through the material spread in front of him. There were diaries, account ledgers, letters, memos, church bulletins, and announcements; an endless array of the minutiae of parish history.

Jankowski sat off to the side drinking coffee from an oversized mug. He watched them with an amused expression.

"You could help, you know," Mark said.

"I'm here to make sure you don't get paper cuts, sir."

Mark growled, and then pushed aside another ledger. His hand fell on a small stack of sheets that were marked in the scrawl the reverend had mentioned—long cursive letters that spelled "Wright." "Here!"

"Excellent!"

Andrew circled the table to look as Mark spread the pages on the table. In the upper left-hand corner of each page was written *Monk Sightings*.

The pages looked like an inventory with single-sentence lines, but the handwriting was small and in such a style that Mark had trouble making out its meaning.

"I'm already lost," Mark said.

"It's not easy to read," Andrew agreed, "but I assumed as a doctor you'd have plenty of practice with illegible scrawls."

"Very funny."

"Let's see . . ." Andrew adjusted his glasses and peered at the pages, moving from one to another and back again. "Some of these are various sightings of the monk: behind a barn, in the middle of a field in moonlight, that sort of thing."

"Does he have anything about the monk when the monk was actually alive?" Mark asked.

Andrew studied the pages further and then slid one aside and discovered another beneath it. "This is the one we want. Apparently Wright is quoting from a letter by Mompesson, chronicling the rumors and gossip about the monk, and I quote: 'Though his appearance be most disturbing, his comforts and consolations hath ministered to the sick . . .'"

Andrew mumbled through a few lines that he must not have found very interesting, then resumed. "'The superstitious speak with consistency of extraordinary appearances and disappearances in the church graveyard. Rebekah Smythe spoke privately to me of following the monk to the graveyard whereupon he vanished before her very eyes in a manner defying nature. Alas, the girl was received unto the Lord shortly after, and before I could discern the facts of her astounding encounter . . .'"

The reverend scanned the pages. "More of the same, I think."

Mark rubbed his chin. "If I heard right, the monk seemed to appear and disappear in the graveyard."

"So it would seem."

"Through the tomb with the symbols?" Mark asked.

"That would be my guess." His gaze fell onto a page that had slid off to the side. He picked it up. "Here are those words again: 'The monk became a scandal to the village after which no one spoke of him except in hushed and somber whispers.' And: 'According to Elizabeth Somers, the oldest member of the parish, the years of poverty were attributed to the curse of the monk, following the scandal which removed him from us.'"

"What scandal and curse?" Mark asked. "What did he do to them?"

Andrew shook his head. "I'll keep digging."

Mark stretched, his muscles still aching from yesterday's encounter with Return to Earth and worsened by the hike today. "I want to have another look at that tomb."

Jankowski stood with his mug.

"Finish your coffee," Mark said, waving him down. "Return to Earth is too busy blowing things up to worry about me."

"There's a comforting thought," the reverend said.

Jankowski sat down again.

Mark stepped out of the rear door of the rectory, crossed the small parking area outside the garage, and walked to the gate. He passed through and headed toward the tomb. Farther up the driveway, near the church center, he saw Joan and Philip. They seemed to be in an animated conversation, but speaking in hushed tones. Actually, it looked as if it was an argument of some sort. Mark didn't want to embarrass them or himself, so he diverted his gaze toward the tomb. He continued on, and when he reached it, he looked over at Joan and Philip again. They were gone. He wondered what they could possibly have to argue about—the altar flowers? The weeds on the edge of the church? Something more sinister?

A moment later, a car started up, and Joan quickly drove past him to the main road. She didn't look in his direction as she passed, which seemed unlike her.

Mark turned his attention to the tomb. It looked as it had earlier in the day: pockmarked, old, moss stained, and, strangely, unidentified. Who was buried here? He had forgotten to ask the reverend if there was any sort of church register identifying all of the graves.

He paced around the tomb twice, inspecting the Lumen Christi symbols and hoping to see something, anything, new. He knelt for a closer look at the base. He realized that, when crouching, the tomb was taller than he was.

He stood up and smiled as his mind went to the magic shows he had seen as a boy: a large rectangular box with a false side into which the magician or his assistant could slip, easily disappearing from the view of the audience.

Mark's smile broadened, and he laughed. It seemed so obvious that he wondered why they hadn't thought of it sooner.

"Hocus-pocus," he said and began to push on the walls of the tomb. The right push on the right panel, perhaps a lever of some sort or a secret latch to lift . . . any one of them might open the tomb, if he could find it.

Jankowski approached and gazed at Mark for a moment. "Sir?"

"Help me," Mark said.

"Help you with what, sir?"

"I need you to go back to the Rose and Crown and get the equipment we used last night. Digger will know. Bring it back to me. I'm going to have a look inside of this. Better yet, I want to *get* inside."

"You want to break into the tomb?"

"It's not a tomb," Mark said. "It's a doorway."

CHAPTER FIFTY-FIVE

INSPECTOR MARTIN DUERR SAT in his office in Lyon, France, sipping coffee that tasted more like the disposable cup than anything resembling coffee.

He gazed at the blinds covering his window. They were lopsided, pulled up too far on one side and not enough on the other. The window was old, smeared. A pigeon pecked around on the ledge outside. *This is a dismal office,* he thought. No wonder he preferred to travel.

He turned to his computer and clicked on the e-mail symbol. Several popped up, mostly internal bureaucratic stuff. One came from an American government system, so he clicked on it. Nora Richards. Did he know Nora Richards? Then he realized it was connected to the photo he'd sent to General Mosley earlier. That Georgina woman on one of the Special Ops teams had been photographed at a Return to Earth rally.

The cover note explained the attachment and Georgina's alleged connection to the rally. Duerr was skeptical and wished he had a few minutes with Georgina to talk about it.

He clicked on the attachment to open it up. At first he thought it was a joke—a close-up of a girl making a stupid face at the camera, and then his eyes drifted right, and he saw a naked man in the background sitting on the edge of the bed. Duerr looked closely at the man's face and suddenly leapt up, his coffee spilling down the front of him. He swore in French, again in English just for good measure, and nearly crawled across his desk to look closer at the photo.

It couldn't be. Yet it was.

Dr. Stefan Maier, the founder of the Return to Earth movement.

"This is a miracle," Duerr said. He couldn't take his eyes off the man, then looked again to check his information. According to Nora's cover note, this photo was from July, just five years ago, the day before the big protest in London.

Five years ago!

"Pretty impressive," Duerr said to the photo of Dr. Stefan Maier, "since you were declared dead nine years ago."

There was a knock on his office door.

"Go away," Duerr said. "I'm having a religious experience."

"I'm sorry, sir," a woman's voice said. It was Veronica, an assistant investigator.

"Come in, Ronny. Look at this," Duerr said, beckoning her.

"There's no time," she said, and her tone of voice caused him to turn to face her. "Daniel has sent the signal."

Daniel was Interpol's spy in Return to Earth.

"Which signal?"

"He's been compromised. We have to get him out right away."

"How long ago?"

"Two minutes. It came through the designated line. We've got the GPS coordinates."

"Where is he? Has he moved?"

"No, he's still in Basel, Switzerland."

"And you scrambled the team, yes?"

"Instantly."

He moved for the door. "Get me on the next flight or bullet train to Basel—whatever will get me there the fastest."

"Yes, sir."

Suddenly, he turned and pointed to his computer screen. "And get that photo to the lab. I want them to inspect every pixel of it."

Duerr reached the elevator and punched the button for the ground floor. The drop of the elevator intensified the butterflies in his stomach. He wasn't nervous; he was worried. The signal from Daniel was a last resort for an agent. It meant the choice between a quick escape and death. Duerr hoped they would get to him in time for an escape, but he had a terrible feeling that they wouldn't.

CHAPTER FIFTY-SIX

MARK STOOD GUARD AT the tomb while Jankowski went for the equipment. He fought against an inflated hope that somehow this would take him to the Blue Monk, but he also recognized that the monk's body, if exposed to the elements, would yield very little information that they didn't already have. It truly was a rabbit chase.

Andrew stepped through the gate from the rectory, looked around, spotted Mark, and came his way. "I wondered what happened to you," he said.

"I'm watching over this tomb to make sure no one steals it."

"Is there something worth stealing in it?"

"I hope so."

The reverend arched an eyebrow. "The Blue Monk isn't buried there, if that's what you're thinking."

Mark wasn't surprised, but asked, "How do you know?"

"According to the church register, this tomb belongs to John Templeton, a wealthy landowner from the late sixteenth century."

"So, I'll find John Templeton inside if I look?"

"Actually, no. John Templeton was a member of one of the expeditions to America. The Jamestown colony, I believe. He died there, but his family erected this tomb in memorial to him."

"You seem to have a lot of empty graves in this cemetery."

"A few. Not proportionally more than any other church this old. Graveyards are sometimes used for bodies and sometimes for memories, but not always both." Andrew waited a moment, and then asked, "Well? Why are you waiting here? There's no body to examine."

"Not Templeton's," Mark agreed, "but I didn't expect to find a body anyway."

"And what, exactly, do you expect to find?"

"A passageway."

At that moment, a car turned onto the drive and came up toward them. Jankowski was driving. Digger was in the passenger seat. Henry sat in the back.

"I didn't ask for a party," Mark muttered.

The three exited the car. Jankowski walked toward Mark and rolled his eyes helplessly. Digger and Henry grabbed the equipment and came to the tomb.

"A little help would have been nice," Digger said to Jankowski.

Jankowski, who looked as perturbed as Mark, simply said, "Sorry, sir."

"I do love a treasure hunt," Henry said with a clap and rub of his palms.

"I really didn't need you to come," Mark said.

"Are you kidding?" Digger said. "The B&B has become a very dour place. Our work is useless; Georgina is under house arrest; I'm . . ."

"Georgina is what?" Mark interrupted.

"I guess she had a fling with some guy who was connected to the tree huggers," Digger said as he set up the scope. "Nora has sent her to her room for being a spy."

Henry frowned. "It's absurd, of course. Georgina is no spy."

Mark hardly knew what to make of this development. "I never would have suspected her."

"Photographic evidence," Digger said, touching the side of his nose.

"I would hate to think of the punishments you'd get if we had photos from your past," Henry said to Digger.

"It depends on the country," Digger remarked. "You'd be surprised what's legal in the Netherlands."

"I don't want to know," Henry said.

Mark noticed that Andrew had been listening to all this, his face a bright red.

"Can we drop the banter and get on with it?" Mark said.

"You're ready to go," Digger said, handing him the goggles. "Same drill as last night—no pun intended."

Mark began to put on the goggles, and then turned to Andrew. "Do I have your permission to drill into this tomb?"

"As long as you find a place that isn't terribly noticeable."

Mark pointed to a low edge along the grass line on the broad north side facing away from the church.

"That'll do," Andrew said.

Mark knelt down and began to drill into the stone. It gave way easily, almost like sand against the high-powered instrument. He reached the emptiness on the other side. Looking at the view on the screen with the scope light turned on he could see darkness, then cob webs, and then, as he angled downward a few feet, horizontal slats of rotten wood.

"I think I've come to a coffin," Mark said.

"That would surprise me," Andrew said. "Is there a body?"

Mark drilled through one of the slats. Initially there was darkness, then what looked like vertical beams. "It's not a coffin. I think the slats were for reinforcement of some kind. Or a hatch door. There are beams shoring up the sides of the grave. Was that normal practice?"

"Not that I know of," Andrew said.

"Anyway, I don't see a body or remains." Mark continued downward several feet, following the beams until they reached the bottom into earth.

"You're eight feet down," Digger said, looking at the markings on the scope line.

Mark slowly turned the scope around, searching. The beams were like walls on all four sides of the hole. Then, his original suspicions were validated. "Aha," he said.

"Aha?" Digger asked. "What aha?"

"It's an entryway to a tunnel. On the north side. Maybe three feet high."

"It's a grave with an *escape* hatch?" Henry asked.

"I want one of those," Digger said.

"It's not an escape for the dead," said Mark. "Try this theory: the Lumen Christi Order knew that this tomb was empty and used it as a means to come and go from the village. I'll bet it leads to their hideout."

"Remarkable!" Andrew exclaimed.

"My dear Watson, you're brilliant," Henry said.

"I see oil lamps and wicks on the floor."

"A grave with lights *and* an escape tunnel!" Digger said. "This is getting better all the time."

"But we still don't know how they . . ." Mark let his sentence drift as he brought the scope up again and positioned it to look at the inside of the concrete tomb itself. He fumbled with the dials. "How do I get this blasted thing to go wide-screen?" he asked.

Digger leaned over and turned a small knob. The camera responded, giving Mark a broader view. More cobwebs and roots. He angled the camera to the top of the panel. "They didn't usually put hinges on the walls of the tombs, did they?"

"Not usually," Andrew replied.

"This is so cool. I want a tomb just like this," Digger said.

Henry put a hand on Digger's shoulder. "Sorry, dear boy, but we're going to cremate you and sprinkle your ashes on a pile of cow dung."

Mark continued to search the panel, bringing the scope down from the hinges. Then he saw what he'd hoped for. "There," he said.

"What is it?" Andrew asked.

Mark withdrew the scope and sat back to look at the panel from the outside. "It's crude, but effective," he said and dug into the bag of supplies. He pulled out a can of pressurized air. Leaning forward, he blasted the air onto the Lumen Christi symbol. Years of dirt blew away and the symbol took on greater depth and detail.

"What are you doing?" Henry asked.

"This is the way in," Mark explained. "There's a mechanism on the inside that has to be turned from out here. It releases a latch which, I assume, will let this panel swing up and open." Mark realized that, to the casual observer, there was nothing special about the symbol. But the more he cleared away, the better he could see how the image of the lamb stood out more than the others, by the mere thickness of a fingernail. He put down the can and pressed his fingers against the top of the lamb and his thumb on its underbelly. It was enough to grab on to. He carefully turned the lamb clockwise. Nothing happened. He tried a bit harder—still nothing. Then, he tried to turn it counterclockwise and it gave way, slowly turning with the noise of grit rubbing grit.

"Good heavens!" Andrew exclaimed.

The mechanism groaned and complained as Mark continued to turn it. Finally, there was a loud *click*, and the panel was released, opening a few inches.

"If this leads to the Bat Cave, I'm going to kiss you," Digger said.

"Let's hope not," Henry said.

Mark pushed the panel and it swung upward. Using his shoulder to hold it in place, he reached in, sure that there must be a way to hold the panel open. His fingers brushed against a large piece of rectangular granite. It swiveled around and rested like a shelf under the panel. He carefully pulled back and the panel held.

"It's like a magician's box," Digger said. "The panel swings in and the magician disappears inside, usually to a trap door. Then the panel falls back into place."

"Flashlight?" Mark asked.

Jankowski handed him a penlight.

Mark shone the light into the grave and saw that it was about eight feet deep. He climbed in, dropped to the bottom and scanned the area. He saw an ancient wood ladder leading up to the panel—the means to get from the tomb to the graveyard—and a narrow entrance to a tunnel.

"I'm coming down, sir," Jankowski said, a protective tone in his voice.

Before Mark could say "It'll be cramped," Jankowski was at his side—and it was cramped.

"I brought another flashlight," Jankowski said and turned it on. It was bright and cast a wide light into the small tunnel.

"Those monks must've been fairly short," Mark observed.

"They always looked that way in the cartoons," Jankowski said. "I'll go first."

Mark put a hand on his shoulder and sized him up. "No you won't. I'll go."

Jankowski looked at Mark, then the tunnel, then Mark again. "Yes, sir."

With the penlight in his mouth, Mark crawled on all fours into the tunnel. Jankowski shone the larger flashlight behind him for supplemental light. The shadows were deep and long. The roof of the tunnel seemed strong, made up of rock. Only an occasional tree root broke through. He went in several feet, but began to feel the kind of claustrophobia he got in an MRI machine. Looking ahead, he couldn't tell how far it went.

He weighed his options and decided to back out again. In the grave, he breathed heavily and wiped his forehead with the back of his hand.

"Well, sir?"

"We can't go in there without proper equipment."

Jankowski looked up at the three faces peering down at them. "Spelunking equipment?" he asked.

"It's too late in the evening to get any now," Andrew replied. "There's a sports shop not far from here. We can go first thing in the morning."

"I could break into the shop tonight," Digger said.

"Is there any chance of finding the owner?" Mark asked. "Maybe we could persuade him to open up tonight—for the sake of national security, patriotism, whatever you think he'll respond to."

"I think paying him extra for the service will do it," Andrew suggested.

"Let's try it."

Mark, then Jankowski, tested the wooden ladder. Trusting it, they gingerly climbed out.

Sitting on the church lawn, Mark appreciated the fresh air and open space.

The reverend leaned into the tomb again. "It's an ingenious rig," he said. "And it explains all those descriptions of the Blue Monk appearing and disappearing in this graveyard."

Mark had to wonder if the ghost he had seen the night before was a ghost at all. Likely it was someone dressed as the Blue

Monk, who knew about the passageway, but who would do it? And why? *We really are in a* Scooby-Doo *episode.* Then again, it was obvious that the tunnel hadn't been used for a very long time, so whomever he saw the other night couldn't have escaped through it.

"You realize that the tunnel may not lead anywhere," Andrew said. "That explosion on the other end might have caved it in."

"It's possible," Mark said, still breathing heavily, "but I still have to try."

"Perhaps you should wait until morning," Henry said.

Mark leaned up on his elbows. "Not a chance. I don't want Return to Earth to have the chance to blow up this end." He looked at Jankowski, who was wiping the dirt off his flashlight. "Jankowski and one of his pals will stay on guard here. Shoot anyone who comes near it."

"He's joking, of course," Andrew said to the soldier.

"No, I'm not," Mark said and climbed to his feet. "This may be our only hope."

CHAPTER FIFTY-SEVEN

INSPECTOR MARTIN DUERR SHOWED his interpol identification to the blank-faced police officer standing guard at the end of the lane. The sky was bruised and the rain fell lightly so the officer wore a plastic-covered cap and regulation poncho over his blue uniform. His hand seemed to come from nowhere, held the ID for a moment, and then handed it back. The officer nodded and stepped aside for Duerr to pass.

Positioned on the border of France and Germany, Basel was a picturesque Swiss city. A shabby industrial park seemed an unlikely fit, with its anonymous businesses set up in anonymous offices and anonymous storerooms. The evening traffic whirred on the Elsasserstrasse to the east, only a stone's throw away. Duerr walked between two single-story buildings with tin roofs and then stepped up to a second police officer by the entrance to office 312. The officer, looking as blank faced as the first, let him in.

A plainclothes detective with a round bald head stood near a receptionist's desk, inventorying the items there. A sign on the desk read R2E Imports/Exports. *Clever*, Duerr thought.

The Swiss detective looked up at Duerr, who flashed his credentials. The detective nodded for him to continue on through the next doorway. Duerr noticed a hall to his left that extended down to other doors. Offices, he suspected, but those weren't his business.

The doorway led to the crime scene, a large open cement-floored warehouse area with steel racks of cardboard boxes and wooden crates. More plainclothes detectives were scattered around, searching, making notes. The center of activity, however, was in a far corner, near the tall, metal docking door. A camera clicked and flashed, sending lightning to Duerr's already hurting head. Duerr braced himself and sluggishly walked the length of the warehouse.

A face he recognized came out of the crowd of plainclothes. A field operative named Lawrence Acklin, who wore the facial expression and clothes of a modest bank manager. He looked so inconspicuous that he could have disappeared into a crowd of two.

"We didn't get to him in time," Acklin said in French.

Duerr appreciated the courtesy. "Meaning?"

Acklin tipped his head toward the crowd. "They tied him to a chair and tortured him."

Duerr nodded, unsure about looking. It wasn't his case to solve, so why give himself nightmares? Yet, he felt he owed it to his agent. Surely he could bear it, if only to show respect and appreciation.

"It was as if they dissected him," Acklin said, his voice shaking. "Like an animal."

Duerr looked to Acklin and wondered if he realized what he had just said. Acklin didn't seem to, so Duerr moved away from him to whatever was left of Daniel.

"Stay clear!" a man in an evening suit shouted at him in Swiss German. The coroner, no doubt, brought in from a dinner engagement.

Duerr looked down and saw that Daniel's blood had sprayed out in a fan. Getting as close as he dared, he peered through the collection of detectives and coroner's assistants to see Daniel— mostly unrecognizable, mostly carved up and blood caked. A bright flash made Duerr turn away and he felt something rise in his throat that he knew he had to get rid of.

"If you must, do it in that rubbish bin," another man shouted at him, also in Swiss German.

Duerr waved a hand at him and determined that he would not be sick in front of these men. He refused to give them the satisfaction.

Acklin was at his side. "I've given the Swiss homicide detectives all the information I felt permitted to give."

Duerr put a hand on Acklin's arm. "I'm sure you've done your best." Small comfort. "Has anyone been to his lodgings?"

"I have a man there to make sure no one touches anything. I waited for you."

Duerr looked at the crime scene again and realized there was nothing for him to do here. Not now. Maybe never. "You drive," Duerr said.

The Old House was a quaint bed-and-breakfast set in a narrow three-story townhouse on the Habsburgerstrasse—a central road not far from the town center of Basel. The owners had worked hard to turn the modern box-like exterior into something cozy and French-like inside. The replica furniture looked as if it had once dreamed of living during the reign of Louis XVI.

On the drive over Acklin explained that the members of Return to Earth had been placed in small inns, hotels, and bed-and-breakfasts all over the area—never centralized in one place in case they were discovered. Kannenfeldpark was nearby and messages were passed between Daniel and Acklin, usually in envelopes hidden beneath a lilac bush near a children's wading pool. Acklin said it was ironic, since there was a police station at one end of the park.

"Do you have any idea how he was found out?" Duerr asked.

"No. We were extremely careful," Acklin's voice lowered with remorse, "but not careful enough, it would seem."

"How did you find him at that warehouse?"

"After we got his message, we went directly to our rendezvous point, but he didn't come. We then came to this bed-and-breakfast, but he wasn't here. The owner, however, was very upset. Apparently there was loud music coming from Daniel's room. He thought Daniel was having a party—what with all the banging. Parties are forbidden."

"What did the manager do?"

"He pounded on the door and told them to keep it down. When the music persisted, he got his passkey and opened the door. The music was still blaring, but there was no one in the room."

"How did they get out?"

"A back staircase and fire door."

"And the room?"

"A wreck. The manager is insistent that somebody pay for the damage."

"We'll see about that," Duerr said, then climbed out of the car and raced through the rain for the front door of the B&B. The door was unlocked and he entered a spacious foyer.

The manager of The Old House was a middle-aged man named Gahr who had blond hair and a sharply line, v-shaped face. His no-nonsense demeanor pervaded his tone, his expressions, and his posture. He could have been an ex-cop. He asked in Swiss German, "Are you the police?"

"Interpol," Duerr replied.

"What does Interpol have to do with my guest? Will they pay for the damage?"

"You'll be compensated," Duerr said.

"How? By whom? When?"

Duerr considered the man, wanting to berate him for being so self-consumed when an agent had been cruelly murdered, but remembered that he was merely a businessman with bills to pay. "What time was the ruckus in Daniel Bovet's room?"

"Four o'clock this afternoon. An odd time to have a party," Gahr said, "but with so much sports going on these days, people seem ready to celebrate something at any time of the day or night."

"Did you see any of the people with Daniel?"

"No. I had gone out into the garden to cover the furniture because of the rain. They must have come in then."

"The room is destroyed, I understand," Duerr said.

"I don't know what's left. I've never seen such a mess."

"Did you search it?"

"Of course not," Gahr said, offended.

"Are his things there?" Duerr asked Acklin, who had been standing by, taking notes.

Acklin nodded. "He didn't have much."

"We'll look in a minute." He turned his attention back to Gahr. "Did Daniel give you any packages to mail or to hold?"

Gahr's expression suddenly changed, as if a memory had landed on his nose and poked him in his eye. "Yes, he did, in fact. Are you Mr. Duerr?"

"I showed you my identification," Duerr reminded him.

"Who looks at that?" Gahr asked.

"Regardless, what about the package?"

"He said I was to mail it tomorrow or give it to you—and only you—if you arrived before." He disappeared into a small room off the foyer and returned with a bulky brown envelope, but he didn't hand it over. "I want some sort of guarantee about the damage," he said.

Duerr took out his wallet and handed him a credit card. "Use that."

"With pleasure," Gahr said, swapping the envelope for the credit card. He disappeared to the back room again.

"What a weasel," Acklin said softly in French.

"He's trying to make a living." Duerr looked at the envelope. It was addressed to him at his office at Interpol's headquarters.

Acklin looked closely at the envelope. "Why would he mail it to you and not to me?"

"It's possible they had discovered your name somehow. To address it to me might have been a greater precaution in case his superiors somehow saw the package." Duerr glanced at Acklin. *Or, he didn't trust you.*

Inside the envelope was a small notebook with a cover depicting two cartoon characters from a popular children's show in Germany. It was the sort of notebook a kid could buy in any stationery shop. Duerr opened it. On the first page, in Daniel's meticulous writing, was the simple inscription: Names R2E.

Duerr breathed in sharply.

"What is it?" Acklin asked and came to Duerr's side to look.

Duerr snapped the book shut. "Gahr's coming," he said and pocketed the book.

Gahr returned with a credit-card slip for Duerr to sign. He did and told Acklin, "I want you and your partner to search the room. I assume your partner is around here somewhere."

"He's already in the room," Gahr said as if some major house policy had been further breached. "I took him some coffee a few minutes ago."

Duerr turned to face Acklin. "I will take your car. Stay here until I come back."

"Where are you going?"

"To follow this lead."

Acklin unhappily gave Duerr the keys to the car. The rain had subsided and Duerr, aware of the book in his pocket, decided against driving. He walked toward Kannenfeldpark to find the police station Acklin had mentioned. As he walked, he watched and listened to the narrow streets: a complaining cat, a couple walking hand in hand, a woman closing the shutters on her windows. It was possible that Return to Earth members were watching him—even following him. It was a risk, but a risk he was willing to take.

The police station was a large white block of a building with an open reception area; in it were tables and chairs, with a scattering of computer terminals. A uniformed officer stepped to the reception counter. Duerr showed her his ID, briefly explained why he was in the area, and asked to use a copy machine. He was taken through to another large open office with more tables and terminals. In the corner sat a copy machine. Someone gave him a cup of bad coffee, and he stood at the machine making copies of each page in the notebook. He then returned the notebook to the envelope, sealed it, and asked the on-duty officer to send it to Interpol headquarters overnight by their most secure means. "Use your chain-of-evidence shipper. Keep it in a safe until it is handed to the delivery service."

The officer looked at the envelope as if it might explode.

"Is there a desk I might use for a while?" Duerr asked.

He was given one in a windowless interview room. He sat down and leafed through the copies of the pages from the notebook. On the last page, written in a hasty scribble, was the name Lawrence Acklin. It was heavily underlined.

Duerr groaned and opened his cell phone. He hit the speed dial for his office. One of his associates, Diane Tournay, picked up. "Martin here, Diane. I'm in Basel."

"Is it true about Daniel?" she asked.

"It's true, but I can't talk about that now. We have a compromised agent, perhaps two. I'll give you their names and the address of the B&B where they can be found. I want them picked up quickly and quietly—and held for questioning."

Duerr gave Diane the names, information, and appropriate authorization instructions.

"Consider it handled. They'll be retrieved within the hour."

"In that case, I'll be there when it happens."

"If you have another minute," Diane said, "I have word for you from the lab about that photograph."

"Yes?"

"They've positively identified the man in the photo as Dr. Stefan Maier." She paused, and then said, "Curious, since he is supposed to be dead."

"Yes. Very curious indeed. Now, I would be grateful if you would patch me through to General Mosley."

"At this hour?"

"He won't mind."

CHAPTER FIFTY-EIGHT

"TIME IS AGAINST US and we have to *wait?*" Mark shouted. He was pacing the conference room at the Rose and Crown.

"I'm sorry," Henry said. "We're doing our best to get the equipment. The owner of the sports shop hasn't been found."

"Throw a brick through the window."

Henry ignored the suggestion. "I've asked Mac, and he's arranging to transport what he can secure from London, but even that will take a couple of hours."

Mark growled.

Nora was leaning against one of the paneled walls, her arms folded. "It's nearly midnight," she reminded him.

"I should have gone in with a flashlight," Mark said.

"And that would have been stupid," Nora said. "You have no idea what you're crawling into or how structurally sound those caves are. You could get part of the way in and a ton of earth might fall on you. You're no good to me dead."

"What a kind thing to say." Mark turned to Henry. "I know you're doing your best."

Henry bowed slightly before leaving the room.

Nora moved to a chair at the table and sat down. "Even if the equipment arrived in the next five minutes, I'd still be hesitant to let you do anything tonight. It's dark, and a storm is coming in from the continent. It should wait until morning when we can do this properly."

"Meanwhile, people are dying in Africa," he said.

Nora groaned. "I hate it when you talk like a character in a B movie."

Mark flinched. "Do I do it that much?"

She smiled at him, but didn't reply.

Mark glanced at the door, then went over and closed it. He sat down next to Nora. "Tell me about Georgina."

Nora frowned. "I don't know what to say. She could be a spy, or not. The evidence isn't clear."

"What's your gut instinct?"

She thought for a moment. "She isn't. My suspicion is that she met a guy who is connected to Return to Earth, and he tried to recruit her."

"Why her? She wasn't a classified government employee at the time, right?"

"That's how it works in espionage," she said. "They recruit people in all kinds of positions and then put them to use when needed. You've already seen how effective they've been."

Mark thought of the lab in Greenland and the helicopter crash in Gabon. He shook his head. "They've stayed ahead of us. The outbreak at the compound could have come from them somehow. Maybe someone who frequented the compound, or someone the pastor trusted."

"We may never know," Nora said. "But the slow and methodical manner in which the movement has put people in places of influence or power betrays a particular kind of evil genius."

"Well, I suppose that's one encouragement."

"What is?"

"For them to pay so much attention to what we're doing here makes me think that we must be on the right track. Or at the very least, they think we're on the right track. If we really were chasing rabbits, they wouldn't bother with us."

Nora tapped her fingernails lightly on the tabletop. "Are Jankowski and Youngman heavily armed?"

"Youngman?"

"The other soldier guarding the tomb. Are they armed?"

"They better be," Mark said. He felt suddenly restless and stood up. "Maybe I'll walk up to check on them."

"Call them."

"I'd rather walk."

"Then take Corporal Westcott with you."

"He's another soldier?"

"Yes, and Brainerd is here, but he's guarding Georgina."

"Is he good-looking?"

"Not very."

"Good. Otherwise I'd worry about how *closely* he's guarding her." Mark headed for the door.

Nora stood up. "Mark . . ."

"I won't let myself get kidnapped," he said, preempting her.

"No, it isn't that." She hesitated. "I think you're doing a good job here. It makes me sorry that I . . . well . . ."

Mark gazed at her for a moment. "You were right to say what you did. Trying to prove you wrong has helped keep me sharp."

She smiled at him and, for a moment, their eyes locked.

He felt as if he should say more, to admit that working with her made him feel confident again, made him feel alive. He considered that there was nothing keeping him from walking the four steps that separated them, taking her in his arms, and kissing her—apart from the possibility that she'd slap him, of course.

She broke the moment by abruptly turning away. "I have to send an update to Mac and the general," she said and opened her laptop.

He smiled. "Give them my love."

Mark and the young soldier named Westcott walked the main road toward St. Lawrence's Church. The night air had a stillness that made it feel like no air at all.

Westcott, like Jankowski, had an air of physical authority that Mark found intimidating. There was no question who would win if anyone tried some funny business.

And it was poor Joan who very nearly got shot when she suddenly stepped out onto the pavement from behind a tree.

Westcott's gun instantly appeared from its hiding place and was pointed at her.

She let out a mouselike squeak and put her hands up. "I'm a friend!"

"Down, boy," Mark said to Westcott.

"You should announce yourself, ma'am," Westcott said to Joan.

"I'm sorry," she said, her voice shaking. "I saw two men walking in this direction and didn't want to be seen until I was sure who they were."

"What are you doing out at this time of night?" Mark asked.

"I was on my way to see you," she said, and Mark noticed that she was looking around nervously and drifting back into the shadows, as if she hoped to melt into them.

"Okay, here I am."

"Not here," she said. "Not in public."

"Then where?" Mark asked. "We can go back to the B&B."

"Not even there. It may be watched."

"By whom? Return to Earth?"

"Them, or . . ." she didn't finish the sentence. Instead she took a few steps back and Mark realized there was a path into the small section of trees where they stood. "Over here," she whispered and went farther into the shadows.

Westcott shook his head, but Mark nodded and said, "If it's an ambush, I'll apologize to you later."

By his expression, Westcott took little consolation from that promise.

They followed Joan down the path. Twenty yards in, it stopped at a small children's playground. A single light on the far end cast muted shadows over the slide, swings, and merry-go-round. She stopped at the edge and turned to Mark.

"Why all the mystery?" Mark asked.

She slipped the bag she'd been carrying from her shoulder. Mark thought it was a large purse, but when she handed it to him he realized it was a leather satchel of some sort.

"What's this?" he asked.

"I want you to know the truth about the Blue Monk," she said, and there was something in her tone that made him feel as if she were offering her only child as a sacrifice.

"What's in it?"

"Everything. Documents only a few people have seen."

"Andrew?"

"No. These aren't part of the church archives. They're private, family papers. Perhaps you'll read them and know whether finding his body will help you, but no one else can see these. You can't tell anyone you have them or from whom you got them. Read them tonight, and I'll get them back from you in the morning."

Mark said, "All right. It's a deal. But I don't understand."

"You will."

"Will it explain the scandal?"

"Yes."

"And the so-called curse?"

"Yes. You'll see," she said, her eyes darting around again.

"Why are you so nervous?"

"There are those who believe I shouldn't be giving these to you," she said.

He hooked the satchel onto his shoulder. "You said they're private family papers. Is that why you have them? They're from your family?"

"Yes."

"But . . . what family are we talking about?"

"*His* family," she said, and the words sounded as if they required an enormous effort for her to say them. Mark could almost hear the shovel digging deeply into the ground to uncover a secret she kept buried her entire life. "I'm a relative of the Blue Monk—Benjamin Hancock. These papers will tell you what happened."

She turned suddenly and headed across the playground.

Mark watched her until she disappeared into the shadows on the far side, and then turned to go back to the main road. Westcott looked at him inquisitively. Mark said, "I guess I'm going back to my room for a little light reading."

PART FIVE

CHAPTER FIFTY-NINE

MARGARET SCREAMED AS THE mob surged forward, John Dicken leading the way. It was only a few steps for them, but she threw herself into their path. As she fell under their feet, she said to Benjamin in a harsh whisper, "Run."

Benjamin's thoughts collided with his instincts. To run was his desire. Years of evading the persecutors of Catholics in Britain had trained him well, but he couldn't leave his sister to the mob that had come for him.

"Don't touch her!" he shouted, his voice wild and angry, and threw back his hood.

John Dicken and the mob reared back, startled by the sound of his voice and the fierce look of his face and raised arms. A few at the back turned tail and ran out.

Benjamin pulled Margaret to her feet; she threw her arms around him and whispered again, "Run. They won't hurt me."

The alcohol that had fueled the mob's hatred had also made them sluggish. Margaret let go and nudged Benjamin to the doorway of her bedroom in the back of the cottage. He glared at the crowd one last time and then propelled himself toward the opening. As he crossed the room to the open rear window, he heard John Dicken roar and shout, "Take chase after the beast!"

He leapt out of the window and onto the soft earth, his robe tangling under his feet, tripping him. He fell and rolled onto his back. He could hear the mob stumbling through the bedroom. Someone shouted to circle the house.

He struggled to his feet and a sharp pain stabbed his right

knee. Still, he drew his robes up and worked himself into a limping run across the field toward the church.

The shouts of the crowd increased behind him and off to his right. Not only were they chasing him through the field, but also attempting to intercept him by coming up the main road. They must have realized where he was going: the church graveyard. Though they probably didn't know there was a tunnel in the Templeton tomb, they apparently guessed that he came and went from somewhere in that area.

He considered making his way to the main entrance to the cave, but the hill was so far away that he didn't want to take the chance of the crowd finding it. Besides, with the pain in his knee he might not make it that far without being caught. He would have to outrun them to the tomb and pray that the night air and the potency of seeing the house of God would clear their heads of madness.

His leg screamed at him, and he again stumbled to the ground. As he got up, he could see the mob: the yellow light of their torches illuminating clubs, knives, and poles. Sweat poured down his face and back. Despite the excruciating pain, he picked up his pace, moving as quickly as he could into the graveyard.

He felt a wave of relief to see that the mob had not made it to the churchyard. He pressed forward, limping, sidestepping tombstones, their places indelibly mapped into his mind. The mob would have more difficulty pursuing him through the cemetery in the dark. He reached the tomb as one section of the mob came up behind him, and the other came around the church itself.

He reached to the symbol of the lamb on the stone, fumbling to turn it so that it would open the side of the tomb. Once, twice, three times he tried, but he was clumsy and his hands were wet. The mob searched for him in the graveyard, their anger still evident in their shouts and curses. He dared not take the time to see how close they were.

Finally, he got a firm grip and turned the symbol. The side of the tomb opened inward and he dropped and rolled, allowing himself to fall to the bottom inside. The pain in his knee shot through his entire body like a bolt of lightning. He muffled a scream and moaned.

The sound of the mob was very close and he pulled himself up, climbing the small ladder to be sure the heavy stone panel was back in its place. As he reached up, the panel was suddenly pushed inward and a torch was thrust into the gap, mere inches from his face. He raised his arm to block it, and flame scorched his arm. He cried out and fell back to the bottom of the grave.

"He's in here!" someone shouted.

Benjamin scampered into the tunnel, both his leg and arm protesting. The tunnel was rough-hewn, but even in the pitch-black, he knew every rock and every turn. He hoped that the mob would fear crawling into the tomb. Most couldn't or wouldn't, and those who would might still be daunted by the tunnel itself, made purposefully small to intimidate any trespasser.

It was only about ten yards of cramped tunnel and then Benjamin reached another passage that opened up tall and wide enough for a grown man. He paused there for a moment. There were voices and flickering lights in the tomb. Some were still following him, though they would have to do it one at a time.

Had he been a soldier instead of a monk, he would have waited where he was and used a rock to knock the heads of those who attempted to crawl into the larger tunnel where he stood. He was tempted to do it, but his conscience was immediately pricked, and he knew he would not—*could* not—commit such violence.

He reached down in the dark and found one of the lamps and the flint the brothers stored there. With trembling hands he struck the flint and lit a wick—and pushed onward into the labyrinth of mine shafts ahead.

His breathing became more labored, and he fought against coughing. They might lose him because they didn't know their way in the caves, but they could easily find him again just by listening. He paused yet again. The voices of the mob echoed back in the caves. They were determined.

He stumbled on, trying to turn his fear of being hunted into prayers. Cool air touched the sweat of his brow, and he knew he was coming to the end of this tunnel. He felt his lungs open up and took in large breaths. He saw the familiar light ahead, the torches that burned day and night, allowing him to navigate the mine in more restful and meditational times.

He was sure he had enough of a lead to reach the entrance to the Cathedral. Once inside, he would be safe. For those who didn't know how to enter, it was impenetrable. Let them stand outside to watch and wait. Let them circle the entire countryside. He would be easily sustained by the stored supplies and, more so, by the sacrament in the tabernacle. He could fast for days on end, as long as he had the body and blood of the Lord for strength.

If necessary, there was yet another concealed passage just below the altar that would allow him to escape the mine altogether and make his way to a safe house in a neighboring county.

Entering the cavern, he felt a sense of security. He stopped to catch his breath. He pulled up the sleeve of his robe and looked at his burned forearm. It was blistered and bleeding.

The sounds of his hunters suddenly echoed around him as if they had been stealthily quiet and only then decided to make themselves heard. They were closer than he thought. He had only moments to escape.

He staggered down a small passageway, quickly coming to what appeared to be a dead end, but there was nothing ordinary, nor dead, about this wall. It was marked with the Lumen Christi symbol and other ancient engravings, representing symbols of the Roman catacombs. This was home.

He glanced back, squinting into the shadows to make certain he was not being watched. Then he moved his hand to the left into a small and unnoticeable niche. He grasped a handle and pulled. A *click* of release, not unlike the latch in the tomb, and Benjamin pressed himself against the wall to slide it to the right.

But it seemed unusually heavy tonight and moved slowly.

There were voices in the mine now growing louder. He threw his light to the ground and covered it with dirt, then resumed pushing the wall to one side. He needed only enough room to squeeze through to the other side.

He finally succeeded, slipping through and then pushing the wall closed again. He peeked through the ever-closing crack and, just before the wall was returned to its proper position, he saw someone move out of the shadows. A young man and he looked directly at Benjamin.

The wall was back in place. The latch fell into the mechanism, locking the mob away. Benjamin slumped to the ground, praying that his ordeal was over—praying that the young man he'd just seen had not observed how he opened the wall. He waited for a moment in the darkness of this new cavern.

The pain of his knee and arm was severe but he forced himself to remain quiet. Benjamin pulled himself to his feet, felt in the dark, and found a new oil-and-tar covered torch. He used the flint to light it, then moved around the cavern, lighting other torches attached to the wall. Once they were aglow, he turned to face the cave—the Silver Cathedral—so called because of the enormous cavern's vein of silver, out of which the monks of the Lumen Christi had carved a place of worship for God.

The altar and the crucifix above it, the chalices for the Eucharist, the tabernacle in which the body and blood were kept, the monstrance, the staff upon which it was carried—all handcrafted from the massive shaft of silver. On the walls, the stations of the cross were painstakingly carved into the silver and also embellished with gold.

The brothers took the unused silver ore, tons of it, and smuggled it to the head of their order, who was able to sell it and provide income for their various secret monasteries, ministries to the poor, and their pastoral work during times of persecution. It was the rule of the order to never speak of this secret place. Few knew of its location.

He went to the altar, genuflected, performed the sign of the cross, and then knelt to thank God for his deliverance. Kneeling sent pain through his body. He prayed for the souls of the men who wished to harm him, asking God to forgive them.

As he prayed, he was taken by a strong sense of his own mortality. He had withstood the sickness that had killed the rest of the order, and he had resisted the plague that devastated the village, but tonight, at this moment, he sensed things were about to change. To suffer and to die for Christ was no longer a distant concept, but a reality from which he might not escape.

Somewhere behind him, the latch clicked on the wall, and it began to move.

The young man must have seen where the lever was hidden. The mob will come for me now. Worse yet, they'll desecrate this sacred place. He thought sadly of his plan to share this place and its wealth with the people of Eyam once the plague had passed. It was to be a surprise, a means to help the village restore itself from this time of devastation. Now, he was certain it would not happen as he'd hoped.

God have mercy. He remained kneeling and listened. A single grunt and footsteps scuffed the ground, echoing around the cavernous cathedral. Then a second grunt and a voice—the voice of John Dicken. "Quickly, pull me through before the others see."

More grunts and then the sound of the wall being pushed back into place.

"I told you," a young voice said. Benjamin recognized the speaker: Joshua Parke, Dicken's young assistant.

"So you did, lad. Well done," Dicken said. He gave a low whistle. "And will you look at this. There's a fortune in here. A fortune to be sure. We wouldn't want the others to see this. Just, look at the altar."

Joshua gasped sharply, but not from awe at the altar. Benjamin imagined the boy had only just seen him kneeling there. "Look," he whispered.

"It is the child of Satan himself," John Dicken hissed, his voice as bitter as bad ale. He shouted at Benjamin, "How dare you kneel at that altar. How dare you feign worship, you son of the devil." His voice came closer. "I know what you are. Is this where you worship, Lucifer? Dare you make a mockery of our most sacred and holy things in this way, you blue-skinned monster?"

John Dicken was right behind him, when Benjamin suddenly stood and turned to face the man.

This time Dicken was not taken aback. His hatred, now burning in his eyes, was not borne of the alcohol, but of something terrible in his heart. Perhaps fear, perhaps bitterness, perhaps even jealousy. In his hands he held a sword, which he pointed at Benjamin.

"Wait! Mr. Dicken—" Joshua Park called, reaching.

"Our Father . . ." Benjamin began as he bowed his head, but was able to say no more. Dicken thrust the sword forward.

Benjamin felt the sword go through him, but was surprised to feel no pain.

And then he felt nothing.

CHAPTER SIXTY

AUGUST 16

JOAN'S COVER LETTER began:

> *Dear Dr. Carlson,*
>
> *I've bookmarked the most pertinent sections of the enclosed documents. There is a bound collection of letters, which will give you insight into the life of Benjamin Hancock, the man known as the Blue Monk.*
>
> *You will also find a bound diary of a man named Joshua Parke and a rather simply drawn map to indicate the network of tunnels and caves leading to and from the Templeton tomb, the Silver Cathedral, and the under-altar entrance, which I now understand has been destroyed by saboteurs.*
>
> *I suggest you begin with Joshua Parke's diary—at the marks I've provided. You may want to do that now, and then return to this letter once you've finished it.*

Mark turned to the bound copy of Joshua Parke's diary, which wasn't an original, but a copy Joan made and then placed in a binder.

Rather than begin at the point Joan indicated, Mark skimmed through earlier entries to learn about the author.

Joshua had begun his diary on scraps of paper provided by Reverend Mompesson as part of a program to teach Joshua to read and write. The early entries—which were in a childish scrawl and even harder to read because of the old English—consisted mostly of simple accounts of Joshua's life: cow milking, sheep shearing, working in the mines to make a "tuppence or two"; then the death of his mother in childbirth, the disappearance of his father, presumably desertion. Then, John Dicken took him in.

Mark's impression of Dicken was that he was cruel and unkind to Joshua, treating him more like a slave than an apprentice, taking advantage of Joshua's orphan status to work him for hours on end, day and night. The tone of Joshua's entries changed, as he seemed to transform from a kind and inquisitive boy to a deeply cynical and hard-hearted young man.

The entries often weren't properly dated, but the first one designated by Joan was chilling:

> This night we dispensed with the Blue Servant of Satan. It was with great honor that our Lord allowed me to see the entrance to his sanctuary and the means to enter. We dispatched the Evil One and disposed of his corrupt body to its proper place of damnation—a deep, dark pit in the cave.

The next marked entry was dated Tuesday, 28 August 1666:

> Master Dicken has prevailed upon me never to mention the Silver Cathedral we found for fear that the others may ransack it for their own gain. It is in my mind that Master Dicken has determined to keep the valuables we discovered for himself, but having nowhere to hide them within the village, wishes to keep them where only he and I know their whereabouts.

Another was dated Tuesday, 4 September 1666:

> This night I have, of my own accord, returned to the cavern, whereupon I discovered the private lodgings of the Blue Beast containing his personal writings, correspondence, and other such incriminations. I hid them upon my person and returned to the hut in the midst of the sheepfold. I hid them until such time as I might read them, to discern the scandalous nature of his attitudes.

Thursday, 6 September 1666:

> Today I saw Margaret on the village road for the first time since that night. She spoke harsh words to me, maintaining the

*lie that the Blue Creature was her relation. She is most anxious
to learn of his whereabouts. For fear of retribution from Master
Dicken, I did not speak. Her final words cut me, as she considered my behavior that night as uncharacteristic of my true person
and held out hope that I was merely under the influence of the
black-hearted John Dicken and would one day repent of my participation in her brother's persecution.*

Saturday, 8 September, 1666:

*I returned to the sheepfold and read with a wary eye, desirous
to be on guard of any wiles by Satan to use the words of the
monk to bewitch me. On the contrary, I was deeply grieved to
discover the simplest expressions of holiness. I must beware, for
the Evil One uses such language for his purposes.*

Sunday, 16 September, 1666:

*Without exception, the cattle have become ill, and sheep are
dying from no obvious cause. This has been a daily occurrence for
the past week. There have been whispers among the men of the
village that it is a curse caused by driving away the Blue Monk. I
bite my tongue for the villagers may well be more alarmed to
know that the monk was not driven away, but murdered. Master
Dicken rebukes and ridicules talk of curses, but I have seen him
privately anxious. One night, while in his cups, he lamented to
me that he would take back that night, for he feared a curse
would be placed upon him alone. I am now afraid, for I was his
partner and, by opening the door, it was the same as if I had
thrust the sword myself.*

Over the next several entries, Mark noted a change in Joshua's tone. The writings of Benjamin Hancock—whatever they
contained—began to work on his heart. The entry dates, while
inconsistent, gave Mark the impression that winter had passed
and he was now reading about events from spring 1667.

Though the plague and the quarantine had ended, the village
now seemed alarmed by the death of livestock, crops that had
mysteriously failed, and unexplained cave-ins in the mines.

Then, in an entry dated Holy Week 1667, something seemed to snap for Joshua Parke.

> *I wept until my eyes burned, in such loud tones that the sheep were frightened and moved away with worried bleats. It was as if our Lord Jesus Himself spoke to me, firmly but lovingly, calling me to account for my actions. I now see that I was party to the murder of a holy man of God who sought nothing but to bring comfort and balm to the village. I now feel as if I, by my own hand, have raised the hammer to pound the nails into the hands and feet of our Lord. I prayed to God for forgiveness, for penance, for atonement. He spoke to me in the most loving tones, but commanded that I should reveal myself to Margaret.*

There was no account of the meeting with Margaret. The next entry declared in dispassionate terms that John Dicken had suddenly been seized by pains in his chest and head, collapsing suddenly and dying three days later. He left a wife and four children.

Joshua Parke was put out into the street but, astoundingly, was taken in by Margaret herself. The entries became far more infrequent, but Mark got the impression that Margaret had not taken Joshua in as a servant, but treated him more like a son, teaching him to advance in his reading and writing, mostly through the study of scripture.

Then, in the next section of Joshua Parke's writings, there was an extended entry. Apparently, Margaret requested, or demanded, that Joshua chronicle the events of the night—the "scandal"—of what had become of the Blue Monk. Mark skimmed through the entry until he came to the fateful part:

> *John Dicken stopped at a juncture of two caves, but I was certain of which direction the monk had gone. I arrived with great stealth in time to see him facing a wall in a dead-end tunnel, which I found curious. Invoking the sign of the cross, he then reached into a secret place, pulling a lever, which also released a section of the wall through which he entered. After which he closed the wall again.*

John Dicken arrived at my side and I informed him of the secret lever, which he entreated me to operate. I obeyed. We both entered a cavern of startling magnificence and I was immediately struck by the sense of having entered not a devil's lair but a church more magnificent than I had ever observed; holy and wondrous in its splendor of silver and gold, with an altar and all things truly of God.

The monk was on his knees before the altar, in a posture of prayer, which John Dicken cursed for its profanity before God. But I knew John Dicken and determined in my heart that he was possessed by the sight of the riches of the cavern and would have them unto himself.

Helpless to understand his intention, I watched as John Dicken drew a sword, which had been given to him by an ancestor, and thrust it into the heart of the monk, who muttered last words of forgiveness, and expired.

I was vexed to my heart by this and fell to my knees with great weeping. Master Dicken struck me and demanded that I help him carry the body of the monk away from this shrine, for fear that the demons themselves might come imminently to wreak their revenge upon us.

Stricken with a greater fear, I gave assistance to Master Dicken, and we carried the body to an adjoining shaft whereupon we found a deep pit that we saw by torchlight had mud and sludge at the bottom. Master Dicken determined that this would suffice, and we dropped the monk in and watched his body sink until naught but a hand could be seen—and then no more.

We returned to the cavern, but Master Dicken feared our discovery by the other villagers still searching the caves. We extinguished the torches, and Master Dicken forbade me to speak of the cavern and its contents to anyone ever, for he had his own purposes for their disposal.

We discovered another passage, under the altar, which allowed us to depart, and in good time rejoined the remainder of the crowd in the church graveyard, feigning ignorance of the monk's whereabouts.

Mark sat back, tapping the pages with the eraser tip of the pencil. "So they murdered the monk," he said to no one. "That was the scandal, and the resulting curse included the odd deaths of their livestock, crops, and miners—not to mention a rash of cave-ins in the mines."

Mark picked up the letter from Joan to see what she had to add.

You see now what became of Benjamin Hancock, left as he was somewhere in a mine shaft. Joshua Parke returned to the cavern from time to time, but never removed another object. Everything remains as it was even to this day. I'll direct you to the proper documents, in particular a letter by Margaret, but will summarize for you . . .

The "curse," which the village felt remained upon it even after the plague had ended, drew endless speculation. Many gossiped that it had something to do with the monk's mysterious departure and those who had called him an "Angel of Death," not an "Angel of Light."

As the curse continued into another two seasons, Joshua Parke took it upon himself to reveal the source of the curse. One night he gathered together the members of the original mob who had attacked the monk at Margaret's house.

For the first time he informed them of how John Dicken had murdered the monk and of his own participation in the act. He publicly repented and begged those in attendance to do the same.

He also announced that the curse might well be the result of the collective sin of the village for their complicity in the monk's death.

Joshua Parke was so eloquent in his appeal that some compared him to St. Stephen and his words to the council in the Book of Acts. However, unlike Stephen, Joshua was not taken and stoned. But the attending villagers begged him to tell them how to lift the curse.

On his own initiative, Joshua said that the family of John Dicken must do penance on behalf of their father, by visiting and maintaining the sanctuary of the Blue Monk as a memorial of his service to them in their great time of need—a service they had repaid with the spilling of innocent blood.

The attending villagers, in their shame, agreed also and com-

mitted not only themselves, but also their descendants to this secret activity, which they swore to guard with their very lives, if necessary. Many took on the responsibility as a way to honor a holy shrine and place of worship; others did it out of fear that, if they refused, they would remain under a terrible curse, but it remained a guarded secret to those families who knew about it.

I suspect you don't believe in curses, Dr. Carlson, but it is worth noting that soon after the penance began, Eyam became a prosperous village, thriving ever afterward. And the legends remain that the Blue Monk appears in ghostlike form as a reminder of his ever-watchful presence and pleasure.

My own family has remained true to the Blue Monk for over three hundred years, beginning with my ancestor, Margaret, who lived to be 101 and who visited the Cathedral regularly. We have all kept the secret. Until now.

I am convinced that if by finding the body of Benjamin Hancock, you may save the lives of hundreds or thousands of people, then you must know the truth.

There are those, however, who will view this act as one of betrayal. How they will treat me if they discover I have done this remains to be seen.

Mark held the letter for a moment and considered the meaning of the last words.

How far would the keepers of a three-hundred-year-old secret go to protect that secret? Might they resort to exploding the entrance to the cavern? Would they resort to violence against the people, like Mark and the TSI team, who were determined to find the monk's body?

Mark felt the stab of a new fear. What if Return to Earth wasn't the only enemy they had to worry about?

"It's getting crowded around here," Mark muttered.

He turned to the other collection of papers to learn about the Blue Monk himself. Maybe there were clues as to how the monk survived the sickness in Eyam for so long, as did his sister.

He picked up the first page and began to read.

CHAPTER SIXTY-ONE

DR. SUSAN HUTCHINSON WAS jarred awake by the shrill ringing of her phone. She had fallen asleep on the small sofa in her office, reports scattered on the floor that she must have dropped when she gave in to her exhaustion.

Stumbling to her desk, she reached for and punched the speaker button. "Hutchinson here. Hello."

"Susan, this is Jim Dillard."

"Hi, Jim," she said and glanced at the time. It was 6:00 a.m., which meant it was midnight where he was at USAMRIID.

"I'm sorry to bother you. It was a gamble. I decided that if you were still at the office, you must be working and I wouldn't be waking you," he said.

"That was a good call." She didn't bother to correct him. "What's going on?"

Jim hesitated. "Is this line secure?"

"Of course it is. What's wrong, Jim?" She felt a deep dread in her chest.

"It's an odd connection, but one I thought I should bring to your attention. It's about the missing boy."

"Okay, go ahead." She looked up at the map pinned to her wall. They had lost Aaron after the incident near the checkpoint.

"You know that a lot of our testing involves animals," Jim said.

Animals? He's calling me about animals? "Sure. You've used guinea pigs and mice to develop a variety of drugs. You gave me a tour of the lab last year, remember?"

"That's right," he said. "Well, since then we've started working with a variety of monkeys and great apes."

"Great apes," she repeated. She must be half-asleep, she decided. She wasn't grasping the thread of their conversation. "Jim, I'm sorry, but you've got to spell things out for me."

He chuckled. "I know. I'm sorry. Look, I got a dispatch from Ronald Smith, a zoologist we support. He has a research lab in a secret location in Gabon."

"Jim, *please* tell me this has nothing to do with Ahaz."

"Ahaz? You're joking. We refuse to work with them. They're sloppy and reckless and—well, you know."

"I know. So, tell me about the dispatch."

"Ron Smith reported that a group of western lowland gorillas they've been following has been wiped out by what appears to be a fast-acting hemorrhagic disease. They suspect it's some new form of Ebola."

Susan felt a chill as she looked again at the map. "Where are they located, Jim?"

"They're in a remote jungle region on the slopes of Mont Ekoumanzork. It's in the middle of nowhere in Gabon."

She found the area on the map. It was an isolated region between Mitzic and Bifoum. "I see it."

"Whatever this disease is it has wiped out every gorilla, young and old, male and female, and has killed them quickly."

"How quickly?" Susan asked as she scribbled notes to herself.

"Beyond belief. The entire group of gorillas was observed in the early morning and they were as healthy as could be. By afternoon, they were all dead. Every one. The researchers were smart enough to keep their distance, but I had a wild thought: maybe the outbreaks are somehow related. Anyway, they're going back to take samples tomorrow using BSL4 protections. They'll also bring back a small gorilla or two to autopsy."

"No, Jim—stop them!" she exclaimed.

"They'll be using double bagging and decontamination."

"Listen to me. If that outbreak is related to ours, the precautions may not work. Your people could die."

"Calm down. The outbreaks may be related somehow, but I doubt they're the same. If I've got my details right, yours was reported on August twelfth from—where was it?—seventy or eighty miles away from our lab. Your outbreak couldn't have been carried by animals that quickly."

"Not by animals, no," she said. "Trust me, Jim. You have to stop your people right now. Tell them not to do anything. Just stand by until you hear from me."

Susan quickly got more information from Jim, hung up, and ran out of her office and down the hall to General Mosley's office suite. Aware that he had a separate room with a bunk and shower, she hoped he was still there. Kevin was not, and a night MP sat up when she appeared.

"Yes, ma'am?"

"Is the general in?"

"Sleeping, so I suggest you—"

She didn't wait for his instruction, but threw herself at the door.

"Wait!" he called after her.

Mosley's office was lit and he stood near a bank of telecommunications machines toward the back of the room. "What in the world?" he exclaimed as he spun around. He looked like he hadn't been to bed at all.

"General, I'm sorry," she said, breathless. "I just got a call—"

The MP was right behind her. "Sorry, sir."

"It's all right. Go find us some coffee." Mosley dismissed him with a slight wave. The soldier retreated. "Go on, Doctor."

She swallowed hard. "A call from US Am Rid. They think they have a rapidly killing Ebola that's wiped out a group of gorillas in Gabon."

"What? Where?" He walked to the maps and papers covering his conference table.

"Somewhere around Mont Ekoumanzork."

Mosley looked over at the map of Gabon on his wall. "Here's the mountain, if you can call a hill that's barely one thousand feet above sea level a mountain." He pointed to an area color coded with green—a remote jungle area. "Aaron must be on the move."

"I have the number for the zoologists, sir," she said and held up the scrap of paper. "They want to take some of the gorillas back for testing."

"No! Let's call them."

"Yes, sir." Susan grabbed the phone and dialed as Mosley turned his attention back to the map. She hit the speakerphone; the line hissed and then connected to a first ring. She pointed to the map. "I believe the research center is somewhere around there."

"It's out of the way," the general observed, "but it would make sense considering the direction he's been traveling."

Susan could see an intersection of three roads, which the general tapped with his forefinger. "One road goes to Lalara and Mitzic." He pointed at the map. "This one goes east and then south to the Congo, while this one heads west, dividing to either go south to the Congo or northwest to Libreville."

Susan continued to study the map while the phone rang on the speakerphone behind them. She saw a line running horizontally through the jungles of Gabon and coming within a few miles of Mont Ekoumanzork. "What is that?"

"That's the Trans-Gabon Railway."

"It looks like it's only a few miles from their research center," Susan said.

"That would make sense," he observed. "It would give them access to the main cities."

The speakerphone clicked loudly and a low, weary voice with an Australian accent spoke softly, "This is Ronald Smith."

Mosley stepped to his desk. "Dr. Smith?"

"Yes, sir. General Mosley? I just got a call from Jim Dillard . . ."

"That's right. I'm calling from the WHO headquarters in Brazzaville. Listening in is Dr. Susan Hutchinson."

"Oh, right. Jim mentioned Dr. Hutchinson. Hello there."

"Thanks for getting up early for us," Susan said.

"No worries. I had to get up to answer the call from Jim." They could hear Dr. Smith chuckle and then clear his throat.

"I assume Jim told you that I'm heading a team working on an Ebola outbreak near Mitzic," Mosley said.

"I've just been told about it, sir. However, we don't see how the animals could have carried the . . ."

"Dr. Smith, we suspect that a boy has carried the virus to

your gorillas. We've followed his movements from Mitzic to Lalara and Alembe."

Smith sounded surprised. "A boy?"

"That's right."

"Just a second, General. You're not going to believe this."

Susan could hear the sound of the phone being put down and the muffled sounds of a discussion in the background. After a moment, a woman's voice came on the phone.

"General?"

"Yes."

"I'm Emily Goodson," she said, with an American accent. "I'm an intern here this summer. I'm responsible for watching this particular community of gorillas. I usually check on them twice a day, photographing them, recording their sounds, taking notes, that sort of thing. I was out there yesterday with a couple of other team members. We were surprised to find an African man and a young white man watching the gorillas. I mean, these gorillas are in the middle of nowhere, so you can imagine our shock."

"A man and a teenager?" Mosley asked.

"Yes, sir."

He leaned forward on clenched fists. "Can you describe them?"

"I can do better than that," Emily replied. "I've got a photograph. I can e-mail it to you if you want."

"Right away, if you don't mind." He gave her his e-mail address. "Do you know where they are now?"

"No. They were with two of the gorillas. The gorillas must have sensed our presence and took off."

"What about the man and boy?"

"We didn't stay with them. Instead, we followed the gorillas. But, at last look, I thought they were headed toward the river. I was worried that they might be hunters or poachers. That's why I went back later in the afternoon. I wanted to make sure they weren't there to hurt our gorillas."

"Thank you for your help," Mosley said. "Please put Dr. Smith back on the phone."

"Yes, sir."

Ronald Smith returned. "Does that help?"

"Dr. Smith, your team must secure the site. Each member is to use BSL4 suits—double, triple the usual precautions. However, do not, and I repeat, do *not* get within a hundred yards of the dead gorillas, and be sure no one else gets to them. Can helicopters land near your lab?"

"Yes, sir."

"We'll have a team there within two hours. Thank you."

As he clicked the phone off, he looked up at the door. The soldier hung there, holding two cups of coffee. "Sir."

Mosley shook his head. "Find Major Maklin and get him in here. I want a team out there ASAP."

The soldier, who seemed unsure of what to do with the coffee, thrust them onto the desk and then turned to leave.

"Wait," Susan said. An idea had come to her.

The soldier stopped, but Susan addressed herself to the general. "We need a schedule for the Trans-Gabon Railway."

Mosley raised an eyebrow at Susan, but tipped his head for the soldier to do it.

The soldier nodded and then hurried from the office.

Mosley's computer beeped. "Here's the e-mail."

Susan stepped around the desk with him to look at the screen. Mosley double clicked on the attachment icon of the e-mail. A blurred photograph came up on the screen. As the resolution improved, a man and a teenager could be seen clearly among the trees, crouching near a field of long grass. The boy was in the foreground, more detailed than the older man, with sandy-brown hair and a gaunt face—similar to the face that looked at them from the family photo on Mosley's desk nearby. The general put his face in his hands and groaned. "It's Aaron."

Susan spun to the map again and followed the symbol for the train tracks. The tracks led directly to Libreville. "If he's going to Libreville, the railroad would get him there."

Mosley joined her at the map. "But where? Where would he go? The American Embassy?"

"Wherever he's headed, his presence in Libreville will realize our worst fears." A thought suddenly came to her. "Here's a question for you, General: Why hasn't he turned himself in? Why is he running?"

Mosley's eyes narrowed, unsure of why she was asking. Finally, he said, "Obviously, he's scared. What he saw at the compound spooked him as it would any of us. His family is dead. Wouldn't that frighten you?"

"Sure," she said, "but I'd run into the arms of the authorities. To get help. So far, he seems to be doing everything he can *not* to get caught. Why?"

"That's a good question." Mosley paced away from her, then turned back suddenly. "The end of the world."

"What do you mean?"

"It was part of my son's theology. The compound was intended to keep them separate from the world's evil influence and to protect them from the forces of evil until the *end* of the world—the Apocalypse. They expected it any day."

That made perfect sense to Susan and explained why Aaron wouldn't surrender to the authorities. Not if he suspected that they were part of the forces of evil.

"The air strike . . ." Mosley added, and his voice sounded choked. "If he saw the air strike on the compound, he might been convinced that he was in the final days. He wouldn't have understood why we did it."

"If he's headed for Libreville, then he must be headed for a place where he'd feel safe and protected." Her eyes went back to the map, followed the railroad tracks, and then fell on the symbol of a small cross near the western terminus of the railroad just to the east of Libreville. "What is that—a church?" Susan asked.

"It might be."

"Do you mind?" Susan asked, and went to the general's computer. She punched in a series of commands, taking her to a computerized map of Gabon, then the Libreville area. She zeroed in on the site where the symbol of the cross sat and a second screen popped up to identify it. "It's a Catholic school, convent, and medical clinic run by . . ." She scrolled further, then read. "The Sisters of Mercy."

"Why would he go there? My son wasn't Catholic."

Susan attacked the keyboard again. A flurry of keystrokes later, she had up the Web site of the general's son and his ministry. She felt uneasy as she came to the home page, which had a photo of David and his wife and a photo of the front entrance to the compound. It had all been so easily wiped away. She quickly found a tab directing her to a page titled "Appreciation." It listed the supporters of the effort in Gabon. The Sisters of Mercy was named there.

"According to this, the Sisters of Mercy was occasionally provided medical backup for your son's commune," she said.

Mosley's eyes widened. "Aaron might know them."

"If he's running out of options, then he might go to them for help," she suggested.

"It's possible. What other leads do we have?"

Kevin appeared at the door, tucking in his shirt, looking as if he had been rudely and abruptly awaked. He gave a self-conscious glance at Susan, then said to the general, "I'm sorry, sir. Had I known you were awake . . ."

"Forget it," Mosley snapped. "Get me air transport to Libreville."

"Yes, sir."

"Also, get the Mother Superior at the Sisters of Mercy in Libreville on the phone."

"Yes, sir," Kevin said, and then did a double take. "Did you say *Mother Superior*?"

CHAPTER SIXTY-TWO

MARK STRETCHED OUT ON his bed and read through the personal papers of the man named Benjamin Hancock who had been known for over three hundred years as the Blue Monk. He was no apparition, but a thoughtful, educated man of flesh and blood who left a collection of journals and writing.

The collection contained mostly letters, some written in Latin, some in French, a handful in Spanish. Joan, or someone, had taken the time to translate parts of the material, a painstaking process resulting in a few handwritten pages and many others that were typed.

The splotchy fonts and uneven lines told Mark that the translator had used an old mechanical typewriter.

The material had been assembled in chronological order; the earliest letters were to or from the members in Benjamin's family. They dealt with incidentals, normal living, and concerns, the worries of a student upon whom high expectations were placed.

He was to become a minister. There were two modest exchanges between Benjamin and Elinor, his betrothed, who eventually became his wife. They had a daughter named Lydia.

Benjamin and Elinor were of one mind and heart spiritually, and together they made a decision to become Catholics. Given that Protestantism was the state religion, this would have been tantamount to professional suicide.

Benjamin announced the decision at a family gathering in Eyam. It stirred quite a reaction in the Hancock family. The elder Hancock immediately and legally disowned his son. Benjamin was left with only his wife and daughter as family. Flurries of letters were exchanged as Benjamin pleaded with his family for their understanding if not their support. He explained his thinking on theological grounds, on a basis of faith, on conviction, on his love of truth. It didn't matter. In the end, the father returned all of the letters with a simple note telling him to never write again.

Benjamin's love for the Roman Catholic Church couldn't be turned into a vocation. He was married and had a child, so becoming a priest wasn't an option. He looked to the deaconate, but had to make a living while he studied. He took on various jobs: blacksmith, farmer, builder, and candle maker. Over the years, there were few things he *didn't* do.

England was going through a painful time of conflict between the Protestants and the Roman Catholic Church. The impact on Benjamin and his small family soon became clear: they had to leave for a safer territory.

They worked and saved and eventually found the money for passage to Ireland, where Benjamin secured a position in Dublin as a teacher of the poor, subsidized by the university there.

During the voyage to Ireland, a storm came upon the vessel. It was battered and took on water. The captain, an inexperienced sailor and certain the boat was going to sink, commanded all to abandon ship.

He ordered the passengers to smaller boats to fend for themselves. According to an account written by Benjamin to the head of the Lumen Christi Order, Benjamin argued with the captain since he believed the ship would be saved while the smaller boats might be lost at sea. The captain prevailed, and Benjamin put his wife and daughter in the care of an older sailor on a smaller vessel. Benjamin stayed behind with a handful of men to help save the ship.

Unfortunately, Benjamin was right. The men were able to save the craft, but only one of the small boats endured the storm. The one with Elinor and Lydia apparently capsized. Benjamin's loved ones disappeared into a watery abyss.

Mark had to put the papers aside for a moment. He could well imagine how Benjamin felt—was aware of the burden Benjamin carried, knowing that his decision had contributed to, perhaps even caused, the death of his wife *and* daughter.

Mark remembered the circumstances surrounding his daughter's death, no longer in a flow of time, but in pieces. He had been away for a few weeks teaching at various seminars—fulfilling his vocation, pursuing his passion. He saw himself before the large crowds, pleased with himself, knowing he was both helping and making a difference as he imparted knowledge borne of hours in study and in labs.

The illness hit Jenny while he was gone. At first, he was dismissive of what he considered his wife's overreaction to the flu-like symptoms. Donna often overreacted to the smallest things: a blocked toilet, a sound under the hood of the car, a sniffle from Jenny.

Everything was a crisis, a reason why she wanted him to rush home. He heard himself explaining that Jenny likely had a minor viral infection, how antibiotics wouldn't help, and how they just needed to ride it out. He heard the condescension in his voice as he watched Donna take Jenny to their family physician. "Yeah, sure, go ahead," he had said, "but he'll tell you the same thing."

The symptoms were deceitful and fooled their physician. Viral meningitis would have been serious enough, but the actual diagnosis was worse: bacterial meningitis. And not only that, one of the worst strains had invaded his little girl's body. Yet, even a disease as bad as this can be beaten if recognized and treated early.

Mark saw himself on a cramped commercial flight, willing the pilot to break all speed records to get him home. He felt bitter disdain for the movie on the screen overhead, the tinny music coming from the earphones of the woman next to him, the offer of pretzels. He allowed himself a single drink—whisky and soda—to ease his anxiety, and he prayed. He prayed as Benjamin must have prayed in the storm.

He wondered whether Benjamin had seen the bodies of his wife and daughter again. Did their bodies float to the surface of calmer waters? Did they eventually wash ashore? Benjamin's letters didn't say.

But Mark had faced the scornful look of his wife as he arrived at the hospital an hour too late. He had faced the serene expression of Jenny, who lay still on the bed. She was lost to him, lost to them forever.

Mark looked down at the pages and was surprised to see water spots like tiny explosions on the print. He was crying again. He wiped his face, annoyed at his emotional incontinency.

There was no point in reading further. Why bother? He knew how it turned out. Benjamin became a monk, helped people, and died as a result of it. Fine. Mark could help people also.

Still, Mark felt a nagging question, one that came to him with the potency of a high-voltage shock: what did Benjamin *feel* as he played out the rest of his life?

Swinging his feet off the bed, Mark sat up fully. Did Benjamin feel anything? Was it necessary to feel anything while doing one's job? While caring for people?

Yes, came the answer, like a voice in the room.

Nonsense, was Mark's response. Leave me alone in a lab, allow me to fight viruses and disease, and I can do it without feeling a thing. Certainly I can work to save humanity without feeling anything toward humans. Why not?

Why not?

Because feelings were personal. Feelings were intrusive. Feelings were risky. Feelings made him vulnerable. His ex-wife played his feelings against him.

No, it was much better to neutralize them, bury them.

Like toxic waste, came another voice.

Mark stood impatiently. This whole line of thought was ridiculous. Pointless. He had work to do.

Like Benjamin.

His curiosity was sparked now. He had to know. *What did Benjamin do with his tragedy? How did he handle it? Did he say?*

Mark turned to the scattered sheets of paper on the bed and reached for the final stack, compelled by a yearning to know how Benjamin rationalized becoming a monk and dedicating himself to others. A clichéd overreaction to a tragedy, he was sure, but for some reason he had to confirm the theory.

CHAPTER SIXTY-THREE

PAULINE MISSABMO AND HER three older children labored in their large family garden as the tropical sun began to race toward the western horizon. She, like her neighbors in the outskirts of Libreville, worked in their gardens in the early morning and late afternoon to avoid the brutal midday sun.

She straightened and stretched her back, glancing toward her home. She knew that some might have considered it only a hut, but Polly, as her friends called her, and her husband, André, were deeply grateful for it. Having grown up in the slums of the city, they experienced the sacrifice and hard work it took to purchase a small home on several acres of fertile land on the banks of the Ogooué River.

During the day André worked at a nearby factory and the children attended the Sisters of Mercy School. Polly was pleased with the Sisters and with her children learning to read and write, but even more pleased to see her children reading and understanding the Bible.

Polly and André were saving as much money as possible in the hopes that at least one of their children could attend college. They knew that, other than backbreaking work and the occasional blessing, education was the best ticket out of the soul-squelching poverty of Western Africa.

Having the land on which she could grow fruits and vegetables while raising chickens, goats, and pigs allowed Polly to not only produce plenty of food for her family, but also to sell the excess at a local market.

The low rattle of the nearby railroad tracks caused her to look up. The afternoon train was approaching from the west. She glanced at the position of the sun in the sky, aware that the train was late. That was nothing unusual; delays in the Gabon transportation system were commonplace. However, what drew her interest was the speed of the train. Rather than speeding past to make up for lost time as it often did at this section of track, risking life and limb of cows and small children, it seemed to be slowing down.

She listened. The train *was* slowing down, but there was no high-pitched squeal of brakes. It was as if it had simply given up on its journey and was coasting to a stop. There was an eerie silence to the moment. The train moved quietly and she thought of the ghost trains that some of her neighbors had sworn they'd seen on moonlit nights. The train was nearly to her property now, a large French-style TGV high-speed engine, scarred and rusted red, crawling to a stop.

Curious, she dropped her hoe and began to walk toward the train, which ran along the river at the very back of their property. Her children began to follow, but she waved them back with a stern warning.

Something was wrong although she was not yet sure what. As she drew closer to the train, she realized no one was moving. The few people she could see through the windows all seemed to be napping.

She walked to the first passenger car. She looked to her left and right. *Strange, no conductors at the doorways.* She turned to her right, heading toward the engine itself. She reached the steps to the driver's compartment and looked up, expecting someone to appear. When no one did, she reached for the railing, but then withdrew, unsure about her right to enter without authorization. She didn't want to get in trouble for her curiosity.

"Bonjour?" She spoke the greeting several times. No one responded. She returned to the first passenger car. The train itself was too high for her to peer into a window, so she went to the first set of stairs and stepped up to the door. She called out in French, "Who is here? Is everything all right?"

Through the window of the coach door she saw what she couldn't see from the ground. The sight before her made her stumble back against the door of the second car. She drew her hand to her mouth, unable to stop the scream that came.

The car was crowded with bodies, twisted and contorted in grotesque positions. The smell of vomit permeated the hot atmosphere. The seats and floor were blood spattered. No one moved. All appeared dead.

Nausea overwhelmed her and she clenched her hand over her lips to press them closed. She felt faint. Struggling against the wave of fear, she saw two of her children approaching. It pushed her to action and she leapt from the train, waving her hands in the air. "Stay away, children!"

"Ma mère!" she heard from her oldest son. "Come here!"

Polly looked to her left to see her oldest son standing near the front of the train. The blood drained from her face and a feeling of dread rose in her chest. "Back away, Louis! Now!"

She began to run toward him, stumbling over the crushed-rock rail bed. To her mounting horror, he didn't move. She rushed to his side and looked into the massive locomotive.

There at the top of the steps leading into the driver's compartment an engineer crawled on his hands and knees, slowly, without any awareness of what he was doing. He whimpered like a sick dog. His face and arms were covered with red sores and claw marks as if he'd been trying to scratch the sores away. The wounds oozed blood that dripped to the deck in front of him. He slipped on it, his arms splaying outward, his head and upper body falling onto the steps and then banging against the steel with a dull thud.

"Mon Dieu!" Polly cried out as she pulled Louis away and began to run toward their home.

Her neighbors came toward them from their own homes and fields. Polly screamed at them, "Get away!"

They came ahead anyway. In desperation, she screamed the words that sent fear into the hearts of most men and women, *"L' Ebola! L' Ebola!"*

CHAPTER SIXTY-FOUR

MARK SAT DOWN AGAIN and began to read what turned out to be a collection of letters translated into English from French. Mark flipped through, trying to discern who Benjamin's pen pal was, and found a small index card with a typed description. It read:

NOTE: Brother Lawrence (Nicholas Herman, c. 1605–1691), the author of these letters, was a lay brother among the Carmelites, known to have lived in a French monastery at the time of this correspondence. He is best known for the classic study of spirituality known as "The Practice of the Presence of God." Brother Benjamin's original letters to Brother Lawrence have not been discovered.

That was all it said, but Mark was astounded. He knew and read the works of Brother Lawrence back when he took his faith seriously enough to study its great writers. With awe he looked at the letters in his hand. This was significant, not unlike finding a few lost letters of William Shakespeare. His hands trembled as he unfolded the first letter.

Dearest Brother Benjamin,
Though it has been several years since your tragic event, I have no doubt that the loss of your dear daughter and wife are the source of your doubt and pain. I will not speak the obvious to you. Eliminating your pain is not possible, so I do not pray that you may be delivered from your pains, but I pray earnestly that God will give you strength and patience to bear them as long as

He pleases. Comfort yourself with Him who holds you fastened to the cross. He will loose you when He thinks fit and bring you to a glorious resurrection as He has promised.

The men of the world consider their losses as a pain to endure, and not as a means from God to demonstrate His mercy and grace. Seeing it only in that light, they find nothing in it but grief and distress. But those who consider the loss of a dear wife and daughter as allowed by the hand of God, as the effects of His mercy, and as the means which He employs for their purification, commonly find in it great sweetness and sensible consolation.

Continue then always with God: 'tis the only support and comfort for your affliction. I shall beseech Him to be with you.

Yours,
Brother Lawrence

Even as he placed the letter aside, Mark wanted to put the rest of them away. *This is too hard. Embracing that kind of pain is too much to ask.* But he couldn't stop and picked up the next letter.

Dearest Brother Benjamin,

I understand, from the tone of your letter, that my words provided small comfort. Still, I encourage you in them; meditate upon their possibilities for your heart. That God often permits suffering should not be a surprise to you. In this world, we must suffer, lest we feel at home here and forget we are but travelers to our true home. Too easily do we forsake the mansion that awaits us, for a small inn by the roadside.

Our sufferings push us onward, ever restless, to be with Him who offers us the ultimate and final comfort.

Our pain, then, purifies our souls, and obliges us to continue with Him. It shapes and forms us, as gold is shaped and formed in the intensity of fire, and as wet clay is shaped and formed in the hands of the craftsman.

I shall endeavor to assist you with my poor prayers. Pray for me, as I do for you.

Yours,
Brother Lawrence

Mark sighed deeply. He struggled to understand how, with all of his theological study and learning, he had missed such basic teaching on suffering.

Still, what did it matter? These were words. Mere words. Nothing more.

And unless Benjamin was a pliable sort of person, these words couldn't have been very helpful. Had someone said them to Mark in the days following Jenny's death, he might have resorted to violence in response. He unfolded a third letter.

Dearest Brother Benjamin,

I am in pain to see you suffer so long. I do not disagree with you when you write that gold and clay are but inanimate things, which neither think nor feel, whereas we are men who do. To that, I would remind you that, while gold and clay do not feel the pain of that which forms them, they also do not feel the love, mercy, and grace of the One who created them. Nor do they understand that their formation is purposeful, as does the child who is cherished and chastised by the parent who loves him.

We are but children, my brother, who daily make a choice in how we respond to the love and chastisement of our Father. We may accept his love ungratefully and be formed as children who are spoiled, unkind, selfish, and of little use to Him in our world. We may also accept the sufferings ungratefully and also become selfish, bitter, and hateful. Or we may be children who accept both love and suffering with welcome gratitude, knowing that they purposefully shape us and, as our beloved Saint Paul has reminded us, enable us to share God's mercy and grace with others who also suffer.

My brother, which choice will you make in this time of suffering? Have you diverted your gaze away from His love, as if it never existed; have you closed your eyes to the many proofs of God's love toward you even now? Awake, my son, open your eyes again, fix your gaze and see Him in that view, and you will bear the pain more easily.

God knows best what is needful for us, and all that He does is for our good. If we knew how much He loves us, we would be always ready to receive equally and with indifference from His

*hand the sweet and the bitter; all that came from Him would
please.*

*I also beg you not to bear crosses that our Father has not given
you to bear. In your words, I see that you have taken upon yourself a burden that is not yours. The storms of life come upon us
and we do our very best to think wisely, to choose diligently, to
respond prudently. Even if the outcome is tragic, we must not
torture ourselves with alternatives, which are not now possible to
put into effect. The past cannot be changed, the future belongs to
God. Ours is to trust Him in the present.*

*He sometimes permits suffering to cure the distempers of the soul.
Have courage then. Make a virtue of necessity. Ask of God, not deliv-
erance from your pains, but strength to bear resolutely, for the love of
Him, all that He should please, and as long as He shall please.*

*He is the Father of the afflicted, always ready to help us. He
loves us infinitely more than we imagine or can ever love ourselves. Love Him then, and seek not consolation elsewhere. I hope
you will soon receive it.*

*Adieu. I will help you with my prayers, poor as they are, and
shall be, always, yours in our LORD.*

> *Yours,*
> *Brother Lawrence*

Mark leaned back against the headboard and closed his eyes.
What was he expected to do with these words? *If we knew how
much He loves us, we would be always ready to receive equally and with
indifference from His hand the sweet and the bitter; all that came from
Him would please.*

He saw himself standing next to Jenny's coffin. In his pain, in
that moment, he didn't ask God for comfort or consolation. He
didn't ask God for anything. He dispensed with God altogether,
just as he concluded that God had dispensed with him.

But now, through the three-hundred-year-old words of a man
whose main job was to wash dishes in a Carmelite priory, Mark
saw that he hadn't given God a chance to either love or chastise
him. He hadn't even tried. He had withdrawn into himself to a
self-reliance that soon failed, to a vocation that became empty, to
an anesthetized existence.

He thought of Nora's words to him in the car and Andrew's brief observations during their hike. *What deal did he think he'd made with God?*

Obviously Benjamin had made his choice, but how did he make it? Did he simply accept the words of Brother Lawrence as they came to him, or did something else come into play?

Mark picked up the last letter.

Dearest Brother Benjamin,

I render thanks to our Lord for your last letter, as he has relieved you a little, according to your desire. You have wisely chosen not to withdraw, as if you were a turtle hiding in a shell. The temptation to do so is great. But you are a man and as a man you have reached out to Him and, in turn, reached out to those who also suffer as you have. You will share their suffering. In that suffering, you will truly become a man of God and lead others to do the same. Of this also I give hearty thanks to God.

You are not alone, my son. The prayers of your brothers and of all the saints are with you.

I know that for you to have arrived at this state has been difficult. So it is, for we must act purely in faith, believing that the outcome is not in our hands, but in the hands of our God.

So, though it is difficult, we know also that we can do all things with the grace of God, which He never refuses to them who ask it earnestly. Knock, persevere in knocking, and I can assure you that He will open to you in His due time, and grant you all at once what He has deferred during many years.

Adieu. Pray to Him for me, as I pray to Him for you. I hope to see Him quickly.

Yours,
Brother Lawrence

Through the lace curtains, Mark could see the gray light of an emerging dawn. He looked at the digital clock on the nightstand and saw that it was after 5:00 a.m.

He carefully brought together all the pages, put them back into their proper order, and placed them in the satchel Joan had given him. He stood and then immediately sat again. Even if he wasn't particularly comfortable with Brother Lawrence's letters, he recognized them as speaking the truth.

All right. Benjamin took his tragedy and allowed it to draw him closer to God and those around him. What have I done with my tragedy? What am I to do with it?

Was it too late to change, to allow himself to be re-formed or reshaped? Would it take a new and painful fire to change the shape he'd become? Can the clay be remolded once it has been in the kiln?

No. It would have to be shattered, ground to powder. The gold would have to be melted. *The bone would have to be broken and reset.*

To change, he would have to suffer. This much he knew, and he wasn't sure he could take that. Yet, he knew he couldn't continue on as he was.

He looked at the last page of the collection: an old map.

There was a gentle knock at the door and it startled him. He didn't want to speak with anyone. He needed time to think.

The knock came again, a little firmer. Then Nora's voice from the other side. "Mark?"

Fighting with himself, he went to the door and opened it.

Nora looked at him, and her pleasant expression suddenly changed to one of worry. "Are you all right? You look horrible." She glanced past him into the room as if she fully expected to see discarded bottles.

There was a lot Mark wanted to say to her. On another occasion, he might have invited her in and poured his heart out to her; she was the one person he could do that with, but this wasn't the occasion. "I haven't slept," he said, nodding his head toward the letters. "Research."

She looked puzzled and then seemed to shrug it off. "The equipment is here. We're going to meet downstairs to figure out how to proceed."

"Okay," he said, but he already knew what he had to do.

She glanced at him again, as if something ought to be said. Then she turned and walked away.

He closed the door and turned to the room.

"God," he said to the apparent emptiness, "eventually we're

going to talk. But, in the meantime, I'm going to do something I haven't done in years. I'm going to ask for your help. Please . . . show me where you're hiding the Blue Monk."

He carefully put all the pages but one back in the satchel.

Moving to the desk, he lifted the lid on the scanner of his all-in-one portable printer and placed the map on the glass. A moment later he had an image on his laptop, and a hard copy to take with him. He then put the map back in the satchel and closed it.

Thank you, Joan, he thought. *You just may have helped the world— and me.*

CHAPTER SIXTY-FIVE

THE TEAM'S MEETING BEGAN with a briefing from Mark, who presented the most pertinent facts he'd gleaned from Joan's documents. He kept it short and was determined not to get lost in the personal history of the monk, explaining only that the Blue Monk had been murdered and the body disposed of in the caves. He held up the map and identified where he hoped they'd find the body in the network of caves.

Mark sat down and watched as Nora introduced Sergeant Jeremy Sickler from the Corps of Royal Engineers, a young and sturdy Englishman with a shaved head and full, friendly face. Sickler went through a cursory inventory of the caving equipment: hard hats with mounted halogen lamps and an extra light that could be attached to the helmet or used as a flashlight as needed; fleece underwear; waterproof overalls with more pockets and loops than Mark had ever seen before; wet socks; waterproof hiking boots with rubberized soles; knee and elbow pads; and insulated gloves. And those were just the clothes he'd have to wear.

Mark felt overwhelmed and asked, "Is all this stuff necessary?"

"You'll find out how necessary when you get down there," Sickler replied.

Digger laughed. "He thought he could dress like Laura Dern in *Jurassic Park*. Light shirt and shorts, a pair of knee socks . . ."

"You're laughing," Mark said, "but you're coming with us, you know."

Digger's face fell. "What?"

"You're our resident grave digger. We'll need your help," he said.

Digger frowned and kicked at nothing on the floor.

"We'll go over the rest at the site," Sickler said, gesturing to the various ropes, bolts, cams, slings, and carabiners. "We've got a few safety tips to consider, as well."

Nora stepped to the forefront. "Well, then, I guess we better let our cavemen get dressed."

Sickler held up a hand. "Pardon the question, but where exactly are we going?"

Mark handed Sickler the old map. "Here."

He looked at it and recognized the identification of the church. "You're going into a churchyard?"

Digger beamed. "We're going into a *grave*."

"Let's be clear about this," Sickler announced to Mark and Digger at the top of the Templeton tomb. "We're going into an environment that is contrary to our natural experience. We can't afford to be overconfident. If you show a hint of claustrophobia—even if you've never suffered from it before—we will abort the mission and come back out." He had given them small rolls of bright yellow tape. "We'll use this flagging tape to mark the caves as we go."

"Is this like leaving a trail of bread crumbs?" Digger joked.

"You bet it is," Sickler said. "A cave that looks familiar one moment can look completely unfamiliar the next. Attach the tape to the stone or stick it out of the cracks so we can find our way back. Now, test your equipment."

Nora watched while Mark adjusted the headset under his helmet. He punched a button on a small walkie-talkie provided by Sickler. It was a top-secret communication device specially designed by the British military to transmit signals great depths into the earth—even through the thickest stone. Mark spoke into the device. Henry, who had been outfitted for the occasion as a backup, listened, and then responded on the other device.

"We're good," Mark said.

Nora watched all this with growing concern. The risks of harm to Mark and Digger in those unknown caves were enormous, and all for a corpse that might not exist. One consolation: Mark was bright eyed and determined in a way she hadn't seen for a very long time. Something happened to him overnight. Something to do with the satchel he'd given her to return to Joan, but only on the promise that she not look at the contents.

The map, on the other hand, was the most hopeful item she'd seen. It purported to navigate the underground tunnels from two directions: through the mouth of the cave to the north, which was now closed due to the mysterious explosion, and through the tomb in the churchyard. Both directions led to a central area marked only as "Cathedral," and to a side spur marked with a "B," which they assumed was the location of the Blue Monk's body.

Nora bit her lip as the men finalized their instructions and offered a prayer for help and protection. She looked over at the two soldiers stationed to protect them in case of any trouble from Return to Earth or anyone else.

She noticed that the men also watched Sickler with a certain amount of competitive disdain. *All testosterone and bravado,* she thought.

Mark, looking encumbered and clumsy in his cave-trolling outfit, hoisted on a small backpack, adjusted the straps, and then approached the tomb. He suddenly looked up and searched around, as if missing something. His gaze landed on Nora. He waved to her, she waved back, and then he descended following Sickler. Digger followed, while Henry lingered around the mouth of the entrance panel of the tomb.

"Nora," Andrew called out from behind her. She turned to see the reverend and another man strolling toward her. She thought it was the detective—Ian something or other—who brought Mark back to the hotel after his hostage ordeal.

The two men came close, and the reverend said, "This is Detective Inspector Ian Glover with the local constabulary. He's here on a possible murder case."

"There's no possible about it," Glover said grimly to Andrew.

Nora asked, "Who's been murdered?"

"Joan Thompson."

Mark now understood Sickler's warning about feelings of claustrophobia. It wasn't a condition Mark ever suffered, but he was willing to make an exception as he crawled forward into the narrow and cramped tunnel. He repeatedly banged his helmet on the rocks overhead and thumped his legs against the uneven rocks to the side.

Every now and then Digger's headset turned on, and Mark could hear Digger's heavy breathing in his ear, along with the occasional profanity.

"Are you all right?" Mark asked. "You sound as if you're going to have a heart attack."

"I'm used to robbing graves, not actually *being* in one," Digger complained.

"Are you still above us, Henry?" Mark asked, puffing as he crawled.

"In every sense," returned the genteel English voice in a burst of static.

"Does that map of yours give any sense of distance?" Digger asked.

"Nope," Mark said. He wished it had. The cool dampness of the tunnel had already begun to work into his joints.

Suddenly, there was static on the headset again and Nora said into his ear, "A question for you, Mark . . ."

"Yeah, go ahead."

"Where exactly did you meet with Joan Thompson last night?"

"Why?" A long, crackly pause. "Nora?"

"She's been murdered, Mark."

The shock stopped Mark where he was. He braced himself against the rocks. "No. How?"

"I don't know all the details."

Mark squeezed his eyes shut and tried to concentrate beyond the last image of her walking away from him. "It was a school playground of some sort, not far from our inn," he replied. "The soldier—Westcott—can show you. He was with us when we met."

"I'll let you know more when you're topside again. Signing off."

Another click of static and she was gone. Mark felt sick. Who would want to kill Joan? It had to be Return to Earth again. Or was it another group, the group that had caused Joan to be afraid for her safety after handing him the satchel? Why hadn't he sent a soldier to protect her? *Because I didn't take her fear seriously. Whom did she fear? Who had her so spooked?*

"Mark . . ." It was Sickler.

"What?"

"We have to keep moving," he said. "I'm sorry about your friend, but we have a job to do."

Mark begrudgingly agreed and pushed himself forward. He had no idea how far he'd gone, but was suddenly aware that Sickler was standing in front of him and that his own helmet was no longer banging and scraping the cave roof. He stopped then turned his head in every direction, flashing the helmet light on the dark walls.

Digger was at his feet, doing the same. "It's opened up," he said.

Mark carefully stood, his muscles and bones protesting as he did. He took in a deep breath of air. It was laden with the smells of the earth, rock, and water. It was not as stale as he expected. He looked at Sickler. "Which way now?"

Sickler studied the map. He then gestured with his helmet light. "This way."

Using the map, they maneuvered the various intersections they encountered along the way, with Digger putting flagging tape at various points. Mark realized that the network of tunnels followed no strategic design, but were dug only where the miners searched for lead ore. The monks had apparently used the existing tunnels and then added a few of their own. Mark knew that without the map they'd be hopelessly lost.

"You realize we've been heading down for quite a while," Sickler observed.

"How far down?"

"We've been walking at such a gentle grade that it's hard to tell."

Mark was surprised to find various torches strewn along the walls. He guessed the monks used them as they made their way through the caves.

Eventually, they came to an opening that led to a taller and wider section of cave. "We should be near the Cathedral," Mark said, studying the map with Sickler. They continued onward and Mark could feel in the backs of his legs that they were ascending again.

"It shouldn't be much farther," Mark said, aware that the map wasn't drawn to any particular scale. For all he knew it could be miles. Who could tell without any markings to establish perspective?

But after another ten minutes and at least a dozen stops to make sure they were on the right track, they reached a wall of solid rock. There was no turning left or right—it was a dead end. Mark looked at the map, the wall, and the map again.

"What is this?" Digger asked. "Did we go the wrong way?"

Mark pressed his palm against the wall. "The Cathedral is supposed to be here," he said. "But I don't know where it is."

CHAPTER SIXTY-SIX

NORA WALKED WITH DETECTIVE Inspector Ian Glover and Reverend Andrew to the rectory.

Andrew seemed to move slower than usual, his head lowered, face drawn and pinched in an expression of unexpressed grief. Nora wanted to say something of comfort about losing Joan, but was at a loss for words.

They paused at a brown Rover that, from the look of the police paraphernalia on the front seat, must have belonged to the detective.

"The playground is where Joan's body was found by a jogger around five this morning," Glover said with a dour expression. "I need details from Dr. Carlson: what time they met and exactly where."

"Corporal Westcott can answer those questions," Nora said. "According to Mark, he was there when they met Joan last night."

"Will he also know why she was speaking with Dr. Carlson at all or what they discussed?" Glover asked.

"I don't know." Nora reached into her case and retrieved the satchel Mark had given her. "It had something to do with this."

Glover took the bag and opened it. "What is it?"

"Documents," Nora replied. "They're connected to the Blue Monk and the work Dr. Carlson is now doing in the cave."

Glover pulled out a bundle of pages and glanced at them without any discernable interest. With raised eyebrows, Andrew leaned in to look.

"Does this mean anything to you?" the detective asked him.

"Diaries? Letters? I'd be glad to take a closer look."

The detective looked at Nora. "Do these documents have anything to do with Return to Earth?"

Nora shook her head. "Not that I know of."

Handing the satchel to the reverend, Glover shook his head. "This was a quiet village until a few days ago," he said, and looked at Nora with undisguised accusation.

A cell phone rang. Nora didn't recognize the ring so didn't bother with hers. Glover reached for his belt and unclipped his phone. He moved away from them as he called his name into the receiver, then his voice fell into a muted tone.

"A nasty business," Andrew said.

"I'm really sorry. Was she married? Does she have family?"

He shook his head. "A widow. Her husband died of cancer a few years ago. They had a son, but he was in the army and was killed while serving as a peacekeeper in Croatia." Andrew paused, averting his gaze from her and looking at a smudge on the Rover's hood. "She was strangled, you know. Who would do such a thing to her? She was as timid as a mouse . . ."

She didn't speak, but hoped talking was of some comfort to him.

He leafed through the pages in the satchel. "I hope this will give us some clues."

"Mark seemed excited about it, but the whole business with Joan was very secretive. I was supposed to deliver everything back to her without looking at any of it. Mark was adamant about that. No one was allowed to see it."

"I wouldn't have put Joan at the center of anything so mysterious," Andrew said. "She's such a simple and uncomplicated woman." The lines around his eyes seemed to deepen and he pressed his lips together tightly.

Nora's cell phone rang. The number on the screen told her it was Mac. She nodded apologetically to the reverend and stepped away. "This is Nora."

"Nora? It's Mac. We have a situation."

"No kidding. You tell me yours, and I'll tell you mine."

"Eventually, you'll be hearing from MI5 or MI6, maybe both. In the meantime, you must make immediate contact with a local detective. His name is Ian Glover."

Nora glanced at Glover, who had his back to her, still on his phone. "I'm with him now. Why?"

"He's about to meet a man from Interpol named Martin Duerr. Have you heard of him?"

"He's the case officer working on Return to Earth," Nora said. "Mark mentioned him—or the general did—I don't remember which."

"In any case, he's coming to you directly. Their agent was killed in Switzerland, but he has some information that may tie into your work there. He's flying into Manchester at . . ." A pause, and Nora imagined Mac looking at his watch. "He's landed, in fact. Give him your full cooperation."

Before Nora could speak, Mac clicked off.

She turned to Glover as he turned to her. "Well," he said with a weary sigh. "It looks as if Interpol is coming."

"How is it going, gents?" Henry asked over the headset.

"Just a momentary pause," Mark replied.

"We seem to have come up against a wall." Digger slumped down onto the cave floor and produced a water bottle from somewhere. He drank and looked at Mark and Sickler. "I'm not in shape for this."

Mark rubbed his aching legs. "Who is?"

"Anything I can do?" Henry asked.

"Not at the moment," Sickler answered. "Unless you know a way to drill through this dead end."

After a pause, Henry said, "Right. Let me know if I can help."

"So, what do we do now?" Digger asked. "You know, the whole thing could have caved in over the years or suffered from the explosion."

Mark stood back from the wall and allowed his helmet light to shine along the edges. Sickler pulled a back-up light from its holster and shone it to double up the brightness. In a shadow above the wall they saw a small section of wooden beam. Mark couldn't believe his eyes—on the beam was the Lumen Christi symbol.

"There's a secret to this," Mark said, looking at the symbol. "I read about this only a few hours ago."

"Where? In a manual?" Digger snorted.

"It was the ancient diary of a boy. His account said that the monk reached into a secret place and pulled a lever. It released the wall and the monk slipped through."

Sickler turned to look at him. "A hidden lever?"

The three men searched the wall and surrounding rocks for anything that might hide a lever. "I don't think it'd be very elaborate. Probably a latch of some sort, like the mechanism in the tomb."

"This is a solid wall, though," Digger said. "It must be on rollers." He pushed himself against the wall and pushed in various directions. The wall didn't move.

"The monk did the sign of the cross," Mark explained.

"What?"

"The account said the monk faced the wall and did the sign of the cross."

Digger looked at him skeptically. "Are you saying there's a seventeenth-century motion sensor hidden in the wall?"

Mark ignored the comment and positioned himself a few feet from the wall. He looked directly at the dark stone and went through the motion of the sign of the cross, hesitating over whether he was to move his hand from the left shoulder to the right, or from the right to the left. He chose right to left— remembering that it was the Eastern Orthodox and Anglicans who went from left to right.

He waited. Nothing happened. He did it again, this time allowing his arm to extend away from his body to the right. His knuckles grazed the wall to his right.

Digger approached him, interested. "The lever is on the right?" He began to run his fingers over the rock where Mark's hand had connected. "Just rock," he said.

Mark thought about it for a moment.

"You're taller than the average man of that time," Sickler commented.

Mark stooped a few inches and repeated the motion.

"Nothing," Digger said after searching the rock again.

Mark stood up straight, stretching his back. "I'm stumped."

"Maybe the Blue Monk was exceptionally tall," Digger suggested. "Or exceptionally short."

Short. The word gave Mark a mental image of the monk standing at the wall and he realized another possibility: "Wait. He was a Catholic monk. He might have genuflected," he said, and did just that. As he did, he noticed in the scuffed dirt of the cave floor a discrepancy. "What's this?"

Sickler and Digger targeted the beams of their flashlights to the floor.

Mark knelt down and brushed at the dirt. Wood—another portion of beam, maybe—was there, with the Lumen Christi emblem. It was only about three inches from where Mark had been standing and was worn and scuffed, as if it had been walked upon many times. "Maybe if I stand on this and do it."

Mark positioned himself on the emblem and genuflected, kneeling on his right knee. He performed the sign of the cross, stretching his hand to the right. This time his knuckles grazed the stone—and a small hinge creaked in the rock wall, opening a small door just a few inches.

"Bingo!" Sickler exclaimed.

"I wonder if it's triggered by the action of the sign of the cross combined with the weight on the emblem?" Mark asked.

"I don't care how it works," Digger said and explored the niche in the rock. "There better not be any snakes in here," he said wincing as he reached into the niche.

"Well?"

"There's a metal lever all right." With some grunting, he seemed to get a grip and pulled. "And voila."

Somewhere in the wall, there was the sound of metal grating against metal and then the wall slid slightly to the right several inches. It was enough for Mark and Sickler to get their hands in and push to widen the space. They pushed hard. The wall wasn't easily moved. Digger stepped up to help and they created enough of a gap for them to step through into the pitch black.

"This cavern is huge," Mark said, as the darkness seemed to swallow the light from their helmets. He reached up to intensify the beam and was mesmerized to see it reflect in a hundred directions around the front of the chamber.

"So this is the Cathedral," Mark said as the three men allowed their helmet lights and flashlights to illuminate what they could of the cave. Mark guessed it was at least five to six stories high, possibly fifty feet wide, and twice that long. Dead torches hung from iron holders along the walls.

Digger walked to a sidewall, pulled out a lighter, and held the flame to the end of a torch. To Mark's surprise, it burst to light as Digger walked toward the front of the room, lighting the torches. The cavern came alive in a blaze of silver light.

Mark stopped in his tracks, his mouth falling open.

"This is the mother lode," Digger said, his voice filled with awe.

The cavern truly was a Cathedral, yet unlike any Mark had ever seen. The altar—and everything in and around it—had apparently been fashioned out of a huge vein of silver. Only the pews had been carved from tree stumps, probably a reflection of the monks' humility. The monks would honor God with luxurious instruments of worship, but not their own backsides.

Digger drifted toward the altar, his voice filled with wonder. "Do you have any idea what this must be worth?"

The monetary value was inconsequential to Mark. He gazed at the beauty and could not begin to imagine the reverence and dedication that must have gone into many decades of backbreaking work by the monks.

He imagined Benjamin lovingly at work with the other brothers, crafting each piece of the altar, the monstrance, the chalices, and the trays. *Was this how he worked out his grief: in the sweat and strain of craftsmanship to create a glorious place of worship? Had Benjamin turned his suffering into an act of worship?*

Mark moved forward, feeling the hair on the back of his neck stand on end. Shadows shifted, rose, and fell upon the dappled walls of rock and the benches. Had their light fallen on the backs of several monks kneeling in prayer, he would have been shocked, but not surprised. Their essence seemed to fill the room.

The three men stood in front of the altar. Set into the rock wall directly behind it was a square crevice carved into the silver, covered by two ornately carved silver doors.

"What's that?" Sickler asked.

"I think it's where they kept the sacrament," Mark said.

Digger looked confused. "What?"

"The bread and wine," Mark clarified. "I think the Catholics call it the tabernacle."

Mark walked over and opened the doors. The three men peered in to see an elaborately carved silver chalice and plate.

"What is it worth?" Digger asked. "Go on. Take a guess."

"Their lives," Mark said. "My guess is that this is what turned the monks blue and killed most of them."

"Taking communion?" Sickler asked.

Mark smiled. "No, drinking the wine out of this silver container. I wonder if it was the source of the silver poisoning that made our monk and the other brothers blue."

Sickler sniffed the air. "Are you getting that?"

Mark also drew in a deep breath. "Fresh air?"

"And a breeze as well," Digger added.

Simultaneously, the three men trained their lights to the right where they saw an archway carved into the rock and a large wooden door beneath it.

"That's where the Blue Monk should be," Mark said, remembering the diagram on the map.

They made their way to the door and examined it. "It's covered with pitch," Mark observed. "Helps explain why it has lasted three centuries." Mark lifted the latch, which opened with surprising ease. He pushed the door open and was greeted by a dim grayness, a contrast to the blind blackness they'd encountered in the tunnels thus far.

"After you two gents," Digger said.

CHAPTER SIXTY-SEVEN

THE MEN HAD TO stoop slightly to get through the doorway and into the adjoining cave. Mark was instantly struck by two wildly different impressions. The first was the stunning beauty of the chamber. It seemed to be made of white translucent quartz.

"It must have taken a million years for the water to carve this out," Sickler whispered. As the men trained their flashlights around the cavern, the light reflected off the massive white stalagmites and stalactites.

At the same time, the foul and bitter smell of dung, mold, and ammonia struck them. The men coughed and Mark lifted his feet in reaction to the stickiness of the floor. "Guano," he said.

Digger lifted his flashlight to the ceiling above them and gasped. It was a moving, rippling mass of bats. "Gentlemen, keep your hats on," he said.

A few yards onward and they found the source of the gray light: a shaft in the ceiling of the cave angling upward to the sky somewhere beyond.

"Light and ventilation," Sickler said.

"Must be how the bats get in and out," Mark observed.

The cave itself was circular with smooth walls glistening with the wet of outside moisture—from the last rainfall, perhaps. On the other side of the circle was a round pit that Mark thought might be a well, built up of uneven quartz stones. Keeping his light shining on a straight path, he went to its edge.

"This must be where they dumped him," Mark said, and he thought of the story from the Bible about Joseph and how his brothers had thrown him into a pit.

"But what's this?" Digger asked.

Mark and Sickler looked to Digger, who had walked to what looked like another altar. Littered on the top of the altar were dried flowers and short, stubby candles.

Digger picked up one of the candles. "Someone bought this at a shop in town for thirty pence," he said, showing the price sticker to Mark.

"There's a group of descendants from the mob who killed the monk that come here to pay their respects," Mark explained.

"Seems freaky to me." Digger turned back to the archway. "I mean, they're not going to come rushing in because we're desecrating their space, right? You wouldn't call it, say, a cult would you?"

Mark paused. Who knew how these kinds of beliefs morphed over the years? What if Joan was murdered by someone in their little group for sharing their secret with him? "Let's keep our eyes open," he said, going back to the well. He shone his light into the hole. Some thirty feet down the beam glistened off something murky and brown. Mark couldn't tell if it was water, or earth, or both.

"Tell me he's not in *there*," Digger said.

"Don't whine." Mark leaned in farther, angling the light into the cavern below. "I'll have to rappel down."

Sickler scrutinized the shaft and shook his head. "It looks like it'll be a difficult rappel. I'll do it."

"With all due respect, Sergeant, I have to be the one. I know what I'm looking for."

Sickler thought a second and then nodded.

The three men set about anchoring a line securely into the cave wall. Fortunately, there were several cracks into which they could insert the spring-loaded cams instead of having to drill into the rock to place bolts.

As he was placing the final cam, Digger lost his grip and the metal instrument fell to the rock, its loud ping echoing off the wall.

There was a flurry of activity above them.

"Down!" Mark called out and the three men quickly dropped. The bats swarmed around their heads and then, en masse, evacuated up and out of the shaft in the roof.

After the bats had gone, Digger stood, trying to wipe the

droppings off his back. He was clearly repulsed. "Bats flying in a mysterious cave. It's such a cliché! You'd think we were in an Abbott and Costello movie."

"You can be the dumpy one," Mark said.

Digger placed the final cam while Sickler checked them all for stability. He then tied equalizing knots and clipped the nylon-knot loops to the carabiners, which were already attached to the cams.

Then Mark, with Sickler watching closely, ran the climbing end of the rope through a GriGri, a hand-sized device designed as a self-locking clutch, used by climbers to prevent a sudden fall. He clipped it onto his climbing harness.

He looked at Sickler, who nodded. "Well done, for an amateur."

"Time to throw the rope into the pit?" Mark asked.

Sickler took the climbing end of the rope and tied a simple knot. "When rappelling into a hole or off an edge without knowing whether the rope is long enough to reach the bottom, you put a knot here. This will ensure you don't rappel off the rope. That would be bad, you see."

Mark smiled. "I can grasp the theory."

After tying the knot on the end of the rope, Sickler threw the rope down the pit. "Sounds like it hit bottom. There should be enough."

While they did this, Digger secured the top end of the rope using an equalized figure-eight knot technique that Sickler taught them. After Sickler double-checked Digger's work, and triple-checked each knot and cam, he nodded. Mark carefully climbed over the stones around the well and to the other side. Sickler and Digger positioned themselves at the edge of the stones.

"I'm off," Mark said. With a grunt, he began to rappel into the shaft, using his feet to steady himself against the rock. About twenty feet down, he was surprised to see a design carved into one side of the shaft, extending to the bottom. At a glance, the design seemed to be made up of a series of squares, each chiseled about four inches into the rock. "There's an odd design here," he said.

Sickler and Digger leaned over the top and hit the wall with their flashlight beams. "It's hard to make out from here," Sickler said.

"Deep squares, like panels for a comic strip," Mark explained. "But they're empty."

"Maybe the monks were going to paint or chisel pictures into the panels," Sickler said. "I've seen that done on cave walls."

Mark perused the design again. "Or maybe I'm looking at it the wrong way. It might be a design made up of crosses. The squares are the spaces between each cross."

"Hey, unless you think they point to your Blue Monk, you ought to keep going," Digger said.

Mark grunted at him and continued downward. A couple of yards later and Mark reached the point where the shaft ended. Suddenly he found himself hanging in open air, as the shaft expanded outward. He looked up at Sickler, silhouetted in the circle above him. "It spreads out."

"What do you mean?"

"It's like an upside-down funnel. This shaft opens out to an underground reservoir or a cavern. The ceiling goes off to my left and right at a forty-five-degree angle and ends at a wall on each side."

Mark let himself down another few feet and hung in midair, unable to hold on to anything but the rope.

"I hope this holds," Mark shouted up.

Mark didn't like the feeling of hanging in the emptiness. He slowly dropped another few feet and then touched bottom. He carefully placed a foot on what he thought would be solid ground. His boot sunk in up to the ankles.

"Soup," he shouted up. "Very, very cold soup."

"Have you touched bottom?"

"It's hard to tell," he said.

He tried to stand and succeeded, but as soon as he took a step, he sunk farther into the muck. Giving himself more slack, he bent to feel the substance of the mess around him. It was soft and ice cold. He brought a finger to his nose and sniffed. "Digger, this is *not* mud down here. It's peat. I think this is a subterranean peat bog."

"Cool!" Digger appeared at the top of the well. His helmet light flashed around Mark like a searchlight.

"That too," Mark said and began to move slowly and carefully through the bog. "But what's it doing here? I thought these things were supposed to be above ground."

"Not always," Sickler called back. "I've come across a few while crawling through caves in Ireland and Europe. Chances are that the opening above us allowed water and vegetation in. The bat guano would help."

Mark scowled. "That was more than I needed to know." He shone his headlamp around the broad cavern.

He shouted up. "I wonder if the monks used the peat."

"It makes for good fuel," Sickler shouted back.

Mark moved sluggishly through the bog and realized the impossibility of what he was attempting to do. "I'm not prepared for this," he called to Sickler and Digger. "I thought the body might be lying down here under a layer of rock, not under all this."

"How will you find it?" Sickler shouted down.

Mark lamented, "We'll need equipment and the means to excavate. This could take days." He groaned. "A man could suffer hypothermia standing in this." He was now up to his knees.

"What do you want me to do?" Digger asked.

"Get help," Mark said.

"I could get a team in from the Corps," Sickler said.

"Let's put it to Henry," Mark said, then turned his headset on again. "Henry, are you there? Henry?"

Henry didn't reply.

"Where is everyone?" Mark called out. The silence worried him. "I think my headset's broken. You guys try."

No one above responded. But Mark thought he heard low voices echoing down the shaft above him.

"Hey! What's going on up there?" Mark positioned himself so he could see up the shaft.

Digger appeared at the top and said in a tentative voice, "Mark?"

"Digger?"

"We have a surprise guest."

"Who is it?"

"You're not going to believe this, but . . ."

And then two shots exploded in the cave.

CHAPTER SIXTY-EIGHT

THE PLAN WAS FOR Inspector Duerr to come to the rectory, so Nora followed Andrew and Glover into the house.

Just before entering the back door, Nora craned her neck to see if there was any activity at the Templeton tomb. The gate had swung closed, obstructing her view.

Andrew fulfilled his ministerial duties in the kitchen by putting the kettle on for tea. Glover disappeared into the dining room, easing himself into a chair with the satchel. He began to paw through the documents. Nora was anxious. Taking out her cell phone, she dialed Henry's number. He seemed to pick up before it rang.

"Yes?" he asked softly.

"Is everything all right?"

"Just dandy. The boys have found a pit where they hope the monk is buried—at least, that's the last word I got from them."

"What about the body?"

"Not yet, but I think they're close."

She paused, praying for Mark to find the body quickly, then said, "I'm with Detective Glover and Reverend Andrew in the rectory . . ."

"All right. We'll find you if anything comes up." He clicked off.

She leaned back against the kitchen counter and watched as Andrew busily went about getting out the mugs, sugar, and milk. *That's something Joan would be doing,* Nora thought and wondered how high the body count would have to reach before this whole crisis ended.

• • •

His ears still ringing from the blast, Mark turned his helmet light away from the shaft and pushed back through the thick bog into the shadows. His heart raced. The shape of the cavern could get him well out of sight, but then what?

All was quiet above as he waited, his mind churning over the possibilities. He tried his headset again, but no one responded. After a moment, he thought he heard a single voice speaking from somewhere in the cave, then silence again. He began to shiver. He hadn't been joking about hypothermia.

He wondered about Digger and Sickler. Had they been shot? He had to assume so, but by whom? Who was the surprise guest?

The cave echoed with what sounded like pounding and then Mark heard the sound of something drop into the sludge. He trained his helmet light in that direction and saw that his rope had been cut and thrown down the shaft. There was no using it to get back up.

Through clenched teeth Mark called out, "Hey, can we talk about this?" and then pushed himself to change positions again just in case whoever was above was trying to track his position by his voice. He was still up to his knees in the muck. It sucked at him like quicksand. He hoped the exertion would warm him up.

"Any chance of negotiating?" He continued to circle around the shaft, avoiding the dull gray light from above, moving back into the shadows on the opposite side of the cave. What could he do?

He stopped. He thought he heard a soft hum. A song. Whoever was up above was humming a jaunty show tune. He also heard the sounds of things being moved around. The surprise guest was busy doing something. Mark then heard the dings of a hammer against rock, each one echoing loudly around him. *What is going on up there?*

He was getting colder. How long had he been in there? Only a few minutes? Longer? It was enough. He pushed onward in his circle, using his headlamp to search the cavern for a means to get out. Suddenly his left leg fell into the muck up to his thigh.

He groaned and struggled to reverse himself. He rocked back and forth, leveraging his weight. His leg slowly came up and out of the peat, and with it came something thin and long. A branch? He almost pushed it aside, but there was something about the shape that caught his attention. He leaned to look more carefully. It wasn't a branch; it was a *hand*. Not the bones of a hand, but a genuine hand, thin and leathery and brown.

The pounding from above continued with the humming.

Mark scrambled to clear away more of the peat around the hand and soon saw that it was attached to an arm. He dug further and discovered that the arm was enshrouded in a dark, rough cloth, almost perfectly preserved. Mark's heart leapt.

The Blue Monk.

Inspector Martin Duerr arrived in a rental car, looking tired and disheveled.

Nora identified his accent as Swiss, but his features reminded her of G. K. Chesterton's famous British detective Father Brown. Short, pleasantly round without being fat, an amiable expression, and sharp eyes behind his round glasses. After introductions he was led to the dining-room table, where he took out his laptop.

"Wireless?" he asked Reverend Andrew.

The reverend nodded.

"Excellent," he said and went through the activity of turning on the machine and loading up whatever it was he had to show them.

"I appreciate your cooperation. We are seeing unprecedented activity by Return to Earth. In the past, they have been a nuisance. Now they are dangerous. They have murdered one of our agents."

Nora looked to Detective Glover, thinking he would mention Joan's murder to Duerr, but he simply frowned and watched.

"Have any of you ever heard of Dr. Stefan Maier?" Duerr asked.

"The Russian researcher?" Nora asked.

Duerr nodded.

"I've read some of his work on virology and genetics. He was considered a leader in the field for a while. He died, though, didn't he?"

"Years ago in a boating accident on the Rhine while helping with an environmental study for the German government. His body was never recovered."

"What does he have to do with any of this?" Glover asked impatiently.

"Dr. Maier's research and the necessary work on laboratory animals, which he hated, led him to radical actions. He secretly established Return to Earth in 1992."

Nora was surprised. "Maier? But I never heard anything about that."

"He was never the public face, but is considered the founder by those on the inside of the movement. His death certified his place as its martyr, I suppose." Duerr paused, then looked at the three of them. "Only, he isn't dead. He was the man in the photo you provided—the man who attempted to recruit your team member."

"Georgina," Nora said. "She told me the man's name was Stefan and that she got the impression he was a doctor."

Duerr turned to the computer and displayed a series of photographs on the screen. Taken in various locations at various points in time, the photos contained a handsome man with a narrow face, broad smile, and, unlike in Georgina's photo, shoulder-length platinum hair that reminded her of Ludwig van Beethoven's particular wild style. He seemed to wear black suits in every picture though what really struck Nora were his dark and piercing eyes.

"An interesting slide show," Glover said, "but how is standing here looking at pictures going to help us? I don't have time for this. I'm dealing with a murdered woman."

Duerr turned to him, alarmed. "What woman? Give me details."

Glover explained to him what he knew so far, but Nora noticed that he left out any reference to the satchel of documents.

"Strangled?" Duerr frowned. "That does not seem like the killing style of Return to Earth."

"Are fanatical murderers so picky?" Andrew asked.

"Yes, in fact," Duerr said. "Strangling is imprecise. You may strangle a person and leave that person for dead without knowing that the person is truly dead. Their methods are more certain."

Nora's eyes fell to the laptop screen again as photos of Dr. Stefan Maier came and went. One appeared with Maier as a dark-haired younger man. He stood next to another man, also young, who looked familiar to her.

"Stop," she said to Duerr, pointing to the screen. "Make it go back."

Duerr looked at her, his eyebrows arched, and then spun to the laptop. "What is it?" He pushed the keys, and the photo returned.

Nora leaned in, and a feeling of stomach-churning sickness washed over her. "Oh, no."

The three men gathered around her.

"Do you know this other man?" Duerr asked. "He was a good friend of Maier's when Maier taught at Oxford. We believe he was also crucial to the founding of the movement. Apparently he is the primary source of money for the movement. His name is Michael Grant and his name remains on their list of members, though he seems to have disappeared."

"I know exactly where he is," Nora said and as she gripped the back of a chair in front of her, she could feel the blood drain from her body.

CHAPTER SIXTY-NINE

GALVANIZED BY THE DISCOVERY of a body, perhaps *the* body, Mark searched more frantically for a way out. *If I were Spider-Man I could climb up the far wall and simply crawl along the ceiling to the shaft,* he thought. *But I'm not Spider-Man.*

Meanwhile, the pounding and humming continued above him. He wanted to kill whoever it was just for the tune he hummed. It sounded like the Disney song "It's a Small World." He hated that song.

Finally, having exhausted his search, he realized what he had to do. But first he took off one of his gloves and placed it on the monk's exposed hand. "I'll be right back," he whispered, his voice shivering.

He turned off his headlamp and moved to the area just beneath the shaft and cautiously looked up. An empty circle of gray light. A pause in the pounding and Mark stopped where he was and waited. The pounding resumed.

Mark turned his headlamp on again and, with trembling hands, pinpointed it to the shaft, being careful not to let the light shine up to the top. *If the monks used the peat as fuel, then maybe they created a way to climb in and out.* But there was no indication of how they may have done it.

The design carved into the rock of the shaft shifted in moving shadows. He positioned himself at an angle and looked at it again. Crosses and squares, he thought.

Stupid man, he groaned to himself as he realized that the crosses and squares weren't part of a religious design, but a crudely carved stone ladder. No doubt it was more efficient and longer lasting than any other material that existed at the time. He moved the flashlight beam as far up the shaft as he dared go. *Yes, it goes to the top.* He shone the light downward again where he saw at the very bottom two iron rings attached to the rock, with an iron rod stretching between them. He imagined that the monks had hooked an additional section of ladder to that bottom rung. Hopeful, he searched around the peat to find the part of the ladder that had probably broken off. He gave up quickly, concluding that it must have sunk and rotted somewhere in the muck.

Moving underneath the ladder, he looked carefully at the bottom rung. It was only a few tantalizing feet away, but well beyond his reach.

So the question was: how could he get to it?

His rappelling rope lay snakelike on top of the peat. He pulled it to him, remembering that it was still hooked to his harness. Maybe—just maybe—he could toss the hook end of the rope up and over the bottom rung of the ladder, reattach it, and pull himself up.

Batman does it all the time. And then he wondered why he was thinking about superheroes so much. Probably because he was becoming hypothermic and losing his mind.

He eyed the ladder again and considered his options. The noise would certainly draw the attention of the guest above, unless the pounding and humming would help cover it. What choice did he have?

He took off his remaining glove to unhook the rope from his belt and then positioned himself beneath the ladder. The pounding went on, so he swung the hook and tossed it at the metal rung. It came back down without touching the ladder at all. He tried again. And again. And on the fourth attempt, the hook tapped the bottom rung of the ladder with a loud metallic clang, then fell back again. The noise was enough to scare Mark back into the shadows.

The pounding went on without interruption.

Mark returned to his position and made two more attempts before the hook and rope looped over the rung. The clatter of the hook banging between the metal rung and the rock wall seemed to get lost in the noise overhead. Mark lowered the hook and rope and secured it again to his harness. His hands shook so violently he had a difficult time tying the loose end to another loop in his harness.

Once he felt securely fastened, he tugged at the rope, hoping beyond hope that it would hold. It did, but complained and slid a few inches before settling itself in place again.

Now for the fun part. He turned off his headlamp, believing that the natural gray light from above would suffice.

At first his hands were too cold and slick to get a proper grip on the GriGri. But he rubbed them hard against the dry part of his shirt and tried again. This time he was able to pull himself up. It took all of his strength, every muscle in his arms and shoulders burning. He fought to control his breathing, sure that a gasp or grunt would be the same as sounding a fire alarm.

The pounding and humming above continued unabated.

Mark wondered if someone was adding a room to the cave.

It was only a few feet, but could have been a mile as far as his body was concerned. The only good news was that he wasn't as cold anymore. The strain and exertion took care of that.

He was within arm's reach of the lower rung, but had to figure out how to transition from the rope to the rung without falling. He hung precariously for a moment, then quickly reached up with whatever was left of his strength and snatched the iron bar.

It bent slightly with a groan but held. Flakes of rust stabbed into his fingers and palms. He winced at the pain and hung for a moment.

Thank you, he thought, unsure of whether he was thanking God or the monks for providing the ladder. *Please give me the strength to climb it.*

The hummer above paused. There was a long silence. Mark held his breath. Then the pounding started up again.

The rungs of the stone portion of the ladder were more like shelves of rock than bars that he could clamp his fingers around. With each one, he had to find a new grip for his hands and a new place to put the tips of his shoes. All the while he kept listening to the pinging coming from above him and attempted to time his movements to coincide with the sound.

Reaching the uppermost part of the stone ladder, Mark was now eye level with the bottom of the piled stones that circled the top of the shaft. He stopped and listened, trying to get a sense of where the stranger was in the cave. The echoing sound made it difficult to pinpoint location, so he decided he'd have to take his chances and peek over the top. He untied the rope from his harness.

Clinging to the stones, he wormed his way up the rest of the ladder and slowly lifted his eyes over the ledge of the stones. He squinted at a new light—white and bright from a battery-powered camping lantern that sat on the altar.

The hummer—a tall man in dark overalls and ski mask—had his back to Mark.

Mark could see that the stranger was systematically nailing ringlets into the walls. To the ringlets he was attaching small explosives. Clearly, he intended to blow the cave to smithereens, leaving Mark, Digger, and Sickler beneath the crush of rubble.

Mark scanned the shadowed cave and made out the forms of Digger and Sickler on the ground. Dead or alive, he couldn't tell.

Suddenly the stranger stood erect. Mark lowered his head behind the stones.

"Blasted contraption," the man muttered softly. Mark heard the soft static of a walkie-talkie. The man fiddled with the device on his belt and then pressed it to his right ear. In a low voice, he said, "Look, don't pressure me. I'm doing my best. Just a few minutes more and they'll be ready."

The voice and accent were unmistakable and Mark's jaw fell.

The stranger was Henry Colchester.

Anger fueled Mark's next moves. Assuming that Henry still had a gun, Mark decided to throw himself over the wall and toward a huge stalagmite that stood near the altar. Mark's knapsack was there—with his own gun inside. He hoped to be able to grab it while using the column for cover.

Henry began to hum again and the chink of the hammer found a rhythm that Mark thought he could use. Counting down from three, he drew himself up onto the stone wall, bringing his full body onto the ledge, crouching to lunge for cover.

At that moment, his headset came alive with Nora's voice: "*Mark!*"

• • •

Nora and the three men stood at the now vacant Templeton tomb.

"Where is everyone?" Andrew asked, bewildered.

"There!" Glover called out. They turned to see three sets of legs, dressed in military trousers, sticking out from behind a large headstone a few yards away.

While Andrew and the two detectives rushed to the fallen soldiers, Nora dashed to the tomb. Not surprisingly, Henry wasn't there. She looked around and found a walkie-talkie lying in the grass next to it. She snatched it and shouted for Mark, but was only able to say his name when she heard a soft pop. Then a corner of the tomb's lid exploded, spraying stone outward, stinging her face.

"Sniper!" Duerr called out.

Without thinking, Nora threw herself into the tomb. She rolled and fell to the ground inside.

CHAPTER SEVENTY

HENRY SPUN AROUND AND saw Mark at the edge of the pit. He instantly dropped to a crouching position as he reached for the gun tucked into his waistband.

Mark threw himself to the ground, attempting everything he planned: the roll, the grab at his backpack, the stalagmite as cover, but his muscles, which had been strained beyond their normal limits, didn't cooperate. He got the backpack, but misjudged the rest of his roll, and slammed against the rock.

Henry fired at him from the opposite side of the cave, the bullet hitting and splintering the quartz only inches from Mark's face. Mark grabbed his backpack and rolled again, this time back toward the pit's stone wall for cover.

"Don't be tiresome, old chap," Henry said. "It's me, a gun, and you."

"Actually, you should be thinking about those explosives," Mark called back, fumbling with the compartment zipper on his backpack. "One stray bullet and you'll be dead too."

"One does what one must for the cause," Henry said.

"Does that include betraying your friends and killing innocent people?"

"The words 'innocent' and 'people' should never be said in the same breath. People are hardly innocent."

"Well, you've got me on that one." Mark finally got the zipper open, but the gun wasn't in the pocket.

"If you're looking for your gun, I have it. It wouldn't have been wise for me to leave a backpack unsearched, now would it?"

Mark slumped. Now what was he going to do? He could hear Henry coming forward, stepping gingerly. He was nothing if not cautious.

Mark searched his backpack for anything he could use as a weapon. Nothing.

"This is so boring," Henry said, his voice close now.

"You're right. So let's do something more interesting. You drop the gun and help me with Digger and Sergeant Sickler. I can't tell whether they're dead or alive. Any clues?"

"Presumably dead. I'm not sorry about that where Theodore Burns is concerned. I found him very annoying."

Henry rounded the stone wall, his gun trained on Mark. "You, on the other hand . . ."

He smiled at Mark. Both hands on the gun, he aimed, and then, unexpectedly, there was a strangled cry in the darkness. It caught Henry's attention and he turned just as Digger threw himself onto Henry.

Henry fell, spinning as he did and landing on top of Digger. The pain must have been excruciating and Digger cried out again. However, it was enough time for Mark to throw himself at the gun in Henry's hand. It went off.

Henry rolled off Digger, who writhed in pain. Henry then swung his fist around and slammed it into Mark's neck. The punch was solid and threw Mark's head to the left—and his body with it. He tumbled, but clung to Henry's wrist.

Henry was like a cat, surprisingly agile for his age, swinging himself around and landing on Mark's chest. All the while they wrestled for control of the gun, with jarring elbows and kicks.

Henry seemed well practiced in his moves and quickly got the advantage, pinning Mark's wrist under his knee. The pain was too much and Mark released his grip on Henry's wrist. Henry sat on Mark's chest and twisted the gun around until the barrel was pointed at Mark's forehead.

"Don't," was as much as Mark could say before an ear-shattering roar burst through the air. Mark flinched, assuming it was Henry's gun going off, but felt no pain. Yet blood and flesh splattered everywhere and Henry's dead weight fell on him.

Confused, Mark pushed him off and struggled to his feet,

kicking the gun away from the lifeless form. A large hole of cloth, flesh, and blood was now where Henry's back had been. Panting, he spun to see what had caused his sudden change of fortune.

Philip, the church gardener, stood only a few feet away with a double-barreled shotgun in his hands, glaring wild-eyed. He panted, his nostrils flaring like a wild horse's.

He clicked the trigger of the second barrel and pointed the shotgun at Mark. "Now it's your turn."

Scrambling to her feet in the tomb, Nora carefully climbed the small ladder to look out onto the churchyard. She was below ground level, but could see Duerr crouching behind a headstone, tense and waiting.

Andrew and Glover were sitting with their backs to another large tomb. Glover pulled a radio set from his jacket pocket and was frantically yelling into it for backup.

There was another pop and a bullet hit the top of the tomb over Andrew and Glover, the spray falling on them like stone rain.

The shooter was somewhere to the north of them, perhaps firing from a point at the far end of the graveyard or farther beyond in the trees. Nora couldn't tell how many there were, and didn't want to be the one to find out.

She ducked down again and called into the walkie-talkie, "Mark, listen—we're under sniper fire out here, and watch out for Henry; we think he's with Return to Earth."

Mark stood perfectly still, his harsh breathing whistling in his ears. He held up his hand as if it could stop whatever the gun shot his way. "Stop, Philip," he gasped.

"Stop nothing," Philip growled. "You come here. You ruin our lives. You steal our secrets. She's dead, you know, and it's all *your* fault."

Mark flinched. "I know, Philip," he said, fighting to keep the shrillness from his voice. "I'm terribly sorry."

"She went to you. You saw everything."

"The documents? It's true. She wanted to help us. To save countless lives."

"She oughtn't to have done that."

"Maybe not, but she thought it was the right thing to do. She was a good and kind woman."

"She betrayed us," he said, and his voice began to tremble. "We're meant to save this place. It protects our village and us. It is our life's work. Generations have given themselves to it and in one night . . ."

Mark took a step closer to Philip. "It's important work. It can continue, but right now—"

"No!" he cried out, his voice booming throughout the cave. "It's over. You've ruined everything by coming here. It's a desecration, and now she's gone." His eyes fell to the altar.

"I know you're angry," Mark said, stalling, looking for the chance to lunge for Philip and the gun. "But we'll get the ones who killed her."

"The ones who killed her?" Philip's violent expression relaxed just a little. He looked puzzled, then annoyed. "Are you a fool? He's standing in front of you."

Mark was staggered. "You? You murdered her?"

"I'm not proud of myself," he said. "'Twas not what I meant to do. But when I saw you and her talking, I knew she had betrayed us. Our families go back generations. *Generations!*"

Mark leapt for the man, pushing the shotgun aside as he tackled him to the ground.

Philip didn't struggle or fight, but let go of the shotgun and raised his hands as if to protect his face. "It's not what I meant to do," he said and Mark realized the old man was sobbing.

Nora was no expert, but she suspected that only one shooter had pinned them down.

Duerr and the others stayed where they were. Sirens

screamed in the distance. She clutched the walkie-talkie and wondered why she hadn't heard back from Mark. Had Henry already reached him? Had Mark and the others already been killed like the three soldiers?

The thought of the soldiers caused her to rise again. She strained to see where they were. If they were still alive, she should be giving medical help. There was another tombstone she could hide behind to get a better vantage point. She positioned herself at the tomb entrance then hurled herself forward and onto the ground. She rolled.

There was another pop, and the grass blew up next to her. She kept rolling until she was behind the other stone.

"Keep your positions!" Glover shouted. "Don't bloody move if you're safe!"

Nora leaned against the stone and drew her legs up. She was about to peek around to identify where the soldiers lay, but then a family of tourists rounded the corner of the church, brochures in hand and cameras ready.

"Get down! Get down!" Nora screamed at them.

They looked up, startled.

Nora bolted from her spot.

"Stop!" Andrew shouted from behind her.

Nora ran, screaming at the tourists, "Sniper! Sniper!"

The father and mother grabbed their two children and dropped onto the ground.

Exposed as she was, Nora expected to feel the impact of a bullet at any moment.

Shots were fired but from a handgun. She guessed Duerr was returning fire in an effort to keep her safe. She slid around and behind another tombstone and waited.

Above her a helicopter flew low to the north. Sirens echoed from the hills.

"He's running!" Duerr shouted.

Nora peered around the tombstone. Duerr, Andrew, and Glover were standing, looking at the field stretching away to the north behind the church. Nora followed their gaze and saw someone dressed in black racing toward the forest.

"Don't shoot him!" Duerr screamed. "I need him alive!"

Whomever Duerr screamed at didn't listen. A volley of gunfire came from somewhere farther up the field, and the runner fell.

Nora sprinted to the fallen soldiers.

"Mark? Are you there?" Nora's breathless voice poured over the headset.

Mark was administering first aid to Digger, trying to stop the flow of blood. "I need help," he panted. "Digger and Henry are down. Sickler's dead."

"Dead?" she exclaimed. "But how do we get to you?"

"Get one of the soldiers to lead you in. We need evacuation help right now."

"All of them are dead or wounded. We've just dealt with a sniper here."

"What?" Mark exclaimed and then knew that the cover fire was the means to get Henry into the caves. Mark turned to Philip, who still sat on the ground, his arms wrapped around his knees, his head lowered. An idea came to Mark. "How did you get in here, Philip?"

Philip didn't speak for a moment.

"You couldn't have come in through the churchyard or the north entrance," he said. "So how did you get in here?"

Philip slowly lifted his head. "There's a third way."

"You can't do anything for Joan, but you can help us now. Redeem yourself! Get up and help me!"

"Mark?" Nora called.

"Wait," he snapped at her and watched the old man.

Philip slowly got to his feet. "I'll show you."

CHAPTER SEVENTY-ONE

USING MARK'S HEADLAMP AS a guide, Philip led Mark back through the Silver Cathedral to a narrow passage on the other side. A few yards into it, Philip stopped at a junction of two caves. "If you go right, you'll run into the cave-in those terrorists caused with the explosion, but we'll go this way."

He carried on, and they walked up a gentle slope, almost like a ramp, for about a hundred yards and then came to a dead end of thick branches and lush green ivy.

"What now?" Mark asked.

"Just push through it, like a curtain," Philip said.

Mark looked at him skeptically, but obeyed. He parted the greenery and stepped through. Suddenly he was out of the caves and in the forest—at the graves of the monks. "Amazing," he said.

Then he heard helicopter blades beating the air. Crouching, he navigated through the monks' resting places and then emerged from under the canopy of foliage. He stopped where he was and gazed up at the sky, small patches between the trees above.

Philip came out behind him and gasped.

Mark turned to him just in time to see a hunting party of a half dozen police officers—all in bulletproof vests and carrying assault rifles—spin around from their various positions in the forest, obviously startled by the sudden appearance of the two men. With a lot of snapping and clicking the guns were instantly raised and pointed at them.

"Don't shoot!" Mark shouted, raising his hands. "I'm one of the good guys."

• • •

Mark led two pairs of paramedics into the cave and worked with them to stabilize Digger, evacuate him from the cave, and get him airlifted to a hospital in Sheffield. Digger was barely conscious when they started to close the helicopter door, but he smiled at Mark and whispered, "You owe me."

"Get in line," Mark teased and closed the helicopter door.

Henry and Sickler were declared dead at the scene. This was no surprise to Mark, who made the same determination when he rushed back to the cave to help Digger, but he regretted losing the information they may have gotten from Henry about Return to Earth. The two bodies were removed by the coroner's officials.

As the helicopter took off, Mark turned to see Nora running to him. At first he thought she was going to run into his arms— and part of him desperately wanted her to do so—but, to his disappointment, she stopped.

"Are you okay?" she asked, panting.

He nodded his head and smiled. Then he held up his abraded and bleeding fingers. "Just some wear and tear on the paws, not to mention some very sore muscles, but otherwise I'm no worse for the wear."

She smiled, and they began to walk back to the cave. She looked exactly like someone who'd just been hiding behind tombstones while being shot at by a sniper: pale, wild-eyed, and disheveled.

"Are *you* all right?"

She nodded and then informed him that the police had stopped all traffic on the road because of the sniper; paramedics had been brought in to deal with any victims, which included the sniper; the soldiers suffered chest wounds and were also transported to Sheffield in critical condition.

"The emergency-services personnel got here fast," Mark commented.

"As it turns out they were already positioned both on the main road and at the top of the hill, barely a stone's throw from where you came out of the cave."

"Who was the sniper?" Mark asked.

"Identity as yet unknown. And he didn't live long enough to tell us. But, we're now besieged by MI5, Scotland Yard, and probably every other law-enforcement agency in Britain. I can't tell if Detective Glover is relieved or upset."

"This is probably more excitement than he's seen in a lifetime."

"He and Andrew are talking to Philip," Nora said. "He confessed to killing Joan out of pure rage. He thought she betrayed them."

"She had. But for a greater cause than theirs."

Nora suddenly put a finger to her earpiece. "Roger," she said, "I'll send Mark back. Under no circumstances are you to let them in." She turned to face him. "The press is swarming the church, the B&B, and now they want to see the cave. I've got to prepare a statement."

"What do we do next?" he asked.

"Go back to the cave and wait for the extrication team who'll remove the monk's body. A professor with some expertise in that area is coming from the University of Sheffield. Then we'll transport the body to Dr. Prentice and her lab at Cambridge."

"Aye, aye," he said. "Where will you be?"

"Back at the B&B. I have to release Georgina from house arrest with profuse apologies."

"You did what you thought best," Mark said, "but flowers and chocolates will probably help. When will we catch up?"

"On the drive to Cambridge," she said and then eyed him up and down. "You may want to clean up."

He looked down at his peat-stained and sweaty clothes. "This is the latest look in bog fashion," he said. He began to move back toward the cave.

"Hey!" he heard Nora yell.

He turned to see her smiling at him.

"Why are you smiling?"

"Because I'm proud of you, Dr. Carlson."

He almost stumbled and fell.

• • •

Removing the Blue Monk from his grave in the peat bog was a delicate and difficult procedure managed by Professor Trevor Huddlesworth from the Department of Archaeology and Prehistory, as well as from the Department of Forensic Pathology at the University of Sheffield.

Dr. Huddlesworth specialized in "bog bodies" and had done work for a number of museums. He took charge of the operation with a finicky attention to detail. Mark watched in wonder as he and his team carefully removed not only the body, but also the peat *around* the body, to preserve as much of the corpse's environment as they could.

"I assume you want to avoid any corruption or contaminants," the professor said to Mark.

Mark agreed.

They eventually lifted Benjamin out of the pit in a large body bag strapped to a stretcher. He was then taken out through the third entrance to the road nearby where a helicopter waited.

"We're going to enjoy going over him at the museum," Huddlesworth said, with obvious relish.

"He's not going to the museum," Mark corrected him. "He's going to Dr. Vicki Prentice at the Laboratory of Molecular Biology in Cambridge."

Huddlesworth's face fell and he turned away in sullen silence.

Mark followed the body to the helicopter, and Nora arrived just as the pilot started the engines. She had changed clothes since he last saw her, but she looked frazzled.

"Is everything all right?" he asked.

She shook her head. "The press at the B&B were relentless and Mac is out of his mind. He's getting pressure from everywhere. Apparently, the epidemic is no longer controlled in Gabon. Our pandemic may have arrived."

CHAPTER SEVENTY-TWO

THE HELICOPTER TOOK THE Blue Monk to Cambridge, while Mark and Nora followed in a sedan driven by a man from MI5, named Adam Pennith.

The parade of people involved in their mission had become so long and convoluted that Mark could no longer keep track of the individuals, their roles, or their jurisdictions. He wondered if any of them were inside agents for Return to Earth.

In the three-hour drive from Eyam, Mark gave Nora an abbreviated account of everything that happened in the caves while she reported to him about her experiences at the church. She took his hands in hers and frowned at his raw fingers, "You've torn them up."

"I hope they have somewhere for me to get cleaned up," he said. "They might confuse me with the bog body."

Gently she began to massage his hands. Their eyes met and he felt a powerful urge to kiss her. He leaned toward her—and then her cell phone rang. She let go of his hads and grabbed the phone from her purse.

"Hello, Mac."

She nodded as he talked on the other end.

"We're on our way to Cambridge, but let me put you on speakerphone." She pushed a button. "Can you hear me okay?"

"I can."

He cleared his throat. "Okay, for the record, you two have done great work. Thanks for everything, but I'm spitting mad about Colchester." He followed the statement with a few expletives to describe his feelings, then said, "I'm on my way to Sheffield to see Digger. I've also given approval for Georgina to meet him at the hospital."

"Give Digger a kiss from me," Mark said.

Mac went on to explain that he arranged for a team to get all of their belongings and equipment out of the Rose and Crown. "But you're still going to have to deal with the local constabulary and MI5. They'll want full statements."

"Actually, I've been getting them while we've been driving," Pennith announced from the front seat.

The man had been silent until that moment, and Mark felt naive for not realizing he'd been listening to their every word.

"We'll deal with all the paperwork after we find out about the Blue Monk," Mark said. "That's our first priority."

"Agreed," Mac said. "Let's touch base at 1800 hours."

It was late in the afternoon by the time they arrived at the stately college buildings of the prestigious Cambridge University. Dr. Vicki Prentice met them at the entrance of the Laboratory of Molecular Biology.

Mark did an embarrassing double take at Dr. Prentice's stunning beauty and stammered, "Nice to meet you."

"Uh-huh," he heard Nora mutter under her breath. He saw her raise an eyebrow. He felt his cheeks burn and he realized what a disgusting mess he was.

Pennith showed his ID and introduced himself as the man who'd be quietly tagging along as their official escort. MI5 was now responsible for their protection.

"Welcome," Dr. Prentice declared to the three of them. "I'm glad you're here; please call me Vicki."

She guided them to a set of double doors, guarded by two fresh-faced young men wearing the Special Air Service pins on their uniform lapels. The pins identified them as members of the British Army's Special Forces Unit.

Mark wondered what they were doing there. The SAS was one of the most renowned and respected special-forces organizations in the world. Obviously, this lab was conducting top-secret work involving national security issues for England.

Dr. Prentice handed them each a security badge. "You must keep this on at all times. If you take it off, silent alarms will cause the entire facility to lock down."

Walking to the door, she gazed into what looked like the padded end of a periscope, looking into the aperture and grasping a metal bar with both hands. "This device reads my iris and retina while it's checking my fingerprints, palm prints, blood type, and credit rating."

Mark and Nora laughed.

"Just joking about that last bit," she said with a giggle. As she stepped away she motioned for Mark to go next. "It will read your badge and then record your data. Anytime you or your badge enter another secure area, it will be sure that you are you. It's a fail-safe security system—at least that's what they tell us."

After Mark's biometrics were recorded, Nora and Penrith did the same. Once they all had green lights, the door automatically opened and they headed down a long corridor—Mark, Nora, and Pennith following the scientist who, Mark noticed, had a catlike walk.

"What have you found?" Mark asked.

"First of all, we were all amazed by the quality of the specimen. Wonderful work, Doctor."

Mark appreciated the affirmation, considering all they'd gone through to find the Monk. "A heavy price was paid for the effort."

"So I've heard," Vicki said. "Our first order of business was DNA testing. Our boy had great protection from decay, thanks not only to the preservation of the peat bog he rested in, but also to its cold temperature. It was a miracle for him to be dropped into such a rarity for caves."

"Well, he was a monk after all," Mark offered glibly.

Nora shot him a weary look.

Vicki seemed to ignore the statement. "We've also found that he has what we're now calling a supercharged CCR5 gene alteration."

"Supercharged?" Nora asked.

They walked through another security door and into a dressing room, where a bevy of technicians surrounded them. "Our team will help you all with your protective suits," Vicki directed. She looked at the agent. "Do you mind staying out here? This is the only entrance and exit."

Pennith nodded.

As the team assisted them with their suits, Mark thought of the compound in Africa, where he last wore protective clothing. It seemed like years ago, not days.

"You were saying about the supercharged alteration?" Nora prompted Vicki.

"Yes," Vicki replied. "Not only did he have the CCR5-Delta 32 mutation, but also he had the CCR5-m303 mutation, and, genetically speaking, he had a double dose of each."

"Double dose?" Mark asked.

"Yes, both the Delta 32 and the m303 mutations were homozygous."

Mark looked at Nora, who seemed as confused as he felt. "Vicki, my genetics classes were a long time ago. Can you explain?"

She shook her head so that her long hair went behind her back. The technicians put a hair net on her and then pushed on her helmet. They did the same for Mark and Nora and then double-checked to make certain that all the seams were sealed. The suits were connected by a wireless communication system so that he and Nora could hear Vicki, and vice versa.

"Okay," she began, as she was checking their suits, "here we go with your refresher of Genetics 101. Genes are units of heredity information that consist of DNA and are located on chromosomes. We get one set from our biological mother and the other from our biological father. If the matching portions of the gene— if both genes—from *both* parents are the same, we call that homozygous. If the two genes are different, we call that heterozygous. In the case of our Blue Monk, he's homozygous for the Delta 32 gene and the m303 gene. He has a double dose, and in the case of the Black Death was doubly protected."

A technician's voice sounded, "Dr. Prentice, I'm opening the door into the antechamber."

A door behind them opened, and they entered a small booth-like room. Then the door behind them was closed. "We'll decontaminate here when we come out."

Then, the door to the lab's morgue opened. Mark was slack-jawed. This morgue was not the usual dank and dark pathology lab, but a bright and shiny facility—everything dazzling, clean, and looking as if it had just come out of a box.

"So, what does this double dose give you?" Nora asked, trying to keep them on track.

Vicki turned to her. "Both the Delta 32 and m303 genes are dominant, meaning that they would have provided him protection even if he had been heterozygous, but being homozygous gave him even more protection. For example, our colleagues at the Institute of Immunology in Moscow have found that if the Delta 32 and m303 mutations are homozygous in humans, they provide complete resistance to sexual transmission of HIV."

Nora looked at Mark and then to Vicki. "So, that helps explain why the fugitive boy has survived this long."

"It does. We've heard from our U.S. colleagues that when they retested Aaron's cord blood sample, they found that he's homozygous for the Delta 32 gene, but only heterozygous for the m303 gene. It would have been better for him had he been homozygous for both."

Mark and Nora were silent. Mark suspected that she now knew, as he did, that this information was likely a death sentence for Aaron unless they could find a cure.

"It's not hopeless, though. Let me show you the surprise."

She turned and led them to the end of the room where two bodies lay on postmortem tables. One was covered with a light blue sheet and unattended. The other had two people leaned over it, in the midst of a dissection.

"Robert?" Vicki said.

The shorter of the two pathologists turned to them and nodded.

"Hello," he said as if they'd just met at a tea party. He was an apple-cheeked man with a pudgy nose and narrow eyes.

"This is Dr. Robert Weisman. He's the head forensic pathologist here at the lab."

The doctor bowed slightly. "I'd shake your hands, but . . . well . . ."

"Understood," Mark said.

"Your body is over here." Weisman, followed by Vicki, walked around the far side of the table and turned to face them over the body. As if giving a demonstration, he pulled the sheet down to midchest, revealing the Blue Monk.

"So that's our hero," Nora said, leaning in closer.

Mark did the same. The monk's skin was bronze colored and leatherlike. He looked like a deflated balloon, shriveled and diminished. Yet the details of his features were startlingly clear: his delicate nose, broad mouth, and large eyes, now closed as if he were merely asleep. Even the dark fabric and ragged edges of his worn robe were evident.

"We've tidied him up as best we could for our purposes," Weisman said.

"Well, it's nice to finally meet him," Mark said, meaning it.

"We've learned several things from our autopsy," Weisman began. "First, the degree of preservation of the body is spectacular, similar to what we've seen in other bodies recovered from bogs."

"Have you seen other specimens like this?" Mark asked.

"Oh, yes. We've done the autopsies on several including the mummies of Cladh Hallan, Scotland, the so-called Yde Girl, and another called the Bocksten Man. These bog bodies, which are also known as bog people, were all found preserved in sphagnum bogs. Unlike most ancient human remains, bog bodies are well preserved."

"What is it about the bog that preserves them?"

"We think it's a combination of the water's acidity and the lack of oxygen. Basically, this combination tans the soft tissues. Some of the bodies retain intricate details like tattoos and fingerprints, as well as hair and facial features."

Mark nodded, unable to take his eyes off the face of the Blue Monk.

Weisman continued, "More than a thousand bog bodies have been found. The earliest, called the Koelbjerg Woman, has been radiometrically dated to be about 5,500 years old. Until your

Blue Monk, the newest was a sixteenth-century woman found in Ireland."

"His skin isn't blue," Nora observed, looking to Mark.

"But there's no question that he was blue when he was alive. Tissue tests showed that he contained toxic levels of silver."

Nora nodded in appreciation to Mark.

Weisman saw their exchange and said, "You knew this already."

"We suspected it," Mark said.

Weisman turned and clapped his hands, causing a computer monitor behind them to turn on. Two rows of pictures appeared on the screen. "Here are pictures of people with argyria . . . er, silver poisoning. You can see how they vary from light to dark blue. Given this man's levels, we suspect he was very blue indeed."

"Would that have eventually killed him?" Mark asked.

"His levels were high enough that the silver would have done him in if the stab wound to the heart had not, but of even more interest is that we found that he was infected with a large number of infectious particles."

"*Yersinia?*" Nora asked.

"Nope," Weisman replied. "Ebola."

"So," Mark commented, "that's even more proof that the epidemic of 1666 wasn't the plague."

"I don't know about that," Weisman replied. "I can only tell you that he has *no* antibodies to *Yersinia*. As far as we can determine, he was not exposed to the plague bacteria, but he has a high viral load of Ebola, and our initial tests show that, genetically, this Eyam Ebola is very similar to the Gabon Ebola."

"That's great news," Nora exclaimed.

Vicki smiled. "Yes, and that's not all. Robert, tell them about the bones."

Weisman nodded and continued, "Bone preservation is usually very rare in these bodies, as the acid in the peat dissolves the calcium carbonate of bone, but because of the extreme cold of the bog in which you found him, Doctor, not only is his bone preserved, but some of his bone marrow is, as well."

Mark tilted his head as if he'd misheard. "You're kidding. Bone marrow?"

Weisman nodded, then pulled the sheet down to the monk's pelvic hair. Mark looked at the opened abdomen. Without looking up, he asked, "Is that what I think it is?"

"Yes," Weisman replied. "All of the abdominal organs have been perfectly preserved, including the liver and spleen."

Nora looked at Vicki. "You said you needed a blood-storing organ from someone who survived a year or more after contracting either the Eyam or Gabon Ebola." Nora turned to Mark. "This could be the break we need."

"Maybe," Vicki cautioned.

"Maybe?" Mark asked.

"Mark, even with the excellent preservation, this tissue may be of no use to us in this condition—in the sense that we may not be able to perform tissue-culture growth with these cells. If so, that means we won't be able to test these cells against the virus and experimental medications."

Mark couldn't tell what she was getting at. "The Blue Monk won't be able to help us?"

"Vicki, there's something you're not telling us," Nora said.

Vicki paused a moment and then said. "Mark and Nora, what I'm about to tell you is for your ears only. Agreed?"

Mark looked at Nora, and they each nodded their assent.

"We're doing some highly secret experimentation here at our lab that may be helpful."

"Such as?" Mark asked.

"We've found we can take the preserved viral and human DNA and RNA, even in this condition, and use it to build a synthetic copy of the involved genes. We can then use gene-therapy techniques to copy the genes into healthy tissue and viral-culture cells."

"So, how will that help us—given the fact that our time line is so short?"

"The folks at Dr. Al Petersen's lab in the U.S. have developed a number of medications that they've been testing in animals. They are called antisense medications. All we need are tissue cultures that match the Blue Monk and a culture of the Gabon Ebola virus, and we can test the existing medications to see which set of medications will keep the virus from getting into the cells of the body and will keep it from reproducing."

"At least until the immune system can eliminate the neutralized virus?" Nora asked.

"That's right," Vicki said. "It's a double-barrel approach and unproven, but we're cautiously optimistic."

Mark was silent for a moment as he looked down on the long-dead monk and considered the implications of what Vicki was telling them. "Then maybe—just maybe—if the experiment works, we could get emergency approval to use these medications on Aaron and other victims. How long will that take?" Mark asked.

"Today. With a little luck . . ." Vicki said.

"We need more than luck," Nora said. "We'll need a miracle."

PART SIX

CHAPTER SEVENTY-THREE

JULY 1671

MARGARET SAT ON THE wooden pew and stared at the vaulted ceiling of the Silver Cathedral. Her eyes drifted down to the beautiful altar and the flickering light of dozens of candles. The room sparkled.

Every year, on the anniversary of Benjamin's murder, Margaret and Joshua Parke, together with the families of John Dicken and the other mob members who chased Benjamin that fateful night—came together in this place to memorialize Benjamin and his order, and to confess their individual and collective sins.

As part of their penance, they gave substantially from their own means to help the poor. They then affirmed their service to the Lord, giving thanks for their forgiveness and the burden of their contrition.

The ceremony and its location were an avowed secret. All the participants knew that severe punishment would be the consequence of any breach of that vow.

Margaret was not in favor of such vows or punishments and thought her brother would disapprove, but she felt it was not for her to judge such things, nor to thwart God's work in the hearts of the contrite. Let them determine their own contrition.

She respected, though, the need to keep this mine and its vast Silver Cathedral a secret—not to mention the vast amount of unmined silver. The greedy would exploit it to evil ends. Kept secret, the order could still utilize the money it gave them.

Margaret prayed for the soul of John Dicken. Yes, he met his justice and his Maker at the time of his sudden death, but the grisly deed he had done to her brother would likely never have been discovered had young Joshua not confessed.

She looked at the young man at the front of the Cathedral and felt a great pride in him, as if he were her own son. She smiled as she watched Joshua and the town's new vicar talking to a handsome, middle-aged man. He could have been Benjamin, as Benjamin would have appeared had he lived.

The man noticed her sitting alone, excused himself from the conversation, and came to sit next to her.

"Sister, are you not cold?"

"I feel strangely warm in this place, dear brother," She placed her arm through Edward's and leaned against his shoulder. "More so, I'm thankful to God that he allowed me to reunite with my two brothers before he calls me home. I only wish Frances could be here."

"Brethren," the vicar interrupted, his voice echoing off the high silver ceiling. "Shall we process to the grave?"

The acolytes, two boys with large candles on elaborate silver candlesticks and a third one with the large ornate silver crucifix, led the small band through the archway at the back of the chapel and into another cavern filled with white crystalline quartz.

Edward walked beside his sister, holding one arm, while young Joshua Parke held her other arm, both there to keep her from slipping on the damp crystalline path.

As they approached the edge of the pit, Margaret could feel the frigid air coming up from the deep, cold shaft. Benjamin was somewhere on the bottom, but no one dared to venture down to find him.

He must be left undisturbed. Perhaps one day someone will find the means to descend into that tragic place, but for now, let him remain where he is, asleep, and not buried.

As the vicar finished the brief ceremony, and candles were lit at the edge of the pit and on the altar, Margaret wondered just how many more years she would be able to visit this place, to celebrate and memorialize Benjamin's faith, life, and service.

She felt no sadness at the thought. She deeply looked forward to her reunion with him, her sister, and her family in their heavenly home.

CHAPTER SEVENTY-FOUR

AUGUST 17

THE CONVENT SEEMED EERILY quiet after the chaos of the crowded streets and traffic of Libreville. Brigadier General Sam Mosley was taken aback by the degree of haze and smoke in the air, and by the myriad motorcycle drivers wearing face masks or bandanas over their mouths and noses. His driver explained that the pollution was normal for this time of year. It was the absence of ocean winds, he explained, and the smoke from the annual burning of overgrowth in the surrounding valley.

God help those with asthma or chronic lung disease, Mosley thought. He was thankful to have been driven from the military air base in an air-conditioned car. He clenched and unclenched his fists impatiently. The news he received only a few hours ago had thrown his entire team into a frenzy of activity.

As he quickly walked toward the administrative office of the Sisters of Mercy Convent, he considered the remarkable peace of the place in contrast to his own inner turmoil. Was it the stillness and quiet inside the large citadel? The spotless tidiness of the grounds rimmed in flowering shrubs and trees? Or maybe it was something of a more spiritual nature that made this a refuge of calm in a world of instability.

He marched up the front walk and the door opened as he approached. A diminutive African woman, whose face was covered with scores of deep, furrowed wrinkles, stepped out. Her face radiated kindness and warmth.

"Welcome to *Le Refuge de la Paix*, General," she said, and held out a small hand.

The Refuge of Peace, he thought, and took her hand in his large calloused palm.

The Mother Superior leaned up to kiss him on one cheek and then the other. "You are a much larger man than I imagined when you phoned." Her smile was wry. "Please come in."

As he entered the cool office, he was surprised by its brightness. The entire back wall was made of glass and offered a view of the white stucco buildings that stretched across the immaculately groomed gardens and grounds as they gently sloped down to the river. He was touched by the serenity of it all.

As the front door shut behind him, he turned to face the tiny woman. Her head and body were covered in a light blue garment that seemed to flow with every movement. Her radiant beauty struck him. With a soft voice, almost a whisper, she introduced herself. "I am Sister Anna Katherine. Welcome to the Sisters of Mercy. May I offer you a mint tea?"

Suddenly aware of the dryness that spread across his palate and the back of his throat, he nodded.

"Please, General," she gestured to an overstuffed couch, "have a seat." She walked to a small rolling cart with a pitcher of iced tea and several cut-crystal glasses. She placed two ice cubes in two glasses, poured the tea, crossed the room, and handed him one as she sat in a chair next to him.

"You are showing remarkable restraint. I'm sure you are anxious to see him," she commented.

"I am, Sister." Mosley reached into his coat pocket and pulled out a photo that Susan had printed off the researcher's e-mail. "This was taken just yesterday—but over a hundred miles from here."

She set the glass of tea on a side table and studied the photo. After scrutinizing it for a moment, she nodded her head. "Yes, General. That's him. The nuns called him *notre petit sauvage*—our little savage."

She lifted her drinking glass and took a small sip. Everything about her seemed to be small and subtle. He wanted her to quickly explain where she had seen Aaron and where he could find him, but he held back. He sensed that there would be no rushing things here in the convent.

He asked quietly, "When did you first see him?"

"Shortly after we heard about the ghost train."

Mosley nodded. The whole nation was now talking about the so-called ghost train since the afternoon before when it drifted to a stop outside of Libreville filled with dead passengers. Rumors spread in every direction. Some said it was mass poisoning, some believed it was the plague, and some said it was a terrorist action. The government was doing its best to maintain calm, but Mosley knew that the true story was likely to blow within the next day. The panic sure to ensue was more than he could think about at the moment.

She took another sip of tea. "Sister Mary first saw this boy walking down the tracks near the river just at the edge of our property. She said he looked lily-white, and when he saw her, he ducked into the brush. Later, Sister Emily saw him digging through the trash behind our cafeteria. When he saw her, he fled, but she could still see him peering out from time to time. So, she put a plate of food out for him. She said it did not take him long to retrieve it, and he ate as if he hadn't eaten in a week."

The general felt a tightness in his chest. The thought of his grandson living like a wild animal was more than he could bear.

The Mother Superior continued, "At dusk Sister Jennifer went out and called for him. She offered him a room, but when he wouldn't answer, she left a pillow, air mattress, and mosquito net, along with snacks. She watched from around the corner as he came to pick up the supplies and take them into the jungle. We assume he stayed out there all night."

"Any sign of him today?"

"No one has seen him, but all the food the sisters have left out for him has disappeared, so we assume he's still out there."

She took another sip of tea as she looked across the compound and then back at him. "I can't tell you why, but for some reason, I think he has either been led here or he sought to come here. I think he needs some time to know that he can trust us."

"Unfortunately, Sister, time is one luxury we don't have." He decided that he could trust the petite woman. "There is only so much I'm allowed to say, but we are on the brink of a possible Ebola pandemic."

The nun searched his face, and then said, "The train."

"Yes. The train was cordoned off before the virus could be spread to passersby or the rescue workers."

"That has not been the only incident," she said.

"It hasn't. There've been others and they all seem to follow the boy. We think he is the host for the virus. If he gets to Libreville . . ."

"I understand," she said. "But I must ask: Are my sisters in danger?"

"They could be, depending on how close they get to him. The virus he's carrying is highly contagious. Have any of your nuns been ill?"

"No, thank God." She thought for a moment, then asked, "How may I help you?"

"I plan to draw him out. So, I'll need a private room with a self-contained air-handling system and complete isolation. Is that possible?"

The sister nodded. "We have a private one-bedroom cottage down near the river. It's air conditioned and has a bathroom and kitchenette. It's where our priest stays when he comes. What else do you need?"

Mosley's gaze drifted to the view from the large window. He noticed the steeple in the center of the convent. "I could use your prayers, Sister, and those of your colleagues."

She nodded. "It's what we do best, General, but how are you going to lure him out of hiding?"

"I'm going to serve him lunch."

CHAPTER SEVENTY-FIVE

MARK AND NORA ARRIVED at the TSI headquarters in London for a late-morning briefing. The frenzied activity of the past few days had given way to an insane period of waiting: waiting for tests, waiting for results, waiting for news, waiting for hope.

The absence of Henry Colchester and Digger, who was in stable condition and recovering in the hospital, was a reminder of all that happened the day before. Georgina remained with Digger in Sheffield.

The news about the train filled with dead passengers near Libreville had shaken them to the core. It was only a tiny hint of what would come if they didn't find a cure right away.

Mac walked into the TSI conference room and seemed taken aback that Mark and Nora were the only ones there. He nodded to them and then strode to the large computer screen and put on the navigation glove. In a moment the screen burst to life, and Mark could see the teams from USAMRIID, Cambridge, and Brazzaville.

"Hello everyone. TSI here. Are we receiving each other?" Mac asked.

"You're clear here," Jim Dillard answered from the United States.

"We're good," Vicki Prentice replied from Cambridge.

Susan Hutchinson seemed distracted, but acknowledged her presence from Africa. "You should have our briefing notes. They were e-mailed to you ten minutes ago."

"Things are getting desperate in Gabon," Mac said.

"They are," Susan replied. "You know about the incident with the train. Panic is beginning to spread. Unchecked, the virus has the potential of spreading through Libreville in a matter of hours."

"Unchecked," Nora said, "but the general has located his grandson, hasn't he?"

"He's close, but he hasn't made contact," Susan said. "We hope to know more shortly."

"Do we have an update on Aaron's health?" Mark asked.

Susan shook her head sadly. "Nothing we've been able to confirm, but we suspect he is in decline."

The monitors were silent for a moment as each team considered the gravity of the situation.

Finally, Jim spoke. "Mac, we've got some news here. We've looked at the genetic tests on Aaron and the Blue Monk, and we've reviewed the genetic fingerprint of the Gabon Ebola virus. That led us to the conclusion that, believe it or not, we already have in-house some antisense medications that might work."

Mac furrowed his brow. "Antisense? Explain that for my sake, if you will."

As Jim spoke, he projected graphics onto the shared screen. "Living cells contain genetic material not only in their DNA, but also in their RNA. A particular RNA, called messenger RNA, is made up of a single strand of genetic information."

"Got it," Mac said.

As Jim projected a picture of an RNA strand, he continued, "These messenger RNA strands are called sense structures because when their message is read by the cell, the cell makes sense of the message and makes a product such as a protein, but the messenger RNA can be blocked if the RNA is mated with a medication; we call these medications antisense medications."

Mac's eyes narrowed and he spoke without confidence. "I think I follow you."

Jim continued, "We've been working for a number of years on antisense medications to fight Ebola, and we've been able to identify a number of antisense drugs that bind to the replication site of this particular Ebola virus."

"Have you tested them?" Nora asked.

"Yes. We've tested a combination of three specific antisense medications called Antisense Phosphorodiamidate Morpholino Oligomers, or what we call PMOs. First we tested the PMOs on laboratory mice infected with a large viral load of Ebola. The medications worked. Then we tested them on guinea pigs and rhesus monkeys."

"What did you find?" Mark asked.

"We found that these three PMOs effectively inhibited the replication of the Ebola virus in each of the animal models."

"And that's good news," Mac said, sounding unsure.

"It is," Jim said. He picked up a sheet of paper as if he wanted to confirm his own information. "We took the tissue cultures from the Blue Monk that Vicki's team sent to us and found that two of these antisense medications duplicate the effect of the Delta 32 and m303 genes. We think that the combination of these two PMOs may not only stop this Ebola virus from entering the cells of anyone exposed to it, but also that these medications may well stop the replication of the virus in those who are already infected."

"Are we talking about a cure?" Mac asked hopefully.

Jim hesitated as if making such a bold declaration was more than he could do. "We think it's a strong possibility. Of course, humans are different from these animals, and there is always the possibility that they won't work in people."

Mac stood straight and took in a deep breath. "But, could we try these medications in Gabon?"

Jim frowned. "Colonel, we've done no tests whatsoever on humans, and even in a crisis like this, it may be very difficult to get approval to do so."

Susan broke in, "Mac, I can get us permission to use these medications. Just give me the word."

"How?" Mac asked.

"When General Mosley went to Libreville, I took over his briefings with the White House and the Joint Chiefs. I'll be updating them in a few minutes. I think I can get permission. If so, we could have the medications on a military jet in hours. Jim, do you have enough for us?"

"Susan, we have enough to treat several thousand people immediately, and we can gear up for the production of more in days, but first we need to test it."

Susan was silent for a moment before answering. "I'm almost certain that the general will approve its use on Aaron. He knows that without medication the boy will die."

Mark looked through his notes, then asked, "There's nothing in our briefing notes about where exactly the general is in Libreville—or how he hopes to encounter his grandson. Can you tell us?"

Susan looked directly at the camera. "He's at a convent near Libreville, and he was insistent that whatever he had to do, he'd do alone. He knows that direct contact will infect him. He knows he could die, along with Aaron."

She was quiet for a moment, and then continued, "He understands the risk, which is why he's counting on us to come through."

CHAPTER SEVENTY-SIX

THE AROMA OF SIZZLING steaks wafted across the trees at the edge of the jungle. Mosley was convinced the enticing aroma would lure his grandson out of the brush. Maybe the boy would even recognize his grandfather though it had been several years since they'd last seen each other.

He purposefully wore civilian clothes since he assumed that Aaron would run from a military uniform. Sighing deeply, he worried about how he might react to the boy's condition.

Mosley took the meat off the grill, transferred it to a plate, and carried it to the picnic table behind the convent's cafeteria. He picked at his own steak and potato, unsure of when he'd last eaten. He wasn't hungry, but busied himself over the food. From the corner of his eye, he watched the tree line.

The picnic table was in the shade, but the sun was at its peak and Mosley felt its merciless heat. He didn't know how long he should wait. He pushed his food around his plate and then took a bite of the steak. At another time, he would have enjoyed its taste. Right now, he didn't care.

His mind went back to a family cookout they had in America before he lost David and his family to the commune. It had been a beautiful day of eating, talking, playing, and resting under the large oak tree in the backyard of his Chevy Chase home. He and Aaron played hide-and-seek that day. But the afternoon was spoiled when he and David exchanged harsh words about David's plan for Africa. They exchanged too many harsh words too often.

If only . . . There were too many "if only's" in his life. If only he had been a better parent. If only he had spent more time with his boy. If only he could have accepted his son's new faith. If only he had taken more time to visit his family. *If only . . .*

He tried to shake off his self-pity. *After all*, he thought, *didn't I give the kids all the things they needed? They had money, good clothes, nice homes, and great schools. What else could they have wanted?*

He bowed his head. *Me.* It was the obvious answer to his question. *They needed me.*

He lowered his head and felt the remorse fill his heart as the tears filled his eyes. Then, even in the blur of his unfocused eyes, he thought he saw a movement over behind a tree.

Or was it his imagination? He sat perfectly still, as if concentrating on his plate. *Wait. There it is again.* A movement at the forest edge.

His body tensed, ready for anything. His breathing slowed to a calm, steady rhythm.

A glint—perhaps a reflection off something metallic—struck his eye.

He remained as he was, an old man sitting at a picnic table eating a meal. He heard, even sensed, the movement by the trees. Mosley tilted his head slightly and saw the boy squatting just where the woods touched the carpet of lawn. He could feel Aaron's nervousness and suspicion.

Without turning to look, Mosley simply gazed ahead and said, "Aaron, I'm your grandfather." He paused, waited, and continued, "I know what happened to your father, mother, and sisters. I've come here to help you."

From the corner of his eye, Mosley saw that Aaron had crept closer while he spoke, but he feared eye contact, or making any move at all that would send the boy back into the jungle.

"Listen, Aaron, I know it's been a nightmare for you. I know you aren't feeling well. Let me . . ." Mosley stopped, his emotions suddenly rising in his throat. He struggled to finish the sentence, his voice cracking. "Let me help you. Please."

Aaron was closer now. Mosley turned his gaze ever so slightly and saw more of the boy. He held back the shock that shot through him. The boy was emaciated, scratched, and smudged with dirt. It had only been a few days, but Aaron looked as if he had not eaten for weeks. Clearly, he was more ill than anyone had imagined.

The boy coughed gently and then asked in a raspy voice: "Why should I trust you?"

The question surprised Mosley and he struggled to come up with a persuasive answer. But before he could speak, Aaron moved ever so slightly and Mosley feared that he wouldn't wait for a response, but would dash off again.

"I don't feel very well," Aaron whispered and his eyes rolled back. He staggered toward Mosley and then collapsed. Mosley caught him and laid him down on the grass. He tugged at his grandson's ragged clothing and saw what he feared the most: hideous sores covering Aaron's neck, chest, and arms.

At the TSI headquarters in London, Mark had just finished reading a detailed report of the medical findings in Cambridge when there was a light tap at his bedroom door.

"Come in," he called out and turned from his laptop to see who would enter.

It was Nora. She looked pale, her face drawn.

Mark stood up. "What's wrong?"

"News from Libreville."

Mark waited.

"General Mosley has his grandson," she said.

Mark didn't understand Nora's tone and expression. "But that's good news, isn't it?"

"It should be," she said, "but he's made *physical* contact. They're both in quarantine at the convent. I have to assume that they're *both* dying."

CHAPTER SEVENTY-SEVEN

AUGUST 18

MARK COULD SEE THE outline of the West African coast as the military jet began its gentle descent. Mile after mile of apparent jungle wilderness met the spotless white beaches—beaches upon which elephants and hippos were often seen.

"Doctor?"

The voice startled him.

It was one of the pilots. "Sorry to bother you. If you pick up the phone by your seat, we have General Mosley on the line."

Mark looked across the aisle at Nora. She nodded and he picked up the phone.

"General?"

"Hello, Mark." Mosley's voice sounded small and uncharacteristically fragile.

"We've begun our descent, General. And, we have the medicine. What's the prognosis there?"

"Aaron is drifting in and out of consciousness. I'm having trouble keeping his fever down and the lesions are spreading across his body. Fortunately, he's not hemorrhaging—yet."

"We're less than thirty minutes from landing at the airport in Libreville. A helicopter will pick us up and we'll be there as soon as possible." Mark paused a moment and fought to control the shaking in his voice. "Tell Aaron to hold on. Both of you hold on."

"I can't make any promises," he said. "Just . . . hurry."

Mark hung up and gripped the armrests of his seat tight enough to turn his knuckles white. *This was all too familiar.* In the air, racing against time, to get to people he cared about before they died. He prayed this time he wouldn't arrive too late.

• • •

Mosley took the cloth off his grandson's burning forehead, dipped it in a basin of cool water, and reapplied it. He then took another, wet it, and touched it to Aaron's parched lips.

As Aaron moaned, he opened his mouth and Mosley gently squeezed the washcloth, releasing some of the water onto his cracked tongue. He turned to wet the cloth again when he heard the soft whisper.

"Grandpop?"

Mosley turned, surprised to hear a name Aaron used for him as a small child. Aaron's eyes were open—ever so slightly.

"I'm here, Aaron."

"I'm thirsty."

Mosley gently lifted his grandson's head and placed another pillow under it. He reached to the bedside table and poured a small amount of sweet tea into a cup. That was one of the details he remembered about Aaron: he loved sweet tea.

He brought the cup to his grandson's lips. "Here's something you'll like, Aaron."

Aaron took a small sip and smiled.

"Here, take some more."

Aaron shook his head, a slight movement. "Later."

Mosley set the glass down and gazed at his grandson—nearly a young man. He felt an overwhelming tenderness and a profound sense of loss. The boy had grown so much without him. "Is there anything I can get you? Anything you need?"

Aaron's eyes drifted over and focused on his grandfather's face for a moment. He nodded.

"What, son? Just name it."

"I know . . . I'm dying."

"Don't say that, Aaron. Help is on the way."

Aaron shook his head. "It's okay. I know where I'm going. I'll see Mom and Dad and my sisters . . ." His voice was faint. "I can't wait to see them—to be with them."

Mosley fought the emotion back and wished he shared even a small portion of his grandson's faith. "There's no need to think about that now."

"I want to think about it, except . . ." Tears formed in Aaron's eyes and then spilled out and down the sides of his face.

Mosley reached out to rub the tears away. "Are you in pain?"

"I'm sad," Aaron said. "I've prayed for you and Grandma every day."

Mosley was at a loss. "You prayed for me?"

The boy's tears began to flow again, and with a trembling hand he grabbed Mosley's shirt. "I want you to be in heaven," he said. "I want you to be there with us."

Mosley drew his grandson close. His own tears came.

Then, something stung his arm and he looked down, expecting to see an insect. However, the stinging was not in one place, but seemed to spread out over both arms. The color drained from his face as he saw a half dozen rosy spots on both arms.

CHAPTER SEVENTY-EIGHT

THE MILITARY CAR SKIDDED to a halt in a cloud of dust outside the Sisters of Mercy Convent. Mark and Nora leaped out, Mark reaching back to grab his black bag. The bag contained not only basic medical supplies, but also vials of the experimental medication. The afternoon heat and humidity assailed them.

Colonel Ronald Cox from Special Forces and Major Kevin Maklin, the general's aide, approached them as they walked to the modest iron gate leading into the convent. The entire area was under the command of the military now, most of the nuns having been relocated to a nearby hospital for testing.

Kevin handled quick introductions and then guided the small group, almost at a run, into the main complex comprising the Sisters of Mercy Convent. Kevin explained, "We've not had any contact from the general for the last hour. When we last spoke, he indicated that he was showing symptoms of the virus."

Mark broke into a run, forcing the others to do the same. They moved through the gardens toward a small white-stucco cottage at the rear of the grounds. Mark was surprised to see yellow crime-scene tape stretched around the area; stationed every twenty feet or so were armed guards in biohazard suits.

"This way," Kevin said and redirected them to a large tent that had been set up away from the cottage near the edge of the neighboring jungle. They entered what was apparently the command center. Tables were covered with communication equipment and maps, while others were set with medical equipment and supplies. The smell of burnt coffee permeated the air. Military and medical personnel were milling around. A small group of soldiers drifted in and out, coming and going with fresh provisions.

As they approached the tent, a woman with blond hair, wearing a white coat, stepped out and walked toward them.

Mark rushed up to her. "Susan."

She looked exhausted, her eyes red rimmed and her pallor white. "Did you bring the medication?"

"Yes. I have it. You're a miracle worker to get through all those bureaucracies so quickly."

She nodded, then turned to Nora and introduced herself.

"You must be exhausted," Nora said.

"Me?" she said. "I'm not the one who's been crawling through caves and dodging bullets."

"What's the update?" Mark asked.

"The situation in Gabon is critical. It appears that Aaron infected the police at a roadside checkpoint, and they, in turn, infected a number of travelers. We've now had over a dozen outbreaks not only across Gabon, but also down into Congo. And you know about the train."

"We heard that the situation was contained," Nora said.

"We thought so too, but two of the first responders who attended the train have come down with symptoms—but only *after* they'd done a shift at the airport. We have no idea who they came into contact with or where those people flew. The aviation authority is running the passenger manifests as we speak, but the virus could literally be spreading across the globe."

Mark's heart lurched. "Then let's not waste any more time talking."

Susan nodded. "Let's get you into a biohazard suit." Susan walked to the technical team in the ops tent that would assist Mark.

Mark looked at Nora. Their eyes met, and an unspoken series of messages were exchanged.

"I hate those suits," he said.

She nodded. "It doesn't have to be you," she said. "I can administer the medicine just as easily."

"I have no doubt," he said, "but you lost the toss. I'm going in."

"I never agreed to a toss."

"You didn't? Oh, my mistake." Mark smiled.

Nora opened her mouth to protest, but Mark cut her off. "This is for Jenny."

Whatever argument she may have had now disappeared in the silence between them.

"Dr. Carlson," Susan called out, "your tailor awaits you."

Mark looked at her and imagined himself walking into that house in a biohazard suit looking like something from the *Creature from the Black Lagoon. It would unnerve the boy,* he thought.

"No," he said.

"What do you mean 'no'?" she called to him, frowning.

Mark picked up his black case and without looking back strode toward the little house.

Susan shouted from behind him, "Don't, Mark! Put on a suit!"

He walked on—more quickly.

Nora's voice joined Susan's. "Mark, don't be stupid! *The suit!*"

"Your saints will protect me," he shouted over his shoulder, and began to jog.

Out of the corner of his eye, he saw one of the guards approach him from the left. He picked up his pace and broke through the yellow police tape like a runner at the end of a race.

The guard shouted at him to halt as he aimed his firearm, but Susan called the guard back.

Mark sprinted toward the door—and a great unknown.

CHAPTER SEVENTY-NINE

THIS MAY BE THE *strangest house call anyone has ever made,* Mark thought as he arrived at the door.

He dreaded what he might encounter. It had been at least an hour since anyone on the outside had spoken to General Mosley, so it was entirely possible that he and his grandson had both died. *Too late again.*

Having reached the door, he realized he didn't know the protocol. Should he knock?

Time was of the essence, he knew, and his hesitation was nonsensical. He pushed the door open, aware of how vulnerable he was. Entering without a biohazard suit was potential suicide.

The silence of the room rang in his ears, and he realized how quiet the entire convent had become, as if it was holding its breath. A feeble puff of cool, damp air swept over him and chilled the perspiration on his back and arms. Any viral particles that were carried by the air would become part of him. He held his breath—as if to forestall the inevitable.

At that moment, he thought of something he read in one of Brother Lawrence's letters: "He is the Father of the afflicted, always ready to help us." It was almost as if he heard the monk say, "Let go, and let be."

Mark tried to relax, struggling to embrace the words, to believe them in a way that would stop his heart from pounding and his hands from trembling. He took a deep breath of the cool, damp air and then let it out. He knew he had made the right decision—no matter the cost.

The cottage had a small kitchenette and sitting room that led to a small hall with two rooms. He stepped into the hall and glanced to the right—an empty guest room. On the left, the door was open, but the room was dark with the shades pulled. He squinted to make out the size and shape of the room and anyone alive inside.

"Sam. Aaron," he called out. No answer.

He imagined the scene: Aaron dead on the bed and Mosley looking up at him just as his wife had, with eyes full of blame and accusation.

He crossed the room, as his eyes adjusted, and he saw a lamp on top of a dresser. He turned it on.

An anemic yellow light cast faint shadows on the walls. Mark turned and saw a bed several feet away. Aaron was in the bed, and Mosley was lying prone on the floor next to it. Mark knelt down and held his hand under Mosley's nostrils. He felt the slight movement of breath. He felt for a carotid pulse. It was there, but very faint.

"Sam," he whispered.

The general moaned.

Mark turned to Aaron. He was covered in a bedsheet up to his neck. His pale face looked as if it were made of porcelain. Mark reached to check for a carotid pulse and the boy's eyes flew open. As they focused on Mark, they grew wide. He tried to sit up.

Mark put a hand on his shoulder. "Lie back. I'm here to help."

Aaron closed his eyes and fell back into sleep or unconsciousness, Mark didn't know which. He placed his black bag on the table and unpacked the supplies. With a speed that surprised even him, he set up and started an intravenous line on both of his patients and increased the flow rate to attempt to hydrate their dehydrated bodies.

As the IVs were running, he removed two vials. Breaking open the seal on the first one, he drew the thick yellow viscous liquid into a syringe. He repeated the procedure with the vial of clear medication. After tapping the syringe to bring the air bubbles to the hub, he expressed the air and then turned to Aaron. He inserted the needle into the IV line.

Mark bowed his head, aware that whatever was about to

happen was truly out of his hands. After whispering a quick prayer, he injected the liquid.

Turning to Mosley, he repeated the prayer and the procedure.

Mark noted the time and then dragged a chair in from the sitting room. He sat down and waited. The room was quiet, and he heard a clock ticking from somewhere. He found himself continuing to pray for his friend, for Aaron, and for himself.

Then, from a quiet place deep within his heart, he felt as if Brother Lawrence spoke to him: "He loves us infinitely more than we imagine or can ever love ourselves: love him then, and seek not consolation elsewhere: I hope you will soon receive it."

He nodded as his gaze fell to another syringe he had prepared on the night table. He didn't know if the virus was in him or not. He didn't know if the medication would help, or harm, or even kill, but he knew what he had to do.

He reached into his black bag and pulled out a tourniquet. He quickly applied it to his left arm, and using his right hand and mouth, cinched it down. After a few squeezes of his left hand, the veins below the tourniquet stood up like pipes heading to a refinery. He swabbed one with alcohol, and as the cool liquid evaporated, took the needle protector off the syringe with his right hand. After the needle entered the bulging vein, he loosened the tourniquet, whispered another small prayer, and injected the medicine.

Nora could not stop pacing. Susan implored her to sit, but it was impossible. Kevin begged her to eat something, but her stomach was churning too much. Her emotions ran the gamut from hope, to desperation, to anger.

It had been over an hour, and there was no sign of life from the cottage. The afternoon sun was beginning to set, and it would soon be evening.

Why hadn't Mark signaled them? Why hadn't he updated them? Had he been taken by the illness? Had the medication failed?

"We'll give them another thirty minutes," Susan said. "If Mark is not out by then, a biohazard team will go in."

Nora nodded. Her eye caught sight of a small chapel on the

opposite side of their operations area. She went in, found a pew with a kneeling bench, and knelt to pray. It was difficult. She found herself lost in tumbling waves of contradictory emotions. She berated herself for allowing him to dictate the situation, considering his emotional state. Going in to help Mosley and Aaron without a biohazard suit was stupid and reckless. Yet she felt understanding and sympathy, wanting to believe that this act was part of his healing.

She wrestled her mind to a point of concentration and went through the various prayers she knew by heart.

She was interrupted when her cell phone vibrated on her belt. She snapped it up and glanced at the screen to see who was bothering her—and saw Mark's cell phone number. Nearly dropping the phone, she got it opened and said, "Mark?"

"Where are you?" he asked in a quiet voice.

"Where are *you*?" she asked. "We've been waiting."

"In my dramatic exit, I forgot to bring a radio," he said. "I just realized I had my cell phone in my bag."

"Well?" she asked.

"I'm coming out," he said and hung up.

Nora raced from the chapel to the barrier outside the cottage, waving frantically to Susan in the ops area. Susan dropped a cup of coffee and followed. The team joined them, crowding as close as they dared.

The front door of the cottage opened and Mark stepped out. He looked in their direction, apparently surprised to see a small crowd waiting for him. He walked toward them and shouted, "Get the ambulance. The general and Aaron are awake. The medication seems to be working." As he spoke, he was looking at the faces in the crowd as if he was searching for someone.

Her.

They made eye contact and he stopped, and bowed to her as if enjoying a curtain call.

A team in biohazard suits rushed at him. They surrounded him, then dragged him back to the cottage.

Nora thought that he wore a particularly serene expression on his face.

• • •

With a radio now in his possession, Mark was able to report from inside the cottage. "The general is awake and Aaron's skin appears to be improving by the minute. We'll need to use quarantine measures to transfer them to the hospital, but I'm cautiously optimistic."

"Did you take it?" Nora asked.

"I took a full dose. We'll have to run tests, of course, but I feel fine."

"Do I have to tell you how reckless, foolish, and overdramatic that little stunt was?"

"True, but how memorable would it have been if I'd followed procedure?"

"You're an idiot. Now hurry up. We have work to do."

CHAPTER EIGHTY

AUGUST 19

MARK PULLED THE CURTAIN behind him and walked down the hallway to the nurses' station. The small hospital at the Sisters of Mercy compound was pristine, quiet, and professionally run. It would be hard to imagine Mosley and Aaron getting better care anywhere else.

Susan Hutchinson was sitting in the station writing a note on a medical chart and smiled as he approached. "How are they doing?"

"Improving by the minute. The sisters are having trouble with them, however."

Susan furrowed her brow. "How so?"

"It seems the older patient is having his staff sneak in contraband ice cream and candy. Apparently it's strictly against clinic policy."

Susan smiled and turned a page in the chart. "Look at this." She turned the chart toward him and pointed to a page with lab results. "It turns out that the general was heterozygous for both the Delta 32 and m303 genes. I think that's what kept him alive. Without the genetic protection, he probably would have died very, very quickly, just like the others. I guess he and Aaron were lucky to be in the same family."

Mark nodded, but suggested, "Maybe it's not luck."

She raised an eyebrow. "Well, whatever it is, you have it, as well."

Now it was Mark's turn to look bewildered. "Why's that?"

She reached to an in-box and pulled out a piece of paper. "Here are your lab results, Doctor. As you see, you don't have either the Delta 32 or the m303 gene. But you did have Ebola antigen in your system. So, without the experimental medications, we wouldn't be having this conversation."

He nodded as he looked through the results.

Susan continued, "And there's no sign of active infection. Your system is as clean as a whistle."

"Indeed," he commented. He handed the paper back to Susan. *No, it's not luck at all.*

She stood and began to gather her things as if she was about to leave.

"So, what's next for you?" he asked.

"I'll remain here in Libreville for a few days. I want to keep an eye on our two patients and make sure there are no further outbreaks. I'll monitor the other victims who have received the medication in Gabon and the Congo. Of course, we're also watching over those who flew from here and had to be treated."

"Where are they?"

"France, Spain, and Germany."

"It could have been a lot worse."

Susan nodded. "We were within days, maybe hours, of a worldwide pandemic, Mark. It would have been awful. I hope you're proud of what you did to stop it."

"Proud of what I did?" he asked, puzzled. "It took teams of brilliant scientists on both sides of the pond—you and your team included. So, there's plenty of credit to go around."

She gazed at him a moment. "Still . . ."

He smiled at her. "It's certainly been an incredible ride."

"So it has," she replied. "And not one I'd like to repeat anytime soon."

"Same here."

She closed her eyes and said with a sigh, "I'd like to have a nice, long hot bath."

"What's stopping you?"

"Later. When I can really enjoy it. For now I'll settle for a nice cup of coffee." She nodded toward the hallway. Kevin Maklin was walking their way.

Mark made eyes at Susan and she stifled a giggle.

"Good work, Doctor," Kevin said.

Mark bowed slightly. "Thanks for all your behind-the-scenes help."

"Ready?" Kevin asked Susan. "I secured a car to drive us to Le Café. They're supposed to have the best coffee in Libreville."

"Excellent," she said. Then, with a wink to Mark, she added, "Even better than the canteen."

"See you around, Doctor," Mark said.

She reached up and kissed him on the cheek. "Under better circumstances, I hope."

He smiled and watched as she walked down the hall with Kevin.

"They look like a nice couple," Nora said, arriving at his elbow. "And I hope the White House gives her some kind of medal for all her hard work."

"She deserves it," Mark concurred. "Maybe they will—if they ever admit officially that any of this ever happened."

"Oh, you can be sure that they will. I don't know a politician on earth who wouldn't want to take credit for averting this disaster."

He turned to face her. "Where have you been?"

"The chapel. I felt the need to touch base." She put her arm through his and guided him in the direction of the lobby. "Come on. We have a plane to catch."

"We do?"

"Yes."

They walked in companionable silence for a moment and Mark's minded flitted through the many events of the past few days. He stopped on one unanswered question and asked, "So, what does your church teach about ghosts?"

She looked at him. "Why do you ask?"

"Because you and I both saw what we believed was the Blue Monk—someone who has been dead for over three hundred years. Not only did we see him but also, in some ways, he helped us." Only now did Mark realize how remarkable and bizarre it all was. "No one has explained it to us."

Nora shrugged. "Will any explanation, one way or the other, persuade you of anything that you don't already believe?"

422 Paul McCusker and Walt Larimore, M.D.

Mark thought about it, then smiled at her. "You're a wise woman."

They reached the front of the hospital, crowded with visitors and patients on chairs and standing around the reception desk. They passed through and reached the black sedan waiting for them in front.

"By the way, where are we flying to?" Mark asked as he held the door for her.

"London," she said, as she climbed into the backseat.

He got in the other side and sat next to her. "Why are we going back to London?"

"I have it from a good source that you are going to be offered a job."

"Am I looking for a job?"

"Didn't you resign from Ahaz?"

"Oh, yeah. I did. So I guess I'm looking for a job."

She turned to face him and said, "TSI needs you."

The driver pulled the car from the curb and guided it into the thick traffic.

Mark turned in the seat to face Nora. "Will you continue to work with them?"

"Yes."

He shrugged with feigned indifference. "Then maybe it's worth thinking about."

She jabbed an elbow into him. "You better do more than think, mister."

Mark reached into his pocket and pulled out an object that he handed to her.

"For me?"

Mark smiled as Nora reached out. Her eyes widened in surprise. "My watch! The one Father Francisco gave me. Where did you find it?" she asked as she leaned over to embrace him. "Thank you, thank you, thank you!"

She pulled away, looked fondly at the watch, and then turned her misty eyes up to him.

They gazed at each other and Mark felt the urge again to kiss her. But his cell phone rang. Groaning, he pulled it out of his pocket. A glance at the screen and he saw it was his ex-wife.

"She can wait," he said as he punched the button to stop the ring.

Nora eyed him. "Are you all right?"

He leaned toward her and whispered in her ear, "I've never been better."

And he meant it.

EPILOGUE

MAC SAT AT HIS desk and finished going over the latest news from Gabon. He would call Nora in a few minutes to get her personal report but, for now, he wanted to sit in the silence of the rainy afternoon and enjoy the relief he felt from having stopped a potential worldwide catastrophe.

His cell phone rang. *So much for that,* he thought. Without checking the number, he simply flipped it open and said, "Mac."

"Hello," a resonant voice said. It was Peter Romero from Ahaz. "We haven't heard from you, in spite of the apparently successful use of the PMO medications in Gabon."

"Since you already know about it, why would you want to hear from me?" Mac asked.

"We expected a report, and the specific documentation of the drugs. When may we expect them?"

"From me? No time soon."

A cold silence filled the line. "I suppose you better explain that statement."

"The explanation is simple. I don't like how you play, so I don't think I'll play with you anymore."

"What are you talking about?"

"You betrayed us. Members of my team got hurt. Your own man was killed, and you set up Henry Colchester." Mac could feel his face turning red. He picked up a pencil and tapped it on the desk blotter.

"Henry Colchester?" Romero asked innocently.

"I know he was *not* an operative for Return to Earth," Mac said. "Though it was clever of you to position him that way."

Romero snorted. "You saw the photos. He was virtually a founding member with that friend of his from the university."

"Old photos taken years ago when the group was dedicated to peaceful solutions about the environment and animal rights. When it became radical and violent, Henry left. He and I talked about it when I hired him." Mac paused and gave the idea further thought. "Or maybe he left because you made him a better offer."

"You're shooting blindly, Mac."

"Am I?" he asked. "What was the plan, Mr. Romero? For Henry to kill Mark, Digger, and Sickler, get the body out through the third entrance, and then blow it all up? Return to Earth would get the blame, and you'd still get the body. Then, miracle of miracles, Ahaz saves the world with an exorbitantly expensive cure."

"An interesting theory," Romero said without a tone of real interest.

"I saw the surveillance photos from MI5," Mac said. "Your people were on the scene in—what was it—a carpet delivery van? Is that how you were going to take the body away?"

Romero was silent for a moment.

Mac continued, "As I said, I won't work with people I can't trust."

Romero's silence left a distant hiss on the line. He was weighing his options, no doubt. Then he said, "Mac, it was never our intention for anyone to die."

"Of course not," Mac said, as he now twirled the pencil in his fingers. "Just as it wasn't your intention for Nathan Dodge to die, or for the virus to escape from the compound."

"Dodge *was* Return to Earth's doing, not mine," Romero growled.

"Maybe. Maybe not. But it was your unauthorized work at an unauthorized site with an untested, unapproved, and unauthorized attenuated viral vaccine that started it all—not to mention that it began an epidemic of unnecessary death and suffering."

Romero paused and then said with obvious irritation, "What is this all about, Mac? More money? Or are you trying to cover your tracks?"

The pencil snapped in Mac's fingers. He didn't reply.

"You want a clean conscience, is that it?" Romero suggested. "You're a little late for that, aren't you?"

"Find some other stooge to do your dirty work."

Romero chuckled softly and then said, "No need to be like that, Mac. Get me that documentation and everything will be just fine."

"I don't think so."

"Do it or your career is finished. You know I have the evidence to make that happen. You could face jail time."

Mac growled in his throat. "Oh, I don't know. If I did a plea bargain with the evidence I have about you guys, I wouldn't be there for very long—if at all. You, on the other hand, could face not only prison, but also malpractice and class-action suits. Those will put a crimp on your retirement and golden parachute, I think."

Romero's anger broke through and he snarled, "Try it and what happened to Nathan Dodge will seem like a skinned knee compared to what will happen to you."

Mac laughed. "Do your worst. You won't get any documentation from me."

Another pause from Romero, then a deep sigh. "We'll be talking again."

Mac leaned back in his chair and realized how hot the room had become. He took out a handkerchief and dabbed at the beads of sweat on his forehead. He was either very brave or very foolish, he thought. Maybe both.

Only time would tell.

AFTERWORD

OUR REPRESENTATIONS OF THE quaint village of Eyam, England, and the epidemic that occurred there in 1665 and 1666 are historically accurate. William Mompesson and Thomas Stanley, the two clerics who decided to quarantine the village rather than risk allowing the disease to spread across the countryside, were historical figures–as were Agnes Hull, George Viccars, and Catherine Mompesson.

Of course, the World Health Organization (WHO), the U.S. Centers for Disease Control and Prevention (CDC), the U.S. National Institute of Allergy and Infectious Diseases (NIAID), the U.S. Army Medical Research Institute of Infectious Diseases (USAMRIID), the Laboratory of Molecular Biology in Cambridge, the British Army's Special Air Service (the 22nd Special Air Service regiment), Interpol, and the U.S. National Institutes of Health (NIH) are very real and wonderful institutions packed with dedicated and incredibly talented individuals. However, the use of their names and functions, for the purposes of this book, are purely fictional.

The Delta 32 and m303 mutations on the CCR5 gene are real, as is the USAMRIID's research on Ebola, an Ebola vaccine, and antisense medications (PMOs). Also, the NIH's (Stephen O'Brien, Ph.D.) research on the Delta 32 mutation in Eyam, England, actually happened. However, all of this very important research has been fictionalized for this book.

Most geographical locations, landmarks, hospitals, and towns of England and Gabon we use in this book all exist. Of course, the events described happened only in our minds.

With various exceptions, all other names, characters, and incidents portrayed in this book are the work of the authors' overactive imaginations. Any resemblance to actual persons, living or dead, events, incidents, or localities is based on fanciful conjecture.

We are grateful to the historical research of John Clifford, the author of *Eyam Plague: 1665–1666* (revised and enlarged in 2003, © John Clifford) and the producers of PBS's "Mystery of the Black Death," which was broadcast on October 30, 2002, as an episode on PBS's *Secrets of the Dead* series (http://www.pbs.org/wnet/secrets/case_plague/).

We are thankful to Nicholas Herman (known as Brother Lawrence, circa 1605–1691) and the collection of his letters in *The Practice of the Presence of God*. The letters found in our novel are adapted from letters written by Brother Lawrence around the time of the events we've depicted. We have striven to keep his voice, theology, philosophy, and teachings intact. An electronic version of his letters can be found at the Calvin College Web site at http://www.ccel.org/ccel/lawrence/practice.html.

We are grateful to Michelle McVay and Paul Multzer for helping us with Gabonese French and to Air Force Lt. Col. Jeff Gray for assistance in helping us understand and accurately (we hope) write about military protocol and equipment. Thanks to Barb and Katherine Larimore for the many hours spent combing through, reviewing, and editing our early drafts of the book. And our gratitude goes to Elizabeth McCusker, who offered notes on the final draft.

We are deeply grateful for the invaluable, unselfish, and sizeable assistance of Reverend Andrew Montgomerie, the current vicar of the Church of St. Lawrence in Eyam, England, and his wife, Mary. Thanks to Jarod Sickler, an expert rock climber and dear friend, for advising us in technical intricacies of climbing equipment and allowing us to use his name.

We're indebted to several physicians who assisted us by reviewing the manuscript for medical accuracy, including epidemiologist Reginald Finger, M.D., M.P.H.; Elaine Eng, M.D.; Paul Multzer, M.D.; Gaylen Kelton, M.D.; Mary Anne Nelson, M.D.; Byron Calhoun, M.D.; Ed Leap, M.D.; Ed Guttery, M.D.; Leanna Hollis, M.D.; and Roy Stringfellow, M.D.

All of Walt's books are reviewed by the Elder Board of his church, the Little Log Church in Palmer Lake, Colorado, for theological and doctrinal accuracy. Thanks to Pastor Bill Story and Elders David Flower, Ron Rothburn, and Dan Smith.

Appreciation also goes to Martin, Regula, Catherine, Marilen, and Frederick Duerr for their help, kindness, and hospitality in Basel, Switzerland. And thank you, Martin, for the use of your name, as well.

We're grateful to the management and staff of the establishments that allowed us to spend endless hours occupying their tables to dream up and write this book: the Coffee Cup Café and Serranos Coffee Shop in Monument, Colorado, as well as Barnes & Noble booksellers, The Egg and I, and Panera Bread, all in Colorado Springs.

As always, we owe more than we could ever express to our wives, for their endless support and encouragement. And to our families and friends who endured (or enjoyed) our absence, our love and thanks.

Thanks to Alton Gansky and Stephanie Evans for applying their considerable talents in editing and improving our book. Last, but not least, thanks to David Lambert (if there's a better fiction editor in America, we haven't met him) and the team at Howard Books for placing their trust in us and applying their considerable skills to making this book even better than the one we first submitted to them.

Irrespective of the substantial assistance we've received from these many experts, any errors in this work belong solely to us as the authors and are not a reflection of the many people or resources we relied upon to write this work.

Paul McCusker and Walt Larimore, M.D.
Colorado Springs, Colorado
February 2009

THE
Author, Book & Conversation

PAUL McCUSKER

Paul McCusker is a Peabody Award–winning writer and director who has written novels, plays, audio dramas, and musicals for children and adults. He currently has more than thirty books in print. He lives in Colorado Springs, Colorado.

WALT LARIMORE, M.D.

Walt Larimore, M.D., is a noted physician, award-winning writer, and medical journalist who hosted the cable television show *Ask the Family Doctor* on Fox's Health Network. He lives in Monument, Colorado.

2

PAUL McCUSKER
WALT LARIMORE, M.D.
THE BOOK

ABCs
THE
Author, Book & Conversation

Q) WHERE AND HOW DID YOU GUYS MEET?

WALT: Paul and I met not too long after I joined Focus on the Family in early 2001 as vice president and family physician in residence. We admired each other's work and began to build a friendship that has only deepened through the years. For me, it has been a terrific privilege and honor to work with Paul on this book. And we're already hard at work on the sequel, *Time Scene Investigators: The Influenza Bomb*. Best of all, we've had a ton of fun working together.

Q) PAUL, AS AN AUTHOR AND SCRIPTWRITER, YOU ARE NO STRANGER TO HIGH-ADVENTURE STORIES. HOW DID YOU COME UP WITH THE IDEA FOR THIS NOVEL?

PAUL: Well, I love speculative fiction that explores the dramatic possibilities of normal people in abnormal situations. So, when I was visiting relatives in the small village of Eyam in England, I was struck by the story of how the Black Plague nearly destroyed the village. What was even more intriguing to me was the sacrificial actions of the villagers and the modern medical mysteries triggered by the event. I began to work on an idea that became TSI—and I quickly realized I would need help from someone with a medical background.

I wondered who I might approach who had medical expertise and writing experience and who I would enjoy working with. Walt came immediately to mind. He had not only written acclaimed medical books but also the bestselling and much-loved *Bryson City* stories, based on his early days as a young physician in the Smoky Mountains. His combination of medical knowledge and storytelling skills made him a great partner for tackling this idea.

Q) SO, PAUL, DID YOU PRIMARILY WRITE THE BOOK AND USE WALT AS A MEDICAL CONSULTANT AND EXPERT?

PAUL: Not at all. We understood from the start that this would be a solid collaboration. We began by developing an outline and story line together, talking through characters, plotlines, and themes. We talked for hours. Walt brought ideas and sensibilities to the project that I don't have. I think we complemented each other—and sharpened each other's thinking. It's a genuine pleasure working on these stories together.

WALT: Once we had the outline and story line, Paul and I began writing first drafts. We each wrote about half of the chapters, with me taking the chapters with more medical issues. Then we'd meet at a coffee shop or café and fuse our stories together. It was great fun.

Q) HOW MUCH OF THE BOOK IS BASED ON FACT?

PAUL: Much of it. The events surrounding the plague and its impact on Eyam, England, in 1666 were taken from history.

WALT: And the medical facts about the Black Plague and the Ebola virus are right out of the medical textbooks. In fact, much of the research mentioned in the book has happened or is happening—although we've fictionalized it.

PAUL: And the possibility of a world pandemic with a mutant virus is a very real threat.

WALT: I think that the most frightening aspect of this book is that it could literally become tomorrow's headlines.

Q) WHAT ABOUT THE BLUE MONK? HISTORICAL?

PAUL: No. That part we made up. However, the disease from which he suffers in the book is real.

Q) AND IS THERE ACTUALLY A TSI TEAM AT THE NIH?

WALT (laughing): Not that we know of.

PAUL: If there isn't, there ought to be.

Q) I PRESUME THE RETURN TO EARTH SOCIETY IS FICTIONAL?

PAUL: It is. But it's based on real people and real philosophies that I witnessed while living in England. Some folks there are fanatical about animal rights and the environment. There are people who truly believe that animals are equal to, or more valuable than, humans. I believe that we're expected by our Creator to be good stewards of the Earth, but not as part of the food chain. We're made in God's image and bear that as unique and loved individuals.

Q) ONE OF YOUR MAIN CHARACTERS, MARK CARLSON, IS CARRYING A LOT OF EMOTIONAL BAGGAGE OVER THE DEATH OF A CHILD AND A BITTER DIVORCE. WHERE DID YOU FIND THE CREATIVE SPARK TO WRITE EMOTIONAL WOUNDS LIKE THIS?

WALT: Barb and I walked through the tragedy of losing four unborn children to intrauterine death. Also, Barb and I have wrestled with raising a special-needs child and have seen the pressure and strain that puts on a marriage—not to mention the spiritual issues it raises when God and his plan simply do not make sense. My memories of walking through that pain and finding help and hope through a personal relationship with God and his infinite wisdom revealed in the Bible have been a great resource for writing about Mark's pain and struggles.

Q) I UNDERSTAND THERE'S A STORY BEHIND YOU BRINGING BROTHER LAWRENCE INTO YOUR NOVEL.

PAUL: Walt and I were looking for a way that the Blue Monk, who tragically lost his wife and daughter to a shipwreck, could speak to Mark three centuries later. We were stuck. Then Walt had an experience at a camp...

WALT: I was serving at Young Life's Crooked Creek Ranch as the camp physician. During this week, I was praying about this particular part of our story line. During a break, I visited the camp store and picked up a modern translation of *The Practice of the Presence of God*, by Brother Lawrence. It was a book I had enjoyed as a college student, but when I was flipping through it, I was stunned to see that Brother Lawrence's letters were actually penned in the fall of 1666—the exact year in which we had placed the Blue Monk in Eyam. These letters were an amazing answer to prayer and we are excited to bring into our story his wisdom and insight about suffering and loss.

Q) YOU GUYS ARE WORKING ON THE SEQUEL TO *THE GABON VIRUS*. WHAT'S THE TSI TEAM UP TO NEXT?

PAUL: Readers of this first book may notice that, early on, the TSI team is examining the body of a WWI doughboy who died of the so-called Spanish flu of 1918—up to 100 million people died from it. Well, in our next story, an outbreak of that virus has been reported in Siberia and looks like it's going to spread. Then our team learns that the original virus may have been a German weapon used in 1918 and has now fallen into the hands of the Return to Earth Society. Suddenly the world is on the verge of another fatal pandemic and our team has to stop it.

Q) CAN YOU TELL US WHAT'S GOING TO HAPPEN TO MARK AND NORA? THEY SEEM TO BE ATTRACTED TO EACH OTHER AT THE END OF THE BOOK.

Walt and Paul just smile and shrug their shoulders.

READER'S GROUP DISCUSSION QUESTIONS

1. The book deals with characters who are Catholic (Nora, the Sisters of Mercy), Anglican (Father Andrew, Joan, Philip the Gardener), Evangelical Protestant (David and Aaron Mosley, Pastor Wyn, and the members of the Compound), agnostic (Mark), and atheist (Sam, Nathan Dodge, and others). To what extent was each faith group accurately or inaccurately portrayed?

2. When General Sam Mosley pushed the button to destroy the underground lab, was he "playing God"? Do you think he may have killed anyone? Was his action justifiable?

3. Ahaz Pharmaceuticals paid David Mosley and his congregation a great deal of money to test an experimental vaccine. What was their motivation? Were their actions or motives ethical? Were they right to do this? Why or why not?

4. On the flip side, were the leaders of the Compound right to participate in this experiment? Do you think they knew all the risks and benefits? If so, do you think they fully (or should have) explained these to every member of the compound?

5. Do parents have the right to subject their children to medical experiments like this? If so, under what circumstances?

6. David Mosley and his congregants chose to commit suicide rather than face a certain and horrible death. They believed a peaceful, painless death was preferable to a horrible death. Was their thinking rational? Would the Bible offer any insight to them? Does the Bible give us any insight into what we should consider when we face pain and suffering?

7. Do you believe groups such as the Return to Earth Society exist? Upon what would they base their beliefs? How do you feel about animal-rights groups that seem to place more emphasis on animal rights than human rights?

8. When Mark Carlson's daughter died, he became angry with God and abandoned his faith. Have you ever had an experience in which you became angry at God? Have you ever felt that God didn't make sense? Did this strengthen or weaken your faith? How?

9. The illness and death of Mark and Donna's daughter put a terrific strain on their marriage, eventually leading to their divorce. Have you walked a similar path? If so, how did you deal with this?

10. Georgina was falsely accused of being a member of the Return to Earth Society. Have you ever been falsely accused of something? How did it make you feel? Have you ever accused someone of something they did not do? Did you apologize? Was it difficult? How did this affect your relationship with the other person?

11. Brother Lawrence was able to help the Blue Monk and Mark Carlson begin to heal from terrible emotional blows. How did his letters impact you? Were his insights and advice helpful to you? If so, how?

12. General Sam Mosley realized a number of mistakes he had made as a father and grandfather. What were they? What do you think he would do differently if he could? What could you do to become a better spouse and parent?

13. In the book, the Blue Monk seemed to reappear as a ghost. Do you believe in ghosts? Do you think the theological explanations given by Mark and Father Andrew are valid?

14. Aaron fled from a number of enemies, both imagined and real. Have you ever felt that you were surrounded by people who mean to hurt you? How did you respond? What gave you hope? What help did you find in your time of need?

15. Margaret, the members of the mob that hunted the Blue Monk, and their descendants returned every year to the Silver Cathedral to honor the Blue Monk, his ministry and his legacy, and to pay homage and penance. Which of their activities would have biblical support? Which would not? Were they right to keep this secret? Were they right to make the vow they made?

16. Margaret chose to forgive Joshua Parke for his role in the death of her beloved brother. Could you have done the same? If Joshua had not asked for forgiveness, would Margaret have been right to withhold forgiveness? Why should she forgive him? What might have happened to her had she chosen not to forgive him?

17. Margaret adopted young Joshua Parke. Why do you think she did this? Why do Christians support and emphasize adoption and care of orphans? How did this change Joshua's life? How do you think it might have changed Margaret?

18. Mark risked his life to bring the medication to Sam and Aaron. In what circumstances would you consider doing the same thing? For whom would you do this? Loved ones? Total strangers? Why?

19. How did Mark's faith change as he was challenged by Nora and witnessed firsthand how faith works in the lives of others?

20. Have you encountered someone whose faith seemed so real that he or she inspired or challenged you? Who was that person? What attributes did he or she exemplify to you? Do you demonstrate your faith in a way that speaks to others? If so, how?